C000269561

MOSAIC

Mosaic

Copyright © Carolann Copland

First Edition

ISBN: 978-1-7392187-3-7

All rights reserved. No part of this publication may be reproduced or transmitted in any form or by any means, electronic or mechanical, including photography, recording, or any information storage or retrieval system without permission in writing from Carolann Copland. The book is sold subject to the condition that it shall not, by way of trade or otherwise, be lent, copied, altered, resold or otherwise circulated without Carolann Copland's prior consent in any form of binding or cover other than that in which is published and without similar a condition, including this condition, being imposed on any subsequent publisher.

This book is a work of fiction. Any references to real people, events, organisations or places are used fictitiously. All other names, characters, organisations, places and events, incidents and all dialogue are the products of the author's imagination and should not be construed as real. Any further resemblance to any actual persons, living or dead, places or actual events is entirely coincidental.

Design & publishing services provided by JM Agency

www.jm.agency

Mosaic

Carolann Copland

Dedicated to my husband,
Neil Copland,
for his love, care, friendship, and support.

Praise for *Mosaic*

- "A beautifully written and captivating, sweeping saga. An evocative story of love, heartbreak and redemption, against a richly imagined landscape."
  Zoe Miller, **Author of A House Full of Secrets**

Praise for *Scarred*

- "The writing is subtle in the best possible way. Without even realising it, the characters creep up on you and are breathing down your neck. I loved it."
Jax Miller, **Best Selling Author of Freedom's Child**

- "The book has a mixture of youthful enthusiasm and adult realism. Carolann is a talented writer who uses gentle language and melodic prose. The story is elegant and has an unique Irishness about it. Very different in style to her debut, this is less of a thriller and more of a study of human frailty. …a breath of fresh air in the genre of contemporary Irish fiction."
Margaret Madden, **Bleach House Library**

Praise for *Summer Triangle*

- "*Summer Triangle* digs deep into the reading psyche…
  the sights, sounds and senses of both locations reading
  authentically… She draws on her life experience to create
  an international thriller with overtones of terrorism mixed
  with mothering domesticity. Her characters are well drawn,
  acting within character from start to finish. The story
  moves from location to location with peaking climaxes
  and a thrilling, unexpected ending."
  Author *Patricia O' Reilly*

- "*Summer Triangle* is such a visual tale that it reads like
  watching a movie."
  Author and Journalist *Billy Keane*

- "*Summer Triangle* is a touching story with many layers,
  encompassing the idealism and desperation of youth, from
  Islamic extremists to a young mother losing her way. It's
  a story that digs deep and I'm already looking forward to
  this author's next outing."
  Winner of Irish Crime Fiction 2014 *Louise Phillips*

- "Carolann Copland has written a story of many worlds.
  The world of intense religious beliefs, the world of teenage
  parenthood and the world of uncertainty…. The Islamic
  narrative throughout the book was progressive and inter-
  linked with the character's story lines, making it subtle but
  important. Skilfully written, this is a book that is not only
  ideal for adults, but would be a great YA read too… a story
  of grief, love and the journey to happiness and fulfilment.

What better way to examine these themes, than through the eyes of young adults?"
Margaret Madden, **Bleach House Library**

- "*Summer Triangle* is a well-crafted tale incorporating elements of thriller, family saga and romance... The Summer Triangle constellation of the title provides a powerful metaphor for East and West."
Anne O' Leary, **Books Ireland Magazine**

PROLOGUE

February 2020

Enrico

I hate having to be grateful. They are being so kind, trying their best, and I'm a miserable old grump. There's a rocking chair in the corner of the terrace that has been bought especially for me. A coffee table stands beside it, at the exact height for reaching over for my drinks and my ashtray. They have thought of everything. A grab rail to get in and out of the bath. A ramp to make the front step more accessible. But all I want is to go home to my own house, where I've been living happily for twenty-three years. Here on the terrace, watching my daughter and granddaughter running their guest house and listening to their busy voices, I'm lonely.

It's only eight o' clock in the morning, and already 'old Enrico', as they call me now, is getting in the way. My granddaughter has been on the warpath this morning. I'm not even allowed to drink my coffee and brandy in peace.

'Abuelo! Move over there with your dirty old cigarettes and your smelly drinks,' she says. 'Do you know what time it is? You're making me sick!'

Easing myself slowly into the chair, I sit back and close my eyes. *If my friend Roberto could see me now*. I open my eyes and look towards the sky.

'Good for you, Roberto, to die while you were still charging at the red flag. You were fit and healthy, strong and respected, and

13

you went out like a bright, shining light: still loved by everyone, remembered and revered as the great Roberto, saviour of the Republican people. Hey, what am I looking up there for? With the badness we've notched up, they wouldn't let us near the place.'

I smile and shake my fist gently towards the ground and the gleaming floor mosaic beneath my feet, that one tile still broken after all these years.

I push myself up out of the chair with the help of my hated cane. I'll walk towards the street; see if I can find a fellow old soul to reminisce with.

I reach for the handle of the door gingerly, afraid that Paulina or Dani will burst through with trays at any moment and knock me over. I know I should really go out through the terrace and leave from the front, but it's such a long way around.

The dining room is full, with about twenty people, and I wonder where have they all slept? I forget that this house is so big now.

'Papá.' My daughter, Paulina, comes towards me wearing her proprietor smile. 'Everything okay?' But I know that what she's actually saying is: *Papá, shut up and get back out to the terrace, out of the way.*

'I'm fine, Paulina. I'm going out for a walk.'

She looks around at the tables, and I know she's wondering how I'll get past everyone without a scene of pushing and shoving and movement. A guest near the door, a girl who has been sitting alone, must have heard our conversation. She stands up and turns towards us and smiles.

'I'm finished here,' she says in broken Spanish. 'If we push this table aside, you could get past if you like.'

Paulina smiles and helps the young woman to move the table. 'Thank you so much,' my daughter says, but she gives *me* a look that says *I'll speak to you later*.

I go to move towards the door and smile my biggest smile for the lovely young girl who has moved mountains to accommodate my age. Wherever she comes from, they obviously respect their elders. The girl is staring intensely at me, and my smile fades as I stand still and stare back at her. She looks exactly like ... But it isn't possible ...

I drop my cane, and when I go to pick it up, I fall forward crashing into another table, sending their pot of coffee spilling across the white cloth.

Paulina stares, horrified, and it's left to the young guest to rush to my side.

'Are you okay?' The girl crouches down, puts her hand out to hold mine, and I let my gnarled fingers fold around hers. 'I'm sorry to have startled you,' she says. 'I look very like her. My grandmother. Sonia Almez. You knew her very well when you were both young, didn't you? My name is Shona Moran. I'm from Ireland.'

I shake my head from side to side. My eyes blur with tears as I look up at what looks like Sonia's younger face smiling down at me. Both she and Paulina heave me back up to standing, and the young girl pulls out a seat for me. I sit and try to recover from the fall and from seeing her.

'Sonia's friend Eileen told me where I might find you, Enrico,' she says. Her accent is unmistakably Irish and brings me straight back to that time when I secretly visited Sonia in Ireland. 'I wanted to meet someone who knew my grandmother. I don't know if she had any other family here, but it would be wonderful if she does.'

The other people in the breakfast room have settled back down now; the spectacle I made is over. I still can't find my speech. What can I tell this girl of the truth?

'Some years back, Enrico, I found out that I was adopted, and I went a bit off the rails for a while. But then my birth sister, Anna, found me, and I've been trying to get to know her and our extended family in Donegal. Then I met Sonia's best friend, Eileen, and she told me all about my grandmother and how she came from here, and she said that if I came to find you that you could tell me more about her and her life before she went to Ireland and … Oh, I'm sorry. I didn't mean to upset you.'

The tears escape and flow and there's nothing I can do to stop them. Shona must be another of Maria's daughters. Anna's sister, she said. Now I'm sobbing openly, for Sonia and all that was lost.

Paulina hands me a napkin and I try to compose myself. I take a deep breath and look at the vision beside me. How can I tell this girl of the story of Sonia and me, and the devastating effect that Franco's atrocities had on our lives? But mostly, how can I tell her what happened after?

Sonia once said that sometimes a lie is the only kindness. But perhaps it's time now for the truth.

PART ONE

CHAPTER ONE

July 1946

The evening sand was gloriously cool to the touch after the burning hot day. Sonia sat and stared at the sea, hugging her knees to her chest and smiling at her thoughts of Enrico. To her right, a couple of visitors sat holding hands, their feet in the water, just touching. Sonia could feel their chemistry from where she was, or perhaps it was her own warm thinking that was making her tummy flutter.

'It's like a great big ball of fire,' the man said.

'But it's just sitting out there on the water. It must be a big ship, all lit up; maybe one of those new cruising ships?' the woman replied.

'It's too far in for that, and it's moving upwards.' He shook his head.

Sonia burst with laughter that she couldn't hold in any longer. These northerners were definitely city people. How could they mistake one of nature's beauties for a ship?

'It's the moon,' she called over. 'Watch now how it rises from the water to its place in the sky.'

The visitors looked at her as if she were mad.

'How can it be the moon? So full of colour? And it sits on the water like an oval ball,' said the woman.

'Watch,' said Sonia. And the three sat in silence as slowly the moon rose up from the water, righting itself into a circle like it was dressing for business. Within fifteen minutes it was sitting in its rightful place in the night-blue sky.

Sonia was filled with an awe that she had never lost in all her sixteen years of watching the day become night in the beauty of Benalmádena. A spectacle that could only be beaten by its rival: the night becoming day, when the pattern was reversed. Sonia would listen to none of her school friends or her brother talking about wanting to leave home to work in Malaga or further away. Sonia was going nowhere but here. Here with Enrico Sanchez.

Today he had said he loved her, and Sonia had been surprised at how this had made her feel: warm and shivery at the same time and filled with a happiness she couldn't even begin to describe. She had always known that he loved her and that she loved him in return … but now it felt perfect.

The moon had joined the stars that would multiply as the dark became more prominent, and the couple were getting up and smiling at her. 'Gracias,' they said, and Sonia smiled back and pitied them their return to city life.

'Sonia!' A roar rang out from the door of the house at the edge of the beach, shattering her smile and the warmth into tiny pieces. Her father was calling, but as long as Sonia had Enrico, she could put all the pieces back together again. No matter what happened, there would always be Enrico, and she whispered his name to herself as she turned towards the house.

'Sonia!' her father called again, and Sonia ran.

'Yes, papá.'

'What do you think you are doing sitting on the beach like you hadn't a care in the world when your mother is slaving away in the kitchen preparing the food for tomorrow's customers? Go inside and help her.'

Sonia braced herself for the slap that would greet her as she walked through the door on her way past her father. Her brother wasn't here to protect her. Miguel had seen their father take up the bottle and go to sit on the terrace and had made himself scarce.

But Sonia had stayed, knowing that the more her father drank, the more her mother would eventually need her. She cried out as her father hit her: not because she was in too much pain, but because if he thought that he hadn't hurt her he would strike again.

'Let that be a lesson to you. Get inside,' he said, and he stumbled back to the terrace and his bottle.

Sonia walked into the large kitchen, past her mother bent over the table, and went straight to the bowl of cool water in the back room. She soaked a clean cloth and returned to where her mother was sitting, holding her shoulder. Sonia pulled back the white collar of her mother's blouse and placed the cool wetness softly on the welt that was forming there. They didn't speak as there was nothing to say that hadn't been said before. Cristina didn't cry but sat and let her daughter nurse her.

When Sonia had done all she could, the two women set about preparing the vegetables for the next day. The house was silent but for her father Hugo's singing: a grating sound ringing out and shaking the house. Sonia worked on and felt the joy of her day slip away. There were some things that even Enrico's love couldn't fix.

CHAPTER TWO

S onia sat upright in her bed as the sun was beginning to filter through the shutters. It must be about half past five in the morning, she thought, and something had woken her. She slipped her feet slowly over the side of the bed. The house wouldn't be waking for another hour, but Sonia felt that she was being dragged from her sleep to go outside.

She shuffled quietly out of her room and tiptoed down the hall. At the door, she slipped on her shoes and wrapped her mother's shawl around her bare shoulders. The heavy black wool contrasted against the light white cotton of her nightgown felt strange and awkward, but something was pulling her. She could hear a light sound in the distance, like something far out to sea, but it was coming from inland. Everything was normally draped in silence at this time of the morning, but the sound was there. She could hear it, and the more she concentrated on the sound, the louder it seemed. Or was it that the sound was travelling towards her?

Sonia shook her head. Bulls in the distance, or nearer? Maybe some had escaped the bull ring and were heading her way right now, charging and dangerous. Sonia turned to go back into her house, but behind her the noise of people shouting and wailing came again. Sonia turned back and began to run towards the cries in the distance. Anger or sadness, or was it keening someone who was dead? Something very bad had happened.

Sonia felt from the noise that this was no natural death of someone old, but sudden and terrible, and it was getting nearer, heading in her direction. Why were they heading towards the coast? If it was one of the fishermen, it would be someone her family knew well. Her steps slowed to a walk and then she stopped. The keening was louder now, over the hill. Sonia stood and stared at the top of a jutting rock as the first men came into sight; their faces set in anger, their feet marching as if for battle. One was Enrico's friend, Alejandro, his face murderous.

'Death to them!' he shouted. 'Death to the killing bastards!'

Seconds later, surrounded by men and women, Enrico reached the tip of the hill carrying something in his arms. Not something, *someone*. He stopped still when he saw Sonia. The crowd moved forward, gentler now, the cries quieter. The marching slowed, then, as they neared Sonia, they stopped. One or two murmured her name, while the stillness of the morning screamed in her ears. Enrico was holding a man in his arms, limp and lifeless; when he and Sonia locked eyes. Enrico's face crumpled, and he fell on his knees and called her name.

'Sonia. Sonia, I'm sorry.'

Sonia let go of the shawl around her shoulders. It dropped to the ground. She couldn't move. She could hear Enrico's cries, and she could see his silhouette in front of her as the sun chose that moment to rise above the hills, as though it had been following him. Sonia could feel the cool of the morning breeze coming behind from the sea, and she could taste the bile rising from deep inside her into her mouth. Sonia could smell the flowers beside her as they opened their petals to welcome the morning sun. All her senses were finely honed, proving to her that she was alive, but she still couldn't move. Then, the world stopped. Sonia swayed, and a woman ran to her and caught her as she fell. The last thing that Sonia saw before her senses left her was the body of her brother, Miguel, in Enrico's arms.

As Sonia fell, Enrico laid his friend gently on the ground. The man whom he had known all his life had been snuffed out like a bonfire quenched.

'Alejandro,' he called. 'Take my place and carry Miguel to his house.'

Alejandro moved back and hugged Enrico as they passed, a small comfort.

Enrico stumbled towards his beautiful Sonia, lying with her head on a woman's lap. With easy strength he lifted her up: her lightness contrasting with the heaviness of her dead brother.

The woman lifted the shawl from the ground and wrapped it around the small, quiet girl now in his arms.

'Sleep, little one,' she said as she covered her. 'Only pain waits for you.' She began her keening once more and the other women followed with their own cries.

The men marched on towards Sonia's house, their anger quieted for now. They had to consider the family: the sister a reminder of the shock that awaited the parents. The men had seen the young man shot down, so their anger at the murderers was to be expected, but the family were about to be told of the death of a son, a light gone from their lives. The keening, humming now, moved towards the house by the sea.

Cristina Almez looked at her useless husband, drunkenly asleep in a corner of the terrace. The house was now empty of mourners as her husband's roars had scared even the hardiest keener away.

She couldn't bear to look at the other man lying on the table on the terrace. *Almost* man. Her eighteen-year-old boy. Her beautiful Miguel. The handsome son who had made her laugh; shown her how to be happy. Her husband was a mistake, but Cristina had lived for her son. Since he was a child, Miguel had been able to quell his father with a look that said *I'm stronger than you. I'm intelligent. Do wrong and I will make you sorry.* Miguel held all the promise of their family in his one big presence. *Don't worry. I'll work it out.*

Who would work things out now?

Cristina rocked herself back and forward and clenched her fists until her fingernails made the palms of her hands bleed.

Sonia sat by her brother, staring at where she knew the gunshot to be; the hole torn in his heart, a mirror of the hole grief was now tearing in her own. Her face hardened. There was little left of her family with Miguel gone: the gentle giant who had protected her all her life.

Sonia looked away from her brother to her father. The man's head lolled to the side, dribble falling from the corner of his mouth to his chin to meet with earlier drool, dried and congealed. The mask of sadness left her face to be replaced with one of disgust.

The gate clicked open and the shadow of Enrico slid across to her side, but still Sonia didn't take her eyes from her father.

'We could take this man now, Enrico; you and I,' Sonia said. 'Carry him to the sea and lower him in. When his body is found on the sand in the morning, we could say he walked into the waves to drown away his grief.'

At Sonia's words, Cristina woke from her rocking. She got up slowly from her chair, walked the short length of the terrace and slapped her daughter full across the face.

The sharp crack made Enrico jump, and Sonia fell in a heap onto the floor.

'Sonia, are you all right?' Enrico cried. He knelt down, lifted her towards him and held her. He couldn't believe what

Cristina had done. 'How dare you treat your daughter like that?' he shouted at her.

'Don't worry, Enrico, it's all right.' Sonia remained on the mosaic tiled floor in Enrico's arms, sobbing. 'Mamá is angry that it is Miguel and not me who is lying there dead. She knows I am little to her, and that I have nothing to offer her – like that worthless piece of dirt that breathes like a sleeping bull in the corner. Miguel was our warm sun, the moon on a dark night, and he had all the magic of the stars. Now the world is empty.'

Cristina's face crumpled once more, and she retreated to her chair and her rocking.

Enrico circled his arms around Sonia and spoke to her gently, his voice a whisper, his eyes fixed on the body of the young man who had been his friend. 'No, Sonia. It won't be like that. It will never be like that. I will never leave you. Miguel knew that we would be together, and even through his teasing and joking, I know that he approved of us. We have his blessing, and we need nobody else. I'm here, Sonia.'

Sonia closed her eyes and let his touch tell her that he told the truth. Enrico would take her to the ends of the earth, and he would never leave her.

'You are right, Sonia. You are nothing to me.' Cristina spoke in monotone.

Sonia sat up and looked over at her mother.

'You are not of *me*,' Cristina continued, 'but of that living heap of wasted anger.' She barked a sharp, bitter laugh. 'The man you talk of with such hate, is the only living blood relation that you have.'

Sonia pulled herself to standing, her mother's words already filling her stomach with fear. She leaned on the makeshift table that held her brother, as if, even in death, his strength could hold her together. She stared at her mother, whose face didn't show the emotion of words of such destruction; words that were right now eating through her daughter. Sonia shook her head and swallowed, trying to find her voice.

'Mamá …' she whispered.

'No, Sonia Almez. Not *your* mamá. Only Miguel. Never you.'

'I didn't mean what I said earlier, mamá,' Sonia said. 'About being useless to you. This day is making us say untruths that have no meaning, and I am hurting as much as you are.'

Enrico turned to where Señora Almez was sitting, rubbing at the blood on her palms.

'Señora, how can you sit and say these things to Sonia, who has loved and protected you from Hugo, alongside her brother, all her life? She is the most subservient daughter on this coast, so I don't excuse your words on the back of your grief. Sonia has lost her only brother and I have lost my closest friend, so take what you said away. Don't make this day worse than it is. Then let us all try to sleep before we say our final goodbye to Miguel tomorrow.'

Cristina stood and wailed. Then she grabbed a flowerpot from nearby. She wielded it in Enrico's direction, missing him and sending it flying, smashing a mosaic tile on the ground.

As she did so, Hugo awoke and stared, horrified, at the damage on the ground.

'My mosaic,' he whispered. 'My beautiful work, destroyed.' He tried to stand but fell forward onto the mosaic he had lovingly created as a younger man. A fisherman sailing away on his boat, the sun rising behind him, while a young woman waved from the beach.

'Fitting,' said Cristina, a smirk on her face. 'Fitting that I should damage the work that you created in memory of your darling *Rosita*.'

Cristina walked up behind Sonia and turned her around to face her.

'This is what you need to know, Sonia. Sixteen years ago, your father brought me and little Miguel up into the Malaguenian hills. He asked me to care for his cousin Rosita. He told me that her family had thrown her out when they realised that she was carrying a baby from a married man. Young and trusting, I felt sorry for the mother and her child-to-be. I remember thinking how kind my husband was to bring his shamed cousin to a farmer's hut and organise her care. I helped her give birth, although I had no idea what I was doing. There were complications and she bled to death, and in my youth, I blamed myself, but her baby girl screamed with life. "She needs a mother, Cristina," Hugo said. "Take her home with us and we will say she is ours. Nobody need know what has happened."

'So I took her back here, and I made her mine and I loved her. But from that day Hugo began to drink himself into a stupor. Whenever he was sober enough, he worked on this mosaic in Rosita's memory. Hugo could have been an artist had he lived a better life, but his whole being became a vessel for his anger and I became the recipient of his punches. On your tenth birthday I found out why. It was also the tenth anniversary of Rosita's death. He told me in a drunken rage about his beautiful Rosita, who was never his cousin. How he had only ever loved *her*, but his family had insisted he marry me, Cristina, the café owner's daughter, and not a peasant from the hills. *You* had been the cause of Rosita's death and *I* had let her die. Hugo never forgave either of us. And he never will.'

Now hearing his name, Hugo stopped staring at the damaged tile and staggered to standing. He tried to register where he was, but all he could see was the gate. He stumbled out into the night in search of some more wine, mumbling incoherently as he left.

Sonia stood before her mother in silence, one hand holding Miguel's lifeless hand and the other gripping Enrico's, who stood, disbelieving and horrified, beside the two women.

'Why now, Cristina?' Enrico asked. 'Why have you chosen today to tell such a story?'

Cristina turned and made her way back to her chair.

'Miguel made me promise not to tell,' she said when she was settled. 'He said that, as long as he lived, his sister was as much a part of this family as he was. But now he's dead, Sonia, and you are not a part of me.'

CHAPTER THREE

S onia chopped the last of the vegetables and pushed them to one side. The fishermen would be ashore soon and looking for drink and food to wash away the salt in their mouths at the end of their hard-working day. Her mother was in bed wrapped in bandages to cover the broken ribs. It had been very bad this time, the 'fall' – bad enough to necessitate the doctor from Arroyo. He had asked what had happened to her other bones. Her nose was misshapen. Her fingers crooked.

'I'm clumsy,' Cristina had said. 'I have been clumsy all my married life.'

The doctor knew but said nothing. He nodded his head and sighed.

'You must stay in bed for two weeks, Señora Almez.'

Sonia had snorted at this, knowing full well her father would never allow it.

'I am counting on you, Señorita Almez, to make sure it happens.'

Then he left. Left her mother lying in her bed, crying in pain – not all of it physical – and left Sonia to the honour of telling her father when he eventually came back with the fishermen.

Hugo had been getting worse since Miguel's death. He still left the house at the same time each day pretending that he was going out on the boats with the other men, but Sonia hadn't smelled the sea on his clothes for a long time. Only the smell of alcohol and tobacco. The people along the coast knew that Señor Almez was not being taken out fishing any more. He was too big a risk to take when all their lives at sea depended on being alert and absolutely sober.

So now Sonia knew that their only income was the café. She had taken it on herself to expand from just the fishermen's dinner in the evening. She packed food for their boat trips, gave them breakfast before they left. She had always been good at mending her father's nets, and now she took on as many as she could. If her mother was to be in bed for two weeks, then she would be working night and day.

'Sonia!' She jumped at her father's shout. 'Sonia! Come out here and bring your tired father a drink.' Sonia looked at the glazed look in her father's eyes and realised he must have been drinking since he left the house that morning. She wondered where the money came from when they had so little. He had no idea that he had left his wife in bed with broken ribs from the beating he had given her the night before. There was no point explaining to him what was wrong with her mother.

Sonia put the glass down in front of her father.

'The other men are coming behind me. I hope everything is ready. They've had ... I mean, *we've* had ... a big haul today so we're all exceptionally hungry.

'Yes, papá. Everything is ready.'

'And your mother. Tell her to hurry. I'm starving.'

Sonia thought about this. If she gave him a lot to drink quickly, on top of all he had already drank, then maybe he might not notice that her mother wasn't around. It was always Sonia who served anyway.

'Yes, papá. I'll tell her.' Sonia ran inside and got herself busy. At least these days, since Enrico had finished school, he was out fishing with his uncle, and he would be in shortly. He would make her feel better. Everything would be all right.

When the other men had left, and Sonia's father was asleep, head down across the table, Sonia and Enrico had a chance to be on their own outside. Sonia explained to Enrico how her father had got worse since Miguel had died. She told him where her mother was and why.

Enrico's face filled with anger, and he stared out at the sea.

'I have a name, Sonia,' he said.

'What do you mean? A name for who?'

'The man who killed your brother, Sonia. I know who it was. He's from the pueblo. He's a staunch Nationalist, high up with Franco's lot. Alejandro overheard him in a bar when a few drinks loosened his tongue. This man was spouting on about how his brother had shot a youth in Arroyo. "Mistaken identity," he said; that the whole country was falling apart if you could shoot a man first and then ask questions later. Alejandro realised immediately who he was talking about. He was lucky. If it was me who had been there, then the brother would be dead, but Alej pretended to befriend him. Got him to spill the beans about his brother; how he had been given the name of a man to arrest; how Miguel was outside this man's house. When he questioned Miguel, he had put up resistance and denied he even knew the man. A scuffle began, and the soldier said his gun went off.'

Sonia was pale. 'Are you telling me my brother's death was a mistake, Enrico? Because I could have told you that already. This whole crazy war was a mistake. Brother against brother. Neighbour killing neighbour. Republicans played their part in their own bloodbath. Then, Nationalists took over from them. Red terror followed by white terror …'

'Don't forget that I lost my family to the Nationalists, Sonia. Gunned down on the road out of Malaga, swatted like flies. If it wasn't for my uncle bringing me up here with my cousins, I would probably be dead now too. They have taken everything from me, and now they start on your family. I want revenge. Miguel was my best friend.'

'And what will you have to show for it? Nothing. This town has lived through too much, and still it comes. Whoever is the winner, wreaks havoc on the other side. So, Miguel is killed. Then you kill his killer. Then, will his brother kill you and where will it end? No, Enrico. You will not kill this man in my name or my brother's.'

Sonia was interrupted by her father's shouts for her mother. 'Cristina! Cristina! Get out here!' She rushed back into the kitchen, followed by Enrico. Her father was making his way towards their bedroom.

'We have enough battles to fight in this house without bringing down Franco's wrath on ourselves,' she said. 'I beg you. Hold your head down and say nothing. Be a fisherman and live life the way we always have.'

Enrico took the chopping knife from the table and ploughed it down into the wood. 'No! You don't understand, Sonia. This man said that an innocent man had been killed and his brother had felt no remorse. He said his brother had laughed when he said Miguel's name. "What's one Miguel from another?" Sonia I'm going to kill this man's brother.'

Sonia pulled the knife from the wood and placed it out of the way. She felt so much older than the girl she had been before Miguel died. She hissed her anger at Enrico. 'Stay out of earshot of my father and the others with that talk. So, you are leaving me and going to make Miguel come back to life for me by killing the man who shot him and ending up getting shot yourself? Or if you do live, you'll be telling your tale from the inside of Malaga Jail.'

'So you would have me sit here, knowing what I know, and letting your brother's death go unavenged as if it meant nothing to any of us? I thought you of all people would understand that I have to do this, Sonia.'

Sonia turned away shaking her head. 'Then you don't know me as well as you think you do, Enrico Sanchez. I value having the one person I love beside me for life, much more than I do losing the two men that can save me from the badness of that imbecile shouting his head off for drink out there. I need you here. If you go … if they kill you or take you from me, what have I got then? A drunken father and a mother who was never my mother.' Her tears fell, and Enrico put his arms around her and held her.

'I can't ignore this, Sonia, but I won't be gone long. I would never leave you to that bastard.'

In answer, she heard her papá's roars come from the room he shared with her mamá, and she pushed Enrico away and ran to her mother's aid.

When she returned, having taken part of the beating that was meant for her mother, there was no sign of Enrico. No one else was there to witness the continuing Almez family horrors.

CHAPTER FOUR

'It's time to go home now, Sonia. There is nowhere left to look, no one left to ask. Enrico is most probably hiding out somewhere. When the heat is off, he'll let us know where he is. But ...'

Alejandro didn't finish. They both knew what he was going to say. That Enrico had either been arrested in his attempt to kill Miguel's murderer or he had escaped and was in hiding. There was no way of knowing without getting themselves into trouble.

'Alejandro, if Enrico was able to come and look for me, then nothing would stand in his way. If he was dead, then the Nationalists would make sure that we knew about it so that they could gloat. He's out here somewhere, Alej, and I'm going to find him. You can run home if you want to, but I'm waiting to hear more.'

'Sonia, he must be in prison ...'

'No! The guards said that there was no one of his name in there. Surely, they would be delighted to tell us of his capture if they had him?'

'Either way, Sonia, he's in trouble. And the more we ask after him, the more we put ourselves in question. I'm not *running* home, as you put it. If Enrico ever found out that I had led you into danger, he would go crazy.'

Sonia sighed and shook her head; the hopelessness of the search was so frustrating. Every so often somebody they knew disappeared from their hometown. Mostly men who were joining the other Republicans to fight underground against the Nationalists, but sometimes women too. A month ago, Sonia had been enraged with Enrico for not keeping his head down and getting on with their lives. Now the thought of joining these men in some way seemed attractive to her. Some of those who disappeared were taken by soldiers with made-up allegations for their arrest. Those men usually didn't come back home. It was like there was only an entrance door into Malaga Jail and the only way out was in a coffin.

But Sonia couldn't think about such things. She looked towards the Malaga hills. Was Enrico hiding out there? If he *was* in Malaga Jail, then she believed he was alive. She would have to go home with Alejandro.

'All right, Alej, you win for now. We'll let the dust settle on our search. I want to go home to see how mamá is doing, but then we will look again. I will leave nothing overlooked until I know where Enrico is. I know that if it was me who was missing, he would not give in.'

'No, Sonia. You are both as stubborn as each other. I need to check on my own family too. And then, if you promise to live life quietly for a while, I will come back under a false name and I will find him. Tonight, we'll sleep hidden on the beach once more, and first thing tomorrow we leave the city and head for home.'

Sonia reached over and embraced her brother's friend. 'Thank you, Alej. I couldn't have survived out here without you.'

Alejandro hugged her back. 'Ha. Do you really think your brother wouldn't find some way to punish me from up there if I'd let his sixteen-year-old sister wander the streets of Malaga city on her own? And Enrico would finish the job for him.' He pushed Sonia away gently and looked her in the eye. 'I believe he is alive too, Sonia. There were three of us always together growing up. Miguel, Enrico and me. I couldn't face being the only one left. He's out there, and we'll find him.'

They turned to walk towards the sea and Alejandro's face fell. Three Nationalist soldiers were heading towards them. 'Hold my hand, Sonia. We are naughty teenagers who got carried away with the time and are hurrying home now to our angry parents. Look coy and embarrassed and let me speak.'

But their attempt at anonymity failed before they had a chance to try it. The soldiers blocked their path and the taller one put a hand on Sonia's shoulder.

'Sonia Almez, at last. I've been trying to find you. And here is Enrico's playmate too. What a catch. We passed you in the car and couldn't believe our luck. Search them.'

The other soldiers looked for weapons but found nothing but a bit of leftover food that Sonia had managed to steal that day.

'Follow us without a word, and you might find that it won't be all bad for you. You've been asking many questions, and there are consequences to asking too many questions. I have a car waiting.'

'I know who *you* are,' Alejandro said quietly. 'You are—'

Sonia watched in horror as her friend got a belt from a gun across his back and fell forward.

'Without a word, I told you. Now get up and try to behave yourself for the rest of the evening.'

Alejandro dragged himself to standing, and Sonia knew he was trying to get her attention to tell her who the soldier was, but she looked away, not willing to give them any reason to hurt him again. Her heart pounded as she remembered scenes of friends and family arrested by the Nationalists who never came back to their families. She was close to tears, but she held her head high and walked between the soldiers.

When they got to the car, Sonia realised that this soldier must be high up in the army to be afforded such a luxury. He held open the door to the passenger seat for Sonia and smiled at her as she climbed in while the other two soldiers bundled Alejandro into the back seat between them.

Sonia closed her eyes against the tears and the unfamiliar territory as they drove through Malaga. After fifteen minutes, they pulled up outside a building adorned with Nationalist flags and pictures of Franco. There were bars on the windows and Sonia realised that this was Malaga Jail. She was sixteen years old and afraid for her life.

Sonia sat in the back seat of the car, contemplating her fate. Why had they only taken Alej into the building and left no one to guard her? She could try to escape, but that was probably what they hoped she would do. *We shot her whilst she was trying to run.* She would stay where she was and see what panned out.

Looking up at the barred windows, she wondered if Enrico was in there. Had he seen Alejandro being brought in? Did he know that she was there, that she'd been asking about him, searching for him? It had all been so futile. In the years since Franco had taken power, so many bad things had happened. Sonia could hardly remember the carefree years of her early childhood. It was so hard to carry on normal life with all the stresses of being on your guard all of the time. People Sonia had played with when she was younger were now people she couldn't trust.

The older soldier was coming out of the building, heading back to the car. He flung himself onto the driver's seat and slammed the door, muttering something about bureaucracy under his breath.

'So, let's get you home, Sonia Almez,' he said, pulling out onto the deserted road once more. 'It's taken me weeks to get to you. Thank God you're such a nosy little nuisance and your many questions about Sanchez helped me to find you eventually.'

Sonia was scared and hopeful at the same time.

'You're bringing me home? What about Alejandro? Is he going home too?'

'Alejandro won't be going home for a while. They're trying to pin something on him to link him to Sanchez. And I don't doubt that they will. Hot-headed Republicans are easy to pick out. Easy to find something they did or said in the past to land them in trouble. And he's nineteen. Old enough to face the music. You, on the other hand, at sixteen are easier to prove innocent.'

The car slowed at a crossroads and her driver waved at another soldier patrolling the street.

'Cover your face, Sonia. I don't want you seen by others. Get into the backseat and hunker down too.'

'I don't understand,' she said, climbing back and pushing her body further down and putting her hand over her face. 'How can Alej be guilty and I'm innocent.? He did nothing. It was me who asked him to—'

'You're right,' said the soldier. 'He is innocent, and I will do what I can to make sure that he serves a minimum sentence and then leaves the country before he lands himself into any more trouble.'

'How can that happen? How can he leave Spain? And anyhow, he won't want to leave. Alejandro loves his country. All his family, his friends, they're everything to him here.'

'I have good contacts. I have power. And if your friend has any sense, he will go where he will be safe.'

They were heading along the coast, away from Malaga, towards Benalmádena. Sonia was looking forward to getting home, but she knew that she would get a beating from her father for going away and leaving all the work to her mother for two weeks. The driver interrupted her thinking.

'So, Sonia. Do you really not know where he is? Enrico Sanchez?'

Sonia stayed quiet, wondering what this man knew of Enrico. If he was asking her then Enrico must be still on the run. He must be safe, or they would have found him by now. If this man had heard about her asking questions, then why had Enrico not heard through his Republican friends?

'It will be better for him, Sonia, if I find him before the other authorities do. He is a wanted man. If I can get to him before—'

'Why? What has he done?'

'Nothing as yet. But he has threatened to kill the soldier who shot your brother. I would like to find him before he does that. If I don't, if he shoots and he is wanted for murder, he will be executed.'

'No! No, they can't. He is angry. He loved Miguel like a brother.'

'I understand that, Sonia, and I am so sorry that your brother was killed. This war has taken far too many innocent by-standers, but it shouldn't have to take Enrico's life too. If you have any idea where he is, you need to tell me. You have to trust me.'

Sonia was so tired. The heat of the spring evening was making her sleepy. She slipped down more in the back seat. Enrico was to be executed if he carried out his threats.

'I have no idea where he is,' she whispered. Then she lay back and cried into the leather seat.

Sitting up with a jump, Sonia rubbed her eyes and looked around her. The car was stopped, and the soldier had been shaking her awake. How could she have slept in the backseat of a car belonging to a Nationalist soldier who had arrested Alej and had lied to her about taking her home? She had some idea where she was. Perhaps on the outskirts of the pueblo. She was so tired. Too many nights sleeping on the cold, uncomfortable sand had caught up with her.

'Where are we?' she asked. 'You said you were bringing me home.' She was a fool to believe that this filthy Nationalist had any good intentions. They might hurt her to get information about Enrico. Her captor held open the door, smiling at her, expecting her to get out. Could she run yet? Would he really shoot her?

'And indeed, I have brought you home. To my home. You are to be my honoured guest until I have decided where the safest place is for you to go. Come on, Sonia. Don't cause a scene here. I don't want my neighbours knowing and telling others that you are here.'

Sonia got out and he closed the door.

'Follow me, my dear, and trust me. If you *are* caught in my house, we are both in terrible trouble.'

It was this last statement that made Sonia decide to follow him into the house; after all, what option did she have? Alejandro was in prison, Miguel was dead, and Enrico was lost. Sonia had nobody else to help her. So she followed the Nationalist soldier into his house, every step filling her with more dread at what awaited her behind those whitewashed walls.

CHAPTER FIVE

The rising sun woke Sonia in the strange room, and she sat up with a start. The soft cotton night gown and the silky sheets felt strange against her skin. A week of sleeping rough on the beaches had helped her to sleep well, despite her anxious thoughts. She could hear men's raised voices down the hall from where she remembered the kitchen was. One belonged to the man who had brought her here and the other sounded similar but harsher. She sat motionless on the bed, so afraid of what was waiting for her on the other side of the door.

Roberto Rodriguez sat face to face with his brother, Alberto, across the large wooden kitchen table. Roberto was determined to get his brother to agree to his plans for their family.

'I have their papers written up, Alberto, and all you have to do is sign them. There have been too many threats from the dirty rojos to harm the girls. Lucia and Dolores have been prisoners in this house, and that's no life for two young girls. Sign the papers, mi hermano, and let them leave for Ireland with Sister Mary-Anne. They will be safe there until we can eradicate the enemy here, and then your daughter and mine can return to live their lives in Spain.'

Roberto waited, trying to read his brother's face for signs of appeasement. Alberto was difficult to fathom. Even Roberto, who had known him all his life, could never tell which way the man would turn in any given situation. He took a breath and let it out slowly in anticipation.

In a matter of seconds, the look in Alberto's eyes went from contemplation to wild anger. He picked up a floral jug of bougainvillea and flung it against the wall. Then he walked over to Roberto, and stood over him. Roberto had always been taller and broader than his older brother, but this did not stop Alberto letting him know who was in charge of their family.

'Roberto,' Alberto said quietly. 'There is no safety in travel at the moment, so our girls would be at risk the moment they left here. The rojos are everywhere, especially here near Malaga, and I will not permit Lucia to travel. You promised to keep her safe here in your house while Eva and I have important work in Madrid with Franco. I cannot believe that you have brought me all the way down here saying that you needed to see me on a matter of extreme urgency. Your duties here in the south are mundane, so deal with them and look after my daughter. Send your daughter Dolores to Ireland with your nun friend if you so wish, but my Lucia stays here in her own country.'

Alberto smiled and ruffled his brother's thick, black curls. Then he calmly sat back down at the table.

Roberto was incensed but he tried to breathe his way through. Forty-five years' experience of living around Alberto had to amount to some sort of knowledge of how to deal with the wickedness that was his brother. An idea was forming in his mind, so he quietly sat beside Alberto and tried again.

'I wish I had your strength, Alberto, but I feel so helpless standing back while Dolores is under threat. I know it's what her mother would have wished had she lived. Please, sign the papers for me to allow her to travel and I'll cross out your daughter's name. I want Dolores to go to Ireland with Sister Mary-Anne, but Lucia can stay here, and I will do my absolute best to keep her safe.'

Alberto stared at his brother and shook his head. 'You are wrong.

This is not the way to do this, but Dolores is your responsibility so put her in danger if you wish. Pass me the papers.'

Roberto pushed over the travel pass to his brother, who signed it without paying any heed to what was written there. Alberto trusted his brother as a fellow soldier on the side of Franco and he was blood. He was quite sure that Roberto would never do anything wrong against his brother or against Franco. And Roberto had used that trust against him many times and would do so again.

The day Roberto had watched his drunken brother shoot Sonia Almez's brother in the street for no reason was the day that strengthened his resolve. At first, he had wallowed in drunken shame, but then he realised what he had to do. Since then, Roberto had used his brother's signature many times to have prisoners pardoned or to have them travel to France or further.

He knew that one day he would be caught out helping the enemy. He and Alberto, two years his senior, had played together when they were children. But he was quite sure that his brother would shoot him dead for his badness. It was a risk he had to take. Everyone in Spain was risking their lives on one side or the other. Roberto felt that he had been born to the wrong family. Everything about Franco's government was wrong, and Roberto would fight to the death to defend his beloved Spain, but he would not risk his daughter's life.

Alberto signed the papers and pushed them back to him.

'Bring Lucia here, Roberto. I wish to speak with her, and I have a letter for her from her mother.'

Roberto rose to go and get his niece. He knew that fourteen-year-old Lucia needed more than a letter from the mother who had abandoned her in Malaga for the society in Madrid; and now, Lucia might be without her cousin Dolores for friendship. The poor girl.

He passed the room where the girl, Sonia, was sleeping. He hoped she had the tact to stay quietly where she was until she was sent for.

He knocked on Lucia's bedroom door and woke the teenager with the news that her father had given him, knowing she would agree to all that was asked of her, but with a broken heart. Quiet, placid Lucia was everything that her parents were not. Later, she would cry but never in front of her father.

Ten minutes later, at the door of the villa, Lucia kissed her father, Alberto, dutifully on each cheek. She wished him a safe journey and sent her affections to her mother. No hugs were exchanged between father and daughter. Lucia's love was reserved for her widowed Uncle Roberto who had brought her up, together with her cousin, Dolores, in a loving, happy home.

Watching the farewell, Roberto realised that Lucia would not manage life without her cousin. He smiled and waved at the back of his brother's car as it wound its way down the path towards the road, but his mind began to refashion his earlier plan for the girls. He knew now what he would do.

He would allow Lucia to go with Dolores, and he would take the brunt of his brother's anger later. 'Another threat arrived,' he would say. 'I acted on impulse to keep your daughter safe. Her name was already on the papers, and there was no time to reach you. Your daughter is alive now because of what I did,' he would tell his brother. 'This was the only way to keep her from harm.'

But he would also send Sonia to Ireland with the girls – dressed as the nun, Sister Mary-Anne. *A silent order of nuns*, Lucia and Dolores would explain to anyone who asked.

When Roberto was sure that his brother was well away from the house, he knocked on Sonia's bedroom door. Sitting on the edge of the bed, Sonia looked frightened and so much younger and more vulnerable than she had by her friend's side the evening before.

'Señorita Almez, I hope you have slept well. Forgive me for intruding and not waiting for you in the family room, but I need to speak to you urgently. You are in great danger outside this house. You are the sister of a dead Republican and the girlfriend of a wanted criminal in the eyes of the Nationalist soldiers. So you have to trust me and know that I am your friend.'

Sonia listened to Roberto's plan for her to accompany his daughter and his niece to Ireland. Dressed properly, Sonia could look much older than her sixteen years. Now, she was to become the silent Sister Mary-Anne and deliver the girls to the safety of the convent in Dublin. In return, Roberto promised to watch out for her family and especially for Enrico. He would keep him from the gallows and send him to her as soon as he could find him.

This last part was what Sonia clung to. No matter where she was, she would be all right as long as Enrico was with her. But inside, her heart was breaking for the country she would be leaving behind.

Sister Mary-Anne stayed in her cabin for most of the journey to Ireland. The ship had called at many ports as the captain and crew dropped and collected cargo as they went, but the three ladies were told to stay on board and to stay out of the way. The captain had been paid handsomely to deliver his human cargo, but Roberto had cleverly held back half until he had news that the girls had been delivered to the convent in Dublin. Captain Juan was taking no chances on not collecting his second half from the Nationalist soldier in Malaga.

'I think I'm going to go mad down here,' Dolores repeated for the tenth time that day.

'You were born mad,' said Lucia. 'No change there.'

Sonia had listened to the cousins bickering like siblings for weeks. At least they had the freedom of letting their frustration out. She was afraid to say anything most of the time in case somebody overheard the so-called nun from the silent order actually talking and became suspicious. If she spoke at all it was in a whisper or using sign language.

When the weather had been particularly bad two weeks before, Sonia had let out a scream as the ship had lurched out of the water, one half seeming to stay up for an age before it came crashing back down to the waves. She thought that they would all die that day.

Eventually, as they lay in their hammocks that night and slept as the storm died outside, Sonia felt her journey taking her further away from her friends and from her Enrico. She was afraid to upset the girls any further, so the tears she shed were silent, and she wiped her face on the rough fabric of her nun's habit.

'I wonder how much longer we'll be on the ship,' said Lucia. 'Captain Juan won't tell us anything. I've never met such a bad-tempered man in all my life.'

Dolores laughed at her cousin. 'You've met your father a few times, Lucia, so you should be well able for the likes of Juan and his grumpy backside face.'

'Dolores!' Sonia whispered loudly. 'Don't speak about your uncle or Captain Juan in that way. Someone might hear.'

'Let them.' Sixteen-year-old Dolores had had enough of ship life, and she wanted off, wherever they were. A few days before, when they had docked in Southampton, Dolores had come up with a plan to escape and to stay there.

'London would be so exciting,' she said. 'I'd much rather go there than stay cooped up in some stuffy convent in Dublin, praying our way through life to a God that forgot about the Spanish years ago.'

That particular conversation had been overheard and reported to the captain. Dolores had been given the brunt of his sharp tongue. And Sonia too.

'Sister Mary-Anne. You may not be able to speak formally to your charges, but sometimes young girls need discipline. I'm leaving you a board and chalk and you can declare your feelings on their behaviour in this way. Keep them from misbehaving, Sister, or I will have to find a way to do it myself. Any attempt at leaving this ship without me will be dealt with severely, I promise you that.'

The wild look on Captain Juan's face was more than enough for the girls to know that he meant it, and so, there was no more talk of trying anything without his permission.

'We must be almost there,' Sonia whispered. 'It's been two days since we left the south of England, so I wouldn't be surprised if we were to dock in Dublin within a day. Be patient, girls, and we'll be in a clean bed very soon and life will be easier again.'

'And then what?' asked Dolores. 'Do we sit in the convent for the next year, while Franco plays guns and murder with the Spanish people?'

'I don't know how long it will be, Dolores,' said Sonia. 'But at least we will be safe there.' She didn't voice her fears, but she had a feeling it would be a lot more than one year before Franco's Spain was a place where they could live in peace and safety.

Sonia shed the nun's habit with great enthusiasm. The clothes that the mother superior had left for her to wear looked horrific but wearing them felt like the height of fashion in comparison to what she had worn for so many weeks on board the ship. Swapping

Captain Juan for Mother Ignatius was similar to taking on a new dictator for the old. The ancient nun had been incensed at receiving Sonia with the two girls instead of the real Sister Mary-Anne. The letter of explanation from her fellow sister in Spain did nothing to relieve her anger.

'What does she expect me to do with three teenage girls,' she asked, 'whose first words to me are "We are never going to become nuns. The very idea"? Well, I'll give you an idea all right. Get yourselves straight back to Spain and get out of my hair.'

The nun was very selfish and narrow-minded, Sonia thought. They couldn't go back to Spain, and there was so much room in the convent they could house half of the homeless Spanish without noticing they were there. The girls had been told to wash and get changed and to be in the chapel within the hour. Sonia was so tired from her journey, she thought that she would fall asleep through whatever prayers or hymns the mother superior had planned for them; but she would get through it because she had a plan of action hatching that meant she wouldn't have to stay too long there.

In the garden, on the way in, Sonia had overheard an elderly nun talking about needing some help for an upcoming trip to visit her family in a place called Donegal. Sonia had understood the bones of the conversation thanks to her communication with some English tourists in her home town; although, she didn't know where this place was or what might be there. But if the nun wanted someone to escort her on her travels, then Sonia would be the one to volunteer. She needed to leave the convent and the sooner the better.

Sonia had tried very hard to grow fond of Lucia and Dolores on the way over to Ireland. But knowing that Lucia's father had shot her brother and had laughed about it later was hard to put aside. Of course, Lucia was not responsible for the sins of her father. She was an innocent girl who needed to be protected from the low-life man that was Alberto Rodriguez, but every time Sonia heard the girl speak of her father, she felt physically sick.

The nun had said that it would take a whole day to travel to Donegal and that sounded about far enough away for Sonia. She could make a temporary life for herself there. It was mean to think of leaving Dolores and Lucia in the hands of the nuns, but she could keep in touch, and it would work out. Maybe she could send for them later. Now, she walked down the corridor with a smile on her face and a lighter step.

CHAPTER SIX

Sonia was freezing. Even on the boat on the way over to Ireland, when she had been soaked through during the storm, she had never known this kind of cold. It had been raining for days. Not like the downpours she had been used to in Benalmádena, when it would burst from the heavens for an hour and then stop. This was constant. Soft. Dripping. Torturous. Cold.

And this was an Irish summer.

She turned over on her mattress and pulled the blankets up around her neck, immediately feeling the cold nipping at her toes. She looked over at her new friend, Eileen, sleeping on the other bed beside her and envied her. Eileen had the covers thrown off her and was sleeping in a short nightdress. Sonia was sporting a borrowed pair of cotton pyjamas and a pair of socks.

'Eileen, are you awake?' Sonia waited for a reply. Nothing. If they didn't get up soon, Eileen's mother would be in, shouting at them. The post office would be opening in half an hour and Eileen's mother liked them behind their counters at least ten minutes before.

It was easy work compared to the work that Sonia had left behind in Benalmádena. Eileen manned the post office itself, and Sonia did her best to run the shop. It had been a stroke of luck that she happened to be buying stamps the day that Eileen's mother fell off the stepladder and broke her leg. Sonia had been in buying stamps to write to Enrico again – care of his uncle in Benalmádena. She was sure that at some stage Enrico would get in touch with him and that he would forward her letters, but six months after she had arrived in Ireland, she still heard nothing. She hadn't heard from her own parents either.

'Girls! Out of that bed with ye! Right now!' Amazing. One shout from her mother and Eileen was up and on her feet in seconds racing towards her clothes.

'Jesus, Sonia. Why didn't you wake me? She'll kill us. Come on. Get going.' Eileen was on the run now.

'I tried to wake you, Eileen, but you didn't hear me.' Sonia reached for her own clothes and when they were washed and ready, the two ran down the stairs and out the door. Easier to chew on sweets from the shop for breakfast than to stay and get an ear-bashing from Mrs McMenamin.

Once inside the shop, Sonia took her place behind the counter of the newsagents and Eileen went to sit in the post office kiosk at the back. It was easier work back there than all the rushing around that Sonia had to do, but you needed perfect English to get through the postal duties. And many of the customers liked to speak their own Irish language there. For the first three months the customers would point to the things that they wanted, but Sonia's determination to learn English paid off, and it wasn't long before she was able to get her head around the basics.

'Speak slowly, please.' The children would mimic her and burst into giggles. Sonia realised now how her southern Spanish accent must have daunted the tourists that visited her parents' café. These Donegal people raced through their sentences as though they were catching a train, the same way the Andalusians spoke Spanish. Eileen was a good teacher, and during their quieter times in the shop, when all the old age pensioners had been and gone home a little richer, the girls used the time to take out the books and copies and work on Sonia's English.

'I would have liked to be a teacher, you know, Sonia,' Eileen said.

'So why didn't you? You would have been very good. I've learned so much already, and that's because of you.'

'Family business, Sonia. Shops don't run themselves and Mam had to take me out of school to help her out in here. I don't mind. I like it here in Balcallan. I'm looking forward to finding the man of my dreams, though; and being married; and to having lots of children. Just like you and Enrico, when he comes to get you.'

Sonia's face turned sad. 'I haven't seen Enrico for over a year, Eileen.'

Eileen reached over and put her hand on her friend's shoulder. 'Are you sure that he'll definitely get in touch, Sonia? I mean it's been a long time, and he must know by now where you are. I love having you here. You know that. But if you want to know if Enrico is still yours, then you should go back to Spain. You should find him and have it out with him.'

'What do you mean? *If* he's still mine? Of course Enrico's still mine. You don't know what you're talking about, Eileen McMenamin. Enrico and I have known since we were small children that we were going to spend our lives together. Nothing could ever change that. You have no idea what has happened to Enrico and to me over the past year. We have lived in danger. Frightened for our lives. I don't even know if Enrico is in or out of prison yet. I don't know for sure if he hasn't gone the same way as my—'

Sonia stopped speaking as she couldn't voice what was on her mind – what she was thinking of all the time. She had received a letter from Dolores, who had travelled with her from Spain and was now living and working in Dublin with Lucia. Dolores wrote that according to her father, Roberto, Enrico was not in prison but was still a wanted man, and that was the last she had heard about him. Her letters to her mother had gone unanswered. Sonia couldn't get the thought from her mind that her beautiful childhood friend, the only man she could ever love, was gone the same way as her brother. She felt that it must be like this because if he was alive, Enrico would know that her heart was breaking over him; that she thought of him in every waking moment; and he would find some way to let her know that he was all right. That he would somehow come to her, or at least, send for her, if he could. If he was ...

A customer walked through the door, and Sonia swallowed her tears once more and painted on a smile for Mrs Carr.

CHAPTER SEVEN

Enrico

I could do without the full moon, but I'll carry on regardless. I've waited for this time since the night I picked up Miguel's lifeless body from the street in Arroyo and carried him home to Sonia. The desire to get this close to the man who pulled the trigger has sat with me all this time, while I've followed up on queries about my target. Numerous pictures of torturing the screaming man before I finish him off have filled my aching head. But now, all I need is to wipe him from this earth quickly and quietly. It will be enough.

Creeping around the back of the villa, I look up to the upstairs windows. I've heard that the wife and daughter have left Malaga, so, if my calculations are right, there is only the sleeping bastard to contend with. I pull back the window that I broke open earlier when the piece of shit was out terrorizing innocents. It's barely large enough for me to squeeze through, but I manage it. Months of hunger have left me a scrawny version of the man I was before Miguel's death.

'I'm coming for you now,' I whisper. 'It's you and me and your precious handgun.' I pat my pocket to feel the comforting shape of the gun I stole from his house earlier this evening, before Miguel's killer returned from his dirt-filled duties. Alberto Rodriguez is no soldier. He is not a man who can conjure any amount of respect from anyone who calls himself Spanish. He's a common criminal murderer, and I'm doing this beloved country the greatest favour by ridding them of this filth.

Leaving my shoes by the front door, I make my way towards the bedroom. The door is slightly ajar. Very handy. Maybe the big, bad bastard is afraid of the dark. This thought makes me slip quietly into his room with a smile on my face. I thought I would be nervous, afraid to kill another man, but I feel nothing but relief that this need for vengeance is coming to an end. The full moon that was awkward when I was outside the house, now makes it easy to tiptoe over to where my worst enemy is lying on his side, the blanket pulled up to his neck. I'm surprised that the man's breathing is so easy. I expected the snoring of the big bulk to drown out the noise of readying the gun before pulling the trigger, but the room is silent.

Later that night, as I sit in the back of the prison truck, I know that I will regret the moments of thought that I wasted, thinking of filling the man's head and heart with bullets. The soldiers that jumped me from behind and knocked the gun from my hand were obviously watching my every move. Before I was dragged from the bedroom, I had to experience the look of victory on that evil face, as he threw back the blanket, revealing himself to be fully dressed and laughing heartily.

'You knew,' I spat at him.

'There is nothing I don't know about you, Enrico Sanchez,' the man replied. 'This is not even my house, but my brother, Roberto's. You have been led a merry dance with your questions, and it has been my utmost pleasure to be your dancing partner.'

And now I am on my way to a prison cell in Malaga Jail, and I think that it might have been better if they had shot me dead.

A gecko crawls in through the open bars and scuttles down the inside wall of my cell. Stupid creature, to have your freedom and to give it up for these four walls. An idiot like me. To have my family and friends, to have Sonia, and to walk into Malaga alone to revenge Miguel's death. How senseless.

But how could I have lived with myself if I hadn't tried to kill the man? I couldn't have married Sonia knowing I had done nothing to rid the world of her brother's killer. But look where it got me. Thrown into Malaga Jail, awaiting trial, and for what? The bastard is still out there, killing more Miguels.

Pushing myself up from the floor mat, I reach across the short space to where the gecko is running aimlessly looking for a way out – as I did with the Nationalists. They were expecting me somehow. How did they know? In this war no one is your friend, and nobody can be trusted. Only a few people knew where I was heading and why; and yet the men were waiting for me to break into the house and to draw a gun on that murderer before they pounced. Waiting to put me here. How many months now? A year?

'Get out of here, little gecko. There is no life for you to feed on within these walls. No fellow geckos to be your mate. Nothing here. Nothing to live for.' I pick the creature up by his middle and put him on the flat of the window. I nudge him out through the bars to the place where I so want to be. He disappears for a minute, but then his eyes reappear around the bars once more.

'Yes. That's right. Come back in here, you imbecile. You're in good company. Stay within these walls with the man who is your like. She told me to stay at home. She begged me not to go away and leave her. Did I listen? No, little gecko. I was as stupid and hot-headed as you. I thought that she would love me more if I bravely killed the man who shot Miguel, but that's not her way. She said that adding to the death was useless. That this war was useless.

But she's wrong, Miguel. You don't mind if I call you Miguel, do you? If you're going to stick around, then you might as well have a name and listen to my rants. It's nice to say that name. Miguel. I loved my friend. He was only a boy on the cusp of manhood.

The gecko comes nearer to the darker corner of the cell. It winds its way around the rough stone ceiling and turns its beady eyes on me.

'Is this better for me, Miguel? This solitary confinement that I keep landing myself in? Yes, it's small, but it's all mine. My own space. And yes, the food's even worse than above, but that's not great either. At least it's peaceful down here. I don't have to listen to men moaning in physical and mental pain. Calling out, so that it's hard to know where the pain in their body begins and the pain in their head ends.

'It's easy to get landed down here. There are so many rules to break, it's impossible to keep track of them all. But it's so hot, Miguel. That's the problem. You'd think in this shade it wouldn't be so hot. But it is. That doesn't help the head either. Sometimes I can't remember what she looks like, Miguel. Imagine. I knew her beautiful face for so many years. Every part of it etched into my head to look at as I wished. But not now. Not in this place. I can't see her smile. Perhaps because she's not smiling. Did you see her out there Miguel? Was she smiling? No? No. Of course. What has she got to smile about? Living with her mother's resentment. Her father's beatings. The absence of her brother in her life. And me. The fool who couldn't even get revenge right. Useless. Yes. I can't see her smile because I took it away from her.'

Boots clatter down the rocky steps that lead to the door of my cell. Keys rattle in the rusty lock and the door opens. Something is thrown on the ground and the door bangs shut once more. I let the steps retreat before I dive on the bread and the water. I hate to let the guards see my hunger. I'll never let myself be beaten by them. Physically, they can do their worst, but they will never wreck my head. When I'm eventually freed, and I will be, I will come back one day and kill every one of these bastards. It's all I can think about in this hellhole. Every day I'm filled with more anger. When I'm upstairs, I listen to the other Republicans quietly vent their fury out of earshot of the Nationalist guards. When I break one of the rules and get a week in solitary, my head is filled with furious thoughts.

I shove the last of the stale bread into my mouth and wash it down with the water. I promised myself that I would make the water last this time. But now it is gone.

And so is Miguel. The gecko is nowhere to be seen in the small space we shared. Perhaps he tired of my ramblings. Or maybe he's cleverer than I thought. By staying still and complying with my ways, he found a way out.

Staring at the empty space left by the gecko, I realise what I have to do. I will give in to this enemy and allow myself to be beaten. I'll confess to my sin. Tell the guards about the rage I felt at the loss of my childhood friend. Do they not feel that too when they lose a friend? I was crazed, had no idea what I was doing. When I stood in that room with the man who had shot Miguel, I had already realised that I could not take away someone else's friend, before they burst into the room and arrested me.

I pace the small cell as I practise my lines for the guards and for those who would judge me.

'I would never have done this dreadful thing. I have never killed a man before. I am a fisherman. That is what I do. When Miguel was shot, I was overcome with grief. But when I stood before the soldier, I realised that he had made a mistake, and that I must not do that too. He is alive because I would not kill him. That is why I paused. When the men ran at me in that room, I did not put up a fight. I was already sorry. Sorry for the thoughts that had led me to that man's house.

'But now I have paid dearly for those thoughts – paid for the sin of anger. Nobody was hurt. It would never have happened. It never will happen. I just want to go back to my pueblo to fish and to live as quietly as I always have.'

They will look at my innocent face and nod their heads slowly. It will take time, and a lot of convincing on my part to turn the guards around to believe that I'm a sorry, beaten man. Perhaps they will suggest that I spy for them on the outside. There are many so-called Republicans who are passing on information, for protection of themselves and their families. I will nod and agree to anything to get to the other side of these walls, and then I will get Sonia and disappear. I can do this thing. I will not be executed in this place for the attempted murder of a Nationalist. I will leave this place and return to see her again.

As soon as I'm out, I will quietly build myself a small army of Republicans. Together we will come and free every good man in this prison and then burn it to the ground full of screaming Nationalist prison guards. When that job is done, I will go to the house of Miguel's murderer, and I *will* kill him slowly. An injury for every day that I have spent in this hell, and then the ultimate shot through his cold heart.

CHAPTER EIGHT

Enrico

The view from the top of the hill is good enough to see what is going on below, but I'm hidden away enough not to attract attention to myself. I will hear someone coming before I see them, and before their presence is a danger to me. My time here in Benalmádena is almost over for now. I'm trying to get in touch with Sonia, but it seems I'll have to go to her house and confront her family. The word is out about why I was freed from prison. The Nationalists have let it be known that I am a traitor to the Republicans and that I have sided with Franco's men. There is a reward now from the Republicans for information about my whereabouts. I couldn't believe how easy it was to be freed from prison. I agreed to spy for them but thought I could disappear and hide. Now I understand the plan they had for me. I have never given them a name of anyone, but still they have managed to turn my own against me.

Crawling down the hill and across the beach, I slip into the Almez family kitchen to look for Sonia. I am sickened by the sight of my future mother-in-law, Cristina, lying unconscious on the floor, her shoulder turned in an unnatural position. Her face is covered in blood and one of her teeth lies beside her on the tiles. I call out Sonia's name, but my voice echoes in the empty place. I run to Cristina's side to see if she's still breathing, then try to put her into a safer position, without hurting her more. Hugo's handywork has almost killed her this time.

I have to think of a way to get help for her, without drawing attention to myself. It's almost time for the fishermen to come in for their dinner. They won't be fed here this evening, but they will be able to get help for the long-suffering Cristina.

I light a torch and bring it outside to set fire to the wood beyond the house. It catches well in the dry heat of the sun. I know it will bring people rushing to the house but will not catch the dwelling. I run back along the beach and hide behind the rocks, and watch. Sure enough, the nearest fishing boat turns around and heads quickly towards the shore. No doubt they think that the Almez house is on fire. Cristina will be well looked after by the people of Benalmádena, but it will take her a long time to recover from her wounds. Hugo is an animal, and the thought of what he has done to Cristina drives me to hatch a plan to make sure that Cristina will never fall at her husband's hand again.

'Buenas noches, Señor Almez.' I walk cautiously towards the man sprawled up against the rock on the beach. He must have had even more to drink in the hours after he beat his wife to a pulp. There is dried drool at the side of his mouth, and his eyes are glazed in the light of the moon.

'Eh?' Hugo tries to place me. I smile and sit beside him. I reach into Hugo's pocket and take out the almost empty flask. I open the top and pretend to bring it to my lips. 'Salud!' I toast the man's health and smile again. It will be easy to get Hugo to finish what's in the flask. He has already had enough to sink a boat. I change my original plan to get Hugo to go out sailing with me. I won't need to spend that much time with him.

'Is it true, Hugo, that you were once one of the greatest swimmers in Benalmádena?' I ask.

Hugo puts down the flask and tries to focus his glassy eyes on me. 'Benalmádena?' he slurs. 'In all of Malaga, you mean. In all of Spain!' He drops the flask on the sand, and I pick it up and hand it back to him.

'Yes, señor. I heard that too. I am also a great swimmer. I swim out to that rock and back often, and no man or boy has ever beaten me.'

'Hah! You never swam against the great Hugo Almez! That would show you to be the sardine that you are!'

'I bet you couldn't still do it, old man! You won't get halfway out, I'm sure.'

The list of expletives from Hugo's mouth is unintelligible as he tries to stand up.

'Let me help you, Hugo. Take my hand.' I bend down and pull the man to standing and whirl him around on his unsteady feet. He stumbles. This is going to be easy. Candy from a baby. Life from a man.

Walking down towards the edge of the water, I recall a picture of Cristina lying on the floor of her kitchen. This is no man. This is a butcher. Visions of the man lying drunk in the corner singing, while his son lay dead in his house enrage me even further, and I get behind Hugo and push him nearer the edge of the sea. I know that as soon as Hugo hits the water he will begin to sober up, so I won't have much time.

'Okay, Señor Almez! Let's see what you can do. We need to get out to that rock. Then we can swim into shore and see if you still have it in you.' I kick off my shoes and remove most of my clothes without bothering to remind Hugo to do the same.

'Come on! Keep going, señor!' I take Hugo by the collar of his jacket and keep swimming. I can see that the water is having a sobering effect on my victim. Hugo's eyes are beginning to register his surroundings. I'll have to act fast.

'From here, señor!' I shout over the waves. 'First one to stand on the beach will have the victory! Are you ready? Go!'

I make a swift push towards the shore, then I look back to see if Hugo is behind me. He is actually swimming well, so this will have to be immediate. I slow down and allow him to pass me out.

'See you sometime, loser!' Hugo isn't even slurring his words now.

Now. It has to be quick. I lunge on top of Hugo and drag him under. I push down with all my strength, but Hugo manages to wriggle out of my grasp.

'What are you doing you crazy boy?! I know you! You're Enrico. The man who—'

But whatever it is that Hugo's about to say will never be known, because my anger has reached fever pitch and I use all my energy and rage to drag the man under. First by his feet, then his shoulders. Anything I can get my hands on. I push the man under until the struggle slows, then stops. To make sure, I hold Hugo under for longer; until I'm absolutely certain that he's gone. Then I finish the dead man's last sentence.

'—the man who has avenged the damage you did to your family.'

I grab Hugo by the shirt and swim further out to sea with him. The tide is coming in and I want to make sure that his body isn't found until I'm well hidden in the hills.

Hugo is dead. Nobody will know the real cause of his death. The revenge is swift, and I will never forget what pushed me to such lengths. I have grown hard watching death come around daily in the prison. I am ready to take my war further.

Now, with Cristina in the hospital mending her wounds, and the villagers preparing for Hugo's funeral, there's no need for me to stay any longer in Benalmádena. I hoped to find news from Cristina about her daughter's whereabouts, but I know better than to visit any other member of my family or friends now. The rumour that I'm to blame for the arrests of local Republicans means that I can't show my face in Benalmádena, where many of my one-time friends would shoot me first and ask questions later. I have even heard my own cousin say that he will kill me if he ever sets eyes on me again.

This deceit is necessary. I have befriended the enemy in order to be released from Malaga Jail. I will have to keep up the pretence, in order to work on my next victim. But Enrico Sanchez would never betray his friends and family. That's the Nationalist soldiers using my so-called *change of heart* in their favour. Doing what they have spent the war doing: turning brother against brother, friend against friend.

Those who know me well should know that I would never turn against the Republican people of Benalmádena. I'm returning to Malaga town now, with plans to recruit a small army and to kill Miguel's murderer. We will free the Republicans held in Malaga Jail, then burn it to the ground.

CHAPTER NINE

Sonia,

Your father is dead. The authorities say that he fell from a rock and drowned. I find that hard to believe. Perhaps the loss of Miguel hit him harder than we realised, and he went out and let himself go under? Your father was a strong swimmer. Even after taking a lot of wine. Our neighbours are saying that he was murdered by the Nationalists, and I've let that be, because he would have liked that. A martyr to the Republican cause.

I loved your father very much, Sonia, when I first met him. But he was a drinker and I spent most of my married life looking after him. I thought that by marrying him I could protect him, but it was I who needed the protection. As Miguel grew, he helped to keep me safe, but since your brother died, your father beat me daily. The morning before he drowned, he left me with a face full of lumps and marks. I do not miss him, but I will never forget him. Hugo has left me with scars and jutting bones that will never heal. When you marry, Sonia, marry a good, kind man.

I miss you. I am so sorry that my grief for your brother made me tell you the truth about your beginnings in the way that I did. I have hated myself for the way that we were when we parted. I am so sorry. You are and always have been my daughter. I hope that in time you can forgive me.

When I went through your father's things, I found some treasure hidden there. Your letters to me. I am sad to say that I never received these gems. Hugo had other ways of hurting people that did not involve physical pain. So, he kept your letters away from me. Now I have read them over and over, devouring every word that tells me that you are safe and with good people.

I heard that you were arrested for your association with Enrico. Then I heard nothing more. I thought that you were dead. That your association with Enrico had taken you from us. I have lost a husband and am showing the world my mourning face but inside I rejoice with my new knowledge that you are well.

I know that you are sad to be away from your beloved Benalmádena, but it is for the best, Sonia. This country is filled with evil. Everywhere I look, I see death and mourning. Friend against friend, brother against brother. Fishermen at war on the streets instead of fighting the battle of the sea, side by side, as they have always done. You are in a good place. I would give my heart to see you, but you must not travel here. Stay safe. For my sake.

And about Enrico. I know from your letters that you have tried to get in contact with him. I am sure you have heard nothing from him as we have. The news I have for you is not good. As far as I know, Enrico is still alive, but trouble follows him on all sides. Shortly after you went missing, he was arrested and was put in Malaga Jail. We heard this through a man who had been released from there just after you left us. Enrico was imprisoned, but eighteen months later, he was set free. We were overjoyed when we heard the news. We had been waiting to hear of his sentencing. Everyone presumed that it would be execution for the attempted murder of the Nationalist soldier.

But it appears that Enrico was freed because he took the side of the Nationalists. I found this hard to believe at first but for every Republican that is arrested now, the Nationalists let it be known that it was Enrico Sanchez who gave them the name. None of his family or friends have seen him since he was freed. And as time goes on, I am not sure what to think. His oldest and dearest friends are screaming for his head. Yes, the world has gone crazy. It was said that he was seen by someone in Benalmádena the night your father died. This fed the locals' belief that the Nationalists had killed Hugo.

Nobody knows anything for sure in this war. But Enrico was heard to say at his trial that he was sorry for ever having thought to kill the Nationalist. That he knew that the Nationalists were right in what they were doing. He said that he just wanted to be left to fish and to enjoy his country. They say he smiled at the judge and called him *amigo*. Whether the life in prison turned his head or that he simply did change his mind, we might never know.

My advice to you my daughter is to forget Enrico. I know these words will fill you with sadness. If this war ever ends, and I feel it never can, Enrico will carry the words that he spoke at his trial. They will follow him like a weight. I want you to have a good life, my darling girl, with everything that I did not have. Maybe you will find yourself a nice Irish man who will protect you. Because that is what you need to be happy. The love and care that makes a good marriage.

I wish I could travel to see you. But your abuela is nearing the end of her days, and I feel it is my duty and my wish to see her through to the last. She was a good mother to me always and she was blessed with a happy and peaceful marriage. I came to her late in life and we were closer for this. Perhaps when she is gone, I will look to coming to your Donegal. It sounds very beautiful. I am happy that you have mountains and the sea to remind you of home. It will keep you close to us.

I will write to you often now. I hope to hear from you too. I know that this letter will bring you great joy and much sadness in equal measure. Know that I love you. Know that Enrico is not for you.

Mamá

Cristina re-read the letter and nodded. It was so hard to say these words to her daughter. Too much for her to have to be the one to shred the young girl's dreams and hopes. But this was a mother's work. To protect her daughter and to give her the best chance in life that she could.

Cristina's parents had begged her not to marry into the Almez family, but she had let her heart guide her, and she had paid dearly for her mistake. Her mother had never said *I told you so*. She had just cleaned up the mess as it happened and waited for the next onslaught. But since her father died and her mother had let old age take her, there had been no one to protect Cristina. Only Miguel.

Cristina put the letter in the envelope and laid it down. She picked up the photo of her son and kissed it. She polished the glass once more.

'Look after your little sister, Miguel. She needs your help from heaven to get it right.'

Mrs McMenamin called the girls down for their dinner for the second time but only Eileen walked sullenly into the kitchen.

'What's the matter with you, girl. You look like you've the trouble of the world on you? And where's Sonia. Is she after an invitation to the table or what?'

'I don't know what's the matter with her, Mam, but I doubt very much that she'll be down for her dinner.'

Eileen's mother made a move to the hallway.

'Leave her, Mam. It's that letter you gave her that came today. I don't know what's in it, but it must be pretty bad. She read it and crumpled in a heap on the floor. She's clutching it to her, so I can't get near it, and she's crying her heart out. You won't get any sense out of her.'

Her mother shook her head and thought about the parcel from Spain that had arrived at the post office that morning. She had seen it while sorting the post and had almost given it there and then to Sonia, knowing how long and hard she had prayed for news from home. But she had thought better of it. Whatever the news, Sonia would probably not have been fit for work today after reading it. At least this way, she might be a bit better by tomorrow morning.

'I'll leave her for now, but she needs to talk about whatever's in that letter and not bottle it up.'

'Give her time. Whatever awful news is inside it, she needs space to take it in herself first before sharing it with us. Leave her with me.'

But by midnight that night, Sonia had not moved from the floor of her room where she had fallen earlier and had not relinquished the letter from her hands.

Maeve McMenamin couldn't stand the sound of the girl's sobs for another minute. She knelt down beside Sonia and took her arm.

'Up, Sonia! Now! Come on. You'll not lie there all night. Get up!'

Sonia allowed herself to be pulled up by Eileen and her mother.

'Now, sit down there and tell us what was in that letter that was so bad that you haven't stopped bawling for hours.'

'My father is dead. And Enrico is ... missing.' Sonia sniffed.

There it was. Everything out in two short sentences. Eileen and her mother looked at each other, and Maeve wondered which part Sonia was crying about most. From what she had gleaned from Eileen over the months, Sonia's father had liked his drink a bit too much and had beaten her mother and anyone else who got in his way. Maeve presumed that most of the tears were for the missing Enrico.

'Go get a small brandy, Eileen. And a few biscuits from the press to soak it up. Sonia needs something for her shock.'

When Eileen left the room, Maeve turned Sonia around to look at her. Her face was a mess of tears and snot and misery.

'Sonia. Is the funeral over?'

Sonia nodded.

'Can you read the letter to me, sweetheart. Is it from your mother?'

Sonia nodded again. It was all she could manage. Sonia didn't know how to deal with all this on her own. She translated the letter to Maeve, heard her shocked intakes of breath and saw the consoling smile on her trustworthy face. It reminded Sonia of what her mother used to say to her when tourists came sometimes to her part of the beach in Benalmádena. *A smile is the same in every language.* Maeve's smile told her that she only had Sonia's interests at heart. Even if her daughter, Eileen, insisted that her mother was a nosy cow most of the time.

As Sonia finished reading, Maeve looked at her with a new recognition. Until now, she had put all the stuff about Enrico down to girlish nonsense. Sonia was two years younger than Eileen. Girls were flighty at that age. But, in fact, Sonia had been working in her parents' restaurant since she was a child, helping a woman who spent a lot of her life mending her wounds and dodging her husband. And Sonia was much more efficient at her job in the post office than Eileen. Maeve's daughter was not spoiled, but she had had so many good things in her life that she didn't have the hunger for work that Sonia showed.

Eileen came in at that moment with the brandy and a sandwich.

'I made you something a bit more substantial, Sonia. I know you never take a drink, so you'll need this to take the edge off the consequences.'

Sonia was hungry now, so she took the sandwich willingly, but she pushed away the brandy.

'Thank you, Eileen. But nothing would ever make me drink that awful drink.' She said this with such vehemence that Eileen and Maeve were taken aback.

Maeve stood up. 'I'll make you a cup of sweet tea so.'

Sonia almost smiled. She was getting used to the Irish ways for treating bad days.

'Tell Eileen about the letter too, Sonia,' Maeve said. 'It's helped me to understand what you're going through, and it will help Eileen too. I'll be back shortly.' And she left the two friends to work things out.

As she busied herself downstairs with the kettle and cups, Maeve mulled over the contents of Sonia's letter. The girl had lived most of her life in a war zone. First with her father, and then with the Spanish Civil War and its aftermath. Sonia had seen her brother carried into her house with a fatal wound. She was in love with a man who had been imprisoned for attempted murder and who then went against his own family and friends to make life better for himself. And all this while she was dealing with her brother's death. It didn't bear thinking about. But Maeve McMenamin knew she would be thinking about it for a long time.

Now she wondered, a little selfishly, what exactly she had let into her home to share a room with her innocent daughter.

Maeve had spent months convincing the people of Balcallan that Sonia was exactly what she seemed to be. A kind, hard-working girl who had had to leave her war-torn country for her safety. And she was all that. But so much more besides.

Maeve would have to work very hard to deal with this one. It was at times like this she felt very lonely as a mother on her own, and she wished she had someone to talk to about this mess.

She put out a cup of tea for Sonia and laced it with three spoons of sugar. She thought she might go back and have that brandy that Sonia had declined.

But Maeve also acknowledged that since Sonia came to stay with them, their house had taken on a new way of being. Eileen and Maeve seldom fought any more. They were almost friends since Sonia had turned up to act as referee. Maeve had grown to like the girl a lot. The girls working together in the post office was working out well. Even when Maeve's leg had healed, she let the young ones take over the heavy work while she supervised.

Going into the girls' room – how quickly it had stopped being just Eileen's – Maeve resolved to spend the coming weeks taking Sonia's mind off this Enrico. No matter which way you looked at the boy, he was trouble. Eileen thought he might be like these boys who joined the IRA. They were all tarred with the same brush.

No, she wouldn't let this troublemaker of a boy back into Sonia's life. She should stay with them until problems in Spain had calmed at least. By that time the girl's feelings for Enrico would have died down. And maybe Eileen could set her up with a nice Irish man if she stayed with them long enough. But no Enrico. That much was certain. Even Sonia's own mother had warned her against him. Maeve would look after her for Cristina. She sounded like a sensible enough woman.

CHAPTER TEN

Sonia was fighting an inner battle. Every morning she got out of bed, washed, ate a small amount of breakfast and went to work. She smiled at the customers and went about her business, like clockwork. She carried the picture of Enrico in her head and in her heart and refused to let go. This boy and man had been part of her being for most of her life, and he was to be her future life also. How could that stop?

Her mother was wrong. She had chosen a bad match for herself, and she presumed that Sonia was doing the same. There had to be an answer to the crazy words her mother had told her. Ever since the day before her brother's funeral, when she had found out the truth about her birth mother, Sonia had found it difficult to trust Cristina completely. How could you believe someone who had spent most of your life telling you the biggest lie ever?

Enrico could never turn against his own. He had even left Sonia because he had a point to prove against the Nationalists. If he could do that, then he had to believe in the Republicans completely. Something was wrong. What was she saying? *Everything* was wrong.

And her father. Sonia couldn't get her head around how she felt about her father's death. Her mother had loved him despite everything. And when Sonia was a little girl, she had loved him too. She had wanted to be his princess, had smiled at him and served him well to gain his respect and attention. But all she had gained as she grew older was the back of his hand when he couldn't reach her with his boot. Because Sonia was the cause of Rosita's death? No. She would not grieve for this man.

But it was for him that the people of Balcallan gave their condolences. As she walked around with her head bent in silence and sadness, the Donegal people helped her to grieve. She had suffered a Mass in her father's memory, organised by Maeve, and a wake to see him off into heaven. Heaven? Nothing could have welcomed her father into that place.

All this time Sonia wept for Enrico. She couldn't believe that she might never see him again. She had sent letters to her family and friends begging them to try to find him. She knew it was too dangerous for her to go back to Spain as yet, but as soon as she could, she would search the country for the only man in the world that she could ever marry.

'Penny for them?' Eileen smiled at Sonia. Again. Eileen and Maeve had been desperate in their attempts to get her out of herself. Only *they* knew the true reason behind her grief.

'Sorry, Eileen. You must be tired of me by now.' Sonia tried a thin smile, but it wouldn't stick.

'I was thinking that maybe you'd like to go on a little holiday, Sonia. I have an uncle in Dublin we could stay with. We could meet up with your Spanish friends. The girls that came over on the boat to Ireland with you?'

Sonia's first thought was how to get Eileen to back down from a holiday without seeming to be ungrateful. But then an idea began to form in her head. Roberto's daughter, Dolores, and her cousin, Lucia – the girls who had travelled with Sonia from Malaga – were working in Dublin. They might have had more news about the situation in Spain from Roberto. Maybe even one of them knew someone who had known, or even better, had heard from Enrico. The thought made her smile a proper smile.

'Could we, Eileen? Wouldn't your mother mind us both taking time from work at the same time?'

Eileen was beaming. She seemed delighted at Sonia's eagerness to do something.

'It's quiet at this time of year, Sonia. And I know Mam'd be delighted to see you getting out somewhere. I'll tell her when we get home today. She can take over from us for a few days. It'll be great. Wait and see.'

'All right. Can we do it soon?'

'Sure. When Mammy comes in later to check if we're working hard enough, I'll put it to her. Then I'll make a few calls to Dublin and see if we can't get a bed for a couple of nights. I'm dead excited already, but don't let any of that show. We're saying that we need a few days off to help you to get over your trauma.'

Sonia was excited about going to Dublin, but not for the same reasons as Eileen. She would find out more about where Enrico was. She was sure of it.

The girls worked hard that day to make it go faster. It was only Tuesday, and they couldn't wait to get to Friday. By the time they went to bed that night they had all the plans in place. They were staying with Maeve's brother, so she was happy that her daughter wouldn't be allowed to go astray. They had called the café where Sonia's Spanish friend Lucia worked and had set up a meeting for Saturday evening. In bed that night, Eileen shared a secret about her own hopes for their trip to Dublin.

'His name's Bart, Sonia. Short for Bartholomew. He's from Gortahork, a village just a few miles from here. I met him before you got to Balcallan. I sneaked out to a dance one Saturday night and he was there with a friend of his. Manus, I think his name was. Anyways, we danced every dance together that night, but at the end of the evening he told me that himself and Manus were off to work in Dublin the following day. I told him I worked in the post office here and to pop in if he was back visiting. But he must be working very hard in Dublin. I haven't heard from him at all.'

'Could he not have sent you a letter to the post office, Eileen?'

'That was what he said he would do but I stupidly told him

not to. I was worried what my mother would say if I started getting letters from strange boys that she didn't know. You know what she's like.'

'I think she may have been more understanding than you give her credit for. She's very kind when I speak to her about Enrico. She was once married to your father, so she knows about love and loss.'

'I know, Sonia. But honestly my mother has changed hugely since you've come to live with us. She's much more liberal. A year ago, she wouldn't have dreamed of letting me go to Dublin without her. But we're getting off the subject. Bart. I'm going to go and find him when I get there.'

'How will you know where to look? Lucia says Dublin is even bigger than Malaga.'

'He started off in a hostel on Dame Street, and I've heard that's fairly central. I'll go there first and see if I can't find where he went from there.'

Sonia got caught up in Eileen's excitement. It was nice to have something positive to think about for a while. But she was worried that so much time had passed, and this Bart fellow hadn't even tried to contact Eileen. *If* they found this person who was somewhere in a city larger than Malaga, would he recognize Eileen after all this time? And *if* he did, would he want to see her? It seemed to Sonia that Bart could have contacted Eileen at any stage, but he chose not to. Sonia didn't feel good about Eileen's chances, but Sonia didn't feel good about most things at the moment, so it was probably her pessimistic mood working overtime.

'We'll go there first thing after breakfast on Saturday, Eileen. Someone there is sure to know where he went to.' Sonia would be positive for Eileen's sake. They would get the search over with early on Saturday, and then they could look forward to the rest of the weekend.

When Sonia and Eileen walked through the doors of the Dame Street hostel at ten o' clock on Saturday morning, Sonia felt she had managed to work hard enough on Eileen not to get her hopes up. They went over to the reception desk and looked around hopefully for someone to speak to.

'Eileen! Eileen McMenamin!'

The two girls turned around to see a man in builder's overalls standing at the door of the breakfast room. He started walking towards them and Sonia immediately recognised the man that Eileen had described to her. She was relieved to see that this man was most certainly delighted to see Eileen.

'Hello, Bart.' Eileen was trying to keep her face neutral.

'You remember me? That's great. How are you, Eileen?'

'I'm fine, Bart. How are you? Are you still staying here? I thought you'd have moved on.'

Bart was trying to make little of his lodgings. 'Ach, you know what it's like, Eileen. You find something comfortable, and well ... the devil you know and all that. Are you still in the post office in Balcallan?'

'I didn't mean that it wasn't a fine place to stay, Bart. Yes. I'm still where I was when we met. You know, the place where you were going to drop in at some stage when you were back visiting in Donegal.'

Bart had the good grace to go red. Sonia thought this was a good time to change the subject and introduce herself.

'Hello, Bart. I'm Sonia. Eileen's friend.'

'Oh my God, Sonia. I'm so rude. I should've introduced you.'

'Ah, sure I thought you were a customer, there, looking for the woman who mans the desk. Pleased to meet you. Bart Sharkey.' And when he shook Sonia's hand, she was pleased to see a genuine shake from the man. Maybe he was nicer than she thought.

But immediately Bart turned to Eileen who was picking up her handbag from the desk looking like she was about to leave.

'Eileen, you're not going already. What brought you here to the hostel? Were you thinking of staying here?'

Sonia knew by the look on Eileen's face, that if Bart didn't know or guess why she was here, then there was really no reason to be here at all.

'No,' she said. 'We wandered in looking for directions. That's all. But I think I remember now the way we need to go. We'll see you then, Bart. Good luck with everything here.' And she linked Sonia and started heading for the door. Sonia couldn't believe they were leaving like that. She stopped at the door and turned around. Bart was staring after them looking distraught. A big change from the man who had been beaming a few minutes ago. She wriggled out of Eileen's grip and walked back to him.

'Bart. Before we go. Why didn't you drop in to Eileen in Balcallan? Surely you were home at some time?' Sonia turned towards a furious-looking Eileen.

Bart looked from one girl to another then back to Eileen. 'Well,' he said. 'In for a penny and all that … Eileen told me not to write to her. She said she wouldn't be able to come to Dublin to visit. Apart from a casual invitation to drop into the post office, she didn't give me any remote encouragement to keep in touch. So … I didn't.'

'And if she had?' Sonia felt she was getting somewhere.

Bart looked away from Eileen's embarrassed face. 'If she had …?' he said. He looked back at Eileen. 'Well, I suppose I would have done a little more than just think about her every day since I met her. I haven't forgotten that night, Eileen. It meant a lot to me. Perhaps I was overthinking it, but I thrashed out what you had said to me, and I came up with the decision that you were trying to fob me off.'

Sonia might as well not have been there by now. Eileen's and Bart's eyes were locked.

'So, was I right? Or not?'

For a moment, Sonia thought it was all for nothing. Eileen looked like she was about to burst into tears. Bart was looking at her, waiting for her to say something, and she was standing there like she was going to disappear into the ground.

'You were wrong!' Sonia knew Eileen would kill her later for being so forward. 'When a girl says you should drop into the post office sometime, then that's what she means. We didn't come here today to find directions. We—'

'Sonia! I can speak for myself.' Eileen moved nearer to Bart. 'As you said … in for a penny. We came here to look for you. I wanted to see you because …'

But she didn't get time to finish because Bart had her up and was twirling her around the hallway of the hostel.

'Put me down!' Eileen shouted, but Sonia could see by her face that she never wanted him to let go of her ever again.

'You don't have to tell me what happened over and over again, Eileen. I was there. Remember?' Sonia was laughing at Eileen's beaming face in their bedroom in Uncle Jim's house.

'I still haven't forgiven you for going back there and telling him everything. I have never been so embarrassed in my whole life.'

'Hah. If I hadn't, we'd be sitting here now listening to you crying your eyes out. I wish you hadn't agreed for me to meet up with you two and his friend Manus later, though. It sounded too much like he was organising a double date with him. You have to promise me you'll tell him I'm not interested. Won't you? I'm promised. You know that.'

'Yes. I know, Sonia. But Enrico wouldn't want you to be sitting around doing nothing all these years. You're so young! You have to live.'

'This is from the girl who is already wondering whether she'll wear a long or three-quarter-length dress for her wedding.'

Eileen picked up a pillow and threw it at Sonia, and they burst into a fit of giggles.

'Sshhh, Sonia. If Jim thinks for a minute that we're not actually meeting up with your Spanish friends at six o' clock in the café, then he'll be ringing my mother in an instant. A date!' she whispered. 'I'm going on a date with the most gorgeous man on the planet.'

'Well, as long as his friend *knows* it's not a double date when I meet up with you later …'

'Oh, don't worry so much, Sonia. Manus lives and works with Bart, and he doesn't want him to feel left out. You'll be fine.'

CHAPTER ELEVEN

Sonia sat and tried to make small talk with the boy beside her. He seemed like a lovely person, but she wasn't interested. All she wanted was to get back to the room in the uncle's house and pour out all of her troubles to Eileen. But the chance of Eileen wanting to leave her man anytime soon was remote.

She smiled again at Manus. 'My English is very bad. I'm sorry.' It worked with a lot of people. If Sonia didn't want to speak to someone, she just acted like she didn't understand, and she usually succeeded. But poor Manus was determined to try hard to get her to grasp what he was saying.

'I said how great it is that you don't drink. Like myself, you know. I don't drink. I mean, I drink, obviously I do. But I don't drink alcohol. Like yourself. I like a girl who doesn't drink.'

And he smiled again. And then he patted her knee again. And Sonia cringed. Again.

She looked up at the clock on the wall. Ten past nine. They didn't have to be home until eleven. Sonia was desperate to get out of there, but she knew if she even suggested going home, that Eileen would be obliged to leave with her, and she'd never forgive her. So, she smiled back at Manus. Her own cares would have to wait for later.

Earlier, at six o' clock, Sonia had been delighted to see Lucia and Dolores in the café where they worked. The three girls had not seen each other since they had been on the boat together from Spain to Donegal. Back then, it had been difficult to get to know each other. Sonia was not able to speak aloud, and the girls had been brought up so differently to her. But they seemed to have grown up a lot since then, and they shared a background history.

When Sonia had turned up at the café this evening, the girls had been there with two other friends they had met who were also from Malaga. It turned out that Roberto, Dolores's father, had organised their escape also. It had been wonderful to chat in her native language. Sonia was sometimes exhausted from trying to speak English all day. But Dolores and Lucia's friends had news for Sonia that she didn't want to hear.

'Your Enrico is in trouble at home, Sonia. You would do best to forget about him. Everyone in Benalmádena, even his own family, believe that he is the man that is pointing the finger at Republican sympathisers and having them arrested. His own cousin was arrested from his house in the pueblo. The soldiers last words to his mother as they left were 'Say thank you to your nephew for this. What would we do without the help of the wonderful Enrico Sanchez?'

'The boy's father has sworn that he will shoot Enrico himself if he ever sets eyes on him. You have to believe it, Sonia. There is no other way that Enrico would have been freed unless he had done a deal with the Nationalist soldiers. He has sold himself to the devil. Don't sell yourself along with him.'

And from the older girl. 'Something very bad must have happened to Enrico during his time in Malaga Jail. Something must have sent him to the edge of madness. I heard that he was a man of honour. A man who would stop at nothing to make right a wrong to his friends and family. But since he was freed from prison, he must have changed. Nobody has seen him, which means that he must be protected by someone, but everyone has heard his name by now. It is a name on the lips of every Republican. Just before they spit on the ground.

'You must forget this man, Sonia. For your own protection. Even if you were to return to Spain now you would not be able to find him. Nobody can. Otherwise, he would be dead by now.

Enrico Sanchez has gone over to the other side to protect his own hide. You must forget about him and stop asking about him, to protect yourself and your mother. Say no more if you value her safety. She has no man in the house to protect her. She is an easy target.'

Later, in Eileen's arms, Sonia had cried until she had no more tears. Now, in this pub, she was numb and had no energy to think up something to say to this nice man beside her. She couldn't leave because of Eileen, and she resented the fact that, while Eileen was wallowing in her new-found happiness, Sonia was drowning in her loss.

Manus was still talking. All Sonia had to do was to nod or shake her head at the right times and he was happy enough. She would not insult him by walking away. But she would not, could not, believe that her Enrico was lost to her. She tried to understand what she had learned. He was free, but he hadn't tried to contact her. She knew from the girls that he had made no enquiries to family or friends about her whereabouts. He hadn't been near her mother to ask of news from her, but the only reason Sonia could come up with was that Enrico was still imprisoned by the Nationalists. Nobody had seen him. It was all she could hold on to, and she had to hold on to something. Sonia and Enrico had always been one and the same person and somehow, she knew that this news was all wrong: that Enrico was good. And he still loved her. Somewhere.

The following morning found them marched off to the church with Eileen's uncle. Even the smell of the incense was different. Sonia felt that she might never fit in in this country. She clipped her mantilla in place. She knelt when they knelt, beat her chest, and she bowed her head in unison with the others. The Latin responses were the same, but when her concentration waned for a moment, she held her hands to either side to pray when the

Irish joined theirs. Sonia knew she would always be catching up with them, her heart would always be with the way things were done back home in Andalucía. Sonia had never felt so lonely.

CHAPTER TWELVE

Enrico

My sobbing echoes in the vastness of Malaga Cathedral. Curled up into a ball behind the altar of The Sacred Heart, I begin to shed a few tears, and once I start, I can't control myself.

Before leaving Benalmádena, I overheard a conversation between two of my uncles. I went to the family house, sure that I could speak to them; tell them the truth behind what has happened; explain to them why I have to make it seem like I'm on the side of the Nationalists. I need the enemy to trust me in order to complete my plan, but it has all gone crazy. The Nationalists have used my so-called defection to their own good. The name of Enrico Sanchez is shit in the whole of Benalmádena and beyond. If I'm seen by Republicans, they will shoot me. If I try to talk my way out of it, and the Nationalists hear about this, *they* would be first to shoot me. I'm facing the firing squad on all sides. I heard them talking about Sonia, about how she knows now about my defection. She is somewhere in Ireland, and I can't ask anyone her address to explain myself to her. The Sonia I know will never believe that I could turn against my own, especially turn against her. But there is no way to know for sure what she believes, and no way to try to send her a message.

My uncle spoke about being punched by his friend, having mentioned that there might be a reason behind my madness. I'm in despair. I can't get in contact with friends without putting them in danger. And even if I do find out where Sonia is, I can't contact her, as that would put her in danger too.

Sitting up, I use the filthy sleeve of my jacket to dry my face. No more tears. I'm a man. When Franco loses power, I will be able to defend myself, so I have to make this war end faster. I need to fight. I've come back to Malaga on a mission, and I'll fulfil it. Every Nationalist I kill on the way will be one step nearer to getting Sonia back.

I pull myself up and brush the dust of the altar tiles from me. I climb over the railing and think of a plan. I'm about half an hour's walk from a house on the edge of the town that's known for its Republicanism. It's a good place to start. Nobody knows me there, I hope, and I might be able to build up a following to help with my mission. I walk towards the great doors of the cathedral and push. It won't give. I push again. Nothing. I'm locked in. Churches are often locked now, post-war making Malaguenians wary of society. Before the war, Nationalists and Republicans stood side by side together in the church. But not now. The church is on Franco's side. The winning side so far. I remember a time when I was little, and my parents were so tied to the church. But my uncle spits if the church is ever mentioned in his house. I know my aunt prays secretly. Some habits are too hard to break.

I'll have to wait it out in the cathedral overnight. At least I'll have shelter. The autumn is setting in and the evenings are drawing cooler. I've been living rough for quite some time now, and I know I could use a wash and a change of clothes. Catching sight of my reflection in the polished brass of the altar, I'm glad Sonia can't see how I look. When all this is over, I'll get myself together and I'll find Sonia. I settle back down in my original resting place behind the statue and close my eyes. I feel the presence of a man looking down on me before I hear or see him. My eyes shoot open, and I jump up.

'Don't worry yourself, amigo. I came over here in the hope that you might have something on you worth robbing, but then I saw that you were even dirtier and smellier than me. And that's some achievement.'

I blink my eyes a few times to try to get a focus on the man in front of me. Can I really be dirtier than him?

'How did you get in? The doors were locked.'

'Oh, I got in earlier. Isn't that what you did? Came for shelter for the night?'

'No. I came in to ... Well, never mind why I came in. I can't get back out, and I have work to do.'

The man laughs at me. 'You won't get past those doors tonight. The curate allows us in to escape the Nationalists and locks us in for our own safety. He will unlock it at first light.'

'Us? You have friends here?'

'Yes. There are probably thirty men or so in the nooks and crannies of the cathedral. We will keep each other company through another dark night and go our separate ways in the morning. Every man here knows who his friends are.'

I look at my new friend warily. 'So how do you know that I am not one of them? The Nationalists. Waiting to turn you all in in the morning?'

'Because you stink like a Republican on the run. You look filthy and hungry.'

'Yes. I am all those things.'

'Come, amigo. God and the curate provide. Behind the altar there is food enough to keep us going. I was sent to check you out before the others crawled out, but I think I can safely tell them that you are one of us. My name is Jaime. Do you have a name, dirty man?'

I think about the outcome of telling this man my real name. What if some of this bunch have heard the name Enrico Sanchez?

'My name is Miguel Almez.'

The newly arisen Miguel – a slight elevation from his gecko status, but not much – heartily shakes his new friend's hand. Then he follows him to the altar where God has provided.

Some half hour later, sitting at the back of the church, I get to know some of my Republican friends. None of them stem from Benalmádena. Nobody recognises me or my dead friend's name, but all men have one thing in common. They hate the Nationalist soldiers. Many of them are on the run having killed or attempted to kill the hated men. Some of them have escaped from Malaga Jail, and that's where I manage to put a seed of an idea together. These men are hardened fighters already. Most either fear or hate Malaga Jail. Can I persuade them to join me to attack the jail, free the prisoners and set the place on fire with the jailers locked inside? That's my plan, but it will take all of these men to help me get it done.

It takes six days in total to earn their trust, set the idea in their minds and plan the attack. Some other men join up with our little band, and I find myself become a leader of an army of forty men. Our plan is ready, and the date is set for the fifth of October. It's Sonia's birthday. A date to remember.

CHAPTER THIRTEEN

Balcallan had gone all out for Sonia's eighteenth birthday. She painted on her best smile and determined to at least look like she was having fun. The school hall had been decorated for the event. Maeve and Eileen had made streamers and banners and hung them around to build up the festive spirit. They had been cooking for days with the help of the aunts and cousins. Maeve had made a fruit punch, and Eileen was given the job of making sure the town yobbos wouldn't add anything stronger to the bowls. Wrong girl for the job.

Sonia had never had anyone make such a fuss of her before. Enrico on his own, yes; but never a group of people all gathered in one place to celebrate Sonia. She knew she should be delighted, and she wanted to savour the moment, but all she could think of was Enrico and how much she wanted him to be there for her big occasion. She needed to keep busy and keep smiling.

Sonia picked up a plate of pastries and went offering them around and accepting congratulations from all of Balcallan's finest and dearest.

'Happy birthday, dear. Isn't this a great party altogether? Eileen and her mam have done you proud, don't you think?'

'They certainly are the kindest people, and they are so good to me, always.' Sonia smiled sweetly at Maeve's sister Dora and hoped it was enough.

'It's just that you seem to be very far away in yourself for someone who should be the life and soul of the party. But sure, what am I saying? You're hardly over your poor father, are you?'

'It's hard. Yes, Dora.' Sonia decided to milk it, to keep the woman sweet. 'And my brother's anniversary was this summer, you know. A lot of loss. I couldn't have managed without Eileen and Maeve. They are amazing.'

'Well, then. You must put away your sorrow for one night, Sonia, love. I'll bet your father is looking down on you from heaven and smiling on the wonderful party his little princess is having.'

Sonia picked a cake off the plate and shoved it into her mouth. The picture of her father loving to see her being spoiled and petted at a party was set to send her into hysterical laughter. She allowed herself to chew slowly to give her time to compose herself before she answered.

'And my mother. She would love all this. You must excuse me, Dora. Eileen is calling me. She must need help with something. Enjoy the evening.'

Sonia walked away and allowed the emotion take over. She expected to guffaw with laughter at the vision of her father smiling down on her from heaven as she was celebrated in her new home town. But the laugh came out as a sob, and she had to go running to the bathroom to pull herself together before she faced anyone else.

After a lot of deep breaths and blows of her nose she came out and dabbed some cold water around her face. Eileen came running into the bathroom looking flushed and excited. Sonia shook her head as she realised that Eileen had obviously failed in her job on punch security.

'He's here! He's here, Sonia!' For one split second Sonia thought she meant Enrico. Imagine how that would feel. One look at Enrico for her would make the world seem right. But she knew it most certainly wasn't him.

'Who, Eileen?' Sonia smiled at Eileen's infectious laughter.

'Bart! He's arrived. I saw him come in, but I needed to get you first. Come on! Come on!' Eileen dragged Sonia out of the bathroom back into the hall and stopped dead.

'All right. There's a problem already.' Sonia looked over to where Eileen's eyes were focussed. She froze at the sight of Bart and his friend Manus standing in the doorway chatting with Maeve. At least she was smiling.

'Sonia, you have to do a favour for your best friend, all right?' Sonia nodded, worried about what Eileen was going to come out with.

'I wrote a letter to Bart, you see, telling him about the party and I didn't think he would be able to come so I was amazed to get a letter back from him saying that he'd love to come, but was it all right if he brought Manus here as he wouldn't know anyone else. Are you following me?'

Sonia shook her head. No.

'I had to tell my mam that they were coming, so I said that we had met them in Dublin and that the Manus fellow was sweet on you, and that I had invited him to take your mind off Enrico for a while, and that he was bringing a friend called Bart to keep him company. Are you following me now?'

Sonia nodded yes in a jerky fashion to show that she didn't like this crazy story of her best friend at all.

'I know, Sonia. I should have told you, but I was so desperate to see Bart, and I had already invited him. Then Mam was delighted that they were coming and agreed with me that it would be a good idea to— I know. I'm the worst person in the world.'

Sonia looked like she might be about to cry. Surely Eileen knew that she had no feelings whatsoever for Manus and that it would be terrible to let him even think anything else?

Maeve was on her way over to Sonia and Eileen with the two men by her side and all the eyes of the partygoers on her, wondering who the two strangers were.

'Please, Sonia. Please!'

Sonia gave Eileen her filthiest look, but then painted on a smile as the trio arrived beside them.

'I believe there are no need for introductions here?' Maeve was delighted with herself. She had completely fallen for Eileen's well-crafted story. If she had known for one moment that it was Bart who was here for Eileen, she would have been hopping mad at her daughter. Even though Eileen was two years older than Sonia. But from the big smile on Manus's face, Sonia was worried that Maeve had already said something encouraging to him, and from what she remembered from her weekend in Dublin, Manus needed no encouragement.

'I'll leave all of you young ones together, so, and I'll get on with looking after the guests,' Maeve said. And off she went with a glint in her eye; her night's matchmaking work was over.

'It's lovely to see you, Sonia.' Manus was straight in with his hand outstretched. She put her hand in his limply and allowed hers to be shaken firmly. Sonia looked over for some help from Eileen, but she and Bart were staring at each other like they were hatching up a plan to escape from the party, fall into one another's arms and devour each other.

Sonia was saved momentarily by Maeve who chose that time to get up on the stage to gather all her friends and family together.

'I think we're all here now, so it's probably a good time to get all the thank-yous and best wishes out of the way. So, thank you all for coming and all the very best wishes to Sonia.' She pretended to walk away and that got her a laugh.

'Seriously, though. I wanted to get you all together tonight to celebrate. Not only Sonia turning eighteen, which is a worthy celebration in itself, but for all of us here to let her know how much her arrival and staying on in Balcallan has meant to us as a family and to the community as a whole. Sonia Almez has had a troubled year which we hope has been made a little easier to bear by the welcome that she got here in Balcallan. And you *are* welcome, Sonia. For myself, I hope that you make this your home for as long as possible. Happy birthday to the girl who has made the little family of Eileen and Maeve McMenamin complete.'

Sonia knew she was as red as Eileen's new dress, as everyone in the hall stood and clapped a loud applause to cement Maeve's beautiful words from the stage. How lovely the people were here; how simple and straightforward. Like Benalmádena used to be before all the madness set in. Then Maeve was calling her up on the stage, and she went even redder at the thought of everyone looking at her. Maeve must have known she wouldn't be able to do this. Why would she ask her such a thing? Sonia was shaking her head and making pleading faces at Maeve and Eileen alternately.

Then this thing – this awful thing that would have such an impact on Sonia's life had she known it then – happened as if in a dream sequence. Manus took her hand and led her up onto the stage to a beaming Maeve and another round of applause from everyone. Sonia, following him, felt her hand burning at Manus's touch. Not burning her in the same way that it did when Enrico held her hand: that beautiful sensation that sent her heart racing. This felt like an actual burning.

When they reached the stage, and in the full scrutiny of everyone's expectant stare, Sonia wondered how she was going to stop herself crying. She tried to smile at Maeve and to extricate her hand from Manus's at the same time, but his fingers were strongly woven around hers in his bid to look after her. Sonia understood that he meant well, but his proximity was killing her. She tried her best to speak to her guests.

'Yes. Thank you. You are all so good to me. I don't deserve all the goodness that Maeve and Eileen give me. I will never forget this birthday and …'

The tears were coming, and she couldn't continue to speak. Maeve reached over to give her a hug and everyone started to cheer once more. Sonia tried to pull her hand away from Manus to reciprocate Maeve's affection, but she had to make do with a one-handed squeeze, and it all got too much for her and she broke down. A collective *awww* broke out as the people there presumed that she was overcome by joy at everything that had happened that night. Sonia allowed Maeve and Manus to lead her down from the stage. If she could just make it to the bathroom once more and give herself time to pull together. Again.

'Manus. I'll speak to you soon. Maeve, you are wonderful for putting all this together. Thank you. I'll be back in a minute.' And she wiggled her fingers out of Manus's grip as he nodded his head in understanding. 'Help yourself to some fruit punch.'

Sonia put one foot in front of the other across the hall to the bathroom and collided with Eileen coming in from outside.

'Sonia—'

'Later, Eileen.'

She ran the last few steps. She ran into the cubicle and closed the door. She would have loved to stay there and cry her heart out with the loneliness she felt, but she knew she had a few minutes at most to try to put her feelings on hold. She let the tears fall down her cheeks silently for a few minutes. *Enrico, Enrico, Enrico* ... Her heart cried out his name. How had she ended up in this place? She was safe from harm. Safe from Malaga Jail or a soldier's bullet, but how could that be worse than being away from Benalmádena and all the places and people she loved? And now this Manus had turned up here determined to win her over. Had Maeve said something in those few minutes earlier to him that made him so sure of her feelings for him? She must have. Eileen must have sold her little story well, and Sonia didn't know how to handle it. She wanted to go home so badly. To Enrico.

She was trying to put away the information in her head, but the facts were flooding in and drowning her. She hadn't heard from Enrico since he disappeared. He was alive somewhere. She knew this. He could find her. He could write to her, but he hadn't asked her mother or her school friend, Rosa, where she was living.

Sonia knew she needed to go out and face Maeve and Eileen's friends and family. She went to the sink and splashed her face with cold water once more. Tomorrow she would do what she always did at home when things got too much for her. She would go to the furthest part of the beach where nobody would be walking, and she would cry her fill. Then she would go into the sea and swim and wash it all away. Begin again.

People were starting to drift out home. Sonia made her way to where Eileen was standing very close to Bart. Manus was drinking the fruit punch like he was dying of thirst.

'Eileen. There is so much food left. Will I see can I give people some to take home? It would be a shame to waste it.'

Manus put down his empty glass and caught Sonia around the waist to her complete astonishment. 'The birthday girl shouldn't be doing any work. Leave that to the two lovebirds there, and you and me'll get to know each other a whole lot better.'

Sonia wriggled strongly out of his grip on her middle and stared at the man who she remembered as being meek and mild when she met him in Dublin.

'Ah come here, would you? What's the matter? I was only having a laugh.' Manus was slurring his words. The glassy look in his eyes was a look she had seen often on her father's face. She looked at Bart who seemed to have also registered that his friend was drunk.

'Eileen, you said that your mother made that punch. That it was just fruit. Has someone been adding to it?'

'Of course, they have. If that's what your friend has been drinking tonight, you may be sure that there was enough alcohol to drown him. How did he get that bad so quickly, though? I don't believe this. If my mother or anyone we know sees him, I'll be banned from even talking to you again Bart. Get him out of here and back to Gortahork quickly before anyone notices. I'll tell Mam that you had to catch yourselves a lift back home.'

Bart looked as disappointed as Eileen. Their time together had been cut short by Manus's swift descent into drunkenness.

'Will I see you again soon, Eileen?'

Eileen could see her mam coming away from her sister and heading their way.

'Yes. I'll write. Go. Quickly.' And she ushered them away as Maeve arrived beside her.

'Are your friends going so quickly, Sonia? What a shame. I was going to invite them back to the house for a cup of tea before they left.'

Sonia looked at Eileen's crestfallen face. She would have loved the chance to have Bart actually come to her house, invited by her mother, all respectable like. Then she would have worked on her mother meeting him again and maybe sometime in the future. The opportunity was gone now, washed away by Manus's obvious problem with alcohol consumption, but with it was Sonia's perfect excuse never to see the man again.

'Such a shame. I was telling your friend Manus earlier, how welcome he was to Balcallan, Sonia, and how he could drop into the house anytime he was passing.'

Sonia's face registered her shock. Eileen's plot could have completely gotten out of hand. Thank God they were gone, but she would have to listen to poor Eileen's tales of woe deep into the night. Sonia knew that Bart had recognised the signs of drunken behaviour in his friend. She was sure that tonight wasn't the first time he had shown his ugly side, and if Bart was happy to still be friends with him, then maybe he wasn't the right person for Eileen. For the first time, Sonia felt the weariness of having to make big decisions without Enrico being around to help.

CHAPTER FOURTEEN

Enrico

The night is hot for early October. It's a perfect time to choose to take the jailers by surprise as they will be sleepy. The good thing about having spent part of my life behind these bars is that I know the timetable of its occupiers like clockwork. Most of the prisoners are aware by now that there's a plan afoot to free them tonight: those who can be trusted on the inside to be calm enough not to alert the guards. I know that not everyone will make it out of here alive. There will unfortunately be prisoners who will die in the fight, and there will be men in my own small army who will not see the morning. The thought that I might not make it myself makes me shiver. There may even be some guards that might escape, but the most important part of tonight is that the prison building will be burnt to a shell, and that the flames of this hell will be seen across Malaga. A fitting eighteenth birthday present for Sonia in her part of the world.

Thinking about her now spurs me forward. I need to move this war on, and the only way I can do this is to kill those on the wrong side. I look up at the top barred window of the jail from my hiding place behind the pillar, and I light a small flame with the torch that I carry. I let it be for five seconds and then I snuff it out. That's Mario's signal to cough three times as loudly as he can. Another signal to the imprisoned occupants that we're going in. I smile at the Nationalist soldier who is our key to Malaga Jail.

'It's time, Rodriguez. Get up!'

'You'll hang for this Sanchez! I'll see to it personally. You're a savage dog.'

'You just keep your side of the bargain and hope that we're kind-hearted enough to see to it that your wife lives through the night.' I push the man ahead of me towards the door.

I'm very proud of this particular part of our plan. This is the man who murdered my friend Miguel. Alberto Rodriguez made it known to all that he was visiting Malaga making him the perfect choice. This soldier is responsible for my year behind these bars. I had to publicly apologise to him as part of my freedom package. It's fitting that we have kidnapped his wife and are using him to gain access to the jail.

'Keep moving!'

Walking calmly towards the door of the prison is made easier in the knowledge that nearly forty other men are creeping out of their hiding places ready to fight their way in as soon as the front gates are unlocked.

'Smile, you filthy cucaracha! Remember what I told you. You're bringing me to see a man who has been wrongly imprisoned. Like myself he is a friend to the Nationalists. Make sure it happens the way I said, and if you're in any doubt, then just think of Eva at home. Make sure she sees tomorrow.'

I hear a clatter of bottles behind me, and a young man's voice shouts a loud curse. I screw up my face in annoyance.

'Your young friends are nervous, Sanchez,' Rodriguez says. 'Hah. You will never succeed in this mission.'

That's all the encouragement that I need. By dawn this place will be razed to the ground. We reach the outer door and I nod at my prisoner. Rodriguez bangs loudly on the door. He has the false documentation ready for the guards, and by the time they realise that they are false, it will be too late for them. It has been easy to lay hands on weapons. Every man in my army was told to acquire two each. One knife for silence and a gun for finishing things off.

The door clangs, revealing a large man with a love for torture that I've never forgotten from my time inside. This animal, Martinez, will get his comeuppance in a few minutes, and I relish the thought that I'll be the one to finish his life.

'Señor Rodriguez? What are you here for at this time in the evening?' He stands back in respect and allows the man immediate entry to the building.

'I have a letter allowing this man access to a man here who is wrongly imprisoned. He is actually a friend to the Nationalists and can help us in our bid to arrest more filthy Republicans.' Rodriguez hands the document to Martinez who makes a pretence at reading it carefully. I smile, hiding my knowledge of the man's illiteracy close to my heart.

'That seems to be fine, señor. I hope this day finds your lovely wife well?'

Rodriguez blanches, and I think he might lose it and prepare myself for the onslaught. It won't matter. The men will be waiting at the door, ready to come in. It might be for the best. I look at Rodriguez for signs and see actual tears well in the man's eyes. I glare at him.

'They are well, señor,' I say. 'We have come from there have we not, Señor Rodriguez? Eva was preparing the evening meal for her husband's return.' This is the picture that I fill Martinez's head with as I watch him turn and walk towards the inner door.

'Yes. They are well. Now, open up, señor! Let's get this done.'

I watch the jailer lead and Rodriguez follow. Rodriguez's head is bent, and he drags his feet. I give him a small push to remind him of what lies ahead, and he walks faster. As soon as the inner door is opened, I shove Rodriguez aside and slipping quietly up behind Martinez, I bring the knife across the fat expanse of his throat. Blood splatters the walls and the low ceiling and I drop the man's body to the floor. This is the second time I have killed a man, and both deserved their fate. I bend down to release the man's keys from his belt and go back to open up the outer door once more. My finger goes to my lips as the men come from the cracks in the walls outside and fill the inner room.

This is to be carried out silently and I can trust these men to execute my plan to their very best. I lied to the men about my age. Twenty is just a boy, but twenty-four, as I said I am, is a grown man with fire in his heart and a belly of iron. The more my plan grew, the more I knew it was the right thing to do. I haven't decided on Alberto Rodriguez's exact fate. I'll see what the night brings and how things pan out, but it seems like I will get to carry out what my heart desires most: to kill the man – and there's nothing at that moment that I want to do more. I have a picture in my head now of Alberto, tied up inside the jail as it burns to the ground. A slow painful death. As Rodriguez has provided for so many Republicans, I will provide for this most hated Nationalist. I nod to my comrades, and they file through the open doors towards the innards of the wretched building, leaving me in the company of Rodriguez.

I don't see the man come up behind me and the surprise of being disarmed and held in a head lock shows on my face. Before I know what's happening, I see Alberto visibly breathe out and a smile spread across his ugly face. I think I might vomit. Surely this cannot be how things will happen? The army of men that I brought with me will be walking through here any moment. I think fleetingly about my own fate. Will I be killed before we carry out the rest of our plan? Most probably. I manage to turn slightly to see that the stinking man who has captured me, is none other than the man I chose as my second-in-command from Malaga Cathedral.

'Jaime.' I whisper his name.

'Jaime, if you like. Or a hundred other names that I've been known as. Take your pick.' And he cackles a loud laugh that can be heard throughout the building. I wriggle, and the man strengthens his grip. I listen as the quiet of the night is deafened by the roars of other men being taken inside the jail.

Alberto straightens up. 'You took your fucking time, Jaime, or whatever you're called. He has killed Martinez already. He will hang for that alone.'

Jaime turns to me. 'No use waiting for your other friends,' he says. 'They are at this moment being locked away in cells in the building they had hoped to burn down.' I can hear their shouts and some dying roars as they are taken.

'Your wife is as good as dead, Rodriguez.' I'm grasping at straws I know, but I want to try to get out alive and Eva Rodriguez is my only hope.

Alberto looks over at the man who I have called Jaime. He nods. 'That is why I was late, Señor Rodriguez. I have freed her and left her with someone to calm her. She is shaken, but she is unharmed. The man who was guarding her is awaiting sentence with the rest of our Republican comrades. I'm sorry we had to go this far, and I'm sorry for Martinez, but it was the only way to capture all of these bastards at once. Did you think that you could go through with all this, Enrico Sanchez?' asks the man who is still holding me. 'How could you be so naïve to think that the great Nationalists would not know of your existence, and not have a counter-plot to your pathetic attempt at freeing your filthy rojos and burning this fine building to a shell. Miguel Almez? You should have thought of a more distinct name than the name of the man who had died at this señor's hands. You will never leave prison now, mi amigo, except in a death cart.'

He turns me around to face him and spits at me, then knees me between my legs and watches me fall to the ground in pain. I stare as Alberto shakes the hand of the man I had chosen to trust with my perfect plan, and I realise that nobody can be trusted and that all is now lost. I close my eyes and think of Sonia, somewhere in Ireland, celebrating her eighteenth birthday on the day we had once planned to be our wedding day. That was all before I ruined our lives with my stupidity, and here I am, wrecking our lives once more. I pray that my end will come soon and that it will be swift.

CHAPTER FIFTEEN

Lying in her bed next to Eileen's that night, Sonia cried quietly as she dreamed of the husband she might never have. Enrico and Sonia should have been spending the first night in their bed together as a married couple. Her eighteenth party should have been a wedding party, with all her and Enrico's families there to help them celebrate the rest of their lives. It would have been shadowed by Franco's influence on their life, but that wouldn't matter as they would have been together. Sonia hadn't shared this with Eileen, but someday she would be able to let it all out to the girl who had become her best friend. It wasn't that she didn't trust Eileen with her secrets. It was herself that she didn't trust. If she opened up, she knew that she would be releasing a dam so powerful that she would never be able to stop the flood.

Eileen had cried because of her problems with seeing Bart again. On into the night she had ranted in a whispered voice of how and when and where she might be able to meet him.

'I can't believe that the night was ruined by that eejit Manus downing the punch the way he did. How could he have managed to get so drunk in such a short space of time?'

'He's an alcoholic, Eileen, like my father. It only takes one or two mouthfuls before they have to drink themselves into oblivion.'

'Sonia!' Eileen raised her voice and her mother banged on the wall in the next room to tell them to go to sleep. 'Sonia,' Eileen continued quietly, 'you can't look at all men who take a drink as being like your father. Manus, God love him, is no drinker. He's obviously not used to drinking, and he thought that it was exactly what my mother told him it was: fruit punch. It didn't

104

take much to get him drunk because he's not used to it. You don't have to be so dramatic about everything.'

And then she went back to talking about her favourite subject again, and how she knew that the only way was to go back down to Dublin to stay with Uncle Jim and to say that Sonia wanted to see Manus again.

Sonia wanted to scream at Eileen. How dare she even think that Sonia could look at the man after the way he behaved tonight? But Eileen dared, and she went to sleep with a plan to put past her mother the next day and it involved Sonia going to see this terrible man. Sonia wouldn't do it – not for Eileen and not for anyone. Her friend could be so selfish sometimes; or maybe it was because, although she was two years older than Sonia, she was very immature in comparison. She hadn't experienced the same life as Sonia had. Yes, Eileen had lost her father at a young age, but she had been protected from hardships and coddled by her mother since then.

Sonia wondered how her own life might have been if her father had died when she was young. Her mother would not have spent her life recovering from inner and outer wounds. He would not have been missed by her family. She thought about the latest letter from her mother that she had kept from Maeve and Eileen. Cristina's letter that day had been filled with news that was beyond imagining ...

Sonia,

Enrico will never be able to return here again. He has disappeared. It has been said that he has changed his name, but more important he most likely will never try to get in touch with you again. You have to stay safe, my love, and even knowing Enrico will be dangerous from now on.

There were times when I found myself wishing to join Miguel and let myself slip out of life, but there was so much left behind. With Franco's men, my mother would never receive the care that she needs, so it is up to me to look after her for the time that she has left. And you, Sonia, my daughter (because you are my daughter no matter what I may have spoken in grief before), I knew that you would try to find Enrico if you could, so I have to make sure that never happens. If you find him, then I will have lost you too.

Perhaps Enrico weeps for you, as you do for him. In another life you were both made to be together, but this life is a different life, and there are new ways to live. You must stay in Ireland for now where it is safe, and you have Eileen and Maeve to love you and care for you. Someday, Sonia, I might make it over to that country to see you, but travel is hard, and my bones still ache from the years of hurt.

I do not grieve for your father. Through his struggles, he left me many years ago. When he first took to the bottle to settle his moods, then I lost him. I should have left him long ago, but with Franco's soldiers it was too frightening to be known to be a woman on her own. That may sound cowardly, but believe me, it was strength that kept me by his side, not cowardice. I would have gone to any lengths, my love, to protect your brother and you. Even staying with Hugo.

But now you are there, and I am here, and Miguel is in heaven. We are all where we are. You and I will be what Miguel taught us to be. Strong. Hold on …

'Be strong?' Sonia thought. 'For what? For whom? Hold on to what?' Sonia couldn't hold on any longer. The tears she tried to silence defeated her, and once more she found herself being consoled by Eileen and Maeve as heartache convulsed her. When she eventually felt that she could stop, she remembered her mother's words about letting life slip away. That was the only thing she could think of doing.

A month later Sonia was still alive and still thinking of ways to keep herself going. She woke in the morning, worked in the post office, came home, ate and went to bed. Somehow, she was able to live by putting one foot in front of the other and one thought in front of the other ... Not too far ahead ... Live for the next thing that had to be done ... And then the next ...

Enrico had not been in touch. Any person linked to him would be in danger. Sonia knew she had to somehow distance herself from Enrico, but she couldn't remove herself from the memory of him. Her every moment was still filled with visions of them together. Until Sonia came to Ireland, life had been all about her and Enrico. Now alone, she just existed. She felt bad that no matter how hard Eileen and Maeve tried, they couldn't pull her out of her depression.

CHAPTER SIXTEEN

Enrico

It is easy for the soldier to drag my weakened body to the ground and sit astride me, holding a gun to my head. 'Enrico Sanchez,' he whispers in my ear. 'My name is Roberto Rodriguez. I wish to speak with you. I have told the prison guards that I have a message for you from my brother, Alberto Rodriguez, the man you wished to kill.' I look up through my swollen face, my eyes full of hate for the man above me.

'Keep up that face,' he says. 'Whatever I say to you today, I want you to glare at me with this hatred. Don't let the guards think that I am saying anything to you that might not be full of venom.' He stands up and pulls me to standing, and I am stunned. What is this man about?

'Sit,' he orders.

I reluctantly sit on the broken wooden stool in the cell I have been dragged to, opposite the man who says he is the brother of the man that I hate. Alberto is still alive, and that is the reason that I am now in the prison that I had sought to burn to the ground. Glaring at this Roberto is the easiest thing I could be asked to do. I want to drag him to the ground and kick his head in.

'This fucking war, Enrico,' Roberto whispers, shaking his head. 'It has ruined all our lives. I don't have long to speak to you, or they will become suspicious. You will find it hard to believe or to understand, but I hate my brother, Alberto, because of what he has become, and I hate everything that he stands for. I had a choice. I could openly turn against him and all my family and end up in prison or be killed, but instead, I don the Nationalist uniform, and I use my influence to try to help other Republicans.' My glare changes to a look of puzzlement.

'Don't change your facial expression, Enrico,' he says. 'If anything, fill your look with contempt. I need to keep my cronies in the dark as to how I live my life as a Nationalist soldier. I have managed to have your death sentence changed to life imprisonment. I persuaded Alberto that it would only be a release to let you die, that you would suffer more in prison instead. You are to be moved up north, near Madrid, and you will stay there indefinitely.'

'You are right, Señor Nationalist,' I say. 'Death would be preferable to prison under Franco.' I'm not finding it hard to keep up the hatred in my look. These words from this man are crazy. All I can see in front of me is a Nationalist uniform and a face that looks so like his brother, Alberto.

'If you are alive, Enrico, then I have a chance to someday get you released, and I will do this if I can. My brother was not always the bastard that he has become. Our parents were killed by Republicans, and he will never forgive them. He is so full of anger and hatred; it eats him alive. I was with him the day he pulled the trigger on Miguel Almez. It was mistaken identity he said, but the truth was that he was drunk, as he often is, and he shot his gun into space as he shouted about how much he hated the rojos, and Miguel walked out into the street and into his line of fire. He walked away and left him dead, and as I watched Miguel's friends scream in anger at the waste of such a good man, I vowed that if nothing else, I would help the family and friends of the man whose life my brother had needlessly taken. That includes you.

'When you are in prison, as much as I can, I will have your back. And Sonia and her family, I will protect them too. I wanted my daughter to leave Andalucía until it is safe to return here. I found a ship going to Ireland, and I put mine and Alberto's daughter on that ship. Enrico. Your Sonia Almez was in Malaga searching for you with your friend Alejandro. Thankfully, I found them before the other Nationalist soldiers arrested them for their association with you.'

'Sonia and Alejandro have nothing to do with all of this.' Now I am alarmed. Whatever happens to me is my own doing, but Sonia begged me to stay home with her, and now I have put her and Alejandro into terrible danger.

'I know that,' says Roberto, 'but you know that the soldiers don't care. The best thing I could do for your Sonia was to get her a new identity and put her on a ship with my daughter. She had to get away from Spain. She needs to be safe, and this was the only way.'

I try to stand up, but Roberto grabs me roughly and shouts, 'I'm not finished with you yet, you filthy rojo!' And he shoves me back down onto the stool.

I shrug him off and take a deep breath. 'Sonia would never leave Spain. You are lying. Messing with my head as all your soldier friends have done before you. If you found Sonia, she would want to go home.'

'If she went home, she would have been arrested and thrown in prison, Enrico, and don't doubt for one moment that the women's prison is any better than the men's. It is a death wish to enter there, and this was her only chance. One day this country will come to its senses. You will be free, and Sonia will return. This madness cannot last so long.'

'And in the meantime?' I feel like I have been given a death sentence. I am completely defeated.

'In the meantime, Sanchez, I will keep you as safe as I can in prison. Sonia is secure in another country, and I will watch over her mother. Sonia's school friend, Rosa, is living with Cristina now, and I will watch her too. There is very little I can do to change the rotten state of things, but I will do what I can. When this is all over, you can bring yourselves back together, but for now, this is the best that Spain has to offer.'

I stare at the man in front of me. Is he genuine? I decide that I have no choice but to believe the man. 'This country and those who hold its reins are sick at heart,' I say. 'I don't hold out much hope for any of us, but I am glad of your help. I am sorry that you are related to that piece of shit, and I would rather rot away in here than have a brother such as him.'

Roberto shakes his head slowly and stands over me. 'Years ago, when we were young, Republicans shot our parents and now Alberto wants to kill Republicans. He shot your friend, and you want to shoot him. We are all Spanish, but the anger spreads through us like a disease, and it will never stop until somebody says *enough, no more,* and shakes the hand of his fellow Spaniard.'

'That is idealistic drivel,' I reply. 'Look around you at our fellow Spaniards. As long as Franco is in charge, we will never have Spaniards. Only you and us. Whites and Reds. It cannot change.'

'That may be so for now, my friend, but I will do my bit to try and change things. Right now, though, I am going to hit you. I will try to lessen the blow, but I want you to look as if I've sent you reeling. I am heading to Madrid tomorrow. It is easy to get my brother to sign orders for me when he is so often drunk, and he is unwittingly sending me to deliver a package up north. You will be following me there, and I will have bribed the right people to keep an eye on you in prison. I wish you good health and much courage, my friend.' Roberto stands back as if I have insulted him, lifts his hand and deals me a blow across the head. 'Shut your fucking mouth, or I'll shut it for you permanently, shitface. May you rot in hell.'

In keeping with the pretence, having fallen to the floor, I turn and spit in the direction of this man's retreating figure.

Two guards drag me into standing and push me towards the door and back into the crowded cell that has been my home for the weeks following my failed attempt at burning it down. The following day, along with countless other Malaguenian Republican prisoners, I am displaced and sent to a prison hundreds of miles away from family and friends: the ultimate punishment, apart from death. As I'm pushed through an opening in the wall, I take one last look at the Spanish street, and I know that I won't be free for a long time to come. No matter how hard Roberto Rodriguez tries, the Republicans cannot bring Franco's soldiers to their knees, and while I and other Republicans fade from memory behind these walls, Spain will crumble.

CHAPTER SEVENTEEN

1951

'Will we dance?'

Sonia jumped at Manus shouting at her over the music.

'My God, Manus. There's no need to roar at me. Let the whole world know your business, why don't you?' Sonia made a big show of sitting down and folding her arms with no intention of dancing.

Manus sat down beside her and smiled. Would nothing thwart the man?

'You look beautiful in your bridesmaid's dress, Sonia. I felt very privileged walking up beside you in the church today. It made me think what it might be like if …'

'Manus! Leave it, please. Not tonight. This is Eileen and Bart's special day, so don't go spoiling it with talk about things that will never happen and then spending the rest of the night sulking because I had to say no again.'

Sonia looked over at the man who had been trying to get her down the aisle for so long and sighed. 'All right. I'll dance. But that's all, Manus.'

When they got out to the dance floor Eileen and Bart moved over for them, and Bart gave his friend a congratulatory slap on the back. Sonia smiled weakly at the beaming Eileen who'd like nothing better than to see her friend give in and get together with the lovely Manus.

Manus had never touched a drop of drink according to him since the night of her eighteenth birthday three years ago. Sonia believed him, but she also knew from her mother that it would only take one drink and he would be hooked again. Manus had opened up to her about the problem with alcohol in his family. His father and his brother were completely wrecked from drinking and had ruined his mother's life because of it. He knew that he'd inherited the problem too, and he was determined to stay well clear from it for the rest of his life.

The music stopped, and Sonia smiled her thanks at Manus and walked back down to her chair. She felt him following behind her and looked at her watch. If it was anything else but Eileen's wedding, she would have made her excuses and left, but she was stuck here until the happy couple were seen off the premises and she knew it would be expected of her, as family, to stay with Maeve until all their guests had left the hotel. And Manus would be there through it all, so she had better just make the best of it.

'How's the new business going then, Manus?'

Sometimes it was worth being nice to Manus just to see the way his face lit up. She smiled a genuine smile at him.

'From strength to strength, Sonia. Sure there's so much building to be done in Balcallan alone, that we're having to take on more men to deal with the building in neighbouring towns as well. The experience we got in Dublin counts for a lot. When people hear we're back from the big capital city with our modern ideas they jump at the chance to take us on. We've Eileen's lovely new house finished for when they come back from their honeymoon week in London. We send people to have a look at the craftsmanship of that house, and they're dying to take us on board.'

'That's wonderful, Manus. Her house is really beautiful, and she can't stop talking about it. But will you manage on your own while Bart's away?'

'Like I said, we've taken on a few lads, so I should be able to keep it ticking over.'

There was nothing said between them for a few minutes, and it was comfortable enough, but then Manus ruined things by bringing up personal stuff.

'Have you had any news from home, Sonia? Did your mother make any decisions whether to come over and visit you?'

Sonia knew that her mother's letter was the last thing that she could talk about right now. Here in front of all of Balcallan and half of Dublin.

'No, nothing recent. I'm sure my mother is enjoying life in peace and quiet, having time to herself since my grandmother died.' Sonia blinked away the tears.

'I'm sure she misses her too though. It'd do her good to come over here.'

'She might, Manus, but travel to and from Spain is difficult. Mamá may find it easy to leave Spain, but it might be difficult for her to return, and she would hate not to be able to go back.'

'Does that mean that you can't go back to Spain yourself? Your family being Republican and all that?' Manus could hardly keep the glee from his voice.

Sonia took a deep breath. The contents of her mother's letter were spilling out, sticking in her throat and she was finding it difficult to breath. 'Ah, Manus …'

'Oh my God, Sonia. I'm so sorry. I didn't mean to upset you …'

But it was too late. Sonia stood up from the table and walked in the direction of the toilets holding her dignity together for as long as she could. She smiled at Eileen's aunt coming out of the cubicle and let herself in and locked the door, then she let her dignity crumble silently down her cheeks.

Two months before, Sonia had written to her mother telling her that she wanted to come home. Sonia couldn't take being away from her family and the place where she had grown up any more. Even if Enrico was not there, at least she would be back where she belonged. The people of Balcallan, she explained to her mother, were the nicest, kindest people you could find, but they were not her people. She wanted her mother, and she wanted home.

Her mother had written a short letter back telling her that her grandmother had died and that she was hoping to come and visit Sonia in Ireland. *Stay a while longer, my love. Wait for me to come to you.*

Last month, she had written to her mother again asking why she wanted to come to Ireland, when Sonia could come home, and they could be together as a family. Then three days ago, she had received a letter from her mother that had put Sonia's life on hold indefinitely.

There is no home to come back to, Sonia. Franco has made sure of this for you. I can't describe the change in our lives on paper, but someday when we are together, I will talk about it to you. This town is a dangerous place for a woman. Even a married woman, protected by her husband has no rights now, but Republican widows and daughters are much more at risk. I felt that it couldn't last like this forever, but we are twelve years on from the war and the Nationalist soldiers get stronger and crueller. Even if you were to get as far as Spain, you would probably end up in trouble before you got halfway to Andalucía.

Last month Miguel's friend Alejandro escaped arrest with a group of prisoners as they were being transferred from Malaga to another jail up north and they ran from there. His family haven't seen or heard from him, though it is rumoured that he was shot outside the town. They grieve whilst not even knowing if grieving is the right thing to do. Others say that he has escaped Spain and is unable to return.

Nobody smiles any more, Sonia. There is not much to smile for but knowing you are safe in Ireland gives me reason to be happy. Not being your birth mother does not mean I love you any less. I want the best in life for you, and the best is not in Spain. Not now or in the foreseeable future.

I don't see how I could get to you, Sonia. I am the widow of Hugo Almez, a known Republican. I am the mother of Miguel Almez, an executed Republican and Sonia Almez, an exiled Republican. I am nobody and that way I can hide away in a corner and stay relatively safe. If I try to move from here, I will draw attention to myself.

And I am poor. I live on the charity of some sympathetic Nationalist wives. Once these women were my friends. I went to school with them, grew up with them, but now … I don't belong here any more, Sonia and neither do you.

I am not sure how I will get this letter to you, Sonia, as the man who helped me with getting letters to you before has disappeared, but I will ask around and find a way. In the meantime, stay safe; and that means stay in Ireland.

There was a tap at the door of the toilet.

'Sonia? Are you in there? Is everything all right? Manus told me you might be a bit upset, love. Can you come out?'

'I'm okay, Maeve. Thank you. I'll be out in a minute.' Sonia remembered her bag under the table in the function hall and knew she would need to top up her make-up and paint her smile back on again for the time being. 'Do you think you could bring me my bag from the table, Maeve? I need something from it.'

'Oh, I see. Is that all? I'll be back in a minute.'

Let Maeve think that she had her monthlies and needed a towel. That would explain why she was not herself as well. While she waited, Sonia came out of the toilet and splashed water over her face, and when Maeve came back, she smiled at her and threw her eyes up to heaven.

'Who would be a woman, Maeve? Eh? And poor Manus. He asked me again and I got cross with him and then got needlessly upset and it was only because it was my time of the month anyway.'

'Grand, Sonia. So, you can go back out now and tell him it was only your hormones talking and actually you'd love to marry the man. Put all of us out of our misery.'

Sonia laughed at Maeve as she walked to the door.

'No chance, Maeve. I'm promised to another.' She heard the deep sigh from Maeve, and she knew exactly what was going through her head.

'For God's sake, girl. Don't you think that it's time to move on?'

'No, Maeve. I don't. It's not as easy as all that. Go on out. I'll be out shortly.'

CHAPTER EIGHTEEN

Sonia typed in the date on the letter she was writing for Maeve: 18th July 1951.

How had she been in Ireland for so long? Four slow years. In Spain, so much had happened and yet nothing had happened. Miguel was dead. Her father was dead. Her grandmother was dead. Alejandro was probably dead. Her mother was trapped. All this was happening, and yet nothing had happened. Sonia had waited three years, since that time when she had followed looking for Enrico, waiting for news that never came. All she had were snippets from people – rumours about where or how he might be – but Enrico had never contacted her.

'God damn you, Enrico, for leaving me that day!' Sonia pulled the typewriter to start the next line, and in her fury broke the ribbon. Now Maeve would go crazy. Sonia knew that if he could, Enrico would have risked anything to see his Sonia, but not her life. If Enrico thought that he was putting Sonia in danger, he would not try to see her. She stood up and put the typewriter to one side. It was time to go home, and she would tell Maeve about the ribbon after dinner. She would make up a story and offer to pay for it out of her wages. Sonia didn't often lose her temper. This was why.

Eileen and Bart were due home from their honeymoon in London this evening. They were taking the train to Holyhead and then sailing to Dublin; then taking the train to Letterkenny and the bus to Balcallan. It would be close to midnight when they got there but Sonia would stay up to greet them. She already missed her friend and wasn't at all sure how she was going to like staying with Maeve now that there was just the two of them. Eileen had suggested that Sonia come and live with her and Bart, but Maeve had flipped.

'How can you even think of starting your married life with the poor man having to share with two women? Don't be ridiculous.'

And so, they were sensible, and Sonia stayed on in their old room and life went on. At least their new house was nearby, and Eileen would still be working in the post office with her, so she would get to see her every day. If Sonia had left and gone back to Spain, she would have really missed Eileen.

Maeve looked at Sonia coming in the garden gate and wondered would this girl ever learn to smile again. Sonia had a wonderful disposition, but she couldn't seem to let go of the sadness that she had left behind in Spain. She carried it around with her like a ball and chain. Maeve knew she had missed Eileen as much as she herself had, so she had expected her to at least be a little bit happy this evening. Maeve had spent the afternoon baking Eileen's favourite cakes and one of them was iced with: *Welcome home Mr and Mrs Sharkey.* Except the *Sharkey* looked like *Shark,* but sure they'd have a bit of a joke of it. She was never a domestic goddess. Thank goodness she'd had her job in the post office all these years.

'Chin up, Sonia Almez. You'd never think your best friend was coming home from her honeymoon tonight.'

Sonia looked up at Maeve and confessed. 'I broke the ribbon on the typewriter, Mrs McMenamin.'

Maeve was about to let loose, but whether it was the return of the happy couple or just the look of pure desolation on Sonia's face she decided to let it go.

'I'll send off for a new one in the morning. In the meantime, you'll have to use a pen and paper for letters. None of your fancy

Spanish swirls, mind you; only honest-to-goodness script. Come on in with you. I've the kettle on.'

'Thank you, Mrs … Maeve.' Sonia kept forgetting that Maeve had asked her to stop calling her Mrs McMenamin at the wedding.

'I don't expect you to call me mammy, but with Eileen gone, you'll be more like a daughter to me than ever. So it'll have to be Maeve.'

They both smiled at the mistake. Maeve noted that when Sonia smiled, she lit up the room. She wondered had there been a time in her life when Sonia smiled a lot. Was there a time when her mother and father and she and her brother were a happy family? Maybe. Maeve was determined to make Sonia smile again. She felt that the girl had been sent to her for that purpose.

'The ribbon was old, Sonia, so it was time to replace it. Don't be worrying yourself about it. Now, I made a banner to hang on the door of the new house, and I wanted you to use your artistic talents to draw a picture of them both on it or something. It's looking very bare at the moment.'

Sonia looked over at the banner laid out on the floor and smiled again. Like the cake it was a labour of love.

'I'll do my best, Maeve. Is there dinner? I'm starving.'

Maeve wasn't sure if Sonia was just trying to humour her over the ribbon thing, because Sonia was never starving. For someone whose mother ran a restaurant of sorts, she never had much of an appetite.

'I was baking so much I never managed it, but I'll throw us something together now.'

'You sit down, Maeve. We have all the ingredients for a Spanish omelette and I'm in the mood for cooking. Why don't you go and have a little siesta for a while now? We'll be up very late tonight.'

'All right, girl. I'll do just that. Don't go to any trouble with the dinner. We can eat lots of cake later.'

More smiles from Sonia. Maybe they were getting there. Maybe.

'Mammy! Mammy! I missed you!' Eileen threw her arms around her mother and hugged her tight.

'Indeed, and I'm sure you didn't give me a thought for the whole week.' Maeve hugged her daughter back and then let her go to her friend.

'Oh, Sonia, I've so much to tell you. Oh, I was going to say "sure we'll catch up in the beds later", and then I remembered that I won't be sleeping with you there. I still can't get used to the fact that I don't live here any more. Not that I wouldn't be married to Bart. I love being Mrs Sharkey, but anyway … I've loads to tell you. You wouldn't believe half the things …'

Eileen was rabbiting on like she always did when she was nervous, and Sonia wondered what she had to tell her that was so amazing. It wasn't like she and Bart had waited to do the bed thing until they were married. Sonia still couldn't believe that Eileen had taken that risk. No, it must be something else.

'Come on in out of the cold,' Maeve said. 'We have the kettle on, and I knew you were coming so I baked a cake.' That got them all laughing.

An hour and two pots of tea later, Bart was shuffling and trying to get his wife's attention.

'I know you've got things you want to talk about, love, but it's been a very long day.'

Eileen looked over at her husband and nodded and stood up from the kitchen table reluctantly.

'I won't come back into work tomorrow, Sonia. I'll be too tired, but I'll start back the day after. All right? And when I wake up tomorrow, I'll come around and help you finish that cake, Mam. It was gorgeous.' She gave her mam a kiss and Sonia a hug and went off leaving both women wondering what it was that Eileen needed to tell them about so much that she was reluctant to go home with her husband to their first night in their new house together.

The next morning the cake was sliced, and the tea was in the cups, milked and sugared. Eileen leaned over and helped herself to the biggest slice. She would need all that sugary comfort to get through this conversation with her mother.

'Come on. Out with it, girl. What's happened?'

Eileen took a bite and made a big effort to swallow.

'Mam.'

'Are you having a baby, Eileen? Is that what you're trying to tell me? That you were pregnant before you got married?'

'No, Mam, no! It's nothing like that at all. But as we're on the subject … I met a man in London that I've been trying to trace. His name's Alan. I've been going behind your back for over a year now trying to trace the man that you said couldn't be found.'

Eileen watched the colour drain from her mother's face. 'No …'

'Yes. It wasn't that hard in the end. I went to the address where you both lived together … in Islington. They gave me our own address as a forwarding address. Imagine. But someone who lived there had been lodging there for twenty-five years. Do you remember a man called Bernard Phillips?'

Maeve hadn't found her voice as yet, but she nodded her head.

'Luckily, we went there as soon as we arrived because Bernie was going to Brighton for a few days, and we would never have met him. He was going to spend a few days with his old pal Alan

McMenamin, and so, the first few days of our honeymoon were spent in that lovely seaside town.

'At first, he wouldn't see us. Are you all right for me to continue, Mammy? You don't look very well.'

Again, her mother nodded and wrapped her hands around her warm teacup.

'But Bernie convinced him it was the right thing to do, and we met in a café on the prom on a lovely sunny day. I was worried I wouldn't recognise him, but I'm the spitting image of my father. He came over and sat down and he couldn't speak for a few minutes. A bit like you are now. Then I told him who I was, and he burst out crying. It was hard looking at a grown man crying like that.

'"My one chance of happiness and I blew it," he was saying. "And I've been blowing every chance I've had since. You were better off without me, Eileen," he said. "I'm not the kind of man that should have a beautiful daughter like you. She begged me to stay with her and get married, and I begged her to go home to Ireland and leave me in peace to mess up my life as I saw fit." And he did exactly that. He spent ten years in prison for armed robbery, Mam. He's a hard man with a body full of tattoos and a shaved haircut. He's trying to pull himself together now in Brighton, but he says he has no friends apart from Bernie, and the only time in his life he was ever able to form a relationship was with you. And he messed that up.'

'I … you knew, Eileen … I never kept it from you that your father was alive somewhere. It was 1928 in a small village in Balcallan, and I had no choice but to make up the story about getting married and being widowed and pregnant. But to you I always told the truth.'

'Not always. You told me that he had disappeared off the face of the earth. That he didn't want me or you …'

'I's true. He didn't want me with a baby. Even back then when Alan was only nineteen, I knew that he was bad news. He was rough. But I had come from such a sheltered existence here, that I looked on him as an adventure. Life was never boring when Alan was around. Scary sometimes but never boring. And then he left me with the ultimate adventure. Returning to a small village in Donegal with a baby and no husband.'

'But you've known for years that he was a friend of Bernie's. That you ... that I could have found him through Bernie any time I wanted.'

'Eileen. Did he tell you that I went to look for him when you were three?'

Eileen shook her head.

'He may not remember much of it. You were such a gorgeous little girl, and I kept thinking that maybe Alan was older and wiser then and might want to know about you. I thought it was important for him to know that you were a little girl and that your name was Eileen because it sounded a bit like Alan. But I went to Bernie, and he brought me to a squat in London where a group of no-hopers lived, all of them a hard-looking scary lot. When I saw your father, he was the worse for drink, and I said what I had to say and left. I had left you with my sister. She knew the whole story too. We made up something about me having to go to England to see your other granny. I raced back to Ireland with my tail between my legs and vowed that I'd protect you from that man for ever.'

'But you should have told me, Mam. You should have said when I was older that I could go to England and meet him and decide for myself. Instead, you let me believe that he wasn't trace-able. You even told Aunty Dora that you couldn't find him. You let us all believe that.' Eileen was crying now.

'Because it was true in a way. I didn't find him. I found a man who was on his way to ruin, and I was afraid that if he was part of our lives that he would ruin us too. I had a three-year-old toddler to look after. You were my number one priority, Eileen.'

'You should have let me decide for myself, Mam. Once I was old enough.'

'I left our address with Bernie. I told him if he ever decided that Alan was on the mend and that he thought that it might be a good idea to introduce you, then he was to get in touch. But all I got, year in, year out, was a Christmas card from Bernie saying: *Hope all's well with you. No change here. All still the same.* And yes, then I let it go. I had to for my own sanity. I was still young, Eileen, and I know it's hard for you to understand of your own mother, but I harboured great hopes of meeting someone else. A lovely, trustworthy man who would take care of us both and … Well, it didn't happen, and we were all right.'

Eileen reached over and took her mother's hand. 'This is not about criticizing the way you brought me up, Mam. In fact, it's not about criticizing anybody or anything. I just got to thinking about it since Sonia came to live with us. She was always putting down her father and not wanting to talk about him, and it made me angry thinking that at least she had someone to call daddy. Then this Christmas when Bernie's card came in the post and this idea came to me again. Who was this Bernie who sent us a card every year and said the same thing every year? I thought Bernie was a woman, maybe someone you had befriended in England, and I decided to start with her. Him, as it turned out. The rest was easy. Except it wasn't. It was the hardest thing I've ever had to do in my life.'

'You should have told me, love. I would have gone with you. Is that why you decided to go to London for your honeymoon?'

'No.'

'No? Just no?'

'There was something else. Poor Bart. He won't forget our first week of married life.'

'What? Something else about Alan? About your birth? I really wish you could have gone with me, Eileen. It can't have been the best place to go for a romantic holiday.'

'No, but it certainly brought us even closer together. I couldn't have managed it all without Bart. He's such a good man, but as I said, there's more, and I need another pot of tea to get my head around this one.'

Sonia was tired out after her day's work and being up into the early hours the night before. She had promised Eileen that she would drop into her on her way home. Maeve had said not to make a habit of it, that a newly married couple would need time on their own to get to know each other. What would Maeve know of newly married couples? And Sonia? Would she ever be in that situation? Yes. If she could just wait it out, she knew that eventually Enrico Sanchez would come for her. They were meant for each other as much as Eileen and Bart were meant for each other.

She knocked on the front door which was a strange thing to do in these parts, especially with your best friend. But it was all new, and they could do it this way for a while to add to the novelty. Eileen came out to her all smiles and dragged her in.

'What kept you? I've the kettle boiled three times waiting for you.'

'I had to write a whole load of letters by hand. I broke the typewriter ribbon yesterday.'

'And she didn't kill you? Well, you're here now. Sit down. Are you whacked?'

'Am I what?'

'Whacked. Like, tired.'

'Oh, yes. I'm ... eh, tired. You must be too.'

'Yes. But I slept in until twelve today. At least that's what I told my mother!'

The girls laughed together.

'I have so much to tell you, Sonia.'

Here it was again. The palaver with the teapot. The getting the telling ready. It was all part of it. The lead up. Sonia had come to expect it from everyone in the village. Eventually, Eileen put the cups out in front of her and sat down.

'Well?'

'Well. Where to start.'

'The beginning.'

'Yes. The beginning ...'

'Eileen?'

'Sonia. When Bart lived in Dublin, he told you he would look after your Spanish friends, Lucia and Dolores while he was there.'

'Are they all right?'

'If you can, Sonia the best thing to do here is to hear me out from beginning to end. Though there might be things you don't want to hear, it's best you know everything. Dolores and Lucia are absolutely fine, but they kept in touch with Bart when he moved from Dublin. He was concerned for them. They're often very sad about leaving Spain, like yourself, so he went down to see them sometimes. Recently, Lucia got herself an Irish boyfriend, so we might be hearing more wedding bells soon.'

'This is a happy story, Eileen, but you look sad.'

'Yes. Two months before we got married, Bart went to see Dolores. She was with Seán – that's her boyfriend – and she had a letter from a friend of hers from Andalucía, from Malaga to be precise, who was living in London. He was another Republican like you who had been jailed and then exiled. He had chosen London because he spoke English, and well ... he spoke of a friend that was with him. An Alejandro Alvarez who had been in jail with him and escaped during a transfer and ran to London with him. She thought that it might be your friend, Alejandro. He was from the same town as you. So we wrote to him.'

'Alejandro is alive? In London? I could go there. Couldn't I, Eileen? It's possible to go there without a passport. I could …'

'Not so fast, Sonia. I went to see Alejandro when I was in London, and he has promised to come here to see you.'

'Oh, Eileen. You don't know what this means to me. To see Alejandro. A friend from home. My brother Miguel's friend. And Enrico's too. Had he any news of Enrico, Eileen? Had he seen him? Heard from him?'

The tears were streaming down Sonia's face as she waited for Eileen's answer to her question. Her life depended on it. Eileen knew that what she was about to say to Sonia would change the way she would live her life from now on. Eileen didn't know how, but she knew that this was going to break Sonia in some way, as if there were many pieces of her left to break.

'Sonia. Alejandro has been in London for six months. Before that he spent time in prison, in Malaga, and he said that Enrico was in that prison with him for a while. He was using your brother's name, Miguel Almez, and that was why nobody could find him. All I know was that Enrico had been working with the Republicans when he was recaptured. There was something about a plan to fool the Nationalists that he was working with them, when all the time he was spying on them. You were right about him, Sonia. He had not turned into a traitor, but he had used your brother's name all this time while he fought against the Nationalists.'

Eileen moved her chair beside Sonia. She took her by the shoulders and tried to get her to steady herself.

'Is he alive, Eileen? Tell me.'

'Yes, Sonia. When Alejandro left him, he was alive. Somehow, he was pardoned from execution.'

'Thank God. If he's alive, Eileen he'll come for me. I know this.'

'No, Sonia, he can't come. He was sentenced just before Alejandro escaped. He was sentenced to twenty years more and moved to a very secure prison in the north of Spain somewhere.'

Sonia called out so loudly that Eileen was amazed that someone from the next house down didn't come running to see what was the matter. 'No!' she cried, over and over. 'No. No. No!'

And then she wept. Eileen had seen her weep for Enrico before, but never had she seen her keen like this. This was new and breaking her heart as much as Sonia's. Alejandro had been very firm that there was no way that Enrico would be freed early. Sonia would be in her forties if she ever saw Enrico again. Eileen held her and let her weep.

Eileen had known she would not have to explain to Sonia that she would probably never see Enrico again. Alejandro had explained to her that he was lost to them, as so many people in Spain had lost loved ones. Not only through death but through displacement, imprisonment and exile. It was a different world, and Sonia knew about this world and knew what life was offering her. Sonia could not return to Spain as long as Franco ruled there, and Enrico would never be free to come to her as long as Franco was in power. In this way, Sonia had been sentenced alongside her Enrico. When Eileen saw her like this, she realised how Sonia had never been able to look at Manus as a possible husband. She had only eyes for one man, and now he was lost; Eileen didn't think Sonia would ever love another man.

Bart came in from work with a big smile on his face that was wiped off immediately he saw the state of Sonia in his kitchen. She had pulled free from Eileen's hold and was screaming and pulling at her hair and her clothes. Sonia kicked the table and threw the chair she had been sitting on across the room and still she shouted. 'Noooooo! Nooo! Nooooo …!'

Bart tried to hold onto Sonia before she did herself or the house some damage.

'Bart, mind her. I'm going to send for the doctor. She's going to need a sedative or something. I'll be back as soon as I can.'

The slamming of the door as Eileen left the room helped to bring Sonia around a little. She looked at Bart. Or through him and past him and fell on her knees on the floor, then curled into a ball. The tears were finished for now, but there would be much more in the days and years to come.

Bart knelt down on the ground beside Sonia and spoke soothingly to her. He had listened to everything that Alejandro had told them about Sonia's past life, about her relationship with Enrico and about her time trying to find him in Spain.

'You've had to cope with too much, my girl. More than most people even hear about in their own lives. You cry it all out, Sonia. You deserve your tears, and we're here for you. Me and Eileen. We always will be here for you.'

CHAPTER NINETEEN

1961

Eileen and Bart hadn't been on a holiday together since their honeymoon ten years before. Normally, Bart's business was his life, and he never took time off from work. She knew he loved her, but he seemed to want to work around the clock. So, when Bart had suggested going to the south of Spain, she had jumped at the chance.

When he had suggested the trip, Bart had given Eileen the seeds of an idea. They could go to Spain and meet Cristina Almez and see if there was any way that she could come to live in Ireland with Sonia. Eileen had been afraid to mention her plan to Sonia at first, but when she did, she was surprised to find that Sonia thought it was a good idea. Despite all her years in Ireland, Sonia still missed her mother greatly. With Franco in no hurry to yield power in Spain, Sonia herself could not risk joining them. But she had made Eileen promise that she would try to find out any news she could about Enrico. Eileen had been reluctant to do so, but the look of distress on her best friend's face changed her mind and she agreed.

Now, here they were on a beach in Benalmádena near Malaga, and it was beautiful.

Sonia hadn't exaggerated anything. The sunrise and sunset, the full moon and crescent moon and the sea and the sand and the siestas. They felt so rested already and the people were so friendly. Especially Cristina.

It had been easy to find her as Alejandro's directions were perfect. Alejandro had travelled to Dublin from London a few times over the years. At first when they met him, all he really wanted was to return to Spain, but then he fell for a woman from Scotland and was content with married life there.

Cristina herself spent her days sitting looking out at the sea and her nights walking the beaches. She was a young woman in years, but her hard life had taken its toll and Eileen didn't think that she would be alive for too much longer. Sonia's mother had given up the will to live. She had no husband, no son and no mother to care for. She might never see her daughter again. But when they asked her to return to Ireland with them, she shook her head and said no.

'You are lovely people,' she said, speaking to them through her nephew Alvarro who was translating for her. 'But I could not put myself into danger at this time of my life. I know my daughter is safe, and I have no intention of changing things for her. If I travelled to Ireland, it would highlight you as the family and friends of Spanish Republicans. I have full sympathy for Republicans still, but I keep my head low and will get on with my life until I disappear to nothing. I lost my religion to the Nationalists a long time ago, and without my family and without faith, what is left?'

'Cristina,' Eileen had asked late at night when they sat on the beach looking up at the stars. 'Do you think there is any way that we can go to see Enrico? I feel I know this man so much from all the years of listening to Sonia talk of him.'

Alvarro, Cristina's nephew, sat up at this and didn't even wait to translate it.

'No!' He was adamant. 'Don't think of this, and don't mention it to anyone. It is dangerous to talk of such things here. You will be watched, and you will bring great danger from the Nationalist soldiers to us. I will not even say this to Aunt Cristina. She will worry, and she does not need that at her time in life.

'You have come to visit a country that has accepted you as tourists. No more. You will eat in our restaurants and lie on our beaches, but you will not question the politics of this country, or you will be going home earlier than you hoped. And behind you will be left a trail of death and prison sentences for all those who spoke to you or helped you in any way. Do you understand? All this peace and quiet, and all this beauty is a multi-coloured veil to hide the ugly face of Franco. Eileen, do not even try to lift that veil. Go back to Ireland and mind our Sonia and make her have a good life.'

'Que vas?' Cristina wanted to know what they were talking about.

'Nada, tia. Eileen wanted to know about Enrico. There is nothing to know. And now we will go home before the soldiers begin to walk the night looking for trouble.'

Cristina spoke to Alvarro, and he translated for Eileen.

'She says not to go looking for trouble and not to open the door to it if it comes looking for you.'

Here, lying on the beach, it was hard to imagine the atrocities that lay under Alvarro's veil. Eileen reached over and took Bart's hand; he squeezed her hand and smiled. Maybe one day this country might be returned to the people who knew how to live again.

Back in Balcallan, the rain and the wind made Benalmádena seem like a million miles away, but at least here it was tranquil inside and out. Eileen didn't always like her so-called friends and neighbours in their small-minded village, but she knew them all, with no hidden nightmares. What you saw was what you got for the most part. Maeve returning home with a baby and no husband all those years ago was probably still the most talked about subject in the village.

'Stick the kettle on, Sonia, I'm back.' Eileen stuck her head around the back door of her mother's house.

'Eileen! You're early. We didn't expect you back until this afternoon!'

'Uncle Jim gave us a lift from Dublin, so we didn't have to wait for the bus. He was delighted with an excuse to show off his new motor. He was waiting for us at the airport and all.' Eileen gave Sonia a hug and sat down. 'It's great to see you, Sonia.'

'It's good to see you too, Eileen. Your mother will be back soon. She's gone to the shops to buy some things for your house for when you get back. She'll be disgusted at you coming back early and spoiling it for her. Do you think you could hide around the corner or something for a few hours till she has it all set up?'

'Don't be worrying about Maeve. It doesn't take much to make her narky these days though. Sure she'll be delighted to see me.'

'Where's Bart?'

'Gone to show Uncle Jim around his new site. What is it with men and their acquisitions? Jim never shut up about his new car all the way from Dublin to Donegal.'

Sonia put the cups on the table and sat expectantly across from Eileen. There was silence for a while, and then Sonia smiled and said, 'Did you take pictures?'

'Yes, Sonia. Lots. I'll bring them to the chemist when it opens on Monday, and they should have them back in a week or so.'

'So, how was she?'

'Good, Sonia. Delighted to see us. Emotional. She's a very beautiful woman, your mother. And your cousin Alvarro too. He was very good to us.'

'I don't remember him very well. He was only about ten when I left, and at seventeen, I didn't spend much time thinking about ten-year-olds.'

'He's a lovely man with a wife and, my God, I don't know how many children.'

'Where did you stay, Eileen?'

'In a guest house in the pueblo. It was so pretty, flowers everywhere, with whitewashed houses and cobbled streets. I loved it. The people there were very friendly. Wary, though. I found that everyone wanted to be friendly underneath but were worried about who we were, and you got the feeling that everyone had been told how to treat tourists and what to say or not say to them. But you knew that they were genuine people by their smiles and their hospitality. Some of your mother's neighbours came to see us when we were in your mother's house. Mostly, Alvarro introduced us as some lovely Irish tourists that Cristina had met on the beach. He was afraid for us and for your family if it was believed that we were coming on your behalf. Or worse – on Enrico's.'

Eileen watched Sonia freeze at the mention of his name. After all these years this man still had the power to stop her in her tracks at the mere thought of him. What a childhood they must have had together. Eileen had spent time in Sonia's country, and it had helped her to understand more of what Sonia had lost and what she missed, but now she would tell Sonia that she would have missed it even if she had been there. Hardly any of her family still lived in Benalmádena – if they lived at all.

And Enrico was lost to the prison; might be dead for all they knew, Alvarro had said. Many died of neglect in there, or malnutrition, or some awful disease that would spread like wildfire with the cramped conditions and any small misbehaviour could result in execution. Eileen couldn't bear to think of it, and she couldn't bear to talk about it to Sonia. It was bad enough that they would always be apart, but it wasn't right for Sonia to know about Enrico's plight.

'There is no word of him, Sonia or of the name he was imprisoned under, and he may have given another name. He has served ten years so far, and Alvarro thinks he may be still there as sometimes if they are moved, or if ... Then the family is sometimes notified. Officially, that is what is supposed to happen, but Alejandro told us that when Enrico was imprisoned, he vowed he had no living family to protect himself from his background but also to protect his family and yours. Even if he has been moved, they would probably notify nobody.'

Eileen was amazed to find Sonia still dry-eyed.

'My poor, poor Enrico. Eileen, I hope he has not had to suffer long in that place. I hope ...'

'What, Sonia?'

'I hope he has gone to my brother. I can't think of him anywhere else but there.'

'Sonia, from listening to the stories about long-term prisoners from Alvarro, it would seem that Enrico may not have made it through these last ten years, but we have no way of knowing, nor will we ever.'

Eileen knew that this was not the time to tell Sonia that her mother had insisted that Sonia leave behind this boy of her childhood and move on. That was for later.

'And my mother. Did you ask her to come? I know that she said no by your face when you came in.'

'She says she can't get up and leave at this stage. She wishes she had done it years ago, but now ...'

'Now?'

'She is quite infirm, Sonia. Well in herself, but not very steady and very hunched over. Too much so for her years.'

'I suppose it's a follow-up from all the beatings she got from my father. My poor, beautiful mother. If I can't go to her and she won't—'

'Can't.'

'*Can't* come to me, then we may never see each other again.'

Eileen wondered if she would ever be able to tell Sonia about the raid on her mother's house after Enrico had been arrested. How the abuse Cristina received from Sonia's father was little compared to what had been done to her that night. To so many Republican mothers and widows. It was best to keep that from her.

'Sonia, you have been given here what few received in Spain: the chance to start over and live a life. Not the life you would have chosen, but a better one than what you would have had if you had stayed in Spain. It is such a beautiful country, but Franco is ruining it, and in doing so he is ruining the Spanish people. Pick yourself up from here, Sonia. This is the message from your mother. Live your life. Live it because of others who can't live theirs.'

Sonia still didn't cry, but she nodded and stood up.

'I hear Maeve coming now, Eileen. I need time by myself to absorb what you have told me before I get the full-blown interrogation from your mother of *what exactly are you going to do with your life, Sonia Almez?* I just need to go for a walk, and I'll be back shortly.'

Eileen stood and squeezed Sonia's arm. She had been talking to Sonia for a very short time, but she knew she had hit Sonia with more hurt in one go than she should have. She would have to look after her well over the next few days or weeks. She wondered if she would she be looking after her for her whole life.

CHAPTER TWENTY

S onia couldn't cry until she hit the beach; then she would find her hidden place and shed her tears until her insides were dry. When she was ready to face the world again, she would go into the freezing Atlantic Ocean and wash it all away, then dress and go home and get through this. For a fleeting moment, she looked at the sea in the distance and thought about going in there and not coming out. Who would miss her?

Rounding the corner where the rocks hid her hiding place, she looked forward to the solitude that this place would bring, where she could let out all the sadness, the hurt and the anger.

She pulled in her breath as she stopped suddenly in front of Manus, sitting on the rock. *Her* rock.

'What are you doing here?' She hadn't meant to sound so loud and so accusatory, but the words were out before she could stop them.

'What am I doing here? Isn't it a free stretch of sand where any man or woman can sit anywhere they like and not be screamed at by some crazy woman rounding the corner and knocking them into the middle of next week? Isn't it a lucky man I am that you've been saying no to me all those years, or I could've been trapped inside four walls with you, listening to the clickety clack of your Spanish temper?' Sonia had never seen Manus in such a strop.

'I'm sorry. I didn't mean … It's just …'

Manus stood up and his face softened.

'It's all right, Sonia. You startled me, that's all. I thought you'd be up with Eileen getting all the news on her holiday, and this place would be free.'

'Yes. I was, but—' Sonia couldn't hold it any more. She had walked stony-faced through the town and marched her grief down the winding lanes towards the beach. She had kept herself together knowing that relief was imminent and now this. Sonia let out a wail that frightened the living daylights out of Manus and he rushed towards her and grabbed her shoulders.

'Sonia. Jesus, Sonia. What? Was there bad news from Spain? Is it your mother?'

But Sonia couldn't hear him. She dropped to her knees like a rag doll and let her grief rip.

Manus tried to sit beside her and hold her hand, but she tugged it away from him and shouted again. 'No! Leave me alone. Go away. You weren't supposed to be here. Go away.'

'I'll sit over there, Sonia, if that's what you want but I won't leave you like this. You know I wouldn't. I couldn't. Oh, God, Sonia I hate seeing you like this.'

He let her go and moved away, but Sonia didn't even notice. She lay down now on the rock and she cried.

Manus sat and watched until he could bear it no more. The wrenching weeping was breaking him, and after a few minutes, he realised that he had tears on his own face. How could anyone listen to that grief without being moved by it? Only the total loss of someone you loved could bring on that kind of noise. He would sit here and wait it out and then see if he couldn't help in some way. What irony it was that Sonia had chosen that hour to arrive.

Knowing that Sonia would be with Eileen finding out all the news about her time in Spain, had made Manus sure in the knowledge that he could go to sit in what he knew was her special spot and not see her there. He had given himself an hour before he would move off home to spend the rest of the weekend with his family in Gortahork.

While there, he had gone over all the difficulties of the last ten years or so. His business with Bart had gone from strength to magnificence. They were riding on a building wave and milking it for all it was worth. He had built himself a house – near enough to the town to be practical but far enough away to enjoy the views of mountains and sea – with four bedrooms and a lovely family room downstairs.

'And tell me, son, are you going to fill it with anybody one of these days?'

His mother was tired asking him and he was tired ignoring her or joking with her or just getting angry and telling her to mind her own bloody business. Manus had every mother of a single woman flinging their daughters at him and he didn't bat an eyelid in their direction. Down in the pub he had to suffer the ribald humour of his building friends and those from his schooldays ribbing him about his sexual tendencies. Why would he not go with a woman? It wasn't natural.

No. It was completely unnatural behaviour to throw yourself at one woman's feet for over ten years and suffer her constant rejections hoping that maybe this time she might relent.

Today Manus had sat on the rock that he knew she favoured, and he had made a decision. He would sell the house he had built out of love for Sonia and move to a smaller place back in Gortahork. He needed to get away from Balcallan and Sonia. She was poisoning him. He had loved her for so long that he couldn't see anything else in his life. Bart was right. There were so many other women around who might make him happy, and Sonia wasn't for turning. Now that he had made his mind up, he should stand up and walk away from here, leave her to her own sorrow. She had given him enough of his own. *Look away, Manus*, he thought. Instead, he looked over and saw her sadness and he went and sat beside her. Manus picked her up and pulled her onto his lap and held her like a child. Sonia put her head into his chest and continued to cry. They sat like that, leaning back against the rock, him caressing her back and her hair for a long time while she cried on.

'Let it out, Sonia. Let it go.' Manus felt a surge of love explode through him that he knew he couldn't let go of, and he let more tears run down his cheeks. Quietly.

Later that morning, or was it afternoon now, Manus had stopped crying and Sonia had run out of tears and they were sitting there wrapped around each other, holding on for life. Manus was afraid to move. His left leg was gone to sleep, and his right arm was aching from the way it had been held around Sonia for that long, but he wouldn't move and break this spell. He didn't want to wake Sonia from whatever she was staring at out to sea. He couldn't bear the moment when she would slip from his hold, declare herself better and wash the tears from her face with the salt water of the rock pools. She would walk back up the beach and he would at least have this. Once, Sonia had lain in his arms and let him hold her.

'Thank you, Manus.' It was barely a whisper and Manus thought he might have imagined it. Sonia hadn't moved but he was sure she had spoken to him.

'I'm here, Sonia, love. You know that.'

'I know. I've been very hard on you for a very long time.'

Sonia still hadn't moved, and her eyes were still fixed on the horizon.

'Sure, I'm an awful eejit when it comes to you, Sonia Almez, and no doubt I will be for some time to come. I actually came to this spot today to give myself a good talking to; try to get myself to move on or something … So, was it your mother, Sonia? Or Enrico? Is he …?'

'Both, Manus. My mother is sick, and Enrico will probably never come out of prison as long as Franco is alive.'

Manus was quiet. He heard both things that Sonia said but he focussed on the latter. He swallowed hard, disgusted with himself at the thought going through his head. The poor man was going through a hell because of something he believed in. Then he registered what Sonia had said first. He sat her up and turned her face around to his.

'What is it? With your mother.'

Sonia shuffled off his lap but to his delight she sat beside him as near as she could and still held his hand.

'Nothing concrete from what I can gather from Eileen, but the beatings she got from my father have taken their toll over the years. She finds it hard to walk and her hearing is going. She's not able to travel even if it was possible for her to go, and I cannot go there, so we will not see each other again.'

'I'm sorry, Sonia.' Manus squeezed her hand, and they were quiet for a time once more.

'In answer to your other unasked question, yes, I will have to let go of him if I am to survive and make something of my life.'

'That's none of my business, Sonia. You don't have to tell me something personal like that.'

Sonia gently took her hand away, but still he felt the spell wasn't broken. He knew better than to think that this man would not be there sitting between them always, but there was something about the way that Sonia was looking at him. She was smiling. Her eyes were still sad, but there was something good in her smile.

'How come you're still around, Manus? I'm glad you are, but how come you're still listening to all my woes and not running in the other direction?'

'You're glad I am? Sonia Almez, that's the nicest thing you've ever said to me.'

'I'm sorry. I know. It's because …'

'I know, Sonia. I know that you're in one country when you want to be in another, and I know that you love a man called Enrico Sanchez who is suffering there, while you're here feeling helpless. I know that you don't love me that way and probably never will. See? I know a lot of things. I'm a very clever man really.'

'To run after a crazy woman like me all these years? That's not very clever.'

'You're still hoping for Enrico when deep down inside, you know that it isn't possible. Maybe you've also decided that if you can't have Enrico, then you'll have no one.' Manus lifted Sonia's hand to his mouth and kissed it. 'I love you, Sonia. I know about Enrico, and I still love you. So, you see, I understand about how you feel and why you keep saying no to me. I understand you because you're a lot like me, but unlike you, I'm not sure I want to spend the rest of my life on my own.

'I made a decision today before you came here. I won't hang around any longer. It'll be hard for me to stay away from you, but I can't keep doing this to myself. If you want to wait into your old age for Enrico, then you can, but I want to find someone to love and who loves me. I want a family. I don't like living on my own. I'll need your help in this, Sonia. If you see me walking towards you, walk away from me. I'm going to move back to Gortahork, but I'll still be working around here, and I'll still see a lot of Eileen as I work with Bart. So, help me out, Sonia and keep well away from me.'

Manus stood up awkwardly on the rock. His legs were still asleep from when Sonia was on his lap. He pulled Sonia into standing, and holding her hand, he forced a smile in her direction. With her other hand she rubbed the sand from her dress and looked up at him. He tried to work out what he could see in her expression, but he couldn't figure it out. She was smiling but her eyes were still sad. Always sad. He had tried for ten years to help let her smile reach her eyes and he had failed. It was time to move on.

Sonia reached around him with her spare hand and hugged him. 'I'm sorry, Manus. I do love you. How could I not? But it would not be fair to pretend to you that I don't have feelings for another man.'

Manus put his hand under her chin and lifted her face up towards his. She was beautiful. He moved his face slowly towards hers and she didn't pull away. His lips were on hers and she let him kiss her. She was kissing him too. When she began to pull away, he held her head in his hands. 'Longer,' he said, and she came back to him, and the kiss went on, and Manus thought that his years of waiting were worth it. It was him who pulled away a little to tell her again what he had told her so many times.

'I love you, Sonia.' Manus's heart was filled with everything he had hoped for. Kissing Sonia was all that he'd wished it would be and so much more. Perhaps he had been wrong to say what he had said …

But Sonia was shaking her head and pulling away from him. 'No, Manus. No. I can't. I'm sorry.'

Manus dropped from his cloud and held out his hands imploringly. 'Sonia …?' But she was still shaking her head and now she was crying again.

Manus could take no more of this. To kiss him the way that she had and to still say no. It was too much. He dropped his hands.

'I'm sorry too, Sonia. I'm going now. Stay away from me if we meet anywhere. I can't let you hurt me like this any more. I won't. Bye, Sonia.' He turned around slowly thinking she might say something, but the only sound was the waves on the strand, and as he walked up the beach, his walking gathered momentum and when he got to the road he began to run, and he ran all the way back to his beautiful house and began to pack.

Sonia watched him run from her until he was a dot on the horizon and then he disappeared around a bend in the road.

She sat back down on the rock that they had shared up until a few minutes before, but this place gave her no solace now. She had let Manus go. He was a good man and a good friend, and she would miss him. With Eileen married, she saw her less and less. Maeve was getting grumpier and was hard to listen to. Her mother was lost to her with all her family and friends in Spain. And Enrico … If she thought about where Enrico was, she would go crazy.

Sonia had nobody.

CHAPTER TWENTY-ONE

R oberto walked past the sentries with his head held high and a strut in his step.

'Good evening, señor!' he would say.

'Another beautiful day in Franco's wonderful country!' would be the answer, or some such words that made the bile rise up onto Roberto's tongue.

To the men that checked his papers as he entered and left the prison, he was their superior. A man with strong contacts high up in Franco's regime. But inside him, every time he walked through those doors, Roberto lost a part of his soul. He waited with dread for the day that he was sure must come, when they realised that he was all show. Roberto Rodriguez was the younger brother of a man who was on the right-hand side of the top man himself. Roberto's brother was Franco's man in the south. Roberto carried that power on the outside, while inside his gut spilled over with fear. He had suffered from such stress for so long that he was sure that he would have a heart attack if a gun did not take him first.

Every year he undertook this visit to this prison and asked to see the same prisoner, hoping that the man had managed to stay alive for one more year. Each visit took on the same order. They would bring Enrico Sanchez into a cell in the depths of the prison, where the prison guards were sure that Roberto could undertake his yearly beating of Enrico, as revenge for the attempted murder of his brother, Alberto. A guard stood outside the door of the room as a safety precaution against the prisoner turning on the soldier.

Enrico would sit on the floor at the feet of Roberto and suffer a kick here and a belt of the hand there as Roberto screamed made-up obscenities at him.

'You filthy piece of shit. Your mother died roaring when we told her of her worthless son.'

At the same time Roberto would whisper as much news as he could manage of Enrico's friends and family in Benalmádena and of Sonia in Ireland.

'Sonia is well. My daughter met with her recently. She misses you. She has never forgotten you.'

As Enrico fell to the floor each time, he whispered back the things that he wanted Roberto to tell people on the outside.

'Tell her my every waking thought is of her, and her face is the last thing I picture when I go to sleep at night.'

Roberto would tell Enrico how things were beyond the walls of the prison and Enrico would tell Roberto what was happening inside those walls. Any guard who was exceptionally cruel or violent would find himself a month or so down the line up on a false charge of Roberto's making and might not be heard of again.

'His name is Fernandez,' Enrico would whisper.

'He is a dead man walking,' Roberto would whisper back.

When Roberto left at the end of his half hour, Enrico would be lying bruised, but inside he would be singing. Every word that Enrico heard from Roberto was music. Every time that he left meant that Enrico would be treated well within those walls.

'Make sure that bastard is still alive this time next year so that I get to kick the shit out of him again. You have no idea how much I look forward to this day each year.' The last thing that Roberto said to the prison guards as he left each time. Nobody else was allowed that privilege except the great Roberto.

'Why not visit more often, señor?' asked a guard.

'The time in between makes it extra special, amigo. Today is the anniversary of the day that he was first arrested for attempting to kill my beloved brother, so it is a good day, but you never

know when the mood might take me. I could come at any time.'
And he and the guards would laugh heartily as he left.

When Roberto made it back to his rooms, he would throw
up violently and his insides would explode with pain. He hated
having to be the person that he was expected to be. Month after
month, year after year, Franco's hold on the country became
stronger, weaker, stronger. Roberto wished with his whole being
that things could be different.

When he was a boy, he had idolized his older brother. Back
then, Roberto was strong where Alberto was weak. He was popular when his older brother only had one or two friends. It was
the younger boy who had looked out for the older boy. But his
brother had excelled at everything academic where Roberto had
been creative. How he had wanted to be a poet, a writer. Hah.
His family would have laughed at him and thrown him out.
When his hero, García Lorca, had been executed, that was when
Roberto had known where his allegiances lay. His brother celebrated the death while Roberto secretly mourned. As they grew,
Alberto used his academic prowess in the most devious way he
could. He was too clever for his own good.

The life of a poet could have been a great life for Roberto, away
from the rot that was at the heart of the Rodriguez family. But after
their parents had been killed by a Republican-thrown grenade in
the street, Alberto vowed to revenge their death by killing every
dirty rojo he set eyes on from there on in. Roberto had seen his
brother kill Miguel Almez and laugh at his mistake. He had wanted
to walk away then and never set eyes on anyone in his family again,
but he had stayed and found another way to fight the badness. If
Roberto's family had any idea that one of their own was using his
power and their majestic name to fight on behalf of the rojos, they
would have had no problem with hanging him from the highest
tree to let the world know what happened to traitors.

So far, he had been lucky. He had saved hundreds of men and women from execution. He had sent hundreds of men, women and children overseas for their own safety. His cousin's daughter had been captured by Republicans and had never been seen again. So, Roberto had sent his own daughter and niece away with Sonia Almez years ago for their safety. He thought it would be a matter of a few more years, that the madness couldn't last forever, but they had never been able to come back. They were grown women, and now with his daughter Dolores engaged to an Irishman called Seán, there was not much chance of them ever coming back.

Every time Roberto saw Enrico, he said the same thing to him.

'We will get you out of here one day, amigo, and we will run to Ireland you and I, back beside the loves of our life.'

A year became another year and Roberto and Enrico survived. Roberto in the laps of luxury that sickened him and Enrico in the filth and starvation that each year weakened him more. Today when Roberto left Enrico lying on the dirt floor of the cell, he wondered how much longer his friend could hold on to life.

CHAPTER TWENTY-TWO

'How old are you, Maeve?'

It was on the tip of Maeve's tongue to say forty-six, but she knew that was wrong. For God's sake, surely she knew what age she was? Best to keep the grumpy face on her and pretend that she was still in a strop for being dragged to the hospital by Sonia and Eileen to be examined by the doctors. As if they thought she was senile or something. Maeve couldn't think of a number right now, but she was quite sure it was not anything near an age where she might be suffering from senility.

'What age am I? What kind of a question is that to be asking? I don't know why I let myself be dragged into coming here today. It's crazy asking me stupid questions like that. What age are *you*?' That should knock the smile off the doctor's face. Doctor? The girl didn't look old enough to be a nurse.

'I'm thirty-two, Mrs McMenamin. Look, you and I know that there's nothing wrong with forgetting a few things every now and then, but if it's something that happens often, and if it's something that stops you from going about your daily life, and the girls here seem to think that it is, then we have to look into ways of helping you to remember things. Would you not want that for yourself?'

Maeve glared at the doctor, then at Sonia. She knew she shouldn't be here and that this was all Sonia's fault.

'Do you know I took this girl in at the age of sixteen?' she asked the doctor. 'I looked after her as if she was my own child and I helped her through all the bad stuff that she left behind in … in … in that place that she came from. And this is how she pays me back. You should hear some of the things that she's been saying to Eileen about me. She doesn't realise that Eileen is my daughter and blood is thicker than water. Eileen has explained everything to me before we came here today. Sonia's become a grumpy cow since she found out she can't go home to … that place, and that she won't see that fellow she likes ever again. I've put up with her mood swings for years but there's only so much a woman can take.'

Maeve stood up. 'Now if you'll excuse me, I'm leaving now. I'm sorry we've wasted so much of your time, Doctor. I only came because I needed to prove to Eileen that all the things that Sonia has made up about me are not true. She's the one who needs some help. And Sonia. When I get back home to *my* house, I want to see your things packed and you out within the hour.'

Eileen was looking between the doctor and Sonia and Maeve. She looked confused. Frightened even. Maeve reached over and took her daughter's hand.

'Come on, sweetheart. My mother'll be wondering what's happened to us.'

Eileen burst into tears and Sonia ran to her.

'It's all right, Eileen. I'm so sorry, but we'll be all right.'

Sonia looked over at the doctor and shook her head.

'Maeve's mother died a long time ago,' she whispered.

The doctor nodded.

'I'm going now. Come on, Eileen, and don't be letting that one upset you any more.'

Eileen sniffed and took a tissue from the box on the doctor's desk. She put her arm around her mam. 'Will you wait for me in the room outside, Mam? I need to talk to the doctor for a few minutes. About Sonia.'

'You make sure you tell her everything I told you, love. Get it all off your chest.' And Maeve stomped out of the doctor's surgery and into the waiting room with Sonia in her wake.

Eileen blew her nose and took a deep breath.

'I'm sorry, Doctor.'

'Don't you be saying sorry to me, Eileen. If I had hot dinners for everyone who sat in that chair and cried ... Looking after people like your mother with symptoms like this is one of the hardest jobs you can do. She's living in her own house at the moment, but unless she has round-the-clock care, she might have to go into a home after a while.'

'But she's only sixty! How can this happen at her age?'

'There's no rhyme or reason to what way dementia can go. Your mother's symptoms seem to have deteriorated rapidly, and she might continue like this, or she might plateau and stay like she is for years. This is the most difficult time for sufferers of dementia, and for the people who have to care for them, because they go in and out of normality. Your mother is angry and frustrated because she knows that there's something wrong, but she doesn't know what it is. At the moment, she's blaming Sonia for everything because she sees her more than anyone else, but there may come a time when she'll turn on you just as quickly. I can't emphasise to you enough, Eileen, that your mother may eventually need constant care – just for her safety, if nothing else.'

Eileen thought about the night when Sonia came knocking on their door at three in the morning because Maeve had gone missing, and they went out in the car to look for her and found her wandering along the beach talking to someone who wasn't there. Questions of her mother's safety were already an issue. She nodded her head. Eileen knew exactly what the doctor was talking about.

'The day is gone when women like your mother would be put into an asylum and left to spend the rest of their days there, Eileen. If your mother goes to the home in Letterkenny, she'll be well minded, but most importantly, she'll be safe.'

'She'll be locked in and shut away from the world.'

'It's not like that, Eileen. She needs care. If she stays in her house, someone will need to be with her constantly, and eventually, she will need to be locked in the house anyway.'

Eileen took a deep breath while she thought about what the doctor had said and let the words sink in. She couldn't turn against her mam. No matter what the consequences.

'We'll manage, Doctor. My mother brought me up alone and I wanted for nothing. She was right when she said that she took Sonia in and cared for her at a time when her world was falling apart. Sonia adores her and between the two of us we'll work something out.'

'We'll leave it like that for now, Eileen, and we'll review the situation in six months or so. In the meantime, if you need help, call the hospital and leave a message for me. You need to remember to look after each other too. It can be very easy to fall out with family over what is safest for your mother. The best of luck to you all. You'll need it.'

Eileen thanked the doctor. She meant well, but she didn't realise what this woman meant to her and to Sonia. They loved Maeve, and they would look after her between them, no matter how hard it got. She walked out and painted on a smile for her mother. She would have to get good at pretending. She tried not to smile at Sonia so as not to rile her mother.

'Come on, Mam. It's time to go home.'

'Grand. Will we be on time for the bus?'

'I think we've missed it, Mam, but we can go in Bart's car. He won't mind taking us.'

Maeve seemed happy enough with that. They left the hospital and walked out to the waiting car with Sonia following quietly behind.

Eileen poured another drop of whisky into her tumbler and then a tiny drop into Sonia's, with water.

'Drink a little, Sonia. We deserve the bit of whisky after the day and night we've had.

'Do you think we should lock her bedroom door, Eileen? In case she goes wandering. Should we do that every night?'

'No way, Sonia. I told the doctor, and I'm telling you, there's no way I'm locking my mother up like some sort of criminal.'

'I don't like it any more than you do, Eileen, but I don't like the idea of her wandering the streets either. She's very agitated after being in Letterkenny for the day.'

'We can lock the front and back door and make sure she stays in the house, but not her bedroom, Sonia. Sit down now and we'll talk about getting a rota going between us to look after her.'

The women sat together in quiet thought for a minute.

'We won't be able to both work in the post office at the same time any more, though,' said Eileen. 'We should take it in turns to work and to be at home with her. We'll need to take on a second person to help in the shop, though. It needs two people to man it, especially with the Irish language students prowling the place these days. One of us could work the mornings and one the afternoons.'

'Mmm. How would you like to have a rest from the shop altogether, Eileen? You could look after your mam during the day when Bart is out at work, and I could look after her when the shop closes and at night. That way you'd be around to get Bart's dinner ready and do some jobs yourself during the day, and you can go home to Bart in the evenings while she's safe with me.'

'You mean give up working after all these years, Sonia?

'I don't think looking after your mam is easy, Eileen. If anything, going to work is probably the easier option. I'm not trying to get out of caring for her, because she needs a lot of care in the night-time also. What do you think?'

'Well, we could try it for a while, Sonia. Bart's cousin Mary has just left school, and she's a bright young thing. She may be just the person for the job in the shop, but we won't make any long-term plans. I think Mam's symptoms are going to change with time, and we'll have to be flexible ourselves as we move along, and, well … your own circumstances might change too.' Eileen smiled for the first time that day.

'What do you mean?'

'Oh, we might find some tall, dark handsome Donegal man to sweep you off your feet yet, girl.'

'Tall, dark and handsome, is it? Well, at least you're not still trying to match me up with Manus these days.'

Eileen sighed. 'No. Poor Manus.'

'What do you mean, Eileen?'

Eileen shook her head. 'Manus hasn't been working with Bart for a few months, Sonia.'

'Why? Have they fallen out?'

'No, Sonia. Manus … Well, you know he sold his house here in Balcallan, and moved back to his family home in Gortahork?' Sonia nodded. 'Let's just say he's busy drinking the money that he got for the sale of the house, and it doesn't look like he'll stop until he has every penny of it pissed up against his mother's back wall. He turns up for work every now and then but never sober enough for him to be any use to Bart. It's getting very hard to keep it quiet. People are beginning to talk about them, and they're losing business because of it. Bart may have to get a lawyer soon to help sort out the mess.'

'That's terrible, Eileen. Poor Bart. And poor Manus.'

'I never thought you'd say poor Manus, Sonia. I was sure you'd say *I told you so* when you heard.'

'I feel guilty, Eileen. It's because of me that this has happened. He was doing so well all these years, but we had words about six months ago that made him realise that we were never going to happen, and I suppose this is the result. I should go to see him, but he asked me not to. He's a good man. My mother used to say that my father was a good man when he wasn't drinking. It was hard for me to believe as I never saw him any other way, but maybe she was right.'

'You shouldn't feel guilty, Sonia. You of all people know what can happen to a man who has a problem with drinking. There was no way you could take that risk with Manus. Now, if you'll excuse me, I need to be getting home to Bart. With the stink of whisky on me, he'll think I've gone the same way as his business partner.'

'Good night, Eileen, and don't worry too much about your mother. She gave you and I the world and we'll give it back to her now.'

CHAPTER TWENTY-THREE

The door opened slightly and a grey-haired lady with a slight frame peered through the slit.

'Yes?' The woman looked Sonia up and down and waited for an answer.

'Mrs Dooley. I'm looking for Manus. My name is Sonia.'

The door opened a tiny bit more. 'So, it's you, is it? I hear you're the cause of Manus's downfall.'

'Did Manus tell you that?'

'Manus tells me nothing, no more than his father or brother. No, it was Manus's lovely friend Bart told me about you. There's nothing for you here, girl. Go home.'

Mrs Dooley went to close the door, but Sonia put her hand in the way.

'Wait! Is he here? Can I speak to him?'

Mrs Dooley opened the door enough to allow her small frame through it and onto the doorstep.

'Sonia. I don't know you and what you and Manus were to each other. All I know is that I had a husband and son who spent their lives in a sea of alcohol and were good for nothing. But I had *one* son who was clever enough to stay sober and run a business and build himself a lovely house. I was proud of him. But pride comes before a fall, especially for people like me. He fell. Bart says he was pushed, but I don't suppose being a Dooley, that he needed too much pushing. I can't get him out of bed in the daytime. I can't get him out of the pub at night-time. If you know what's good for you, then you should run a mile and leave him to me to sort out. Lord knows, I've enough experience of it.'

'Mrs Dooley. My mother says my father was a good man, and I have to take her word for it because I hardly saw my father sober a day in my life, but Manus I *know* is a good man. I've seen it for years with my own eyes. I want to speak with him and try to make him see reason. He gave up drinking once before and he might do it again.'

Mrs Dooley shook her head. She stood aside and pushed the door open fully. 'Be my guest, Sonia. If you think you can make that man see sense, then by all means, go and try. If I knew you well, I would probably insist that you leave well alone and save yourself, but he's my son and I don't know you, so I'm going to let you have your way. On my side, I have nothing to lose.'

Sonia walked past Manus's mother and went down the hall into the kitchen. She could see Manus's and Bart's handy work visible in all the modern conveniences within the house. No wonder the woman wished that she could have her son back.

'I'll go up and tell him that you're here, but I can't promise you that he'll take a blind bit of notice.' Mrs Dooley went down the hallway and Sonia heard her tread lightly on the wooden staircase. She decided not to leave it up to Manus as to whether or not he wanted to see her. She followed his mother up the stairs and stood outside Manus's room and listened to the conversation between mother and son.

'I'll not see that dirty, foreign cow! Get her out of here this minute. Who does she think she is? I told her to steer well clear of me. And get out you too. You know I don't like you interfering in my life. Get out of here and leave me in peace!'

Mrs Dooley froze when she saw Sonia standing outside the room. She stared unbelieving at her and barred her way. The two women glared at each other until Mrs Dooley gave way. As she said herself, she had nothing to lose.

Sonia opened the door of Manus's bedroom and scrunched up her nose. She was immediately brought back to the times when it was left to her to clean up her father after a particularly bad night when her mother was in bed nursing her wounds. She knew she should run right there and then. She could hear her mother's voice telling her *I knew he had a problem when I married him, but I thought I could save him from himself. I was wrong, Sonia.*

Sonia walked quietly across the room and sat on the end of the smelly bed.

'I told you to go away and leave me alone, woman.'

'You did. But here I am.'

'Sonia.'

'The very woman.'

'You're the last person in the whole world I want to see right this very minute. Get out.'

'Make me.'

Sonia waited in the quiet room, wondering would he indeed make her. Would he do what her father would have done if anyone had challenged him in this way and lash out at her? She stood her ground and sat on the bed and waited. There was no sound for a while. Then Sonia thought she heard a sniff. Still, she said nothing.

Eventually, Manus spoke. She hadn't realised that he had been crying until now when she heard the shake in his voice. He barely sounded like himself.

'What do you want, Sonia? You've had all of me. There's nothing left to take.'

Sonia heard the words of the man who felt he had lost everything and resolved to give it back in the only way she could. Sonia had nobody. She had nothing else in life, but with Manus Dooley she might be able to do some good. She hadn't forgotten the way he had kissed her. She knew that the kiss was charged with all the love a man could give a woman, and it had felt good to have that love when she had lost so much of everything. It would be good for her and for Manus. It would give her life purpose. She would give them a chance. She leaned down towards Manus and whispered to him.

'I missed you, Manus. I just wanted to tell you that.' She kissed his forehead and brushed back his untamed hair. 'I'm sorry for what's happened to you, and I want to put it right. Get washed, Manus, and go back to work tomorrow.'

'Bart's sacked me. He's seeing a lawyer.'

'Is that what you want?'

'I can't have what I want.'

'I missed you, Manus.'

Sonia stood and left the room. Walking passed Mrs Dooley on the landing she squeezed her arm and smiled at her.

'Well?'

'Let's wait and see.'

The next day, walking into the office to see Bart, Manus knew he was doing the wrong thing, but he couldn't help himself. He knew in his heart of hearts that Sonia Almez did not love him, but she had given him a little bit of hope that she might be able to be with him. She missed him she said. Missed him. What did that mean? She missed him. Did it mean that she'd realised she loved him? Or did it mean that she missed all the head-wrecking that she caused him. Anyway, it was no bad thing to try to pull himself together. He was washed and shaved, and he hadn't gone out drinking the night before. His mother was smiling from ear to ear when he left that morning, and he knew if she had a medal, she'd give it to a certain Spanish girl.

But Manus was shaking. Shaking for want of a drink and for want of his life back and for want of Sonia. First, he had to convince his best friend that his want of his former life was stronger than his want for a drink.

'Bart.'

'Manus. Sit down.'

Manus did as he was bid for fear his legs would give out from under him. This was as much his office as it was Bart's, but he felt like he was here for an interview. He guessed he was.

'Tea?'

'Yes.'

Bart went out and asked their secretary for the teas. Moll had been working for them for years and knew exactly how they took their tea. He'd say nothing, but Manus would love to tell her to put a truck load of sugar in his, but that would show Bart how weak he was feeling.

Sitting back down, Bart waited for Manus to start the conversation. He wasn't going to make it easy for him by mentioning his wash and brush-up. Bart knew from experience that that was only the start of an uphill struggle to be dry. They had been down this road years before and Manus had won the battle then. But not the war.

'I wanted to come in and say hello, Bart. That's all. For now, anyway.'

'What's changed?'

He might as well come clean. Bart would find out sooner or later.

'Sonia came to see me.'

'Disaster.'

'Maybe. But I'm going to try again. The alternative wasn't very pretty.'

'No.'

Moll came in with the teas. She winked at Manus, and he smiled back. She was a good egg was Moll. Manus sipped his mug of tea and smiled again. There were at least three spoons of sugar in his tea. There was nothing that woman didn't know.

'So, how's business, Bart? Did the contract with Mooneys come together?'

'We started on that a month ago.'

'Grand. And it's going well?'

'Aye.'

'You're not making this easy, Bart.'

'Hah! Easy, is it? Is that what you came here for? A little bit of easy? Well, easy doesn't fit the life that I've been leading here by myself for the last few months, Manus. So, if it's easy you're looking for, you might as well knock back that tea and go back to the mammy. 'Cause you won't find easy here.'

'Now, that's more like it. At least you're talking to me.'

'Oh, I've a few words I'd like to say to you, all right, and none of them are nice.' Bart put down his mug and leaned into the desk, pushing a load of paperwork out of the way. 'If you've come waltzing back in here this morning to pick us up from where you dropped us in the cesspit, then you can think twice. I've kept the place ticking over, Manus, without you; and I was able to move on when I didn't have to babysit my business partner any more. We're doing really well, despite your absence.'

He sat back and folded his arms. 'Some would say *because* of your absence. So, what do you say you turn around there now, Manus, my old friend, and go out the way you came in and leave me in peace? Sonia had the right idea before. She knew what she would have been letting herself in for. You've said some choice things to me over the past months, boyo, and you'll not come swanning in here this morning and expect me to simply put it behind me.'

Manus looked Bart straight in the eye and nodded.

'You picked me up after a fall once before, Bart, and I can't expect you to do that again. I've some money put aside from the sale of the house, and I can live on that for a while. I wanted to come in and say hello to you this morning and let you know that I'm going to try to pull myself out of the pit again. And I'm sorry my drinking had such a terrible backlash on us, Bart. I'm truly sorry for that.'

Bart sat stony-faced, his arms still folded, his body taut. No. He wasn't going to make this easy. In fact, the way he was, he might well never speak to Manus as a friend again, never mind as a work colleague.

Manus put down his empty mug and stood up.

'If you can find a minute, Bart, you're always welcome in my mother's house. I'd love to see you whenever you can spare the time.'

'Ah, sure I can come over, Manus and we can share a bottle or two together. I'd look forward to that, of course.'

Manus cringed at the level of sarcasm in his oldest friend's voice.

'I'm going to do it this time, Bart. I am.'

He turned around and walked past Moll, giving her his best smile. 'Thanks for the tea, Moll. I'll not be needing it that sweet the next time you see me.'

'Please God now, Manus. Take care now.'

Keep walking, he told himself. *Hold your head up now*. Manus willed himself to keep it together as he passed the workers in the yard. He nodded at those he recognized.

When he got out of the yard, he walked faster, past the garage and on past the post office. She would be in there now, smiling and greeting the customers and working her heart out as she always did. He stopped outside wanting so much to go in and see her. He wanted to show her that he was up and washed and dressed and sober, but he couldn't trust himself to speak to her. He wasn't strong enough yet and he didn't know how long that would be. He saw Eileen walk towards him with her poor mother by her side.

'Hello, Manus,' said Eileen. 'It's lovely to see you so …'

'Go on, Eileen, you can say it if you like. So sober. Well, I've a bit to go yet, but I'm determined to put my heart into getting a life back again. It's lovely to see you, Mrs McMenamin. It's a beautiful day. I'll see you soon, Eileen.'

He walked on past the graveyard and stopped outside the church. He hadn't been to Mass for months. His mother said he wasn't fit to be served at God's altar. Well. Maybe soon.

'Hello, there. Manus Dooley, isn't it?'

The priest was standing behind him as he turned around.

'Oh, hello, Father. I was resting from my walk.'

'Sure, come inside with me, Manus and rest properly with a cup of tea in your hand.'

Manus tried to come up with a quick excuse as to where he had to be, but when he couldn't think of one, he realised that a cup of tea with the parish priest from Balcallan was something he thought he might like. He was a kindly man. Very humble. Not at all like their own priest in Gortahork.

'That would be lovely, Father, if you're not too busy.'

'Not at all. The morning Mass is over, and the bit of shopping is finished.' The priest held up the small bag of groceries in his hand. 'There are some chocolate biscuits in here that I only allow myself to take out for visitors, so don't think it's your company I'm after. Purely an excuse to tear open a packet.' Manus joined in with the man's infectious laughter.

When they were settled in the kitchen with a mug of tea each and a few biscuits in front of them, the priest spent no time waiting to speak frankly to Manus.

'I heard you weren't well there for a while, Manus.'

'That's a very polite way of putting it, Father.'

'Sure, what other way is there of putting it? It's a sickness, Manus. I hear from Bart that there's a few others in your family suffer from it too.'

'The one who suffers from it most in my family is my poor mother. That woman's a walking saint. I swore when I was growing up, I wouldn't touch the stuff, and when I saw what it did to my brother from an early age, it strengthened my resolve. Now that's the second time in my life that I've let life's little problems take over and stooped to the bottle. Today's the first time in months that I've woken up sober, Father, and I'm dying for a drop, since the moment I opened my eyes, to take the edge off the world.'

'And the bit becomes an extra drop, and the extra drop becomes a second tumbler full and that becomes a bottle …'

'… and the world feels like a better place for a while. I can't believe I'm having this conversation with a priest. Father Gates below in Gortahork would have thrown me out for a waster and a sinner at this stage. No badness intended to Father Gates. He'd be well within his rights to throw me out.'

'There's the sickness in my family below in Sligo too, Manus. I believe it's inherited. I decided myself at an early age not to try it out. When I took the pledge for life, it wasn't for want of a place in heaven that I did it, but in the hope that I could steer clear of the fate of my father and uncles. I know that it's with God's help and my own prayer that I'm still hanging in sober at the age of sixty-five.'

'You're never sixty-five, Father. You don't look a day over fifty.'

'Another good reason not to drink the hard stuff, Manus. Sure, the odd chocolate biscuit is the nearest I come to addiction.'

'To what, Father?'

'Addiction. That's what it's called, Manus. When you need alcohol so badly that you think you can't face life without it. It means you're addicted, and the only cure for it is abstention. The longer you go without a drink, the easier it gets and the easier it gets, the longer you can go without it. It helps to have someone who's there for you and can help you get through the worst of it. The next few weeks, if you can keep going, will be the worst.'

'I have a very good friend who helped me through the bad times the first time this happened. I don't think he's ready to go down that road again with me.'

'Eileen's husband, Bart? He's a good man, Manus. He'll be there for you in the long road. I suppose you have to try and prove to him that you mean it and you really want to stay sober.'

'I do, Father. I want it because of something else as well.'

'Sí. And a very good reason she is too.'

'Is there anything in the parish that you don't know about, Father?'

'No, Manus. It's a burden to carry, but unfortunately there's nothing that's not related back to me in the course of my work here. Now, might I suggest you go and say hello to the lady on your way home today? Let her see the effort you've made. Drop it into the conversation that you've been in having a cup of tea with me. For some reason, I'm very popular with the ladies of this parish.'

Manus stood up and walked to the door, laughing along with his new friend. God, it felt good to laugh. This man had filled him with hope, and he was ready to take on the world.

'Whenever you feel like a chat come in and see me, Manus. Now's a good, quiet time of the day, and there might be a chocolate biscuit going as well. Take care now. God bless you.'

CHAPTER TWENTY-FOUR

The house where Manus had grown up may have been small, but it was cleaned within an inch of its life. Mrs Dooley was fastidious about cleanliness, which must have been a huge task when you were clearing up after two, sometimes three, drinking men. Manus had seated Sonia at the head of the table as soon as she came in the door and Mrs Dooley had been only too delighted to relinquish her seat for the esteemed guest who was her son's saviour and his hopeful ticket to a life of sobriety. Sonia stood to clear the plates from the table.

'Sit down there now, Sonia. I'm sure you do enough in that house over in Balcallan without running around after us here.'

'I don't mind doing the dishes, Mrs Dooley. It's the least I can do after eating such a delicious meal. I loved that apple tart. I've never been able to put the ingredients together so well, like they fit. It always tastes like there's too much or too little of something and I can't quite figure out which.'

Sonia knew she was letting her words tumble out nervously over the table, but she couldn't help herself. It had been a difficult meal. In her efforts to make her feel at ease and comfortable, Mrs Dooley had suffocated Sonia so much she felt that she couldn't breathe. Certainly, she couldn't talk. She had come here for her Sunday lunch today feeling that she was to be interviewed by her future mother-in-law, but it was Manus's mother who had been the one who had tried desperately to paint herself and her son in a glowing light. She was trying too hard. Nobody had talked about where Sonia came from or why it had taken Sonia all these years to give in and say yes to Manus.

When Manus had left Balcallan, Sonia had missed him. She realised then that she had grown to love Manus in a way. Manus Dooley had been a part of her life for so long, that she hadn't realised that she relied on their friendship as much as she did. When she heard what had happened to Manus, she had felt a huge sense of regret. And hurt. Not an overriding passion to run to him and take him in her arms and whisper her undying love to him, but a feeling that this wasn't the way things should be. Sonia knew that she had the power to put things right.

'You can't go out there marrying a man because you feel guilty about him, Sonia.' Eileen had been adamant in her opinion. 'Do you think he's going to change so much because he's put a ring on your finger?'

Sonia didn't know how long or how well Manus would do as a husband, but if the alternative was to sit and grow old while she looked after Maeve, she would go quietly senile herself. Manus was a lovely man when he was sober. He was intelligent and determined to do well in life. And they were friends. How many newly married couples could say that about themselves? Manus and Sonia understood each other. They each were bringing a load of baggage to the wedding table, and they would both have to work hard to accommodate the other's past life. They had discussed it long and hard on the beach late into the night last week and had made what Sonia believed was the right decision.

There was one other thing that had swayed her decision. Sonia wanted a baby and Manus did too. She knew that being married didn't automatically give you motherhood. Poor Eileen had been struggling for years to have a baby. Sonia hoped her friend would cling on to her latest pregnancy for the length it would take. Then if Sonia could also get pregnant, perhaps they might even have two little girls to bring up as best friends for each other.

'Would you like a nice cup of tea to wash that down with?'

Sonia snapped out of her reverie.

'Yes, please, Mrs Dooley.'

'Manus, bring Sonia into the sitting room there and let her relax. I'll have a pot of tea in to you shortly.'

Sonia smiled at Mrs Dooley. They needed to be on their own for a while to let the tension of the afternoon abate a little. She followed Manus the short few steps into the sitting room and sat on the chair that Manus indicated.

'Do you think she likes me, Manus?' she whispered.

'That was never going to be in question, Sonia. My mother had her heart set on you the minute you turned up on her door-step to bring her youngest son back to life. And you did exactly that, sweetheart. I feel wonderful and it's all down to you.'

'All I did was turn up here giving out to you, Manus. It was up to you to do the really hard work, and I have to say I'm very proud of you. No matter what happens in the future, what you've done lately has been the hardest job of all. I saw what you were like those first few days not drinking, shaking and sweating and looking awful, but look at you now – you're a new man.'

'Ready for a new life, Sonia, with the most beautiful woman in the world.'

'Ha. I can't believe you waited all those years, Manus.'

'You needed time, Sonia, to … let go, and before you say anything I know you haven't let go completely, but if you had agreed to marry me before now, it would never have worked. I needed you, but there was nothing you needed from me. Now, I feel that you need me too. Walking away was the best thing and the worst thing that I've ever done. It nearly destroyed me, but it made you say those words that I'd been waiting for half my life. *I missed you and that must mean that I love you.* Most of all, I felt that you needed me, and it feels good to be needed.'

Manus reached over and gently drew the back of his hand along Sonia's cheek.

'Ahem. Sorry for intruding, but the tea is well drawn now. Any longer and we could walk across the top of it. Mind you, Manus looks like he could probably walk on water with that grin on his face.'

The trio laughed, and Mrs Dooley went to set down the tray on the table. A loud banging from upstairs made her drop it in fright, sending cups and tea splattering everywhere.

'Fiona!' Mr Dooley's booming voice filled the room with the problems of the house. 'Fionnaaaaaa!'

'I'll go, Mam.'

'No, love. It's not you he wants to shout at.' Mrs Dooley recovered her wits very quickly, like a woman who was well used to such an invasion of her head, but even after all these years it still made her jump. 'I'll be back down, shortly.'

Manus and Sonia looked at each other. 'Don't worry, Sonia. He'll be fine once he's had his cup of tea and a bowl of porridge. If Mam can get that into him, she'll be onto a winner. At least Dad's here and in his bed. Pat didn't come home at all last night. God only knows what ditch he's asleep in today.'

'I'm not worried, Manus. You forget, I was reared on such behaviour. Your father's roar was like an echo from the past, that's all. Will she be all right up there?' They could hear the shouts and abuse coming from the bed; that meant Mrs Dooley had arrived in the room.

'Oh, she'll be fine. She has it down to a fine art by now. She's had to suffer that man for years, and Pat along with him. Me for a while there, and that must have been terrible for her. To see me go the same way when she had looked on me as her pride and joy. Pat is much worse though, a very violent man. We've had the Gardaí to visit more than a few times, and maybe one of these days they'll drag him off for good. It would be the best thing for him, but the worst for Mam. There's plenty families where the men have a love of the drink, but a son in prison? She'd never survive that.'

'Hopefully, it'll never come to that.'

'We'll see. She's very worried about the wedding, though, Sonia. It's hard enough for her to have to put up with it all on a day-to-day basis. but at a big showy event where the spotlight is on the family for the day might be too much for her. I'm not sure what's for the best.'

Sonia smiled, realising she now had a get out clause. She'd been dreading being scrutinized for a whole day by everyone from Balcallan and Gortahork.

'What's the smile for then?'

'We could go to Dublin to get married. Or London. It doesn't have to be in our own parish. I have no way of obtaining my baptismal certificate, so we could make up some story about having to go somewhere else to get married.'

'Sonia. I've waited all these years to show you off to the people of Balcallan and Gortahork as my own, and now you talk of running away like we've something to hide?'

'No, Manus, we're not hiding, but it would save your mother from any embarrassment. We could bring Eileen and Bart because we'll need them as best man and matron of honour, and it might help to cement things between you and Bart. Maybe your mother might stay with Maeve for a while, because she'll need looking after while we're away.'

'You have it all worked out already. Were you thinking about this all along?'

'No, Manus, but you have to admit, it would be the best thing for all. Or we could bring your mother and Maeve with us on holiday. That would mean a lot to your mam, wouldn't it?'

Manus was quiet. Mrs Dooley was coming back downstairs, and she came into the room with her head held high and her dignity in her boots.

'Sit down, Mrs Dooley. We were waiting for you before we had the tea. I'll pour.'

'No, Sonia. That tea's a mess and not fit for drinking. Let's not pretend that nothing happened. Manus get a cloth and clean that lot up and make a fresh pot till we start again.'

'Honestly, Mrs Dooley. It's fine.'

'It is not fine, Sonia, and I'll be Fiona from now on if that's all right with you. There are times when it feels just too much of a chore to be called after that thing in the bed upstairs. Don't look at me like a wounded puppy, Manus. If the girl's going to be part of this family, then there are things that she needs to get used to. Now, go and make me some tea.'

Manus gathered the things on the tray and left his mother with Sonia. Sonia smiled at his nervous look to put him at his ease. When he had left the room, she let out her breath and realised that she had been on edge for most of the afternoon.

'Mrs Dooley … Fiona …' Sonia shifted forwards in her chair. 'I know about this life, because it's what I left behind me in Spain. Some are for saving, and I think your Manus is one of them. I may need your help along the way, though, and if ever you need to talk, or to clear up after anything, then come to me. We can help each other.'

'Indeed, and I won't have any need of that, young lady. Now poke that fire up. It's getting chilly in here.' Fiona sniffed and pulled her cardigan around her, but Sonia could see her shoulders relax and a half a smile forming on her face.

CHAPTER TWENTY-FIVE

Sitting at the large, wooden table to eat was not as easy as it used to be, and as Sonia reached for her peas with her fork and spilt most of them over her bump, her husband broke into a fit of laughter.

'It's amazing how fat you can get when you're not even able to get a bite to eat,' he said.

Sonia smiled mischievously and flung the remainder of the fork's contents across the table showering Manus in peas and potato.

'That'll teach you to call me fat,' she said, her eyebrows raised in daring for him to get back at her. He answered her by showering her with a load of his own peas and the two of them kept at the pea fight until they couldn't laugh any more.

That was all that Sonia, now two weeks overdue with her first baby, needed to get her going, and her laughter turned to gasping as she held on to the table with the sudden onset of pains.

'What? You're not …?'

'It must be,' she said. 'I've been feeling it a bit all day but not like this. Oh, Manus, this is terrible.'

'No, it's not, you gorgeous woman. It's the best thing that's ever happened in the whole of my life. Let's get you out of here and into Letterkenny before you give birth on the kitchen floor in a pool of peas.'

Sonia looked down at the floor at the mess of peas and began to laugh again – enough to send her waters rushing down her legs and she screamed.

Twelve hours later, in the small hours of the morning she held her beautiful, sleeping baby daughter in her arms. Called Fiona Cristina for her grandmothers, Sonia couldn't take her eyes from her. For the first time since she had arrived in Ireland, she felt a sense of belonging. She had somebody here who was a part of her. She had sent the reluctant Manus home to catch up on some sleep and she was enjoying the quiet time before Eileen and Bart came in to see her.

'Fiona Cristina Dooley. I love you. You're so very perfect.'

Manus walked into the kitchen in the dark. Something wet and hard squelched under his feet. He stopped, then smiled at the memory of the pea fight and Sonia's waters breaking on the kitchen floor. He backed out of the room. The mess would keep until morning. He was wrecked. He hadn't wanted to leave the hospital and his beautiful baby daughter asleep in the cradle, looking like a gift from heaven. That was exactly what she was. A gift. Who would have thought that the love of his life, Sonia Almez, would agree to marry him and that they would go on to have a beautiful baby girl? When Sonia had shrieked with pain in the hospital, he had held her hand and told her it was all right. He loved her. Their baby was almost there. It had taken some persuading for the midwife to let him stay for the birth.

But when Sonia became delirious in the last minutes before the birth, it was that bastard's name that she had called. Enrico. Manus hated every letter of that name.

CHAPTER TWENTY-SIX

The room was silent. Manus's mother sat in her chair in her kitchen. Hers but not hers. Leaving her drunk husband and son had seemed like the best thing to do when Sonia had suggested it. A new start.

'You're fifty-five years old and have plenty of life left in front of you, Fiona. All you're doing with that pair in your house is facilitating them.' Sonia's words rang true.

She loved the newness of the house. The smell of paint interwoven with the smell of her daughter-in-law's delicious Spanish spices. Her bedroom was an absolute delight. Fit for a princess. She should never have shared that stinking bed with that whisky-mouthed man all her married life.

Manus had moved her in while Sonia was in the hospital. She had brought some of her own things, but when she had to choose, there was little worth having. Most of the furniture in her family home was broken and battered, but she had lots of lovely photos in their faded frames. Memories of when the boys were children, and her husband, Mick, only drank on Friday nights. Those evenings she went 'on holiday' to her parents in the next village and dropped the boys to a neighbour on Saturday afternoons while she went to clean up after Mick's excesses. She couldn't remember exactly when the Friday extended to two, three, seven nights, and when Pat left school, he drank himself through four jobs before he let himself drown in his own sorrowful life.

When Manus went the same way, it had broken Fiona's heart, but then Sonia came, like an angel, and the wedding rescued him.

'Please, please God let the drink not take my son again,' she prayed, 'and bad cess to that pair I've left behind.'

To cook and clean for Manus and his new wife was a pleasure, and when Sonia came home from the hospital with Fiona's gorgeous namesake, that would be the icing on the cake. Sonia would return to working in the post office and Fiona would mind the baby. The village could talk as much as they wanted about working mothers not being normal, but they weren't a normal family. The gossips weren't finished plastering Fiona's own name in the dirt since she left Mick and Pat to their own mess. To hell with the lot of them. She, and Sonia too, were due a bit of happiness, and Fiona would make sure that they got it.

The sound of the potatoes bubbling over got her to her feet. Turning the gas down, she lifted the lid on the bacon and cabbage to check that it was still covered. The one thing she missed from her house was the stove, but she would get used to the gas cooker, a small price to pay. The smell of the bacon brought her back to her newly married days when she was so excited cooking for her husband. It was the first thing she prepared for him, and his appreciation of her efforts should have been enough to send her running back home.

'It's grand, Fiona,' he told her. 'You'll get the hang of it. Ask my mother about how she does it, and you'll get it right with a bit of practice.'

That was the only time he had ever commented on her cooking. After that he only shovelled whatever she gave him down his ungrateful throat and left her to the cleaning up. Fiona watched with pride how Manus always cleaned up alongside his wife. Sonia wouldn't have it any other way. Here they were now, pulling into the gravelled driveway of this glorious house. Fiona left the dinner to finish itself and ran out the side door to greet her beautiful new granddaughter.

Three months later, Sonia still had the baby in the middle of the bed between herself and Manus. Nothing was spoken about this arrangement. There was no need. Sonia knew that as soon as she put baby Fiona into her cot in the beautiful nursery her daddy had built for her, that Manus would want to resume marital relations again. She tried to put the thought out of her head as much as she could and get on with the daily rituals of washing, eating, playing with her baby and sleeping when Fiona slept. She was a good baby, and Sonia knew there was no reason to keep her in the bed with her. Her mother-in-law tackled her about it one morning after Manus had gone to work.

'Sonia, love. I know that this is none of my business, but I feel that I need to ask you. Why is little Fiona not in her own room yet? She's getting bigger and she must take up so much of that small bed you have up there. I think it would be more comfortable for her to be in her own room. Better for all of you, don't you think? The longer you leave it the harder it will be. Think about it, Sonia, but don't leave it too long.'

Sonia thought about it. She watched Manus watching her with what she knew to be absolute lust. She watched her mother-in-law watching them both for signs that things were good between them. Fiona offered to babysit while they went out, or better still while they went off for a weekend together. Sonia made excuses. Sometimes before a date, or at times when they were about to walk away and leave her with her grandmother, she would suddenly find something wrong with the child as a reason for them not to go.

As Fiona got older, though, Sonia ran out of excuses, and eventually, she had to concede and allow her daughter to sleep in the nursery. Fiona loved it and slept through the night from the beginning, with her mother running in and out to check on her far too often. When Sonia found herself shaking the baby awake in the middle of the night to stave off a particular look she had seen in Manus's needy eyes, she knew she was going to have to pull herself together and get on with her married life. What must her mother-in-law think of her? She was not acting like an ordinary married woman should act.

Sonia lay in her bed each night and hoped that this was not the night that Manus would want her. When he did, she smiled at him and lay back and undressed. She allowed the act to happen and wondered was there something intrinsically wrong with her that made her dislike sex so much. She knew that Eileen loved her *nights in the sack* as she called them. When Manus was finished, he would always hold her face in his hands and say, 'I love you,' and Sonia would always smile at him and say, 'I love you too, Manus.'

And she did love her husband. He was such a good man to her and his daughter and his mother. He even went back to his childhood home once or twice a week to straighten the place out and to leave food for his father and his brother to live on. He would go in the evening when he knew they were out drinking. If they ever wondered who their magic elf was, they never mentioned it. If Sonia ever passed her brother-in-law or father-in-law anywhere, there was never a word spoken in recognition of each other. She was the reason their woman had left them to fend for themselves. They would never forgive her.

When Eileen gave birth to her daughter, Deirdre, soon after Sonia had Fiona, the women knew that they had no option but to put Maeve into a home for her safety and their own sanity. Maeve had moved in with Eileen and Bart when Sonia got married, and they tried to mind her between all of them, but the change in her environment made her much worse. It broke their hearts, but no amount of love could keep her out of harm's way. Eileen had waited years for her baby girl, and the pregnancy and the birth had left her exhausted. Sonia had strength enough for the two of them.

Manus, Sonia, Fiona and her grandchild continued in this way for years and they did all right. Sonia never let on to her husband that she was doing the unthinkable thing of taking contraceptive pills. Sonia had had a difficult time finding a compassionate doctor in Dublin who gave her the illegal tablets, but once she had found her, poor Fiona waited in vain for a second grandchild that could never come. She never told Eileen either, as her friend continued trying but failed to produce a second child. When she had lost a fourth baby, Bart insisted that they stop trying and Sonia managed to get Eileen to contact her Dublin doctor and to take the pill for the good of her health.

When Sonia was forty years old, Maeve McMenamin died in her sleep in the nursing home in Letterkenny. Everyone at the funeral agreed that it was unbelievable that the amazing woman with such a great heart could be gone from them. Sonia and Eileen, who had watched their beloved Maeve spend her last months in the gentle care of people who knew how to care for such things, were filled with grief, knowing she had been a mother to them both.

Sonia held her friend in her arms that evening and sobbed with her. 'She showed us how to be real mothers, Eileen. We can pay her back by being the best mothers we can to our own two lovely daughters.'

Although Sonia was the best mother that she could be, she struggled to be the wife that Manus wanted. When his own mother was diagnosed with cancer and was gone within six weeks, Sonia held Manus in her arms at night and comforted him in the only way she could. But with her mother-in-law gone, there was no need to keep up the pretence, and Manus stopped trying to make love to Sonia. She knew that it was her fault: that the man could not keep up a want for a woman who didn't want him back. She hoped he would find a lover. It would help her guilt. But as the years passed, Sonia could see no signs that Manus had any interest outside the home and his business. She still thought of Enrico so much, and she got news of him occasionally from her friends in Dublin. How was he lasting out in prison? She wished she knew.

CHAPTER TWENTY-SEVEN

1975

Enrico

I peel the brown uniform from my body, scrunching my face in disgust. It feels like taking off a layer of dirty, unwanted skin. I have worn Franco's shit-coloured clothes for so long, I can hardly remember the crisp white shirts and the wine-coloured trousers I favoured in my teens. Mario's aunt puts her head around the door without knocking and her face doesn't even register my nakedness.

'Here are some of my late husband's clothes and underwear,' she says. 'He was a much bigger man than you, not so tall, but stockier. There's a belt here to help you hold yourself together. We'll have to fatten you up, you scrawny man. Mario was the same when Franco's prison spat him out onto the street. I've run a bath for you and dinner will be ready in an hour. It will take that long to scrub that dirt off. All right?'

I smile at the elderly lady who welcomed me into her home an hour ago, and so far, has treated me like a long-lost son.

'You are too good, señora. Thank you for everything. I can't—'

'Say nothing more. You are welcome in my house. Every one of Mario's prison friends have passed through here on their way from that hellhole to their home towns. Many have been freed in the past week, so hopefully my house will be filled with Franco's ex-prisoners in the coming months.' The woman in widow's clothes turns and leaves me swallowing the tears I've been trying not to shed since this morning.

I woke early on my mattress on the floor of my cell, as I have every morning for too many years. A prison officer called out my name from a list while we were eating our morning bread. *The morning list.* The bread stuck in my throat with the fright of hearing my name on this list that has been the execution sentence for so many prisoners before. Not my name, but the name I have used for years here, Miguel Almez. I told them that I have no family, so nobody will be notified of my death.

I coughed on my food and stood slowly to join the frightened, unbelieving group of men and stumbled with them through the building to the outdoor square. The word inside the prison for the last few days has been that the game was over for Nationalist Spain. Over the past few weeks, we heard that more men were being released each day from the hovel that they had lived in for so long, but some had not been so lucky as the daily executions were still being carried out. The terror of Franco would last until his bitter end. The horror of almost completing your sentence only to face the firing squad after all was on everyone's mind.

We were marched down a corridor and then shoved through a gated hole in the wall with the butt of a Nationalist rifle. I found myself, with twenty or so other men, standing outside on the street. Then the prison officer pulled the gate closed behind us. No explanation. No speech of freedom.

After a few moments, the reality began to set in. Some of the men began to screech and jump, pushing and hugging each other with the joy of being outside the prison, but I could only stand in shock. I felt the anxiety of all the years wrap around me and keep me still. All normal life was suspended for me the day that I first lifted my friend Miguel's dead body up off the street after he was mistakenly shot dead. Had I woken up from that nightmare now? I was not sure if I was still living the hell or if it was actually at an end.

When Mario's name was called some weeks earlier, he thought he would be shot, and he whispered the name and address of his aunt to me before he was marched away. 'In case you get out of here, amigo. I think my time is up, but you might be luckier. If you do get to her, tell her to give my mother a hug from me.' He shuffled towards the guard who had called his name, shaking his head in disbelief. Then he looked back at me once more before the soldier grabbed hold of his arm and dragged him out of our cell. When I was released, I thought that maybe Mario had not been killed that morning. Perhaps he was gone to his aunt's home? So that's where I went too.

Walking aimlessly at first, and then falling into a rhythmic shuffle as fast as my dilapidated body let me, I found the house within an hour. As soon as the aunt saw me in my brown prison uniform, she stood back and welcomed me in. Mario, she explained, had also been released, and for the first time today, I felt the emotion of my liberation and what it means to be free.

She also tells me Mario left here two weeks ago, to try to find his sister and brother. So many people in Spain will be picking up the pieces of their lives and trying to put their families back together again.

Standing in the bedroom in the aunt's house, I think about who I will look for. My parents are gone. I have no idea how many years I have been away. I don't know what age I am. Forty-something? But there is Sonia in Ireland. My Sonia. And Alejandro is out there somewhere. I will find them and take life from there.

Lowering myself into the hot water tub, I feel the beginning of the strain of the wasted years drain from me. I lie back for about ten minutes, trying to erase the bubbling thoughts in my head, and the familiar anger creeps in. Sitting back up, I reach for a small towel and begin to scrub. I try to rub all the years of dirt from my body, but no matter how much I tear at my skin;

I still feel the dirt of the prison cling. Eventually, I give up and pull myself out of the bath. My energy is used up, and it's with great difficulty that I put on the unfamiliar clothes and shoes that belonged to a man who died in that prison long before I ever got there. Mario told me how his uncle was arrested for having Republican connections and died of typhoid two years into his ten-year sentence.

'Enrico! Come and eat!' The woman calls from down the hall. I can smell dishes that I remember from my far, distant life. Sonia's mother's kitchen. Yes. The fisherman's café always smelled of home cooking. I've tried not to think of Sonia for so many years, so thoughts of her would not drive me mad. I might as well have stopped trying to breathe. As soon as I felt the ground of freedom beneath my feet that morning, my thoughts turned immediately to Sonia. I yearn to see her.

'Would you like some more?'

I look down at my empty plate and smile and nod.

'That was so good, señora. I had forgotten what real food tasted like. Thank you. And to be asked if I would like some more? Oh, the luxury. And to sleep on a real bed tonight in a room without twenty snoring, smelly men. It's hard to believe. This time yesterday ...' My words trail off. I don't want to remember yesterday, or any other yesterdays in that place.

'Never mind yesterday,' says Mercedes, putting a fresh bowl of stew in front of me and pointing to the pile of bread, nodding her head. 'But don't get too used to sleeping on your own in that room. Mario gave my address to many men, and from tomorrow, I'm expecting more knocks on my door.'

I raise my eyebrows questioningly as I stuff more bread, soaked in gravy, into my mouth.

Mercedes' eyes fill with tears as she chokes out the words of happiness that will fill so many Spaniards with absolute joy. 'I hope that we will be sharing our food with many more Republican men, Enrico. Remember this date in your heart. The twentieth day of November 1975. Today Francisco Franco closed his eyes for the very last time.'

I close my own eyes and allow those words to take rest in my head and my heart. 'May he rot in hell, señora.'

CHAPTER TWENTY-EIGHT

Enrico

S itting in El Vaso, sipping a small beer, I look around at the familiar but strange, worn faces and crumbling walls. I came here straight from speaking to my cousin and his wife and I feel defeated. They didn't recognise me at first. My emaciated body and bald head look nothing like the big, healthy, eighteen-year-old who was arrested so long ago. So many years of my imprisonment under Franco's bastards were not enough to soften the memories of the local people from my pueblo. The rumours that encircled my family and friends of my collaboration with the prison guards in Malaga all those years ago has hardened every Republican heart in the town. I have been gone so long that people do not believe I am the same Enrico who ran these streets as a boy, squashed beside them on school benches and who fished with them on rough seas as a teenager. To them I'm now Enrico Sanchez, the man who shamed his family and his town by turning in a list of Republican names to the Nationalist authorities. That lie served me well before, but now, how will I get them to believe the truth? That it was I who was arrested at aged twenty, whilst trying to lead the Republicans in fight.

Franco's men have done a great job of smearing my name with dirt. When I first tricked my way out of prison, the Nationalists at the same time arrested the men and women on a so-called list of mine. When I led a charge against Malaga prison a year later, I used a false name and kept that name through all my years in prison in order to keep my family and friends safe. The town's hero was Miguel Almez, shot by Nationalist soldiers. A mistake they had said. It was a mistake that nobody here had forgotten: a killing they had needed to vent their anger about, and the arrests that were made in my name were the perfect target.

'I should have known this is where you would be.' Snapped from my maudlin thoughts, I look up to see a woman with greying hair, of about my own age, looking down at me. Her face is familiar as are so many others around me, but I can't place her.

'I heard you were in town,' she says. 'Señora Almez is spitting your name in disgust at the poor fishermen trying to eat their dinner in her café. I believe you had the audacity to go there asking after her daughter, Sonia. You idiot.' She laughs and then I remember the laugh of Sonia's school friend, who endeared everyone to her back then with her sense of humour in the face of any woes sent her way.

'Rosa.' I stand beside her. 'It's good to see you. So good. A familiar face smiling at me. I can't remember the last time that happened.' Much to my horror, I feel my eyes grow wet and Rosa holds open her arms to embrace me. When I stop shaking, she releases me and shouts at the locals around her.

'Go back to your drinks and your bad thoughts. This man is a hero and one of our own.' A few grunt and mumble but none argue with Rosa, a woman whom they have known forever and who is most definitely one of their own. 'They'll have us both married off now, Enrico, for hugging in public. You're doomed.'

I smile and feel Rosa's warmth wrap around me and hold me. I don't think I will ever forget that hug. It pours life back into me as we sit down.

'So, mi amigo. Tell me. What hellhole have you been hiding in all these years? Because from the state of you I can see that you haven't been living it up in Nationalist circles. You poor, poor man. The last I saw of you is when you vowed to avenge Miguel

Almez's death, but like everything else in this forsaken country, the punishment was yours. My Alejandro is married in Scotland and may never come back, and your Sonia is married to an Irishman, with a daughter, and so tied to that island for life.'

I stare at Rosa. I knew from Roberto that Sonia was in Ireland, but I had no idea of the life she was living there. This flat statement from her best friend, delivered as old news, sucks the air from the space around me.

'You didn't know? I can see from your face. I'm so sorry, Enrico. Franco may be dead, but it's too late for some of us. He's already taken so much from us.'

I still can't speak. I can barely breathe. Sonia is married and has a child. I knew it was too much to have hoped that she would wait all this time for me, but we made promises. There was never going to be anyone else we could love the way that we loved each other. I understood the best thing that Sonia could do was to leave Spain while she was in so much danger. The last thing that I wanted was for her to end up in a prison like mine. She had to go somewhere like Ireland, but now it's time for everyone who has been displaced to come back. Roberto Rodriguez lied to me about Sonia. She should be spending the rest of her life with me, making up for those terrible years, but that will never happen now.

'Do you have somewhere to live, Enrico? Are you staying with your cousin? I heard you went to visit them.' Rosa smiles at my puzzled face. 'Do you not remember what this town is like? Not everything has changed. Everybody still knows what everyone else is doing.'

'No, my cousin ran me from his house. It appears Franco's lies still fester in everyone's minds here.'

'I'm working and living with Cristina so let's go back to her. Sonia's mamá might be all fight on the outside, but she needs some male help and protection in that place. I'll make her take you on and give you a place to sleep, and I will work on the lies that the people believe about you. Everything will get better, Enrico.'

I follow Rosa and find myself staying in the house where my love had grown when me and Sonia were young; sleeping in the bedroom that still held her childhood in its walls; and every night before I sleep my heart breaks a little more.

CHAPTER TWENTY-NINE

Enrico

Leaning against a rock, I have an excellent viewpoint to observe her. I breathe her into me, desperate to reach out to her. She sits in a position on the sand that is familiar to me from our teens. The beach was always Sonia's escape back then. Is she escaping from something now, or is that only my mind hoping that she hasn't made a new life without me in it after all? I want to believe that thoughts of me are paramount in her head. A wave splashes at her feet, and Sonia allows it to circle her without acknowledging how cold it must be.

Sonia is married to a man called Manus and has a child called Fiona. That much I have managed to learn from the villagers without giving away anything of myself. Now is a good time to turn around and walk back the way I came, through the fields to where the bus goes to Dublin, then to the airport and back home to Spain. I came to Ireland to make sure that Sonia was all right, and I have heard that she is doing fine. We can't go back to that time before. It's too late. We have our new lives, and we should let the past be. Maybe I should try to love Rosa. She's a wonderful woman. She's free, and Sonia is … She's crying now silently. Only a few tears escape, but I can't bear to look at the sadness on her beautiful face.

'Sonia …' The strangled word escapes me before I have a chance to check it.

Sonia jumps up and wipes the tears away and she looks around towards the place where she heard the voice calling her name. I step out from my hiding place and say her name.

'Sonia,' I say again. Quieter this time. 'Do you know me?'

Sonia steps away from me and catching her bare foot on a rock, she falls backwards. Her ankle is cut, but she pays no heed to it as she tries to scramble away from a man that she hasn't set eyes on in so many years.

'It's been so long, Sonia. I couldn't stay away any longer. I know that you have your own life now. I wanted to make sure you were all right. That's all.'

Sonia tries to stand up but calls out when she tries to put some weight on her injured foot. I move towards her.

'You're hurt, Sonia. Let me help you.'

She allows herself to be gently lowered to the sand once more.

'Enrico,' she whispers. 'You came back from the dead.'

I busy myself cupping salt water in my weathered hands and pouring it over her cut. Then I kneel in front of her and take her face in those hands and smile.

'You were worth coming back for.'

CHAPTER THIRTY

It was time to collect Fiona from her Irish dancing class. The two hours on the beach had been the longest and the shortest hours she had ever lived. Sonia put one foot in front of the other. She felt as if she was floating, and she couldn't figure out if she was angry or happy at what had taken place that day.

Enrico. So many years of hoping, imagining, wishing for him, trying to let him go so she could make another life for herself, and almost getting there. Next week, Sonia would go to Dublin on her own for a few days off to be with her Spanish friends, take some time away from motherhood and work.

'Mammy!' Little Fiona ran out of the hall and threw her arms around Sonia, bringing her mother back down to the here and now. She smiled at her nine-year-old daughter and showered her with kisses, enjoying that she still wanted to be hugged. In a year or two she would be an embarrassment to her daughter. Sonia lived for the contact with her beautiful baby girl. She was everything.

'You smell funny, Mammy,' said Fiona. Sonia laughed nervously and felt the blood rising to her face.

'What a strange thing to say, Fiona.' She smiled at her daughter. 'I'd better have a bath when we get home if I'm smelly.'

'Not smelly like bad, Mammy. Only different or something. What's for tea? I'm starving. Miss Wobbles danced the legs off us today.'

'Don't call her that. That's not nice, Fiona Dooley!' Sonia looked around to make sure that no one was listening to her daughter's name for the ageing dance teacher. She took Fiona's hand and started walking towards home.

'But when she dances, Mammy, it's hard to keep from laughing when you're standing opposite her. Today she said, "Now girls and boys, I want you to copy everything I do," and Séamus got a fit of the giggles and she sent him out of the hall, but it was too late. We were all gone off on one by then and Miss Wobbles went red in the face she was raging so much …'

Sonia was glad that Fiona was in such a chatty mood, and she tried to keep her mind focussed on her childish humour, in a vain attempt to keep away the thoughts and feelings creeping in and taking over.

'What did you say, Mammy?' Fiona took her by surprise.

'Nothing, bebita. I said nothing.' Had she spoken her thoughts out loud?

'Yes, you did, Mam. You said something like "me and eeko". Is that something in Spanish?'

Sonia felt her heart race at the thought of her daughter knowing what she had been thinking. 'Oh, I might have. I'm not sure. Nothing important. I was remembering my own Spanish dancing when I was your age. I loved to dance.'

'Will you teach me, Mam? To Spanish dance, I mean. And could I get a Flamenco dress with big red spots on it? And could I get those clickety-clackety things?' Fiona began to twirl and stamp her feet and click her fingers and her mother joined in and they both laughed.

'Hah, we'll see, bebita. We'll see.'

'Don't call me bebita. I'm not your baby girl any more, Mammy. I'm *nine*!' And they continued their journey home, each thinking their own excited thoughts. Fiona about her future Spanish dancing, and Sonia about the man she would have to be careful about never mentioning aloud again. *Mi Enrico.*

She would see Enrico in a week in Dublin.

'Mr and Mrs ..?' asks the hotel manageress over the rim of her glasses.

'Sanchez.'

'Almez.'

Sonia and I answer at the same time.

'You have different names?' The woman straightens up and glares at Sonia who is fingering her wedding ring and looking guilty.

'Sanchez,' I say. 'We're newly married. It will take my beautiful *new* wife some time to get used to her *new* name.' I smile my most charming smile and Sonia smiles shyly.

'Right so. And it's the two nights, is it?'

'Yes,' I say. 'The weekend.'

She fills in our names in the ledger asking me to spell them out to her very slowly. She takes a key from the hook behind her and hands it over to the bellboy who walks up behind us. Sonia frowns when he winks at me as he picks up our separate pieces of luggage.

'Room 214, second floor,' she says. 'Breakfast is served from seven to ten.' I can feel the nervousness radiating from Sonia.

'Go raibh maith agat.' Sonia thanks the woman in Irish, causing her to smile for the first time.

'Aren't you great altogether,' says the lady. 'Not many foreigners would try to learn a few Irish words to come here. Enjoy now.'

'We will,' I say, returning her smile, and I lead my *bride* towards our bedroom for the first night of our long-awaited honeymoon.

Up in the room, Sonia makes a big play of unpacking her bag. She babbles about the weather and the lovely room and how nice the staff are. I stop her mid-sentence.

'Shhhh, mi Sonia. I know that you and I have a lot to talk about but that can come later.' My arms are around her and she reaches up and pulls me towards her.

'I'm sorry. I'm talking about nothing. I'm nervous, Enrico. After all these years of wanting only you and here we are. It's a miracle.'

'Oh, it's real, Sonia. This is all happening, and my body is desperate for your touch and to touch you. I never knew the meaning of being on fire before, but now I do. Do you not feel some of that, amor?'

'I feel like that too, Enrico. I've never felt like this before. When you and I were together in Spain we were only teenagers. Now we are both so ready to be with each other.'

Sonia moves back and begins to undress as if it is the most natural thing in the world. She knows that I'm feeling the same way as she is. We both want nothing more than to lie down together on the big hotel bed and let nature take its course. She smiles invitingly at me as I remove my clothes quickly. When I am naked, Sonia gasps. I should have warned her of the scars and the jutting ribs. She takes a deep breath and reaches out to caress one particularly large gash that almost took my life in the early days of prison, before Roberto intervened and kept me alive. I forgive him now for his lies. Sonia is mine after all. When we're both ready, Sonia takes my hand and leads me to the bed. We lie down and wrap ourselves around each other and drown in a slow passion that neither of us ever hoped to experience.

Sleeping with Sonia in my arms tonight, I want her to run to Spain with me and never go back to Donegal, but she has Fiona, and she knows that she will never be able to take her away from her father. This weekend is all that we have, and then we will go our separate ways. I can feel the pain already taking hold. Life is cruel.

CHAPTER THIRTY-ONE

Enrico

I can't figure out what it's all been for. All those years waiting to leave prison, determined to get through the sickness, the beatings and the verbal abuse from prison officers. If it hadn't been for Roberto, I know I would have died in that place. Sitting here on the stony beach, I feel no thanks for being saved for what this life is throwing at me now. So, Roberto sent Sonia to live in Ireland for her safety. Then that do-gooding bastard did as much as he could to make my stay in prison as easy as possible. Easy. Roberto may have eased his own conscience but all he did was lengthen my misery.

At least I enjoyed one wonderful weekend with Sonia. We poured a whole lifetime of love and passion into those two days in Dublin, but I wasn't able to persuade Sonia to leave Dublin and come back to Spain with me.

'I have made Manus suffer enough,' she said. 'All those years he waited for me while I pined after you. He was patient. He's a good man, Enrico. I couldn't take Fiona away from him. She's his princess. And I certainly could never leave her. Life has been so hard for you and me, but we have to make the best of what is left to us.' She watched me walk away through the airport and she went back to her nice, neat life in Ireland. Except it isn't nice and it certainly isn't neat. She's married to a *good* man, a *kind* man, but where was the unending love and passion that she would have known if we were allowed to be together?

So, I'm back in Andalucía and working for Rosa and Cristina.

'To pay back the money for your flight to Ireland,' Rosa says, 'and once that's done, we will see what life brings.'

Somehow, while I was away, Rosa has worked on the people of our town, person by person, and slowly built up a new version of Enrico Sanchez. Overnight I seem to have gone from 'Sanchez the traitor' to 'Enrico Pablo Sanchez, the hero of the pueblo'. I am the man who built up an army of Republicans to take down the Nationalist prison officers in Malaga Jail. My attack may not have been successful, and I may have spent more than half my lifetime in prison, but I have earned the badge of hero. Now the local people know who I truly am, and why I had to let them believe that I was a traitor before, in order to trick the Nationalists into freeing me. I returned from Ireland to a fiesta in the town that lasted two days, celebrating the return of their hero. The people need a reason to celebrate after years of misery and they have willingly grabbed hold of Rosa's version of me and made me a man who will go down in history.

But without Sonia standing beside me it feels worthless. Now I'm living with Sonia's mother, Cristina; sleeping in the bed that Sonia slept in for the first sixteen years of her life; waking up to the things that she held dear. When she left the house that morning to go in search of me with Alejandro, they had no idea of the trouble that would lead them to. Of our childhood friends, Sonia is in Ireland, Alejandro is in England, Miguel is dead; and though I have been free these last three months, I might as well be still in prison. In there, I had hope. Now what am I to do?

Rosa has been spared. She is still here living her life and she is prepared to help me to live mine, and all I have to do is allow it to happen. Her proposal on my return to Ireland seemed preposterous. I love Sonia and Rosa has always loved Alej.

'Enrico, think about it,' she said. 'Sonia and Alej are not coming back. You and I will never love anyone else in the way that you love Sonia and I love Alejandro, but we have to think of our own lives. Perhaps I'm being selfish. You can live your life alone here and probably thrive as the town hero, the toast of everyone, but for me and Cristina, it's harder. Even now in 1976 with Franco gone, and with Spain trying to put itself back together, it is a dangerous and lonely place for women living on their own. If I could be with you, I could be someone here. Together we could run the café for Cristina and help her in her old age. It's the only life that makes sense for you and I. Perhaps … we could find another way to love each other. We are good friends, and we understand each other. Think about it, Enrico.'

It was the longest speech I can ever remember hearing from Rosa. She has obviously thought long and hard about it. She sowed the seeds of my heroic deeds in my absence. She persuaded Cristina to offer me a place to live and work. Rosa is right. Living alone is a frightening option for a woman. Roberto promised me he would look out for Sonia's family and friends, and he tried, but those years when I was in prison were horrendous for Rosa and Cristina. Rosa mentioned days when they had been abused beyond imagining. I don't want to think what she meant by that.

I could manage alone in the future, but I would be lonely. Rosa is offering me, us, a better life. Something to live for at any rate.

I watch a plane fly over in the clear blue sky, and at the same time, the boats are sailing into the harbour with visitors. Tourists are beginning to flock to Andalucía for holidays. Cristina's café has become less a place for fishermen to eat at the end of the day and more a haven for tourists to sample flavours, while looking out at the Mediterranean Sea. Rosa says they have plans to extend the house to become a guest house in the future. They need a man around the place and I'm getting used to the routine of my days as Cristina's verbal punch bag. Almost on cue, she puts her head out the door and yells at me.

'Enrico Sanchez! I don't pay you to sit on your backside staring at the waves. I need barrels moved, so get in here and get working.' I jump up and walk towards Cristina.

'Even in prison I got more breaks than I get here, Señora Almez. You have me worked to my bones.'

'You're lucky to be here, Enrico.' Cristina wipes her wet hands on the back of my shirt as she shoves me in the door. 'If it wasn't for Rosa, you wouldn't have this job. You are the reason my Sonia had to leave this country. If she and Alejandro hadn't run off looking for you all those years ago, they would be here now. Poor Rosa would be married to Alejandro, and I wouldn't have to depend on useless men like you to help me.'

I stop and turn in the doorway. 'Do you think that I don't think about that every day of my life, señora? That I could be your son-in-law now? That I might not have had to spend more than half of my life in Franco's hellhole? I did what I did out of love and respect for your son. Miguel's death changed everything in all our lives. So, if you want to scream at someone, go point your finger at the man who pulled the trigger on your beautiful boy. That was not me.'

I walk around the back of the building and heave a barrel over on its side. As I roll it in the direction of the kitchen, Cristina follows me.

'So, Enrico. What will you do now? Will you marry Rosa? Will you give her back all the goodness that she has given you?'

When we reach the kitchen, I right the barrel of wine and turn to face the woman who has been one of the few constants in my life. Even though Sonia is not truly hers, she loved her as much as she could. Cristina lived through a loveless marriage and now she is asking me to do the same.

'I don't know if it would be fair to Rosa to marry a woman I don't love, who doesn't love me. How is that right, señora? You of all people know the agony of that. I love your daughter. Rosa loves Alej. How can we live a life of pretence?'

Cristina sits on a stool beside the wooden table and leans her elbow on the decades of niches in its fabric.

'Enrico Sanchez. The day my husband drowned was the day that I was freed from an endless life of abuse. Hugo's life may have been a sham, but I was left without a male figure in this house for protection. A Republican widow on her own was fair game for any Nationalist soldier passing by, but Rosa and I helped each other through. If it wasn't for her, I might not be alive now. Sonia has offered me a home in Ireland, but I don't want to go to live with strangers. This is my home.

'I have come to depend on Rosa for everything. Marry her, Enrico. You love each other as friends, and since you came back from prison, she has nursed you and fed you back to health. You will look after each other. After all that you have both been through, surely that life will be enough? This house can be your home. Unless Sonia ever comes back here, which is highly unlikely, I could leave all this to you and Rosa, and hopefully, to your children. I'm sure that this is what Sonia would want for this house. So, what do you say, Señor Hero of this town? Don't you think that we all deserve a little bit of happiness? Maybe not happiness but at least contentment?'

I lean my back against the whitewashed wall and fold my arms. I think about my time in Ireland with Sonia. She loved me and left me. Her commitments are not to me any more. I know from our weekend that she still loves me as much as I love her, but she's settling for Manus. So, perhaps I should settle for Rosa, a loving friendship.

'I will marry Rosa, señora, and I will be who you want me to be. We will never replace your son or your daughter in this place, but we will take care of you as best as we can. You say that you were better off having a man in the house with Hugo, but he had beaten you so many times without even knowing. He had abused Sonia almost every day of her life. She may have been the reason that her birth mother died but that was not her fault. You should have no regrets where Hugo is concerned. With his death you were saved, not lost. I will marry Rosa and I will do as you wish here, but we will never mention Hugo's death again.'

For some moments we stare at each other, the memories of the past chasing through our minds. She looks at me with her face scrunched in puzzlement or anger or both. I have been too outspoken of my hatred of Hugo. The last thing I need is to sow seeds of doubt in people's minds as to how he died.

Eventually, Cristina pulls herself slowly to standing. 'I hear foreign voices along the beach. Go and welcome them in this direction and turn on your best Andalusian charm. If you are to be family, then bring in the customers to your family restaurant.' She nods her head and smiles, and reaches over to me, kissing me on each cheek.

Perhaps this life will be all right. It's the best I can hope for with Sonia gone from me. I hurry towards the entrance to the café, and opening my arms to the English customers, I give them my widest smile with a twinkle of hope in my Andalusian eyes.

CHAPTER THIRTY-TWO

Sonia walked around the back of Eileen's house after work. She was cold and wet from her walk from the post office in the village, and so tired. Eileen's face beamed at the sight of her friend at the door.

'I thought you'd be putting Fiona to bed about now. Bart is upstairs reading Deirdre a bedtime story. This is a nice surprise.'

'I asked Manus to put her to bed tonight. I was catching up at the post office and I came straight from there.' Sonia sat down on her own chair in Eileen's kitchen. She had favoured it for all the years that she had been coming to her friend's house for chats and parties and news of crisis in their lives. This wasn't a crisis, not exactly, not if she played it properly. She had to tell Eileen the truth, though. She couldn't keep it to herself any longer.

Eileen was warming the teapot when Bart came into the kitchen.

'How's my favourite Spanish señorita?' he smiled at Sonia. Ever since she had married his friend Manus and brought him back to the fold of the business, Bart had nothing but good to say about Eileen's best friend.

'Hah. Señorita indeed. My señorita days are well behind me, Bart. Señora is what I am now and have been for many years.' Sonia felt her face heat up. She was very aware that she hadn't lost her looks and the years had been kind.

'You're the best looking woman Balcallan has ever seen, Sonia, and well you know it,' said Eileen. Although Eileen was still slim, she was getting wrinkles and her hair was a little greyer with each month. 'I should stay well clear of you, so I should. You're showing me up. Even my own husband fancies you.' With that remark, Eileen gave Bart a friendly smack across the head with the tea towel in her hand.

'Oh stop, the two of you,' said Sonia. 'You're embarrassing me.' And the three friends laughed together, easy in each other's company.

'Are you having tea with us, Bart, love?' asked Eileen.

'Well, I was going to stay in, but seeing as you have a gossip partner for the evening, I might head to the pub for a swift one. What do you think?' He looked at his wife, his eyes full of mischief.

'Go on with you so, but don't be gone till all hours.' Bart had the anorak on and was out the back door before she could change her mind.

Sonia envied her friends their easy ways with each other. These days she was constantly thinking about what her life would have been like if she had been married to Enrico Sanchez, instead of the hard work it took to be always nice to Manus. Since she came back from Dublin, it had been even harder. How could she take a lifetime of it? And now she had a huge problem to get over.

When the teacups were out and the tea was poured, Eileen came straight to the point. 'Come on then, Spanish señorita. Out with it. What's happened?'

'I told you. It's señora.' Sonia tried to smile but then she broke into a sob.

Eileen was over to her side of the table in a shot. 'Ah, Sonia. What's happened?'

'Oh, Eileen,' Sonia managed through her tears. 'I'm having a baby. I'm pregnant.'

Eileen pulled back. 'But Sonia, darling, that's fantastic news. Why the tears?' She reached over and pulled out a tissue and handed it to Sonia who blew hard before she spoke again.

'Oh, I know how hard you and Bart tried for another baby, Eileen. It seems a bit cruel for me to be having one without you.'

Eileen shook her head. 'Seriously, Sonia? Is that what you're crying about? No way.'

'I'm too old to be having a baby.' Sonia looked up at Eileen to gauge her reaction.

'Is there something else, Sonia?' Eileen frowned knowingly at her.

'You know me well.'

Eileen sat back down, but this time on the seat next to Sonia and took her hand. 'Nobody knows you and me, Sonia Dooley, as well as you and me. What is it?'

Sonia took a deep breath. 'It's not Manus's baby, Eileen.'

'Oh, Jesus Christ, Sonia.' Eileen's voice was deadpan, but Sonia could see the look of incredulity in her eyes. 'Whose baby is it?'

'Three months ago, Eileen, I went to Dublin to see my Spanish friends.'

'Oh, Sonia. You didn't sleep with some strange fella down there, did you? Do you even know who he was? Oh, God, girl. Listen, I'm glad you told me but you're not to tell anyone else. And Sonia. Tell me this. When was the last time that you … you know … *slept* with Manus? Please tell me it was recent.'

So that was it. She could get away without ever mentioning Enrico's name, even to Eileen.

'Two weeks after I came back, Eileen, I did a terrible thing. I had already missed my monthlies. I seduced Manus, even though there had been nothing between us for years. I was so scared. I knew that I needed him to believe he was the father of this baby. I got him drunk and pretended that I was also drunk, and we ended up … doing … it. He hadn't had a drink for so many years, and I persuaded him that one drink would do neither of us any harm. I said that I'd had a couple of glasses of wine with my friends in Dublin and had enjoyed it. It was over with quickly and without fuss. If Manus was suspicious, he never mentioned it. The next day he said that he would prefer not to have a drink again as the lack of knowing what he was doing the night before had scared him. I asked him did he remember making love and he said no. He actually apologized. Oh, Eileen. I'm the worst woman in the world.'

'Indeed, you are not, Sonia Almez. You made a mistake and that's all. With any luck, this baby will come out as dark-haired as you and not look very different to Fiona. Though her features are like her dad's. Whatever the baby looks like, you can say he or she is the spit of some uncle or cousin that Manus has never met. It'll be fine, Sonia; better than fine – it'll be wonderful. Another baby is exactly what all our lives need right now. It's the best news ever.' Eileen reached over and gave Sonia a bear hug.

Sonia pulled back a little. Eileen was being so wonderful with her. She would have to tell her the truth, and so, she did.

'Eileen, there is more to this. I know I told you that Enrico was free, but I didn't tell you that he came to Ireland. We had two beautiful days in Dublin together and then I had to walk away. He cannot stay here, and I cannot leave Fiona. I told him that we wouldn't stay in touch, so he doesn't know about the baby. It's complicated, but he is going to marry my childhood friend, Rosa, and he will work in my family restaurant for my mother Cristina. This is the only way that it can be, Eileen. I am so happy that I'm having Enrico's baby, but my heart is breaking every time I think that I might never see him again.'

Eileen pulled back and was quiet. She got up and began to wash out the cups at the sink. Eventually, she turned to Sonia. 'Thank you for telling me that, Sonia, but you must never tell another soul about it. I've never kept a secret from Bart, but I'm going to make an exception with this. If it had been some random person that you had met, that would have been different, but this baby's background should never be mentioned after tonight, for your sake and Manus's and Fiona's. You're having Manus's baby. If he finds out the truth of this baby's fathering, it will wreck him. Only you and I know the real truth, so let it stay this way.'

Sonia got up and the friends embraced each other. 'Thank you, Eileen,' said Sonia, but she had a feeling that she had broken something in their friendship, something that might not be fixed. 'Good night. See you soon.'

Sonia walked home to her husband and daughter, clutching her secret to herself. The most beautiful thing that could happen was that she was having a baby that was made by her and Enrico, but she knew that she could never tell that to anyone else ever again.

CHAPTER THIRTY-THREE

1995

On the night before Maria's nineteenth birthday, Sonia lay in bed staring into the dark. The years without seeing Enrico had been turbulent years in Sonia's life. Their daughter, Maria, was wild and wonderful. Sonia loved every dark strand of hair on her beautiful head, and was well aware, that in trying to make up for her lack of a father, she had spoiled her youngest child.

Enrico never knew he had a daughter, but Manus knew from early on that Sonia had tricked him into believing that Maria was his. She and Eileen had not predicted how easy it would have been for Manus to find out about Enrico's visit. He still had friends in Dublin from his building days, he told her, when she was seven months pregnant. She had been seen with her Spanish man. Manus had sat her down very quietly and told her what she should do.

'I'd like you to turn around and go back to Spain. You've ruined my life and I want no more to do with you. It's easy now,' he had said. 'Franco is dead, and there's nothing stopping you, but you can leave Fiona here with me.'

Sonia stared at him like he was mad and then she had stood up and continued to make the meal and said nothing. They were the last words of any significance that Manus had ever uttered to her. He had left her in the grand bedroom that he had carved with his bare hands so lovingly and gone to the smallest room in the house with his few belongings. This night, nineteen years ago, when Sonia had been in labour in Letterkenny hospital, he had gone drinking.

For the first years, he had continued to look after his darling little Fiona, but when his daughter became a teenager, Manus had slowly rolled himself into a drunken stupor from which Sonia was sure there was no return. Poor Maria grew up calling him daddy, but never getting any recognition for her attempts to gain his attention. Any kindness left in Manus Dooley was kept only for his daughter, Fiona, and later, for his son-in-law Gerry, when Fiona married and moved into her new home.

Eileen and Bart had tried to keep Manus from falling apart but their attempts fell short of fixing their friend's broken heart. He lost his half of the business once more, and although Eileen blamed Sonia for his downfall, she still allowed her old friend to work in the post office, and between them they looked after Maria.

Sonia had tried so hard to make things bearable for her girls. They were ten years apart but very close. Fiona was often the only one who could get Maria to behave when she went off the rails, but lately her second child had been getting better. She had knuckled down over the last few months and studied for her exams and Sonia was quite sure that even with her bad beginnings she would do very well when the results came out. Maria was clever, but she didn't always use her sharp brain to help her academically. More often than not, she came into her best when she was getting out of scrapes that she had let herself get mixed up in.

Sonia was looking forward to that day. She had made a chocolate cake, Maria's favourite, and iced it with the words *Happy 19th Birthday, Maria.* They would make it a special day. She had taken the day off from the post office and …

It was still the early hours, but Sonia was sure she heard the click of the back door. She slipped her feet over the side of the bed and reached for her dressing gown and slippers. She went downstairs and opened the back door in time to see her younger daughter's familiar frame against the backdrop of the sunrise in the fields at the back of the house. Where could she possibly be going at this time of the morning? She was about to call out to her but then decided to let her go. Wherever she was going she would have seen the cake in the kitchen that her mother had stirred her love into and would come back.

By seven o' clock that evening Sonia arrived at Fiona's house distraught with worry.

'Hiya, Mam. I was on my way round to you. I thought we were going to have the birthday cake at home.'

Sonia walked past her into the hall and began speaking a mile a minute. 'I can't find her, Fiona. I've looked everywhere, and I've asked any of her friends that I know of. I didn't want to worry you, but I had to come. She's gone, Fiona. Her rucksack is missing and lots of her favourite clothes and shoes.'

'Slow down, Mam. What do you mean? Where would she be gone? She can't be. I know she can be a little brat when she wants to be, but she'd never go away without telling *me*. Come in and sit down and we'll talk about it.'

Sonia followed her daughter into her lovely new kitchen with all her gadgets and state-of-the-art cooking equipment.

'As far as Gerry is concerned, nothing is ever good enough for his beautiful Fiona,' said Sonia, smiling now that she was with her calm, practical daughter. 'Unlike Eileen's poor Deirdre. Your friend should never have married that strap of a man who got her pregnant on their first date.' Sonia's mind was glad to be elsewhere after the worry of the last few hours looking for Maria.

'At least he stood by her, Mam, which is more than most men would have done.' Fiona always saw the good in everyone.

Sonia didn't envy Deirdre and Rory McGee their loveless marriage, but maybe they would make a go of it. She had hoped that would happen for herself and Manus –but look where that had got her.

That was it. Perhaps Manus had said something awful to Maria after all these years, on her nineteenth birthday, marking it in a bad way for her. Would he really have stooped that low she wondered?

'What are you thinking about, Mam? I've asked you twice if you wanted a cuppa.'

'Sorry, Fiona. I'm trying to work out what's happened to your sister. I know she's been hard work over the last few years, but I thought she was settling down. She's worked hard lately for her Leaving Certificate exam. You don't think your dad said something to upset her, do you?' Sonia sat back in her chair.

'Like what, Mam? They never talk to each other. Why would Dad choose today to say something to Maria?' Fiona stopped making the tea and stared hard at her mother. 'What's been going on in the house that I don't know about?'

'Nothing, Fiona. Nothing unusual anyway. Manus and Maria haven't even seen each other as far as I know for a long time. Maria makes sure that she's well out of his way when she's coming and going.' Sonia needed to change the subject before it started to get dangerous.

'Why? Do you think Maria might have challenged him, Mam? About why he never acknowledged her? Do you think she might have been asking him was there more to it than her birth coinciding with the breakdown of your marriage?'

Sonia knew her face was burning. Did Fiona know more than she was letting on? Had Manus said something to her? Maybe when he was drunk? But she would have tackled Sonia about it, she was sure. Fiona was all about honesty at all costs. That was why Sonia had never been able to let her know that she had lied to her about Maria since the day her sister was born.

'No, Fiona, you're right. As I said they haven't even seen each other. He can't have been responsible. I mean, not responsible but …'

'Responsible or not responsible for what, Mam? After all these years, what could Dad have said to Maria? C'mon, Mam. I'm a grown, married woman. What is it?' Fiona sat down and ignored her earlier offer of tea for her mother.

Sonia was cornered. She needed to tell Fiona, but she knew that the deception of all these years would make her daughter very angry. She had no choice now though. Maria was missing, and they had to find her and that meant being honest. 'Okay, love. I'll tell you.' Her voice was shaking. 'There is a good reason why your father hates your sister, and why he hates me.'

Fiona stared at her mother. Sonia knew that Fiona had asked her many times over the years why her father had changed from a loving, caring father into a drunken man prone to violent outbursts. The father that Fiona had known as a child was hard-working and always had time for his family. After Maria was born everything had changed. Fiona had suffered. Maria had suffered. Sonia had been miserable. Manus had probably suffered the most. She would have to be totally honest and tell Fiona exactly what she had done and take what was coming to her.

'When I lived in Spain, I was engaged to a man called Enrico Sanchez.'

'You left Spain when you were seventeen, Mam. How could you have even had a steady boyfriend, never mind been engaged?' Fiona was smiling now, expecting her mother to tell her that she had been holding a candle for some childhood sweetheart.

'Enrico and I were promised to each other. There was never any talk of anybody else. When my brother was shot, Enrico was eighteen. He wanted to avenge Miguel's death. He got himself into trouble and spent more than half his life in prison under Franco. When he was freed, he came to look for me, Fiona, but by then I had given up waiting for him. Your father had asked me so many times, and I was so lonely, so I married him, and we had you. We were happy enough. I loved Manus enough to be married to him. We were good to each other.'

Fiona looked like she was on her guard, waiting to hear about some disaster. 'And when he came to look for you? When was that?'

'Almost twenty years ago, or so, and we were together … for a weekend. He wanted me to come back to Spain with him and with you, but I couldn't do that to Manus, or to you. You and your father adored each other. So, I came back and …'

'And you had Maria? And my father couldn't bear to look at the child that came from another man?'

Sonia couldn't hold the tears any longer. She was devastated, and she knew by Fiona's look how angry she was. She had never seen such darkness in her daughter's face. 'Oh, Fiona, I'm so sorry. It's been so hard, but Manus made me swear that I would never tell you or anyone else. He didn't want the shame of being a man whose wife had strayed with another man. I promised him, Fiona. I couldn't tell you.'

Fiona was on her feet. 'So you're telling me now, when I'm twenty-nine years old, that my mother and father have been living in a world of lies for nearly twenty years. Actually, more than that. You married poor Dad because he was a handy substitute for the man you had left behind in a prison in Spain. Dad could stand in until the bold Enrico was freed and came running to save his Spanish childhood sweetheart. You never loved my father.'

The chair screeched as Sonia came around Fiona's side of the table and clutched her daughter's shoulder. 'I did love Manus. I knew he was an alcoholic when I first met him, but he chased after me for ten years, and he didn't drink in all that time. He built up a business with Bart and a house for us. I told him over and over that I was waiting for Enrico. Eventually, he gave in and stopped pestering me, but he started drinking and his life fell apart. I couldn't bear to watch him, and I felt guilty that he was drinking because of my rejection. So, I went to him and—'

Fiona pushed her mother away from her. 'And you saved him from himself with your pity and you took care of him … and lied to him.'

'I never lied to your father. Not back then. He knew how I felt, but he accepted it, and for years it worked. We managed to enjoy each other's company and we had a good life. If Enrico hadn't come to Ireland, perhaps things would have been different.'

'Perhaps? Are you mad? Of course things would have been different. We would have had a great life and my father wouldn't have drowned himself half to death in a vat of whisky.'

'Something would have triggered it eventually, and Eileen agrees with me that your father's drinking is because of an illness, not because of Maria. He had this before I met him …'

'But he had it under control until you wrecked his head. What did you do when you came home? When you realised you were pregnant? Did you shag my father so he would think that Maria was his?'

'Fiona! Don't use words like that.'

'Why not? It's true. You couldn't exactly call it making love now, could you? Hang on. Did you say Eileen knew about Dad? Did Eileen know all about your little secret? You told her, but you couldn't tell me.'

'Of course, I couldn't tell you when you were a child, Fiona, and I had already told Eileen before your father made me promise not to tell anyone.'

'You can't seriously be sitting there saying that this is my father's fault. You ruined his whole life, Mam, and mine with it. I lost my proper dad the day that you ran off with your Spanish lover.'

'Oh, Fiona, I'm sorry, but Enrico and I should have been together from the start.'

'Don't be ridiculous, Mam, you were only kids. A seventeen-year-old girl doesn't make promises that she's expected to keep for the rest of her life.'

'I loved him, Fiona. The same way that you love Gerry.'

'Except that *you* had children from two different men and expected the world to believe that we were sisters.'

'You *are* sisters, Fiona. Of course, you are, and you love Maria. You always have, and what I've told you can't change that. You have to help me to find her, Fiona. I'm so worried about her.'

'You know what I feel like doing, Mam? I feel like throwing you out that door and never letting you back in. I want to tell you to look for your wayward daughter yourself; that I don't want anything to do with you.'

'You can't do that, Fiona. I gave it all up for you, my previous family and my life in Spain. I gave up Enrico and stayed here. I never even went back to see my mother in case I met Enrico again and stirred up who Maria really was.'

'Well, you should have gone. You might as well have, for all the good that your staying did for Manus. My poor father, and all those years he never told on you. He took all the blame for his drinking on himself and never told the world that you were the cause of it all.'

'I did not turn your father into an alcoholic, Fiona. It's inside him. It always has been and there's nothing that me or your poor granny or anyone could have done to change him.'

'And my poor sister. Maria must have always known that she was the cause of Dad's misery. He was always so mean to her, and you spoiled her to make up for it. A fine pair of parents you two were, and now she's done a runner. And do you blame her? She must have overheard a conversation or something. Have you and Dad had an argument lately that Maria might have overheard?'

'We have not. Myself and Manus haven't said a word to each other for years, except when we're in company and we have to try to be polite. When we're at home I make his meals. I clean up after him in between my work hours. He still pretends to go to work, and he sleeps at home when he's not too drunk. Maria would never have heard any of this from me, but she may have heard it from Manus. He might have snapped after all these years.'

'And would you blame him?'

'Yes, actually, I would. It was never Maria's fault that she was born into that house, and he's made her life a misery since the day she could sit up and take notice.'

'No, it isn't Maria's fault. There's no doubt whatsoever as to where the blame falls for this mess.'

Fiona moved towards the cooker and put the full kettle on the boil and Sonia sat down on the chair that she had left. Fiona stood over the kettle with her back to her mother and said nothing while Sonia mulled the situation over in her head, trying to work out how she could make all this any better. Maria was gone somewhere. Something had filled her mind with such a loathing for her family that she had packed her bag and left them. But to where?

A few minutes later Fiona set a cup of tea in front of her mother.

'Thank you,' said Sonia, trying to come up with something more to add. 'Are you going to help me look for her? Maria. We can't leave her to be by herself.'

'She's nineteen. She's allowed to leave home if she wants to.'

'But she has nowhere to go, Fiona. She'll be out all night. She knows nobody outside Donegal.'

'Yeah, well, we'll start with her friends here in Balcallan. I'll make a list and you can take half. If we've no luck by tomorrow morning, then we'll … go to the Gardaí.'

'Thanks, darling. I knew you would understand.'

'Understand? Are you bloody well joking? I understand all right … That my long-suffering saint of a mother, who is pitied by all and sundry the length and breadth of Balcallan, is actually an out-and-out floozy, and in shaming her husband all those years ago, she wrecked his life and that of my poor little sister. I *understand* that you couldn't keep your hands off a man who wasn't your husband. I *understand* that while bringing us up to believe that honesty was everything in life, you were lying about everything that was important in our lives. I *understand* that somehow my beautiful little sister has somehow learned about her background and run away from the wreckage. So yes. I'll be helping to look for the poor girl, but no, I do *not* understand what you were thinking of, or why you would do such a deceitful thing to us all.'

Sonia barely made it to the kitchen sink before she threw up. She was still retching when Fiona walked over to a drawer in the corner and pulled out a notebook and a pencil, completely ignoring her mother's distress. She wrote down three names before she came to a stop. Then she handed it to her mother who was sitting back at the table, shaking. Fiona filled a cup with water and banged it down on the table in front of her mother. She sat down beside Sonia.

'I can't think of anyone else. Maria chopped and changed her friends to suit the weather when she was a kid, and she's been so moody over the last years that she lost any friends that she had.'

Sonia spoke, her voice breaking as the aftermath of her retching tried to right itself. 'I don't know any more of her friends' names now, Fiona. I've already been to two of those houses. You know, she wasn't miserable this last year or so. She worked hard for her exams and there was something or someone that was making her happy. I asked her one night was it a boy that she had met, but it was the one time of late that she bit the head from me and told me to mind my own business, but something was definitely making her happier for a while.'

'Okay. You go home and wait there and see if she turns up. I'll go and knock on this other girl's door and come back to you when I'm finished. If I hear nothing by tomorrow morning, I'll go down to the Garda station and report her missing.'

CHAPTER THIRTY-FOUR

Enrico

Rosa is sitting up in bed with her pillows propped up around her. She has a book open, but her concentration is not on the words on the page. I'm sitting at the end of her bed with my feet up, reading the newspaper.

'Your feet stink, Rico. When did you last wash?' Rosa's words come out slurred. The side of her face is so badly dropped it's hard to recognize her. My smiling wife, so full of laughter before, looks and sounds like an alien when she tries to speak; her contagious good humour is almost gone. When Rosa laughs now, people around her freeze, scared by the sound that comes from her shrunken mouth.

'Nothing wrong with you, woman, if you can still nag me like that. I had a wash at Christmas, and I'll have another at Easter if you leave me alone. The one good thing I can say about General Franco is that he was never fussy about my hygiene all those years I was his guest in his five-star hotel.'

I turn the page of my paper. 'Speaking of Franco, look at this, Rosa. They're pulling down the monuments to that monster. He'll be turning in his grave. In a few weeks, when you're feeling better, we'll go to watch one of the destroying ceremonies. I'd love to get the chance to kick his face in as he falls to the ground. A lump of stone is all he ever was.'

'A lump of stone didn't do the damage that he did, but let it go, Rico. I've told you so many times, don't let him eat up any more of your life. Listen, it's stifling in here. Do you think you could help me to dress and carry me outside to sit on the terrace?

I'd love Paulina to see me up and about when she comes home from school. I promise to sit around the back, and I won't scare away the tourists.'

I concentrate hard to take in all that Rosa says to me. It's a long speech, and it's difficult for her to get it all out and even more difficult for me to translate it into something I can understand. Sometimes when I get it wrong, Rosa gets so frustrated, and the doctor told me to keep her as stress-free as possible. That could bring on another attack, she says, and Rosa might not survive a second stroke.

'Okay, Rosa, love. Let's do this. Slowly and carefully, all right? First, I'm going to tell your cousin Alba to start getting the tables ready for lunch and I'll come straight back to you. Five minutes.'

I slide off the bed and walk towards our bedroom door. Well, Rosa's bedroom now. She needs so much room to make her comfortable that we decided that I should move to another room. I feel very guilty that I enjoy not having to share a bed with Rosa. I grew to love her more with every year, but not in the way that a man should love his wife. In my head it's still only Sonia. Rosa probably knows, but we rarely discuss it, I'm sure she still pines for Alejandro. In the early years we tried to make that part of our marriage work. We were ecstatic when Paulina was born. Afterwards, though, it was more and more difficult for me to perform in that way, and now I'll never be expected to again, but what a price we're paying. Poor Rosa is as good as lost to me.

'Rico.' Rosa calls me back as I get to the door, and I turn around. 'Rico, I'm sorry you have to suffer this. So sorry.'

I shake my head. 'Rosa, how many times have I told you that you are never to be sorry for having a stroke? You didn't bring it on yourself.'

'It was my idea for us to get married, Rico. I thought that you needed looking after when you came out of prison, and I wanted to help to put you back together again. I thought together we could help Cristina, and now …' She leans back, exhausted by her attempts at speech.

I take a deep breath and lean against the doorframe for support. 'And now, Rosa, we get to look after you. It's your turn to be minded. You gave, and now you have to take.'

We look hard at each other and drink in each other's strength as we have done so often over the years. 'You're still my rock, Rosa. Nothing changes that. Even today, when you want to put little Paulina's wellbeing over your own comfort, shows that you are still there for us.'

'Will you manage on your own, Rico? Will you manage Paulina?' Rosa lies back against the pillows, breathless after her outburst.

I know there's no answer to that. I'll never manage the way Rosa wants me to manage. I'll never have her strength, her good humour, her determination.

'I think Cristina's calling me my love.'

'Go, Rico. She'll get upset if you leave her alone too long. Her blindness is so hard for her. Frightening. She actually gave out to *me* this morning.'

'First Miguel, then Sonia, then Hugo, along with my mother. And now you. Everyone leaves me,' Cristina had said.

Rosa smiles wearily at the memory. 'As if we were leaving her on purpose.'

Rosa laughs, and I too laugh loud and hard as I run towards Cristina's anxious voice to help calm her.

When I return to help Rosa up, she is sleeping off her medication. She is eerily quiet, and I put my fingers to her wrist. When I feel her weak pulse, I'm reminded of what little time we have left with this paragon of a woman who saved my life.

Six weeks later, Cristina gets her wish to join her family. She falls down dead from a heart attack, two days after her beloved ally, Rosa, eventually succumbs to her own illness.

I call Eileen in the hope that she will bring Sonia home for their funerals, but the news that she gives me leaves me grieving in a way that I never thought possible. Sonia is busy trawling the streets of Dublin looking for our own beautiful daughter.

How could she have kept a daughter a secret from me all these years? I try to be there for Paulina, the daughter I've always known about, but I'm so angry at the loss of the daughter, Maria, that I never knew existed. And now she is missing, so perhaps it's too late.

CHAPTER THIRTY-FIVE

Two years after Maria disappeared, Sonia still woke up every morning in a daze. She had been to Dublin with Fiona many times since last year, after it was reported that Maria had been spotted in a café in O' Connell Street. Every time they came back, they had been devastated all over again. Sonia had even been in touch with Enrico. She had heard that Enrico now knew about Maria from Eileen, and she thought that somehow Maria might have found out about him and gone to look for him.

She knew he had married her childhood friend Rosa soon after he left her in Ireland, and that they had a child called Paulina, but poor Rosa had died two years ago, along with Cristina, and Enrico was alone with his daughter.

Enrico had come to Dublin as soon as he got her letter and they had met in the same hotel as before. He had been so angry with her at first for keeping their child a secret from him, but after a while he caved in, and they had spent another beautiful weekend together. This time Sonia had promised to come back to Spain with him as soon as she had worked out where their daughter was. She couldn't take any more of living with Manus. In fact, she thought that he might even be better without her.

Fiona was kinder with her than before, but there was still a coldness between them that might never be mended. Fiona had Gerry, and Eileen was caught up with her family and grandchild. They were still good friends who shared a history from their teenage years, but Eileen had never got over the deceit that Sonia had scattered in the wake of her and Enrico's weekend in Dublin all those years ago.

Manus was still drinking away his life and she was the last person who would be able to change that. Unless she left. That might help him to recover. Would anyone really miss her if she was gone? Fifty years of her life had been spent in Ireland, but Spain still called her. She wanted to go home.

'You and I have had enough of misery in our lives, Sonia,' Enrico had said before he left. 'It's time for us to be together and spend the rest of our lives looking after each other.'

'It's true, Enrico. I have spent my whole life trying to do the right thing by other people and it's got me nowhere. As soon as I find Maria and settle her, we'll go. She might even come with us.'

'My friend Roberto died two years ago, and he has left me his house in Benalmádena. We can live there, and nobody will bother us. I think that you can get a divorce from Manus if you want to, and we can get married.'

'Divorce might be legal in Ireland now, Enrico, but I couldn't drag Manus through the courts after all we've been through. When I leave, I will go quietly and let the Balcallan tongues wag behind me. It will hurt Manus badly, leaving him to the gossips. I wish there was some way to …'

'You're right. We don't have to go through all that hassle, Sonia. It's time for you to do the things in your life that you want to do, not the things that you feel that you have to do.'

Enrico was right, but Sonia had one thing she had to do before she left them all. She had to find out what had happened to Maria. It was tearing a hole in her heart that she couldn't get over. As the months and then years went by with no word, it was hard to accept what the police were saying. Maria was twenty years old now, and for whatever reasons, she had decided that she didn't want to come home. Sonia adored her daughter, and she knew that Maria had loved her. That was what made it all so difficult. Maria *had* loved her, but it seemed she had rejected her mother and Fiona for another life. No matter how much Sonia had given her daughter it hadn't been enough.

Fiona was leafing through the local paper when the doorbell rang. Looking out through the sitting room window, she was shocked to see a Garda car parked outside and two Gardaí she knew from the local station standing on the doorstep. She rushed to open the door to them.

'Mrs Martin?' asked the taller of the two.

Fiona stood stock still.

Something's happened to Gerry, she thought. *Oh please, God no.*

'Can we come in?' asked the other Garda.

'Of course, sorry.' Fiona stepped aside and followed them through to the kitchen.

'Let's sit down, Mrs Martin.'

'Of course, sorry.' She sat, and they followed her example.

'Mrs Martin, it's about your sister, Maria.' The younger Garda – Fiona couldn't remember his name – looked like he might be about to cry. 'I know we should be talking to your mother, but I've heard she's not been well, so …'

Fiona was so relieved to hear that Gerry was okay. And here they were saying that they'd found Maria too. Her smile filled her whole face, and she reached over and patted his hand.

'Oh my God, you've found her. Oh, thank God. Where is she? Did you bring her home? Is she all right?'

Both Gardaí shuffled uncomfortably in their seats.

'I'm so sorry. There's no easy way to tell you this.' The younger fella was talking again. What was it his name was?

'We've found a … girl that fits Maria's description, Mrs Martin. The girl was found dead in a squat in Dublin, having overdosed on heroin. I'm … so sorry, Mrs Martin.'

Fiona sat still in her chair. 'You're wrong, Jimmy,' she said to the older Garda whom she had known most of her life, but who was now telling her something that was completely alien. 'It isn't Maria. Maria loves life. She's wild, but she enjoys living, so she would never do that to herself. This girl that you've found, where is she?'

'In Dublin. In a hospital morgue.' Fred. That was the young fella's name. A silly name for a Garda, Gerry had said when he'd turned up in the village.

'Mrs Mar— Fiona,' continued Jimmy. 'We need someone to go to Dublin. You know … to …'

'Yes, I'll drive down this afternoon.' Fiona couldn't believe how calm she was being, but it was all wrong anyway. They had gotten it all wrong and some other family was going to have to go through all that heartbreak.

'We'll tell them to expect you. We're so sorry.'

All the way to Dublin, Fiona convinced herself that it wasn't Maria, because it couldn't be her. Maria was too strong. She was too full of life to be—

When she was finished with the business of looking at this poor girl, she would resume her search for her missing sister, her beloved Maria. There had to be something they hadn't thought of, somewhere they hadn't looked. If anyone could feel their way to Maria, she could. Two years was so long. She must be ready to be found.

'I'm coming Maria. I'll find you. I'll bring you home.'

CHAPTER THIRTY-SIX

Fiona and Gerry let themselves in the back door of her parents' house. There was no sign of Manus's destruction through the kitchen, so she thought he must still be out. She hoped he wouldn't come home that night upsetting Sonia any more than was necessary. They quietly crossed the kitchen into the sitting room where Sonia was lying on the couch fast asleep.

Fiona sat on the chair facing her mother. It would be the hardest night of her life, waking her mother to the news that her youngest daughter had been found. The news that they had clung to hearing someday was that Maria had been found alive and well in Dublin or somewhere, and she had wanted to stay clear of Manus and that was why she had stayed away. Now Fiona was going to have to tell her mother that her daughter's overdosed body had been found in a dirty drug users' squat in Dublin.

'Will we leave her sleeping for now, do you think?' whispered Gerry – always a man who wanted an easy life. 'We'll make us all some dinner in the kitchen here and let her wake up naturally.'

'No, Gerry.' Fiona wasn't whispering. Her voice was monotone. She had hardly spoken at all since she had identified her little sister's body in the morgue. 'I have to tell her before himself comes charging in. In fact, I wanted to see if we could move her over to our house for a while. No doubt Dad will be shouting the odds here, saying horrible things about my poor sister who never did anything to him except remind him of his wife's infidelity, as if that was Maria's fault. His ranting will make things ten times worse for Mammy.'

'Okay so,' said Gerry. If he was thinking that he didn't want his mother-in-law staying in his house indefinitely, then he never said a word. 'That's probably for the best.'

Sonia's eyes opened slowly, and she took in her familiar surroundings and sat up suddenly when she saw she had company.

'Ah, Fiona love. And Gerry. This is a lovely surprise. How are you?' Then she took in the look on their faces and she stopped. 'What, Fiona? What has happened?'

Fiona moved over beside her mother and turned her to face her. She looked to her husband and caught his eye, taking from him the strength she would need to tell her mother. How could she say it? No matter what she said it would change nothing.

'Mammy.' She took Sonia's hands in hers. 'We were in Dublin today. The Gardaí called me. They had terrible news, Mam.' She couldn't get the words out. She couldn't tell her mother this.

The back door burst open on them, and Manus came crashing through to the sitting room. Fiona looked up at her dad to try to take in what level of drunkenness he had reached. He was glassy-eyed and red in the face but standing straight.

'Ah, Fiona, my girl, and Gerry too. Isn't it lovely to see the pair of you.' He was barely slurring his words. If you didn't know him, you might think he was only a bit tired. 'Are you here for the dinner? But sure, there's no smell of food at all from the kitchen. We'll have to have a drink or two, Gerry, while we're waiting.' Manus sat down heavily on the spare armchair in the corner.

Gerry looked over at his wife and rolled his eyes and shook his head. Sonia hadn't taken her eyes from her daughter. Fiona wondered if she had taken in what she had been told. Did she understand what was happening?

'G'wan there, Gerry and pour us a few swifts. What's with the pair on the couch anyway? You'd think someone was dead or something.' Still nothing happened. Manus stood up, unsteadily now. 'Jesus, I don't know what's wrong with the lot of you. I'll get the bloody whisky out myself.'

Fiona squeezed Sonia's hands. 'Mam,' she said softly. 'Maria's gone from us. She was taking drugs and she overdosed.' Fiona burst into tears and put her head on her mother's shoulder. She could feel Sonia shaking her head, then she heard a noise come from her, a gentle whimper, as Fiona's words began to take shape in her mind.

'No,' her mother said. Then 'no, no, no,' over and over, and the women held onto each other and cried as if their hearts would break.

Manus turned back and handed one of the filled tumblers to Gerry. 'Drugs, is it?' he said. 'Sure, what else would that one have done, with what she came from? Probably been prostituting herself around the city for the last couple of years to pay for her dirty habits.'

Gerry slammed the untouched drink down on the coffee table, shocking Sonia and Fiona into pulling away from each other and looking over in time to see Gerry pushing past his stunned father-in-law and knocking him back into his chair.

'How dare you, you young strap.' Manus went to get up from the chair but caught sight of Gerry's discarded glass on the table and settled for that instead. 'What in the name of Jesus is going on with those two?' he asked, then sat back in his chair and knocked back the large whisky.

Gerry lifted Fiona gently away from her mother and helped her into standing. 'Come on, love. Let's get your mam over to ours. You can come back later and get her things.'

Fiona in turn put her arm under her mother's, to help her up. Sonia allowed herself to be led outside to Gerry's car and into the back seat where she lay down, still sobbing. 'No, no, Maria, no.'

A few days later, Fiona brought Maria's body back to Balcallan. Her beautiful baby sister was home, but instead of organising a party, they were having a funeral.

When Fiona came back from Dublin and sat Sonia down to tell her that Maria was dead, that she had taken her own life, her mother felt rejected once more. Wherever Maria had been and whatever had happened to her, she had felt that taking her own life was easier than coming home to her mammy and asking for her help to sort out her problems.

The effort of organizing a funeral was too much for Sonia, and Fiona and Gerry had to do most of the work. She did manage to get in touch with Enrico though. He had come as fast as possible, but he was no match for the Irish way of burying their dead so quickly and he missed the funeral. He stood by her grave with Sonia and sobbed openly for the daughter he had never met. *A relative from Spain,* Fiona told anyone who asked about him. Manus never came to the church or the cemetery, which had the tongues of Balcallan wagging.

'Maria's father's poor heart is broken, and we all have different ways of grieving,' Sonia told anyone who asked after Manus.

Enrico begged Sonia to come back with him.

'We're not getting any younger,' he said, 'and enough time has been wasted in our lives.'

But he went home angry, following Sonia's declaration that Fiona needed her here. She had said no for the last time. Sonia had put her family before her own happiness again. Their separation was complete. But in the weeks and months after she buried her daughter, all Sonia wanted was Enrico's arms around her. She yearned for that touch. Nothing had changed the way she felt for him in all those years.

For a week Fiona practically lived by her sister's graveside, talking to her. Two years of talk. 'Why did you leave us

Maria? What could have been so bad that you couldn't face us? We loved you so much. Where did you go? Why did you hide? We tried so hard to find you, Maria. Where were you? Were you punishing us, Maria? Were you punishing yourself? Where were you …?'

Fiona sat on the grass beside her sister's grave asking her all these questions and telling her all the things that were good and bad in her life. By trailing back through Maria's time in Dublin, she had worked out that her sister had left Donegal because she was pregnant. That she had left her baby in the hospital and written a letter to say that she would be back for her as soon as she had sorted herself out.

'But you never sorted yourself out, Maria. Why could you not have trusted me? Or Mam? I was always there for you.' The grass was damp, but Fiona didn't care. She came here every day in all weathers. Perhaps she hoped that she would find some understanding of her sister's actions by sitting beside her.

She told her all about what they had found in Dublin after they had looked back into her past. 'We found your baby, Maria. Little Anna is such a dote. I feel like you've left a gift for me and Gerry. Thank God she hadn't been adopted yet. It's like she was waiting for us. We'll be thankful for her every day, but I wish it could have been different, Maria. I wish I could have watched you bring her up. I would have helped you.'

Fiona caught her breath and stopped for a moment. 'Gerry is completely in love with her. Everything is *Anna this* and *Anna that. Did you see what she did there, Fiona? Did you hear what she said there, Fiona?* He's gas. Oh, she's beautiful, and she's changed our lives all right, that's for sure. What's that poem you liked by Yeats? With the line in it about a terrible beauty – that was it. I will love every bone in her body, but I wouldn't have loved her instead of you, if the choice had been there.'

Fiona pulled herself up from the damp grass and smoothed down her clothes.

'Oh, Maria, I miss you. I always will, and I'm angry at the senselessness of it all. All you had to do was say, *I'm in trouble, Fiona*, and I'd have come running to you. Never mind Dad. Did you know he wasn't your dad, Maria? Did you guess? I never did. Not until Mam told me the day you went missing. She's lost since you died, Maria. I thought when I told her about Anna, her own granddaughter; that she would have bounced back, but even that wasn't enough to shake her. I don't think she's even registered what we're trying to tell her. She's lost so much in life: her brother and her parents; Enrico and her friend, Rosa; her home and her sense of belonging. I was so angry when I found out about her and Enrico. I thought she had set Dad on the road to ruination, but he was always sick, Maria. It was inevitable. She turned him down so many times before they got married and he knew where her heart lay. They both took on second best. What a sad life.

'But Dad and Mam gave me my life, and then Enrico and Mam gave us you. I loved every moment of our nineteen years together, sis. When I saw you dead in the morgue, I thought I would never stop crying, but I think Anna will give me strength to live without you. I hope she'll give the same strength to her granny. Mammy is wasting away. Losing you is killing her. She told me that it's awful watching Dad drink his life away, and she feels that she's done that to him. I'm trying to pull her back, because sixty-six is too young to give up on life. Though you gave up so early. Did you mean to do that? Was it an accident? Oh, Maria, my gorgeous baby sister, how did it all go so wrong for you? Drugs are a curse. Mammy says her father was an alcoholic. Is addiction in our blood? Perhaps you had no choice. Did you fall in with the wrong people?

'I'm going home to Gerry now and I'll see if I can get Mam out of bed. In a few days we'll be able to visit Anna again and one day soon we'll bring her home. I'm living for that moment. I'll never pretend to her that I'm her real mother, I'll tell her all about you, everything. I won't bring her here and tell her you're here, that would be too confusing. I'll keep you alive in the stories I'll tell her. I love you, Maria, and I'll be back again soon.' Fiona blew a kiss towards the headstone. Then changed her mind and blew a kiss towards the sky. She shook her head. The only place Maria was, was in her heart.

The rain had stopped, and the sun was trying to come back out as Fiona made her way out of the cemetery. She would have to make her life with Gerry, and now with Anna, without Maria and without the people her mam and dad used to be. She would be happy with her new family. It would be okay. It was getting easier. Maybe she could try to bring her mother back to her, and to lessen her father's drinking. There was still a chance that they could both pull something together for what could be another twenty or thirty years of life. The first ten years of Fiona's life had been lived in a house full of love and happiness. She would try to bring her parents back to that again.

Fiona and Eileen had never spoken much since Fiona had found out that Eileen had known about Maria's background but had never said a word to her. Now, with her worry about Sonia, Fiona felt she had no option but to meet up with Eileen and talk. They were sitting in a café in Balcallan and sharing a pot of tea.

'I can't seem to get through to her, Eileen. I've been trying to get her to come to Dublin with me to help look through the aftermath of Maria's life there. I've found something amazing, or *somebody*, actually.' Fiona was dying to share her news with someone other than Gerry. Her mother wasn't well enough to take in the news about Anna properly.'

'In Dublin? Was there a man after all?'

'Yes. Well, I don't know who, but there must have been some-body here in Balcallan. When my sister left here two years ago, she was pregnant. This is why she ran. Whether she ran to the father or away from him we'll never know, but she had a baby, Eileen. A little girl.'

Eileen reached over and clutched Fiona's hand. 'That's won-derful news, Fiona. Is there any way that we can see her? Do you know what happened to her?'

Fiona wasn't altogether comfortable with Eileen's familiarity, but her news overcame her feelings. 'It's better than that, Eileen. Anna, that's what Maria called her, was in a home and was fos-tered, but they couldn't have her adopted because they were looking for her mother. Maria had left a note saying that she was in difficulties, but she would be back to get Anna as soon as she could. It turns out now that if myself and Gerry would like to adopt her, we can. Gerry's been down to Dublin to meet her, and he's completely fallen in love with her. We've never been able to have a baby of our own, and Anna is beautiful. She's my niece and all we have left of Maria. We're going to adopt her, Eileen. Isn't that amazing?'

Fiona let her recent difficulties with her mother's best friend go, while she was so enamoured with the latest developments in her life, and she held Eileen's hand across the table.

Eileen was delighted with Fiona's news and what it meant for the childless couple. 'It's the best news anyone around here has had for such a long time, and is your mammy delighted? When did you tell her?'

'I'm not sure she's taken it all in. I don't know, Eileen, she's been so unstable since Maria died. Retiring from the post office was all very well, but since she lost that, she's had no focus in her life. I cook Mam and Dad's meals for them now that Mam has gone back home, and leave them in their house. I'm afraid that finding out that Maria had a baby; that she was pregnant when she left here and didn't feel that she could tell her own mother; that Mam's taking that as yet another rejection.'

'She shouldn't feel that, Fiona. I know she blames herself for Maria's leaving, but if Maria was pregnant, then really, it's the fault of the baby's father that she left, don't you think? Having Maria's baby around should be all that she needs to bring her back to us properly.

'I've been hard on her over the years about her and Manus, and I know that you two have had your differences over the last two years about Enrico, so maybe it's time for us to put this behind us and let Anna be a new focus for us all. I can't tell you how happy I am for you, Fiona, and for Gerry too. I know what it was like for us when we didn't have a baby for all those years. Then Deirdre came along at the same time as you, and it was like the world was a perfect place. Go home now, Fiona, and talk to Sonia. Tell your mam what you've told me.'

Eileen stood up and came around to hug Fiona. It was awkward, but it was a start. Things would get better for everyone.

CHAPTER THIRTY-SEVEN

Sonia slipped off her tiny shoes, smiling sadly at the blue ribbon that Fiona had woven through the edges with daughterly love. She looked around for a safe place to put them. There was a damp, mossy shelf below the rocky hillside. They would be far enough away from the crashing waves, but easily found before the sea claimed them, so that they would know what she had done. This part of the shore was notorious for its dangers. Nobody would be able to swim here and tackle the strength of these waves, unless they were hoping that they would be taken far out to sea, so far that they would never be found. The cold spray strengthened her resolve as she wandered closer to the edge of the water. She could taste the salt on her lips and the familiar smell of seaweed calmed her.

The moon hid behind the dark, racing clouds, and Tory Island was hidden from view. She shivered in her light red dress and the feel of the chilled sands beneath her bare feet. She would never see Tory again, but this was something she had to do. She had thought about it over and over. Last week, when Manus had drunkenly demanded his dinner, then had fallen asleep into it halfway through eating, and she had had to mop up the mess. Last night, when he had come into her room when she was undressing and had started to grope her. All she had wanted was Enrico's arms. Enrico's touch. She hummed a song she remembered from her childhood, something she had learned at school, when the world seemed such a hopeful place, where she and Enrico were to be together forever, and nothing could stop that.

Fiona was happy with Gerry. They would give Anna all the love she needed, but her granddaughter would forever be a reminder of the reason her daughter had left. Sonia could take no more of Manus or what their lives had to offer. She waded further into the freezing waves knowing that this was the only answer.

Eileen opened the door slowly and when she saw it was Fiona outside, she stood back to let her in. 'Fiona. It's yourself. Did you talk to your mam? I've the kettle on.'

'Eileen, I haven't come for tea. Do you know where Mammy is? Did you see her today? Was she here? When did you see her last?'

'Enough of the questions, for goodness' sake, girleen. She's probably gone for a walk, that's all. You know how she likes her walks. She'll be gone to the beach, below the dunes, even in this weather and at this time. Sure, you know your mammy could sit there for the night and forget what time it is.'

'No, no! She's not. She's not on the beach. I've looked. I've looked everywhere.' Fiona dropped a shoe on the ground and bent to pick it up.

'Why have you Sonia's shoes in your hands? Aren't they the ones you bought her?'

'That's what I found, Eileen. That's all I found, these shoes that I got her in Dublin. She never liked them. She said they were too flashy for Balcallan, but she wore them today. They're all sandy. They were on a rocky shelf in the hillside. Eileen, where is she? The shoes were put out of the way of the water, I think.'

'What are you saying, Fiona? What are you saying about the shoes? Why would Sonia leave her shoes on the beach? She'd never have come back barefooted, would she?'

'I've looked everywhere that she might be normally. Her car is at home in the driveway. Her handbag is in the house, with everything still in it. If she walked, she didn't mean to go far or to stay too long, but she hasn't come back yet, and it's pitch dark.'

'Ah, Fiona she'll be fine. Have you asked around? Look, you're getting all in a bother because you're thinking of the way Maria left us, but Sonia is not Maria. Your mam is one of the strongest women I've ever met. She's been to hell and back in her life and she's still always there for you and all of us. Now stand there and I'll get my coat and we'll go out and look together. She'll be around. She's probably stormed out of the house because Manus is upsetting her or something.' Eileen leaned in and grabbed her coat from the hall press and followed Fiona back out.

The next morning the boats were coming back to shore; each one as empty as the other. A neighbour walking the hills had seen Sonia walking barefoot on the beach the night before.

'I thought it was a strange time of the day and the year to be paddling,' he told the Gardaí that morning when the village went on high alert, 'but I walked on and thought no more of it. Sure, the Spanish woman was a little odd at the best of times, and she had definitely not been the full shilling since she lost her daughter. I'm sorry I didn't do more now, but …'

Every boat from Balcallan to Gortahork was out looking for Sonia. Or Sonia's body. Nobody could deny now that Sonia had decided that she couldn't take any more of what life was giving her. Eileen, Bart, Gerry and Fiona sat on the sand waiting for news. They had searched everywhere in the hope that Sonia had wandered off somewhere, but nobody had seen her. The only clue that they had about Sonia's whereabouts were her shoes that were left on the cliff and the man who saw her in the water. At some stage a boat would find her, or she would be washed up on the beach when the tide turned.

Bart touched Eileen on the shoulder and pointed to the man at the edge of the beach looking on at the proceedings. Manus was sitting on a rock with his arms folded around him and rocking back and forward. Bart stood and walked towards his old friend.

'Manus. How are you doing?' A stupid question he knew. Manus was crying and shaking. Bart sat on the rock beside him and put an arm around him. He thought Manus might push him away, but Manus turned his head into Bart's shoulder and sobbed.

'I drove her to this, Bart. I've been such a bastard to her for too many years. She was always honest with me. She never pretended to be someone she wasn't, but I loved her so much and I thought that I could turn her around. Until Maria came, I thought that was possible. I might as well have pushed her under the waves and drowned her myself.' Manus sniffed and looked in his dirty pocket and took out an old rag of a tissue. He blew hard and put it back in his torn coat. He was a wreck.

'Indeed, you did not drive her to this, Manus Dooley. She's not been well since Maria died. Her heart was broken, and there was nothing you could have done to change that.' Bart straightened Manus upright again and sat himself to face him. 'You and Sonia were wrong for each other. It was not your fault you fell in love with her, and it wasn't her fault that she met the other fella before you. If she hadn't had Maria, and if he hadn't come back looking for her, then maybe you might have made a go of it. I for one never thought we'd see hide nor hair of him again with all the shenanigans going on in Spain.'

Manus shook himself, as if the very thought of Enrico was enough to make him shiver.

'And poor Maria. She never asked to be brought into the world. I made every day of that child's life as miserable as I could, and if I'm responsible for Sonia's drowning, then I'm equally responsible for Maria overdosing in Dublin. She ran away from me because I hated her, and she couldn't take that, and why should she have to? I'm an out-and-out bastard, Bart. I should walk into those waves after Sonia. At least I would get to spend eternity with her, even if we weren't meant to be together here on earth.'

Bart stood up and looked down at the wreckage of his oldest friend. 'Enough of that this minute, Manus. Do you think that's going to help anyone here? Hasn't Fiona suffered enough without you adding to it, and do you think you're the only person around here who's full of guilt? Do you not know how hard it's been for me to look at you all these years drinking yourself half to death, messing up Fiona's and Maria's little lives? I've wanted to intervene so many times, but I was too stubborn. You had made your bed I said over and over to myself, and you could damn well lie in it. A right little shit of a friend I turned out to be. Got on with my own life while yours was falling apart.'

'Ah, Bart, sure you couldn't have done any good. Would you look at me this morning from the want of a drink? I'm shaking and sick and sweating. Every day is like this. Sonia and Fiona tried, but I was stubborn too. If my drinking hurt Sonia, then I used it as the perfect weapon. I ruined my mother's last few years too. Joined the rest of the men in my family. A right lot of heroes we are … the glorious Dooleys. Stupid, whisky-soaked brains, every man.

'Bart. Do you think it might be a mistake? Do you think she might have only gone away somewhere? The night before last, I … I did something terrible. I was mad drunk, but I remember some of it. I went into her bedroom, Bart, and I … Well, I'm not sure exactly what happened but …' And Manus started to cry again like he might never stop.

A shout went up from one of the boats coming into the shore and everyone on the beach ran towards the men dragging the boat in, but they didn't have Sonia.

'We found this,' said the man, his voice catching with the emotion of what he was giving to Sonia's family. 'It was caught on a rock near the hills,' and he handed a large piece of torn, red cloth to Fiona's outstretched hand. Fiona ran her fingers over the sopping fabric and nodded. She couldn't speak. There was no doubt in her mind that this was a torn piece from the dress that her mother had been wearing when she was last seen yesterday.

Manus was the first to speak. 'We'll go home, Fiona, love, and wait for more news.' And he put his arms around Fiona, and they walked away from the beach.

Fiona rocked her eight-year-old daughter on her lap and held her tight. She loved reading stories to Anna, but more than that, she loved to tell her stories about her mother and grandmother. Fiona had never lied to Anna about her beginnings in life, except for the endings of Maria's and Sonia's lives. That was too much for an eight-year-old to handle so she always told her that they were very sick and that they died. So far, Anna had always been okay with this. Other people she knew got sick and died. She had never known her mother or her grandmother, so it didn't mean too much to her about how they died.

'Another story, Mammy, please.' Anna was in her pyjamas, all ready for bed, but she had always been difficult to settle at night-time. Ever since they had brought her back from Dublin six years before, she had made bedtime a hassle. 'I want you to show me the Spanish dancing my granny learned you. Will I go and get her castanets? Will I put on the music?'

Fiona couldn't manage all these memories tonight. It was enough that it was her sister's anniversary, without Anna pushing her to think any more than she had to about her sister and her mother. Sometimes she wondered if they were both subject to depression, and if they were, would Anna have inherited this trait too? Her anxiety about going to sleep at night worried Gerry as well as Fiona. Only having one child was a problem in some ways. Her friend Deirdre had two girls, without a father around, and she never worried as much as Fiona.

'Not tonight, sweetheart. I'll stay upstairs with you until you sleep, though.'

'Will you stay upstairs all night with me, Mammy?'

'I'll try, love. Now let's go up.'

'Sometimes you say you'll stay upstairs, Mam, and when I wake up, you're not there. That's not telling the truth.'

Anna had made her first confession the week before with the rest of her class at school and was to make her First Holy Communion soon. She was all about the truth and never telling lies.

'Your friends don't have their mammies stay upstairs with them every night, Anna. I bet if I asked them, they'd say that they say *night, night* and that they go to bed like good little girls.' Fiona didn't want to push her with the religion thing, but she'd try anything to get a good night's sleep.

'I am a good girl, Mammy. Was my mammy a good girl? My mammy who had me in her tummy before she died?'

Fiona swallowed and tried to control her emotions. She hoped Gerry would be home soon. Tonight was not a night to be answering questions about her little sister's behaviour. But sure, what chance did poor Maria ever have to behave in the right way? When she compared the fathering that Anna got to what she or her sister had as children, then there was only one answer to her daughter's question about the mother she had never known.

'Your mammy was the goodest little girl in Ireland, Anna, and I loved her almost as much as I love you. And she always went to bed when she was told.'

That was definitely a lie. Maria was almost as bad as Anna at going to bed. The only thing that got her up the stairs was the appearance of Manus in the house, then Maria was gone up the stairs as quick as she could.

'Now. Get up the stairs and get into bed, you little scamp.' Fiona pretended to chase her daughter towards the stairs and her squeals of delight were like music.

If only she and Maria had had the glorious childhood that Anna had. If only her dad had been able to be kinder. Manus had left the house he had shared with Sonia and lived now with his brother in their dilapidated cottage; tending to his dying brother and never touching a drop of alcohol since the day he had found that his wife had drowned. He was a doting grandfather to Anna, although they both knew that they were not related by blood. If only Enrico had stayed in Spain. Would Sonia be still alive? But then there would never have been Maria or Anna. So many *if onlys* that could never have happened.

PART TWO

CHAPTER THIRTY-EIGHT

February 2020

Walking along the corridors of Malaga airport to the queue for passport control, Shona Moran breathed in the sense of freedom that was Andalucía. Away from the stares and pointing fingers of Dublin, she could enjoy the relaxation of not being known to the people who passed her by. Here, in Spain, she looked forward to shaking off the Irish judges and the begrudgers, who were not happy with her, Shona Moran, walking away free from Dublin's Criminal Courts of Justice.

Shona hoped she could lose that gripping fear of what might have become of her. She would never allow such things to happen to her again. She had had all the excitement she needed in life in her first twenty years, and since then, life had been quietly, boringly normal.

She was pulled from her thoughts by the sound of her young daughter pulling along her little Princess Jasmine suitcase.

'Mammy, can we go to the beach when we get there? And can we go to the water park?' Ruby was skipping and looked like excitement would explode in her. Shona looked over at Ruby's daddy, Tommy, and they laughed together. Shona and Tommy couldn't wait for this holiday too – their first together as a family. Extending Ruby's half-term for an extra few days would do her no harm.

'We'll get settled in this evening, Ruby,' Shona said, 'and tomorrow we'll decide on our plans.'

With only this in her mind, she smiled at the customs officer as she handed him her passport. He didn't return her smile. He looked at her photo and looked back at Shona. He typed a few words into a keyboard in front of him, shook his head and shrugged his shoulders.

'No,' he said, and gestured to another official.

'What's going on?' asked Tommy. Then two policemen appeared and apologised to Shona, whilst asking her to accompany them into a side room.

'Where are you taking my mammy?' asked Ruby, clinging on to her daddy's hand now.

Here it was again, Shona thought. It was never going to go away. She may have been found not guilty in Ireland, but from now on, no matter where she went, was the name Shona Moran going to be a noose around her neck waiting to be pulled?

'Por qué?' she asked. The two officers looked over at each other, a disbelieving look on their faces.

'You don't know why? You are Shona Moran. You must know why?' The shorter man smiled at her mockingly.

Shona closed her eyes and tried to blink back the tears. She knew that the only thing that she had been guilty of in her teens was falling in love with the wrong man: Jameel Al Manhal. But in the eyes of the Irish people, she had brought trouble to their shores. She had sat beside Al Manhal while he threatened, unknowingly to her, to blast a whole tram full of people to smithereens, and then she had fled with him to Wales, unwittingly becoming his alibi.

She had been sucked into believing that he was everything she thought she wanted. She trusted he was kind and understanding; passionate, in a way that even now, knowing who he really had been, made Shona sometimes miss him. Jameel had helped her to free herself from her addictions and made her see her own worth, and she would have followed him wherever he wanted her to go. Jameel – or Majid as she had discovered was his real name – had her besotted. She had almost let go of her whole family to be with him, even her gorgeous baby girl, Ruby. Somehow, Jameel made her accept that she would be better off in life without her family constantly making her feel guilty. He managed to persuade her that baby Ruby would be better off with her daddy; that Shona should move on and make her new life with Jameel. Until that day when she woke up and realised that it suited him better to be without her.

When Shona had seen his dead body thrown across that car bonnet, a part of her had broken. Even when she knew where he came from, knew who he was and knew how much he had used her, she had still missed him. Was it only that feeling that she had missed? Was it only the way he had made her skin burn with passion for him that she had pined for? She knew that all those feelings had been false, but they had felt as real as life itself.

That was all in her past, though, and now her life was all about Tommy and Ruby and building her life around them.

'What is the nature of your visit here, Ms Moran? Where are you staying and who are you seeing whilst you are here?'

'I am staying at this guest house,' said Shona, scrolling through her phone for the address of the place that Eileen had given her. She handed the phone to one of the men, who looked at it and keyed the words into a desk computer in front of him. The other man looked over it and dialled the number that was on it.

'Hello? This is the airport customs police here, señorita. I wonder could you help me with something? I have a young woman here who is saying that she is booked into your guest house from today. Can you verify that Shona Moran is staying with you? And for how long?'

Shona listened, straining to hear what the lady on the phone was saying, but she couldn't catch anything.

'So,' the officer said at last, putting down his phone. 'Señorita Daniela Sanchez says that you are indeed staying with her, along with Tommy Farrell and Ruby Farrell.' He smiled without letting the pleasure of it reach his eyes.

'And why are the three of you staying in this particular hostel? And for how long? As I asked earlier, what exactly is the nature of your visit?' The other man folded his arms, already looking bored. Perhaps he had hoped for a bit of excitement, an arrest of a woman of Shona's background. *Would this follow her all her life?*

'I was hoping to find some of my family. I'm adopted, you see, and a few years ago, I found my birth family in Donegal, in Ireland, but apparently my grandmother was from Malaga,' Shona explained. 'I'm hoping to find *her* family, and perhaps to meet some people who are related to me. My grandmother's friend in Ireland said that this was the last address she had for my grandmother. We plan to stay for a week.'

Shona wiped some perspiration from her face. It was hot and humid in the tiny office, but the men would probably think she was sweating because she was afraid. And she was a little afraid. Not for right now. Not of the two men in front of her, beginning to stand up now to get on with their evening. Shona was afraid of her future and how her recent past would impact on her and her family. Would it always be like this, because years ago, she had ended up in the wrong place at the wrong time with the wrong man?

The larger man stopped, his face scrunching up in remembrance of something. 'Your father, he is also a terrorist. Am I right? I remember reading about him in the newspapers. It was the Spanish connection that made it interesting, you know? An IRA man from way back, who had been hiding out in our beautiful Costa for almost twenty years.'

Shona stood up. She'd had enough. 'My father is Des Moran. A kind and good man, who brought me up and loved me all my life. The man that you are talking about, my *birth* father, is not my real father. I met him a few years ago. Once. I hardly know him, and I'm not and never have been a terrorist. I met up with the wrong person. I …'

She took a deep breath and battled to hold back tears. She was angry at the two gobshites in front of her and angry at herself. Fear had made her slate her birth father, who she loved. Jameel was in the past, but not her adored birth father, Danny O' Grady, who was, right now, serving a short sentence, most of it suspended, in Cloverhill Prison, for a small crime he committed against his will decades ago. She shook her head, shaking the tears away. Leaning her hands on the table, she looked up at the man nearest to her. 'Please,' she asked. 'Can I go now? I'm so tired.'

Shona hung her head. Those years had been the worst of her life, and she didn't think she could go through much more. She had stupidly thought that it was all behind her, but it would probably be here on the way back next week, and every other time she wanted to do something that other people would find easy, would be a mountain for her to climb.

The man nodded. 'Okay, Ms Moran, no need to be so upset. We are waiting for your suitcase to come back to us and then you will be free to go. Apologies for the inconvenience.'

As he finished speaking, a woman wearing plastic gloves that looked like they had spent a whole day going through other people's dirty laundry walked in dragging Shona's flowery suitcase behind her. She handed it to Shona with a look that followed the length of her body, obviously interested in what it was that made up Shona Moran.

Shona thought of the contents of the bag, now sullied by this horrible woman and her mucky gloves. Ruby's pretty sun dresses next to the dresses that Shona had bought in the hope of gaining Tommy's admiration. Tommy was the key to her future, and if she could persuade him that they should stay together, then her life would change. He could protect Shona; literally save her from her crazy self. She loved him, but not like she had loved before – not in an all-consuming passionate way. Shona Moran loved Tommy Farrell in the way that a woman should love and trust a man she wanted to spend the rest of her life with.

She had been a terrible mother, girlfriend, daughter – all-round bad person – and somehow Tommy was still here beside her. He said they would always be friends, but in the last year they had become so much more to each other. Shona wanted to be with the only person in the world that she trusted completely, and with whom she had fallen in love over their last few years of shared parenthood in a way that she knew was real. The hope of what the following week would bring carried Shona out of that awful office back to Tommy and Ruby, through the airport, into the taxi, and all the way to the guest house where she would spend the next week of her life in peace and quiet.

CHAPTER THIRTY-NINE

Enrico

I hate having to be grateful. They are being so kind, trying their best, and I'm a miserable old grump. There's a rocking chair in the corner of the terrace that has been bought especially for me. A coffee table stands beside it, at the exact height for reaching over for my drinks and my ashtray. They have thought of everything. A grab rail to get in and out of the bath. A ramp to make the front step more accessible. But all I want is to go home to my own house, where I've been living happily for twenty-three years. Here on the terrace, watching my daughter and granddaughter running their guest house and listening to their busy voices, I'm lonely.

Easing myself slowly into the chair, I sit back and close my eyes. *If my friend Roberto could see me now.* I open my eyes and look towards the sky.

'Good for you, Roberto,' I say. 'You went out like a bright, shining light: the great Roberto, saviour of the Republican people.' I smile. 'Hey, what am I looking up there for? With the badness we've notched up, they wouldn't let us near the place.' Instead, I shake my fist gently towards the ground and the gleaming floor mosaic, that one tile still broken after all these years.

'Abuelo! Move over there with your dirty old cigarettes and your smelly drinks. Do you know what time it is? You're making me sick!' My granddaughter, Daniela, is on the warpath.

'At least I've had eight hours of sleep. I'm entitled to get up and have my breakfast. Have you even gone to sleep yet? You're a waste of good young life. Your mother lets you away with murder, Daniela.'

I glare my granddaughter out. She gives up and goes to the kitchen. I haven't lost it. If I can tell Dani what to do – my daughter's only daughter – and get away without having my ear chewed off, then I'm still respected in the house. But I'm still in the way. I know.

I would never have allowed her mother to go out at night and not return until morning. Does Paulina not realise Dani isn't sleeping here? And if she isn't sleeping here, then she's sleeping somewhere else, *with* someone else. No such thing ever happened when I was that age.

Would you listen to yourself, Enrico? No such thing ever happened when you were that age. As if you were an angel ...? But you never flaunted it in your abuelo's face.

'Papá! I could smell that you were out here before I even walked down the stairs. The place stinks. Do you think I can make breakfast in there with your smelly habits? Close the door to the terrace.'

I don't have to turn around to look at my daughter to know she has a face on her like a bull in full charge.

I stub my cigarette out on the saucer under my coffee. I lift the brandy to my mouth and down it in one. I haul myself up and back into the kitchen, flinging the cup and glass into the sink and emptying the ash into the bin. I scowl at my daughter and go to leave the room.

'Just one more thing, papá. Things happen differently now than in your younger days. I won't have you making my daughter feel bad about herself when she is good enough to get up early in the morning and come back home to help out before she goes off to study. She's a good girl. Leave her be. It's not like you led the life of a priest since my mother died, is it? You're a hypocrite, Enrico Sanchez.'

Paulina hands me my cane, with a look that says she would like to hit me over the head with it. I take it and blink. I straighten my back as much as I can at ninety-one and walk back out to the terrace. When I get to the door, I look back to the kitchen to say I'm sorry, but Paulina is gone. When she comes back, I'll apologise. When my Daniela comes down, I'll make it up to her. I must be wearing them down. I'm tired of myself.

Paulina is looking out the upstairs open window and she smiles and waves. I blow her a kiss. My daughter has heard me talking to myself. She'll send for the men in white coats if I don't start to behave myself. I close my eyes again. Paulina is so like her mother. Rosa was good and kind and gentle. Saintly. Our short marriage after my release from prison was quiet. Exactly what I thought I needed.

I try to snooze, but the brandy that should have been sipped slowly for an hour has had a bad effect on me and I'm wide awake. I'm remembering my school days and sitting beside a young girl. Sonia Almez only had eyes for Enrico Sanchez. Since we were teenagers, we knew we belonged together. Sonia and Enrico.

I'm smiling to myself. Thoughts of Sonia always bring a smile that creeps up and wraps itself around me and stays with me. I doze off with that smile.

Someone is shaking me gently. I open my eyes and look into the caring eyes of my grandchild. Dani is also good and kind and gentle.

'Abuelo, I am sorry I was cross earlier. I was out of order. Lo siento. We're running a guest house, and if we are found to be smoking near the kitchen, we will be closed down. You have to understand.'

'My dearest girl, you have nothing to be sorry for. I was completely wrong for being so grumpy with you. I will stay out here in the mornings. I will stay out of your way.'

'You're not in the way, abuelo. It is just the health regulations. Okay?'

I smile. 'I have never been very good at keeping rules, but I will try harder, I promise.'

'No, abuelo, don't change too much. We love you as you are. Now, your breakfast is ready.'

'I have had breakfast.' I wrinkle my eyes mischievously.

'A coffee and a brandy? I don't think that is exactly the best breakfast you could have. You need something now to line your stomach against all that poison. Come on. Up you get.'

Dani puts her arm around me and pulls me from the chair. She hands me my stick and together we make our way slowly back into the house.

'Would you like to eat here in the kitchen, papá, or will you eat with the guests in the dining room?' Paulina is still whirling around the kitchen, piling trays with food.

I look up at my daughter and try to make the right decision.

'I don't know, Paulina, am I a guest or am I family?'

'That's not what I meant, papá! Please don't turn everything around to make it sound like an insult. The kitchen is busy with Dani and I running in and out to the guests and the dining room is relaxing. That is all that was meant, but you are right, you are family, so, sit down there and wrap all of the cutlery in napkins for me and make yourself useful. You can have your breakfast later with the rest of us.'

Paulina gives Dani a conspiratorial grin, and I give them both an earful of loud, hearty laughter. Maybe it won't be so bad around here after all.

Paulina is right. The next hour or so is manic in the kitchen. Orders are called in the door and food is flung out to Dani at an alarming pace. The heat from the pans and the hot plates is stifling, even though it's not yet hot outside. Each time the door to the dining room opens, I can hear the calm sound of a Spanish guitarist floating from the tiny speaker. The quiet chat of Spanish and English comes from tables, mostly peopled with couples. Only one girl sits alone, her back to me. It looks nice out there, and I like meeting and chatting with new people. Paulina knew this and that's why she suggested the dining room. As usual, I will have to learn to curb my tongue. Its sharp point never leads me where I want to be.

Paulina comes back into the kitchen, and I put down the napkins and cutlery. My arthritic fingers are no use with jobs like this.

'I think you were right, Paulina. I would like to sit in the other room, and I am making a mess of your napkins anyway.'

'Papá, not now, I haven't time. You'll have to wait. It's got very busy out there just now, and I wish to God you would make up your mind what you want to do.' She grabs the plates that Dani offers her, her face like a wildfire, and then she's gone out the door all smiles and courtesy.

She has a sharp tongue too. Perhaps she's a little bit like her father after all.

'Dani,' I sigh. 'Have you another job for me? One that doesn't need delicate, artistic hands.'

Dani looks at me in panic. 'Abuelo ... I can't right now. It's just *this* hour every morning. We only offer breakfast here, so, it has to be good. It's all a bit crazy for an hour, but it will quieten down soon, and mamá will have more time for you ... I'm sorry.'

On her way past me she squeezes my shoulder. I push the cutlery away from me and grunt. I'll go out. I might not be able to walk very far, but at least I'll get out from under their feet, and I'll come back when this has all died down. I haul myself up from the table and pull my stick towards me. Nobody has any time for old people now. When I was a boy my abuelo and abuela were like gods in our house and I resented all that respect. I hated running around after them. I was no better.

I'll walk towards the street, see if I can find a fellow old soul to reminisce with. I reach for the handle of the door gingerly, afraid that Paulina or Dani will burst through with trays at any moment and knock me over. I know I should really go out through the terrace and leave from the front, but it's such a long way around.

The dining room is full, with about twenty people. Where have they all slept? I'd forgotten that this house was so big now.

'Papá.' Paulina comes towards me wearing her proprietor smile. 'Everything okay?' But I know that what she's actually saying is: *Papá, shut up and get back into the kitchen.*

'I'm fine, Paulina. I'm going out for a walk.' Paulina looks around at the tables and I know she's wondering how I'll get past everyone without a scene of pushing and shoving and movement. A guest near the door, the girl who has been sitting alone, must have heard our conversation. Perhaps being on her own in the dining room has made her more tuned in to what is going on around her. She stands up and turns towards us and smiles.

'I'm finished here,' she says in broken Spanish. 'If we push this table aside you could get past if you like.'

Paulina smiles and helps the young woman to move the table. 'Thank you so much,' she says, but she gives *me* a look that says *I'll speak to you later.*

I go to move towards the door and smile my biggest smile for the lovely young girl who has moved mountains to accommodate my age. Wherever she comes from they obviously respect their elders. The girl is staring intensely at me. My smile fades, and I stop in my shuffle. *Madre mia* … It looks like … But it isn't possible … She is … And …

I drop my stick and when I go to pick it up, I fall forward, crashing into another table and sending their pot of coffee spilling across the white cloth.

Paulina stands horrified and it's left to the young guest to rush to my side.

'Are you okay?' The girl puts her hand out and holds mine. I let my gnarled fingers fold around it. 'I'm sorry to have startled you,' she says. 'Apparently, I look very like her. My grandmother, Sonia Almez. You knew her very well when you were both young, didn't you? My name is Shona Moran.'

I shake my head from side to side. My eyes blur with tears, and I look up at what looks like Sonia's younger face smiling down at me. Both she and Paulina heave me back up to standing and the young girl pulls out a seat for me. I sit and try to recover from the fall and from seeing her.

'Sonia's friend Eileen told me where I might find you, Enrico,' she says. Her accent is unmistakably Irish and brings me straight back to that time when I secretly visited Sonia in Ireland. 'I wanted to meet someone who knew my grandmother. I don't know if she had any other family here, but it would be wonderful if she does.'

The other people in the breakfast room have settled back down now; the spectacle I made is over. I still can't find my speech. What can I tell this girl of the truth?

'Some years back, Enrico, I found out that I was adopted, and I went a bit off the rails for a while. Then my birth sister, Anna, found me, and I've been trying to get to know her and our extended family in Donegal. When I met Sonia's best friend, Eileen, she told me all about my grandmother and how she came from here, and she said that if I came to find you that you could tell me more about her and her life before she went to Ireland, and … Oh, I'm sorry. I didn't mean to upset you.'

The tears escape and flow, and there's nothing I can do to stop them. Shona must be another of Maria's daughters. Anna's sister, she said. Now, I'm sobbing openly: for Sonia and all that was lost. Paulina hands me a napkin, and I try to compose myself. I take a deep breath and look at the vision beside me. How can I tell this girl of the story of Sonia and me, and the devastating effect that Franco's atrocities had on our lives? But mostly, how can I tell her what happened after? Sonia once said that sometimes a lie is the only kindness. But perhaps it's time now for the truth.

CHAPTER FORTY

'So, tell me about your aunt, Fiona, and your sister, Anna. Are they keeping well?' I ask Shona, once I've got over the shock of seeing her in the breakfast room earlier: a living, breathing image of Sonia in her youth.

'Well, yeah,' said Shona. 'I suppose. Will we sit here for a while? It's hard to walk and talk.'

I'm sure she means for me and not for herself.

We sit on a bench in the Plaza. Shona breathes in the scent of oranges from the trees above us and waits while I settle my walking stick beside her.

'I'm the wrong person to ask about Fiona. I hardly know her, and I'm not her favourite person.' She shuffles uneasily on the bench.

'You don't like her?' I ask. 'Why?'

'No.' Shona shakes her head. 'I don't mean I don't like her. She doesn't like me. Well, she doesn't trust me. She feels I'm a bad influence on Anna.' She shrugs her shoulders. 'She's probably right. Since I met Anna, I've caused chaos in their lives.'

Shona explains a little of how she came to meet her birth family in Donegal. How she found out about her mother, Maria, dying in Dublin shortly after she was born.

'Fiona thought that Maria had only had one child, but she had me too. Anna's birth father led me to my own birth father. It seems he and Maria had got involved with the wrong people in Dublin, and he ran to Spain to hide for years after Maria died. He's now serving a sentence in prison on the back of that. He's a good man though, Enrico. We've all done things in our past that we regret, right?'

'I spent a few years behind bars myself, Shona, and I definitely made some bad choices when I was younger. Your sister, Anna, was Maria's first child? Am I right?' I ask.

Shona smiles. 'My half-sister. We have different fathers.'

'Hah. Maria was a bit of a wild girl then,' I say.

'What do you know?' Shona stands up and faces me, the smile replaced with a glare. 'She and my father fell into bad company. They were unfortunate. She was our mother, Enrico. Mine and Anna's, and you've no right to judge her.'

She turns and goes to walk away. She's right. What do I know of Maria?

'Shona! Come back and talk. You don't know your way around here. You'll get lost.' I feel around for my stick and slowly pull myself to standing. 'Shona, I'm sorry,' I shout. Shona stops walking and turns around. She waits for my plodding steps to catch up with her. I take my time, my stick tapping on the cobbles as I walk. When I'm standing right beside her, I put my hand on her shoulder. 'Shona, querida, you're right, but I know more than you think I know. With her family background, Maria may always have had problems.'

Shona reaches for my weathered hand on her shoulder and holds it. 'I feel that you're going to tell me more than I came to Spain to find out. What are you saying, Enrico? I know Maria's father, Manus, was an alcoholic, but from what I heard, he's not wild. Anna says he hasn't had a drink since the day Sonia died.'

'Perhaps, my dear Shona … but I need to tell you a story.'

'Oh, you're a great one for the stories, Enrico. I don't know whether to believe half of them or not.'

'Well, this one is most definitely true. It's a happy ending story … Well, for some it is … One that didn't have happy beginnings – for me, anyhow. And it might be quite shocking for others. For you certainly, and I know that there are those back in

Donegal who will be very angry with me when, or if, they find out. But I will tell you, and I will leave it up to you to decide if they should know, or whether it would be kinder to them to leave them ignorant as they have always been.'

'Hah! No pressure, so, Enrico. You don't know me well enough yet to know that I'm shite at making decisions. I will most probably make the wrong one and cause absolute havoc.'

'We'll take it one step at a time then. All right?'

Shona nods.

'Fiona and Eileen told you the history of your family, about Manus and your grandmother Sonia, who you were called after. The love of *my* life.'

'The woman of your dreams. Go on, so.'

'You see, Shona, Manus Dooley was not Maria's father. There was someone else in Sonia's life. Someone she loved more than the long-suffering Manus.'

Shona's face gives away her shock.

'Take my arm and let me lean on you, Shona, and we'll talk.' We walk quietly past the whitewashed houses, each in our own thoughts until Shona stops.

'Enrico,' she says at last. 'Are you telling me that you are Maria's father? Are you my and Anna's grandfather?'

'I've stories to tell you. I hope you're ready to hear them. Manus and Sonia should never have married. It was cruel for both of them. For Sonia, because she could never love him, and for Manus, because he let her rejection send him to the bottle and lost half his life in it.'

'And Sonia too. It must have been awful for you to hear of how she died, knowing that she couldn't continue without you ... or Maria.'

'Well, that's where I need to change the direction of the story. Manus and Sonia's marriage was a failure, but back then in a small village in Donegal, nobody would ever leave their husband. It was unheard of. Maria had died. Her sister Fiona was married by then, and she and her husband Gerry were adopting Maria's daughter, Anna. I don't believe that they knew of your existence. So, Sonia was left with a choice: to hold on and nurse Manus through drunken rages for the rest of her life or …'

'Or to end her life. So tragic for you both.'

'Stop interrupting me, Shona. Do you want to hear the rest?'

Shona nods, and as we walk slowly home, I tell Shona the story of Sonia Almez and Enrico Sanchez and how Shona herself came to be. It's a beautiful but harrowing story, and its ripples will spread far; and for some, it will be a story too hard to handle.

We arrive back at the guest house, Shona's arm linked with mine, as Tommy and Ruby are leaving to go to the beach. Ruby's eyes light up when she sees her mamá and she lifts up her two little arms to be hugged. Shona reaches down and wraps herself around her daughter.

'Ruby, sweetie. Look at you, already in your cute little swimmers and hat. Mammy has some very special news to whisper into your little ears today.'

Tommy raises his eyebrows questioningly, and Shona grins at me. I return her smile tenfold.

'Will you give me five minutes to get changed, Tommy? I'll follow you down to the sea.'

'Yeah. Okay … But what's the big news? I'm intrigued.'

'I'll tell you on the beach.' Shona looks over at me. 'It's okay to tell Tommy, isn't it? I mean, it's all about Ruby, and Tommy is her dad.'

'Of course,' I say. 'Soon we may have to explain it to every-one, and there'll be a few people who are going to feel very bad, very hurt. I have a lot of people to say sorry to, and that's going to be hard. Let me sit and talk to my granddaughter, Daniela, about it today, and we'll work out the best way to deal with it.'

'Enrico, you don't have to mess up your life on account of me and Ruby. Perhaps it's enough that *we* know; that we don't have to hurt anyone else.'

Tommy stares at Shona. 'I haven't a clue what all this is about, Shona Moran, but I can't believe that you of all people are thinking about keeping truths from others, after what you've been through yourself.'

'I know, Tommy, but Enrico will have to shake up his life so much. I'm thinking of his daughter, Paulina, and the rest of his family.'

'No,' I insist. 'Tommy is right that it's time for the truth. Honesty might hurt, but lies cut so much deeper. Leave it with me today, querida, and enjoy the beach.'

'You missed a bit on her arm there, Shona.'

'Where? I think I can sun-cream Ruby without a lecture from you about childcare, Mr Dad of the Year.' Shona pretended to squeeze the cream at him.

'Jaysus,' Tommy laughed, lay down on the towel and closed his eyes, as Shona slapped more cream on Ruby. She had marched down to the beach, a woman on a mission, eyes ahead, bursting with the news she had heard from Enrico that morning. Tommy had asked for a few minutes' peace under the heat of the Andalusian sun before her dam exploded and his life had to open up to make room for more of Shona's *stuff*. She had come here to find out a little more about her grandmother, and it seemed she had heard a lot more than she had expected. Never a dull moment in Shona Moran's life.

'I give you full access for the next half hour, Ms Moran. You obviously need the practice in parenthood more than I do.' Tommy sat up slightly and gave Shona a wink and was rewarded with a handful of sand over him.

'I'll make sandcastles, so, and we'll bring her into the water when his majesty is ready.'

Tommy looked relaxed, with another potential row averted. They were getting good at this: joking with each other, when before they would have ended up in a huff. Shona was trying so hard, and they were enjoying each other's company. Tommy was especially enjoying sharing the care of Ruby. He adored his daughter, but she was a handful. Her first few years without her mammy around had really shaken and exhausted him.

Once the castle was complete, Ruby woke him with her happy little screeches. Shona was very proud of her mound of sand with a surrounding moat and shells for windows.

'A work of art,' said Tommy. 'Now let's get this kid splashing. We'll make a water baby out of her. She'll love it.'

A few minutes later, while Ruby was loving sitting at the edge of the gentle waves, Shona told Tommy Enrico's story.

'This man, Enrico, Tommy. He's my grandfather. My mother, Maria, was the result of him and Sonia having a short affair in Ireland when he got out of jail after Franco died.'

Tommy reached over and held Shona's hand. 'What a story, Shona. In a way, that's lovely. Enrico seems a good man, not like Manus. I'm glad *he's* not your grandfather. The things we heard about him hitting and shouting at Maria when she was a child when he was drunk.'

'Yes, but he's different now, according to Anna. Apparently, he knew that Maria wasn't his, Tommy. They kept up the pretence to save face, but my poor mother never knew. She suffered his rejection of her all her short life, and Tommy, I know that's enough to be getting on with, but there's more.'

'Hah,' said Tommy. 'It wouldn't be a Shona Moran story if there wasn't more. Spit it out.'

So, Shona did. 'Sonia Almez, my grandmother … She's not dead, Tom.'

'What?' Tommy sat up quickly.

'I know, I know. She left her shoes on the beach, and walked into the waves all right, but she didn't drown. She climbed up the side of a cliff with Enrico's help and the two of them disappeared back to Spain.

'She's here, Tommy. Sonia left her drunken husband and started a new life back home with her childhood sweetheart, but she left her daughter and granddaughter, Anna, too. She didn't know about me. She's been ill recently, and she's recovering in a nursing home at the moment. Enrico visits her every day, and we're going to meet her later.'

Tommy sat with his mouth still open for a moment, trying to take in all that she was telling him. 'Are you sure you want to meet her? I mean, are you not even a little bit angry with her and Enrico, Shona?'

'What do you mean? She's my grandmother and she's been alive all these years. Of course I want to meet her.'

He took Shona's hand in his. 'She lied, Shona. Fiona and Anna think she's dead. How could she do that?'

'I know, Tommy, but she's my granny, and I want to get to know her. I'll talk to her about what they did, but I'm not going to judge them yet.'

Tommy sat there staring at Shona smiling and shaking his head and Shona's heart filled with warm, longing emotions. This feeling was ten times better than anything she had felt with Jameel.

This was real. She reached over and kissed him, and he responded with all the love she had yearned for, for so long.

'This evening when we get back, I'd like to bring my little princess and her lovely mammy for a slap-up meal. We'll go somewhere on the beach and eat and drink and watch the sun set and the moon rise. Our little family. What do you think, Shona?'

Shona couldn't speak. She smiled back at him and wondered if she could bottle this happiness. She had it all at her fingertips. Tommy, Ruby and Shona could be a family. Her grandmother had got what she wanted in life, eventually. Maybe Shona wouldn't have to wait quite as long.

The old woman sat in her room waiting. She knew that Shona and Ruby were in Malaga, as she had asked Jorge, her nurse, on the hour.

'Do you know if they are here? Did Enrico telephone?' Her mind rambled in the mornings when she woke up, but by midday, she usually managed to gather her thoughts.

'They are here,' Jorge had said. 'He called me last night, but you were already asleep.'

'You should have woken me, Jorge. Were they here?'

'He only wanted to tell you about them. He seems smitten. He texted photos. They're beautiful. Here. Where are your glasses? Look for yourself.' Jorge scrolled down through the photos Enrico had sent him. 'So like her grandmother.'

She had told Jorge her story and her history. He knew all about her life in the wilderness without those she loved, and of the lies told from love or truth. That had been her choice and she had chosen love. She had lived long enough without it.

'They're here, Sonia.' In her excitement, Dani ran into the room without knocking.

Sonia was sitting on the bed in a state of dishevelment, with discarded clothes and jewellery tossed around. Dani pulled her to standing gently. 'They're in the family room and Jorge is bringing them tea.'

'How do I look, Dani?' Sonia asked. 'Is my dress too colourful? Should I change? Enrico sent such rubbish when I asked him to send me in something nice to wear. Silly man said I would look beautiful wearing a black sack. I haven't even brushed my hair, little as there is of it.'

Dani smiled. 'He was right. You look beautiful, as always. How many changes of clothes have you had already? Enough now.' She turned her around to sit in the wheelchair. 'Easy does it.'

'Do I have to go in that? Can I try to walk to her?'

'And risk falling over in front of them? I don't think so.' Dani settled her into the chair and wheeled her towards the door and down the corridor.

'What are they like, Dani? Are they like their photos?' Sonia asked.

'Apparently, Shona looks like her mother. And *her* mother before her. You loved Maria, so you will love Shona. Especially as Maria called her after you. She bites her bottom lip the way you said Maria always did. The child's father is with them.'

'Oh, I didn't know she was married. Stop a minute, will you. I can't hear you behind me.' Too many wallops across the ear in early life had left her slightly deaf, and her hearing aid didn't always pick up important details.

Dani came around to the front of Sonia's chair. 'She's not married, but who are you to talk about marriage and you shacking up with my grandfather all these years?' Dani laughed, and Sonia swiped at her playfully. 'Now let's go. You know they'll love you.'

A collective inhale of breath, and they journeyed down the corridor and into the sitting room where four silent faces sat waiting to meet the woman who had cheated on death and cheated on her family.

Enrico moved forward. 'Sonia, darling, this is our Maria's daughter, Shona. She's *our* granddaughter.'

The two women looked across the room at one another, one seeing what the past years had changed and the other wondering what the future years would bring.

CHAPTER FORTY-ONE

Shona's first sense when she woke was that she was being rocked gently to and fro. It was a good feeling. She felt safe. Though when a soft breeze touched her cheek, she opened her eyes in fright, shocked to see grey clouds low in the sky directly above her. A seagull was perched nearby, staring at the intrusion to his quiet night. She looked around. Two oars lay down in the bottom of the boat she had been sleeping in. Then the realization dawned.

'Shite,' she said, her voice hoarse. 'I'm in trouble again.'

'Are you often in trouble?' Shona sat up suddenly and looked up to see someone dressed in a long coat looking down at her. The quick movement made her head swim.

'That's my boat you've been sleeping in. Time to get out, I think. Don't you?'

Shona slipped off her high heels and tried to stand while pulling down her short black dress. Her purse and the hat she had bought in the plaza the day before were beside her. With absolute dread, she climbed over the side, waded in and stood beside her accuser. Still feeling as if she was being rocked back and forward, Shona fell against the person beside her and dropped her belongings.

The stranger laughed and reached out to steady her. 'You're in a right mess. Where are you staying?'

Shona couldn't think of the name of her guest house, so she shook her head. She was shivering and felt sick. Physically and mentally.

'Dunno. But I need to find Tommy, and I need to see Ruby.' Then Shona started to cry. Big drunken sobs.

'Look. I live over there on the first floor. I was on the balcony, looking down over the marina when I saw you face up in my family boat. I thought you were hurt, but I'm happy to see that you're only drunk. Come and sleep it off, and in the morning, you can try to get back to wherever you're supposed to be and whoever it is you're supposed to be with. All right?'

The trip back to the apartment was not without its troubles, but they managed, and then Shona passed out on someone else's bed.

Two painkillers and a pint of water later and Shona was beginning to feel human again. They had been left on a tray beside her, with a flask of coffee and a ham and cheese sandwich. Presumably, it was the same person who owned the double bed she had woken up in. She tried to remember how she had ended up there. There was a boat and someone in a long coat? Then lots of stairs. Shona couldn't remember much more. She had no idea where she was, but she knew that this was not the bedroom at the guest house where she had spent her first night in Spain.

She reached for the sandwich and took a few unwelcome bites. Then she tried the flask of coffee. It was very sweet as she liked it. There was a note beside it from someone called Toni in beautiful handwriting, written on squared paper.

Hi, Sona.

Why had he called her Sona? *Sona*?

I found you last night lying in my boat. You were lucky not to have ended up out at sea, as it had been untied from its mooring. The water was very calm, and you didn't float very far. You must have had so much to drink to be that way. I live nearby, so it was easier to bring you here to my apartment. I am gone to work now and will be back this evening, but I have scribbled a map for you on the back of this in case you want to go back to the guest house you tried to tell me about.

Shona tried to sit up a bit more in the bed to make it easier to read. She shivered and pulled the covers up over her. She hadn't a stitch on. Had she undressed herself or had this Toni undressed her? Or …? The evening had started out so well … Oh, God. Had something happened with Toni? Shona looked over to the other side of the bed. There was a dent in the other pillow, so someone had slept there beside her. She swallowed a sob that was threatening to spill then continued reading.

I had to wash your dress, but it is nearly dry with your other things. I will leave them outside my bedroom, and you can have another shower if you want. Help yourself to more food and coffee.

Toni

Another shower? Shona had no recollection of having a shower. Had she managed alone, or had she had help? She couldn't bear to know.

The best thing to do was to go back to the guest house and forget about it. For now, she would get washed and dressed. *No tears yet*, she thought to herself. Plenty of time for self-indulgent shame later in the day. It was almost 1 pm.

Lying her head back down on her pillow, she willed the pain and the dizziness to ease. Face up in a boat? How on earth did she get into that predicament? From the sound of it, Toni had saved her from who knows what. A boat that was untied, ready to float out to sea? Who had brought her and left her there? Or had she gone there herself? She might never know. How could she have walked away from a beautiful night out with Tommy and walked into this nightmare? Tommy didn't deserve this. In one night, she had undone all the goodness that she had built up over the last few years.

'You're a stupid bitch, Shona Moran,' she said out loud to herself. 'You swore you would never let this happen again.'

Last night, Dani had offered to babysit to let them go out alone. They had jumped at the chance and were in the middle of their wonderfully romantic night out when Shona brought up the subject of her grandmother again. It had been a stupid row about whether or not Sonia and Enrico had been right to lie to their family or not. Shona had said that they deserved some happiness, but Tommy argued that they had a choice to be together without all the lies. A couple of glasses of wine had weakened her. Tommy had asked her not to drink, but she had been sure that one or two would do no harm. One or two had led to many more, as it always did in the past.

Storming off to the toilet, she had got chatting to a drunk Irish girl who offered her a swig of vodka from her bottle, and then she had gone off with her, out the back of the restaurant and into the night. They had met up with a crowd of other Irish people Shona's own age, and she had gone with them to a pub, then a club, then she didn't know where. She had been away from her parents, Tommy, and her daughter.

Independent and free, twenty-three-year-old Shona had let herself go. But Shona Moran was an alcoholic, and she shouldn't – and couldn't – let herself go. Who was this person who had found her and cared for her? Or had he cared for her? She wanted to lose him and hide away in her guest house room from the shame she felt about it all. Tommy had always told her that drinking the way she did left her vulnerable to all sorts of awful things. She had worked so hard to put her drinking days behind her.

First steps first. Shower and dress. She eased her legs out of the bed and allowed them to lead her to the bedroom door where her clothes from the night before were sitting folded neatly ready to be worn again. The bathroom was in front of her. Her mobile was sitting on top of her clothes and there were three missed calls from Tommy. She was amazed he had called her. Surely, he should have given up on her by now.

Whatever happened today, Tommy must never find out that she had slept with someone. Not that she knew for sure if she had, but he mustn't know how bad her drinking had been. This Toni must never meet with Tommy. From the note, he seemed like a lovely person. *Too good for the likes of you, Shona*, she thought. She wondered if she could pretend to Tommy that she had gone off because she was so overwhelmed by her new family. Could she make it believable but better? Sure, Shona. Tell a lie. Isn't that what you're best at?

Half an hour later, Shona was out on the balcony having coffee and a big sticky slice of cake that she had found in the kitchen. She was enjoying it immensely, despite her churning stomach.

Perhaps she shouldn't have come to Spain so soon after all the other crap in her and Tommy's life, but she felt that they could do with a holiday. Shona wondered what she had told Toni about her trip. She had come to find out more about her grandmother's life in Spain and had uncovered so much more than she had bargained for.

She had hoped that she would have more time to spend with Tommy. More time to work on their relationship. For so long,

Tommy had been more her on-and-off friend than her boyfriend, and Shona had tried so hard to get to where they were now. Well, she had certainly let Tommy down last night. Her stomach heaved with the memory. Shona was desperate to go back to the guest house to sleep off the excesses of the night before, but Tommy was there and how could she face him?

Could she take the coward's way out and text him an excuse about last night? She took out her phone and started to key in the words.

I'm sorry, Tommy. I was so embarrassed by what happened last night at the restaurant. I'm so sorry I walked off on you. I'm going to see Sonia and I'll be back soon. Shona. X

She pressed send before she could change her mind. Tommy came back to her immediately.

Yeah? Well, don't mind me awake worrying about you all bloody night and don't mind me looking after our daughter all day today.

No name or the usual *X* that came with his texts. She should stop being a coward and ring him, but she wasn't able for it. The bed looked so inviting. She would love another few hours to get over her hangover, and she did want to see Sonia again soon.

Old Eileen in Donegal had given her some background, but there was so much more that she wanted to know. Shona's birth mother, Maria, was Sonia's daughter, and she had died just after Shona was born. When Shona asked why Maria's headstone had a memorial to Sonia, Eileen had explained that her grandmother had drowned, and they had never found her body, so there was no grave. That must have been so hard for the family. But if they knew the truth, wouldn't that be so much harder?

Shona knew that she needed to go back, but for now, she had to put herself together to be ready to face Tommy and Ruby. She wouldn't be doing their relationship any good if he found out everything about what had really happened last night.

Shona couldn't keep the tears back any longer. If Tommy found out, it would be the end of their friendship, never mind the end of any hopes she might have for the two of them. Would he hear it from Toni? Shona wondered. Was this anything like one of those small Irish towns where everyone knew each other? She hoped not. Her future was all so very fragile, and she needed to be more careful of who she was with and where she went to. The last few years had been the best that Shona had ever known, and it was up to her not to muck it up. Great start.

It was breezy outside, and Shona was shaking from her hangover. She decided to borrow the long coat on the door hook to keep her grounded and to cover up her short evening dress from last night. She could drop it back later, that way she could find out who her benefactor was. Who the man she had spent the night with was. She shivered and wrapped the coat around her.

'Don't bother,' Tommy raised his hand to dismiss whatever excuse Shona was about to give him for her absence. 'The state of your red eyes says it all. Go to bed.'

'But where's Ruby?' Shona looked around the guest room.

'Your new family wanted to get to know her, and I didn't argue. I'm wrecked. I've brought our flight forward to tomorrow evening. We're going home. Back to the way we were before we came over, except for one change. Ruby's going back to her *old* childminder.'

'No, Tommy. Please. Listen …'

'No, Shona. Please listen, my arse. I'm going out,' He left quietly, closing the door softly, leaving the room behind him charged with his anger and disappointment.

The bed looked too inviting to ignore, and Shona curled up on Tommy's side, hugging his pillow to her.

'I'm sorry,' she said to the closed door. 'Again. Will it ever go away, Tommy? Will I ever stop using vodka as a blanket to wrap myself in whenever I get overwhelmed?' She had been weak. Had she lost her best friend again? Who was she kidding? She wanted Tommy to be much more than a friend. She was in love, and she had great hopes of turning her life around, getting him to love her the way she loved him. This holiday had been a dream for her, and she and Tommy had been getting closer. There had been hope that they could be a proper family – until she had screwed up again.

The smell of salt and seaweed on the coat she had borrowed brought her back to the evening before. Whose boat had she woken up in? Whose coat was she wearing? *Who cares, Shona?* she asked herself. *You got upset and you got drunk in a heartbeat. You're a useless piece of shite.*

Her eyes were closing. She needed sleep. It wouldn't change things or make the bad go away, but it would help her to face up to it. No running away this time.

She woke up sometime later to a knock on the door. She sat up and wondered if she'd dreamt it. It was getting dark. Jesus, her head still hurt, and her tongue felt like she'd drunk half the bay.

Another knock and a call. 'Tommy? Shona? Can I come in?' It sounded like her cousin Daniela.

'One minute.' Shona's voice came out hoarse and ragged.

She got out of bed and buttoned up the coat she was wearing to cover up last night's dress again and to make it look like she was getting ready to go out.

'Sorry, I was in the loo,' she lied. 'Hello, Ruby love.' Shona held her arms out for her daughter. 'Did you have fun with Dani?' She gave her cousin her biggest smile and hoped she could get her on side. 'Come in.'

Shona immediately regretted the invitation. Tommy's leg had been bothering him too much to bend since his trip over, and *she* had been so busy running around enjoying her new discoveries. Their room in the guest house was pretty disgusting, even by Shona's standards. She sensed Dani's sharp intake of breath.

'Sit down.' Shona swept an overflowing suitcase off the chair onto the bed, sending half the contents scattering to the floor. Dani sat.

'Thank you for having Ruby.'

'It was a pleasure.'

'I hope she wasn't any trouble.'

'Of course not. My grandfather is in love with her, but I think we may have tired her out in the play park.'

'Maybe I should stay in, let her sleep for a while.'

'Were you going out?'

'Eh, yeah. For a walk only, along the beach.'

'It's warm out, for a coat.'

'Maybe. I thought it was a bit chilly earlier, but I think we'll stay in anyway.'

'You might as well take it off then, and I'll take it back to its rightful place, if you don't mind.'

'Sorry?' Shona had no idea what she was talking about, but from the look on Daniela's face, she felt something horrible was about to kick off.

'The coat you're wearing. I bought it, so I recognize it, as there's a small rip on the pocket. It's not your coat. I left it in Toni's. Where did you get it?'

Shona sat on the bed, willing Ruby to say something to change the subject, but her daughter was so tired that she lay down on Shona's bed and closed her eyes.

Shona looked away from Daniela, trying to figure out how to answer her without having to tell her that she had no idea how she came to be in this Toni's apartment. She looked down at the long, black coat with different coloured and shaped patches. No two buttons were the same, the pockets were in different places and the collar was ruffled. It was the kind of coat that she would love to own.

She looked back at her cousin who was staring at her, almost through her, and she felt that this girl could see inside her head. She felt she could read Dani's thoughts too. She was thinking that Shona didn't deserve her beautiful Ruby, that she would never amount to being anybody and that Tommy Farrell was wasted on the likes of her. Turning towards Ruby, she caressed her daughter's face and spoke to Daniela.

'It's gorgeous, your coat, I love it.' Shona began to unbutton the coat, knowing that she was about to expose that she was wearing the clothes that she went out in the night before. She slipped it off her and handed it back.

'I'm not sure where I ended up, Dani.' Shona sat back down on the edge of the bed. 'I haven't a clue where I spent last night. We were having a beautiful night, but I drank wine, and I shouldn't drink. I have a problem. Tommy and I had a sort of misunderstanding in the restaurant, and I remember heading to the loo. I met a girl there. We chatted and drank vodka and we left to get more drink. I walked away from Tommy, and I have no idea why. Very early this morning I woke up in a boat in the marina, and then later, in a stranger's bed.

'The last few days here with Tommy and Ruby have been amazing. I had hopes for the three of us becoming a real family, but now I've screwed up again.'

'Again? Is this something you do regularly? And this stranger's bed you were in, is that where you got the coat?'

There was a quiet in the room. Ruby had fallen asleep with her thumb in her mouth. Shona looked around for a blanket, but Dani was beside her, covering Ruby with the coat that was still warm from her mammy. Once Ruby was covered, Dani placed her hands on Shona's shoulders and spoke to her in a loud whisper.

'I hate you, Shona Moran. Before you arrived, I had a grandfather who was all mine. We lived in a house that was ours because its original owner had disappeared after the war and never came home, and then you turn up and take my abuelo Enrico for yourself. He only has eyes for you and your Ruby. Apparently, my mother tells me that this house is legally yours too. Then you turn up today wearing *my* coat. If I find out that anything happened between you and my Toni last night, I will personally fuck up your life a lot worse than you think it already is. Leave my coat on the terrace when Ruby wakes up.'

Dani turned and left, leaving the door ajar and Shona's stomach heaving at the thought of what might have happened with some guy called Toni, who apparently belonged to Daniela, the night before.

CHAPTER FORTY-TWO

The early morning saw Shona walking the beach, with Ruby running in and out of the lapping waves, her soft singing a soothing background to Shona's racing thoughts. The sea was calm after the cold rain of the night before and the soft waves hugged her bare feet as she went.

Tommy had booked their flight for seven that evening and was busy packing their bags while she kept Ruby out of the way. The ring of her phone stopped Ruby in mid-chatter.

'Hi, Margaret,' Shona was relieved to hear her aunt's voice.

'Shona. How's the sun, sea and sand?'

'Beautiful, Margaret, but we're, eh, coming home early, this evening actually.' *Please don't let her blame me*, thought Shona.

'Why, Shona? What did you do?' Shona could feel, rather than hear, Margaret's sigh on the other end.

'Fuck off, Margaret. You're as bad as everyone else. Everything always has to be Shona's fault, as if nobody else in our family ever puts a foot wrong.'

'Did you drink, Shona? I asked you not to. I begged you. This was your chance, love, to put everything right.'

Shona said nothing. What could she say?

'Are Tommy and Ruby all right?' asked Margaret, her tone softening on mentioning her adored great-niece.

Shona took a deep breath.

'*Saint* Tommy is perfect, Aunty Margaret, and Ruby is wonderful. She's loved Spain, but in case you're even a little bit interested, Shona Moran is not all right, not even a little bit. She can't get her head around her new family, and she can't get Tommy to love her. Her new cousin has decided that Shona is the shit on the end of her shoe. Her new grandmother is shaking her head and muttering in Spanish that Shona is exactly like Maria and will no doubt meet a bad end like her mother. She doesn't realise that I understand every word she says in Spanish.

'So, yes, the night before last I drank. I woke up face up in a boat and I have no idea where I went to or what I did, but everyone here has decided that I obviously got up to no good. The only person who is speaking to me is a ninety-one-year-old ex-terrorist who faked his girlfriend's death decades ago so she could run away to Spain with him.'

'Shona, what are you talking about? Listen. Is that Ruby I hear beside you? Where are you?' Shona could hear that tone in her aunt's voice. The one where she was walking around on eggshells with Shona.

'She's here, Margaret. We're walking along the beach. Tommy is packing, but I'm not ready to go home yet. I don't want to go back to a family who think I'm such a fuck-up that, as soon as I say that we're going home early, they automatically presume that *I've* done something wrong. But do you know what? You're right, oh wondrous, all-knowing godmother. I have fucked up. Again. And I'm not coming back home. Right now, this very minute, I'm walking up to a strange man heading towards me and I'm going to hand him Ruby. Then I'm going to go for a very long swim and do you all the best favour of your fucking lives. And no, Ruby is not within earshot of my potty mouth if that's what you're wondering.'

'Shona, for God's sake, stop that now. For once in your life will you think of someone else before yourself—'

'Or what? You'll get Tommy to take Ruby away from me again? He's going to do that anyhow.'

Sonia pressed the red phone icon and flung the phone onto the sand.

'What's the matter, Mammy? Why are you crying?' Ruby was crying now too. Shona felt the tears on her own face, realizing she had upset her daughter. She wondered how many times in Ruby's short life she had cried because she understood how useless her mother was.

CHAPTER FORTY-THREE

'Sorry, señorita. Only four people are allowed in a cable car at one time. You and your sister need to go in the next car.' The operator stood back, nodding his head for effect, as the door of the cable car closed, holding Enrico, Tommy, Ruby and Paulina. Shona took a breath and turned to Dani.

'You and I are not getting in there together. This was supposed to be a last treat before I get on the plane, and I am not sharing it with the cousin from hell who seems to want me dead with one withering look. Sisters, my arse.' Shona looked around at the queue behind her and contemplated having to walk all the way back through the waiting throng. Dani laughed at her and climbed into the next car.

'Get in, Shona and stop causing a fuss.' She reached out her hand and caught hold of her cousin and pulled her in. Before Shona had a chance to protest, the doors were closing, and they were following the rest of the family.

After the original swoosh, the car settled down to a slow hover-like state and soon the ghostlike carousels and roller coasters of the closed-down Tivoli Park were dots beneath them.

Dani and Shona sat opposite each other, looking out different windows. Shona's view of the Malaga mountainy terrain, rocky and grassy, dotted with sheep and horses, was blurred. She swallowed, determined to keep the tears that were threatening to fall firmly behind her eyelids.

'So, this is cosy.' Dani smiled at her cousin, her teeth gritted.

'Look, Dani.' Shona clenched her fists to stall her temper. 'In a few hours, myself and Tommy and Ruby will be getting back on a plane to Ireland, and we'll be out of your hair. Then your precious life will be all yours again.'

'Oh, it's that simple, is it? You come here for three days. You suck up to my grandfather and make him all yours. You wow abuela Sonia into thinking that she has been waiting her whole life for the moment that her granddaughter and great-grand-daughter appear in her life. You leave my poor mother shaking with the thought that the house that she has lived in her whole life, the guest house that abuela Rosa had given her life to, is actually legally yours. And your parting gift …? You get drunk and you sleep with *my* Toni. She won't even answer my calls since yesterday morning when you arrived back wearing her coat. She has obviously fallen for your lies and false charm.'

Dani was standing, leaning over her, shouting in her face. 'Did you sleep with her, Shona? I need to know. Think. Remember. Get hold of some of your drunken brain cells and shake the memory out. Where did you sleep the night before last? Did you wake up in her bed or the couch? Why did you come home wearing my coat? Tell me. I have to know the truth.'

Shona knew she was being petty, but she was still trying to keep her emotions together, so she said what came to her first. 'Get your grammar together if you're going to accuse me of all sorts of crap.'

'One thing I know, Shona Moran, is that my English gram-mar is perfect,' Dani snapped. She sat back on her bench and the car swayed back and forward, increasing Shona's apprehension.

'You said *she* and *her* when you meant *he* and *him*.' She couldn't believe that in the face of such a serious argument she was being so disgustingly trivial. The heat of the car was making her sweat, and their arguing was taking up the little air around them. Shona felt that the ride would never end, and she wished that Sonia had never suggested going up in the cable car to Enrico. What were two nonagenarians thinking of – doing such a crazy stunt as this? So typical of her grandparents, though, constantly trying to make up for their lost years, stolen by Franco and his bloodthirsty war.

Dani was looking at Shona with a curious smirk spreading across her face. 'Shona, do you remember any of the night you were drunk? Anything at all?'

Shona's temper was rising. Dani was seeing something funny in Shona's troubles. She was obviously going to take refuge behind laughing at her if she couldn't get her to confess what she had or hadn't done.

'What has that got to do with it, Dani? If you must know, then no. I remember walking away from the restaurant out the back way when I came out of the bathroom with another Irish girl. I went to a club or something, and then the girl who had given me vodka was nowhere to be seen, and another girl told me to come back to her apartment for a party and she'd try to find Tommy for me later. I suppose I wasn't making much sense. I guess I didn't make it there. I ended up somehow in your Toni's boat, then went back to his apartment. Oh shit, Dani, I'm sorry. You're going to have to ask Toni what happened when you see him.'

'Her.'

'Sorry?'

'*Her.* Toni is short for Antonia. *She's* my girlfriend. Surely you remember if you'd slept with a boy or a girl, Shona.'

'Fuck off, Dani!' Shona was the one standing in the car now. 'I have never slept with a girl. I do *not* have a thing for girls. It didn't happen, all right? There is no way that happened, I can guarantee you.'

'Okay, okay. Sit down and hold your knickers or whatever. I'll have you know that Toni is a very beautiful girl.'

'That may be so, Dani, but I like boys. I have never fancied a girl, and not only do I not have a problem with you being with a girl, but I'm absolutely delighted. It takes me off the hook completely. I definitely did not have a thing with your Toni. I think I borrowed the coat to stop me from shivering, but it wasn't a gift from my lover. Or even *your* lover. Okay?'

'Okay.' Dani was giggling now. 'Point taken. I wonder how you did end up in Toni's. As soon as we get home, I'm going over to her to try to find out what happened.'

'Good idea. Though, I'm not sure I want to know what really happened that night. I'm ashamed of getting drunk in front of my new family. I've let Tommy and Ruby down again, but most of all I've let myself down. I'm such a good-for-nothing, Dani.'

The girls sat quietly for a few minutes, looking down on the hills coming nearer. Dani reached over and took Shona's hand. Shona squeezed it lightly and tried to smile. 'Thanks for forgiving me, Dani.'

'Forgiving what? I was angry that you had been with Toni, and you weren't ... and ... eh, you know ... I don't think we should tell Toni that I thought that she had ... You know ...'

'Why not?'

'She'll be furious with me for not trusting her. Toni and I have been with each other for two years, and I should've known better. I think I was so annoyed at you taking over my grandfather, and possibly my house, that I got carried away.'

'Dani, I've no intention of taking anything from you. I came here to answer some questions about where I came from. I'd like to come back to visit but not to take anything from you.'

'Look,' Dani answered. 'We're coming to the top of the peak now. You have to go home this evening, so we don't have much longer to try to get to know each other; and the time that we've had, we've been too busy snapping at each other to make use of it properly. So you must come back again. Soon.'

'Or you could come to Ireland, Dani. Meet your other cousin, Anna, and Aunty Fiona.'

'Hah. All the shit will hit when you get home and tell Fiona that her mother is still alive.'

'I'm still not sure if that's a good idea, Dani. Too many people will get hurt.'

The car came to a juddering stop and Dani got out and reached her hand in to help Shona out. 'Dry your tears, Shona, and try to enjoy this amazing view on your last afternoon.'

After coming back down in the cable car over Tivoli Park, the two girls linked arms and headed towards the rest of their group. Ruby was holding her daddy's hand, and pulled away to run towards her mammy, but Tommy made a face and held her back. Turning towards Paulina, he said, 'I think I'll take a taxi back to the house now. I might get Ruby to have a few hours rest before we have to get to the airport.'

'I'll come with you, Tommy,' said Paulina. 'Dani, you can take my car and bring Shona to see Sonia in the nursing home with your grandfather.' Paulina handed her keys over to Dani.

Shona tried to talk to Tommy to tell him what she'd found out from Dani, but he kept ignoring her and walking away from her. She could feel his anger rising with each attempt.

He was already walking towards the taxi rank, and Shona followed him. 'Can I take Ruby with me, Tommy? To see Sonia?'

She tried to ease Ruby from her father, but Tommy was holding fast.

'No. Shona, leave her. Ruby, jump in the car with Paulina.'

Ruby took a quick look at her mam and dad before climbing into the taxi. She clearly wasn't sure what to make of all the tension going on.

'Your daughter's not a piece of meat to be picked up and thrown down whenever it pleases you. Unlike me. I don't know how Dani has forgiven you so easily. You obviously managed to turn on the charm with her like you do with everyone else.' He lowered his voice to a whisper. 'So you slept with me one night, and you slept with some Toni the next night, but it won't happen again.' He walked away, but Shona walked beside him.

'Tommy, I didn't … you know … with Toni. I know I didn't. I was sure I couldn't have, but Dani kept going on about it, and in the end, I believed it happened. And you overheard Dani shouting at me about it. But—'

'Save it, Shona. You don't remember, so how would you know?'

Shona took hold of Tommy's arm to try to slow him down. 'Dani's boyfriend is actually a *girl*friend. It's not short for Anto*nio* but Anto*nia*. There is no way that we, eh … were together like that. You of all people know where my preferences lie. It didn't happen.'

Tommy stopped and stared at Shona, and she continued. 'We have to talk about it, Tommy, but right now I need to go back to see my grandmother one more time. We're going home in a few hours, and I still need to ask her so much about my mother and why Sonia left Ireland. I'll need answers if I'm going to speak to Fiona and Anna.'

'Could we not have had one week, Shona, without you complicating things? You're a law unto yourself. Even if you didn't sleep with that Toni person, you still got pissed drunk again. How are me and Ruby supposed to put up with that? She's only little now, but she can't grow up with that kind of uncertainty in her life. Look, go and talk to Sonia for now, but this conversation doesn't end here. We need to put a line under you and me, then make plans for supervised access with Ruby. I can't handle you, Shona Moran, and I don't even want to try any more.'

Shona caught the filthy look that Tommy shot in her direction, and swallowing a lump in her throat, she tried to reach out to him again. 'Tommy we were doing so well. You've no idea how sorry I am.'

But Tommy wasn't having any of it. 'Do you know how many times you have apologised in the years that I've known you, Shona? But it's always the same. You may have kept up the charade for longer than normal this time, but you still ended up falling into your black hole.'

Shona tried to put her two hands up to beseech Tommy, but he used his stick to push her away again. 'So, you didn't sleep with Dani's girlfriend, and you think you're bloody wonderful. I'm not pissed off about that,' he said, in a loudly whispered rant, his eyes filled with tears. '*This* is because you fell off your fragile wagon so easily on the second day of our holiday. One minor sensitive misunderstanding and you did a runner, not only on me, but on Ruby too. We're not having any more of your fuck-ups,' he said. 'You can go to hell.'

Shona watched him climb in beside Ruby and swallowed a sob. She was such an idiot. She had paradise in her hands this week, and she'd let it all go. As she looked at Tommy with Ruby on his lap, she felt such a longing to be part of them – to be Tommy's other half. She remembered her mother's words as she was growing up: *You always want what you can't have, Shona.*

CHAPTER FORTY-FOUR

Shona and Sonia sat side by side in the family room in Sonia's nursing home. Maria's mother and Maria's daughter. The wild, young woman who connected these two women seemed to be in that room with them, willing them together, while Enrico and Dani were having a coffee together in the café.

'Another day or two and I'll be going home to Enrico. Isn't that great news altogether, Shona?'

Shona nodded and tried to smile. It was funny to hear her Spanish grandmother speak English with such a Donegal accent – a reminder that she had spent so much of her life there.

'But in the meantime, Shona, my love, I have all the time in the world to listen to your troubles. I failed your mother, because as much as I loved her, I could never get her to conform to the ways of our small village. I realised too late that I was wrong to try and change her. We should have welcomed her differences and celebrated her talents, instead of always trying to stifle her. She was beautiful and intelligent. Manus knew from the beginning that she wasn't his, so he turned back to drinking and he treated Maria terribly. I tried to come between them. It was terrible to watch him speak to her in the same way that I had been spoken to – as the bastard daughter in my own childhood home.'

Shona frowned, puzzled.

'Yes,' said Sonia. 'Another story I'll tell you sometime, about my own upbringing. I deserved everything Manus gave me. I ruined his life, Shona. I ruined a good man. Manus loved me and that was his downfall. I loved Enrico and that was mine.'

Shona looked over at her elderly grandmother. It was hard to know if she was telling the truth or rambling through memories, but it all fitted together, so it must have been true.

'How is Fiona, Shona? And Anna? I was going to go to my grave with this secret. It seemed kinder to everyone, except to me. I would give anything to see them again. To hold my daughter in my arms and to see my other granddaughter. It was a terrible thing to do. A crazy decision. I wanted to go back so very much or contact them some way, but I kept leaving it a bit longer, deciding to enjoy life with Enrico for a while. For the first time in my adult life – actually, in my whole life – I was almost happy. I'm not saying I didn't love my life with Fiona and Maria, I did, but when I lost your mother, I fell apart. It was easy for Enrico to ask me to leave Donegal. I messed up by marrying Manus. I should have stuck to my decision to wait Franco out, then go home, but I was lonely, so I gave in. Poor Manus.'

'And poor Fiona. According to Anna she never got over your death, Sonia. She blamed herself. She said that she and Maria were never enough for you. She knew that you always wanted something else. Someone else.'

'Ach, lay it on me, why don't you? I wanted to *belong*, that's all – to love and be loved. Call Anna, Shona, and tell her for me. I would give anything to meet her again. See what she thinks about talking to Fiona.'

'I know full well what she'll think, Sonia, but I'll call her anyway.' Shona reached forward and hugged her grandmother. 'I'm so glad I've met you. I, of all people, know what it means to need to belong to someone, so meeting you has made life more meaningful. I'm going to ring my sister, and I'll come back to you shortly.'

'Hi, Anna.'

'Shona! How are you? How's Spain? How's Ruby? Is it hot? Did you find any of Granny's family?'

Shona took a deep breath and steadied herself. She could spend this conversation talking about the weather or she could get right into it and tell her sister the incredible news that she was still trying to digest herself.

'I'm fine, Anna. Spain is beautiful and very warm. Ruby thinks she's in sand and sea heaven.'

'And Tommy, Shona. Have you fallen out with each other yet, or have you fallen in love?' Anna laughed.

'Hah. You're hilarious, Anna. No. We were getting on very well with each other, actually. We were being very grown up about everything. Well, until …'

'What? What did you do, Shona?'

'Jesus, Anna. I did nothing. Thanks a bunch. It was Enrico who's upsetting the cart this time. You know? The man who was Granny's ex-boyfriend.'

'Go on.'

'Well, it seems he wasn't such an *ex*-boyfriend after all. Are you ready for this?'

'Okay. I'm sitting down now. Shoot.'

'Enrico came to Ireland after he was released from jail when Franco died.' Then Shona went on to tell her the wild tale that followed his visit and how it affected them all. Anna was crying.

'They didn't mean to hurt you all. It happened, that's all.' Shona was trying to gauge Anna's reaction, but she was silent. 'Say something.'

'Fuck sake, Shona.'

'Your mammy's obviously not within earshot,' said Shona. 'She's going to have a fit, and I wouldn't blame her.'

'She's not going to have a fit, Shona. I'm not going to tell her. She's lived in ignorance of what actually happened all these years. You can't tell her either. And what about poor old Eiley? The deceit. They *grieved*, Shona. Years of healing later, I'm not going to let some auld fella in Malaga get something off his chest, so he can feel better and die in peace. What about the rest of us? Mam is never going to hear this shite. It's not going to happen, Shona. I'm not having someone coming to tell my mam that my grandmother didn't die years ago, and that she's living in Andalucía with a fella she ran off to Spain with.'

Shona sighed. She felt that whatever she did with this new information about their lives, it wouldn't matter. If she didn't open up and tell the truth, then Enrico and Sonia would be upset. And if she did … well, the hurt would travel far between Ireland and Spain.

'That fella she ran off with is our grandfather. I'll leave it with you, Anna. Think about it for a while. I love you, sis.'

Shona was getting that awful feeling again, where she felt that everything that was going wrong was always her fault. That she was somehow responsible for getting her new birth family into this predicament. She had wanted to find out about where her grandmother came from. The grandmother who had walked into the waves on a beach in Donegal full of grief when her daughter died. But Sonia hadn't done that. She had climbed a cliff and left Ireland with Enrico. Her grandfather.

'Can you come to Spain, Anna? Could you bring Fiona do you think?'

'Shona, you never cease to amaze me. You think that everyone can always drop everything and run wherever you want them to be. Real life is not like that. I'm studying for my masters right now.'

'You could study here. Your mam would buy that idea. I could do with some help, Anna. I was supposed to be going home today with Tommy and Ruby, but I want to stay on here for a bit longer. To find out more about this family history. I'm out of my depth. I *need* you here. And maybe your dad could come. We could do with his practical head on the situation.'

'Shona, my dad will go through you for a shortcut. We're getting over the fact that you found out Maria didn't overdose; that she was murdered. My mother grieved all over again for her sister. I can't do this to her with her mother as well. It would hurt her too much.'

'So, we sit back and live a life of lies? Do you think that Fiona would want that? I've already been the victim of being lied to all my life about my adoption. If she finds out in the future, I don't want her to feel the way that I do now. Think about it, Anna. I'll ring you later.'

'Yeah. Thanks for that, Shona. No pressure.' Anna's face disappeared and the phone went dead.

There was no point in Shona wondering whether she had done the right thing or not. The damage was done. Not by her, but by Sonia and Enrico, and before them, by Hugo and a poor woman called Rosita. A long line of deceit by people who never meant to be dishonest but fell in love with the wrong person – just as she had with Jameel. That was in the past, and though she felt a sadness around her when she thought of how Jameel died, she knew that she was over him; it had never been the right kind of love, only a passing passion.

She knew that what she felt for Tommy was real, and she had to do something to rectify the mess she had got herself into. One small problem in her life and she had poured vodka down her throat like it was the last bottle in the world. It was time to face up to the fact that she could never have a drink. She would tackle that problem when she got home. It was the only way back to Tommy. But for now, she needed to stay here for a week or so and try to put the whole story of her past into something that made sense, and Sonia was the person who would show her how to do that. She walked back to the family room and Sonia looked up at her expectantly. Hopefully. She would have to tell her the truth about what Anna had said.

'I can see by your face that the call didn't go down very well, Shona. I'm so sorry that you were the one who had to make it.'

Shona sat down beside her grandmother. 'That's an understatement. So, what would you say to Fiona or Anna or even Eileen if you did have them here in front of you?' Shona was still reeling from the difficult phone call she'd had with Anna. 'Not that I think there's ever a chance of that happening. My sister says that there is no way that she's telling her mam that you're still alive. She says the shock would be too awful.'

'Until you got here, Shona, I had decided that Enrico and I would go to our graves with our secret. It was easier on everyone in Ireland and in Spain. We were terribly selfish, but I felt at the time that we had all suffered enough. Me and Enrico and Manus. I couldn't desert Manus in Balcallan, it was unheard of. So I died. Poor Fiona and Eileen. I'm sure they're the only ones who noticed my leaving once the initial horror of it had died with me, but I'm sorry now.

'I realise that we were naïve to think that we could keep a secret like that. The world is a much smaller place than it was many years ago. It's so much harder to hide away now than it used to be. Somebody was always going to find us.'

Sonia turned away from Shona and stared out the window at the sea. It was hard to admit how wrong she had been. She felt tears gathering and a lump forming in her throat.

Shona reached to the small table and poured the coffee that had been left for them.

'Sit back, abuela, and drink up. You followed your heart for the first time in your life. You had been selfless all those years in Ireland. Staying with Manus and letting Enrico go back to Spain must have been so hard, but you did it. Lying to your family was wrong, but you did it for all the right reasons. I've been doing that all my life. Doing wrong for the right reasons. I'm delighted to know that I got it from somewhere.'

The two women laughed in a giggly, girly fashion and sat back and sipped their coffee.

'Ah, I love Spanish coffee,' said Shona. 'But seriously, I'm nothing as nice as you. Mostly I always did the wrong things for the *wrong* reasons. I go off the rails quite regularly in life. My poor mother, Norah, has had to put up with an awful lot of crap.'

'Well, there you are,' said Sonia. 'Maria was a little brat too, but I loved that child so very much. When I found out that she died, took her own life all alone in that big city, I was heartbroken.'

Shona spluttered on her hot coffee. She had forgotten that Enrico and Sonia had no idea that Maria's death in Dublin had been no suicide.

'Are you all right, Shona?' Sonia was concerned.

'Yes. I'm fine. It's hard to think about … how she died. That's all.' Shona wondered was this a secret that she *should* keep from them. Shona hated secrets, but how do you tell a mother that her daughter was actually murdered? That the man who had killed her was dead now too?

'Honestly,' she said. 'I'm fine.'

Sonia shook her head. 'I went *off the rails* as you called it when Maria was found dead. You say that I was selfless, that I was following my heart, but I would never have done those things if Maria had lived. Friends and family would not have been surprised when they heard that I had also killed myself. I had been behaving strangely for so long. Enrico used that knowledge to make them believe that I had walked into the waves on purpose. It was almost a year after I came back to Spain before I realised the terrible cruelty of what I had done, not only to Fiona and Eiley, but to myself as well. To know that your daughter, granddaughter, and your best friend were only a plane ride away, and that I could never go back to see them, made me go crazy some days. But by then, how could I go back? This seemed like the only way.'

'So, what will you do now, abuela? Let Anna say nothing to Fiona and Eileen, or let them know that you're still alive?'

Shona was thinking of her own deceit. If Sonia decided to tell the truth, then Shona would tell her grandparents what had actually happened to Maria. But if Sonia and Enrico decided to keep their secrets, then maybe Shona would be entitled to keep hers too.

'I don't know, querida. I remember how I felt when Enrico came to Ireland after he was released from prison. I had thought that he was dead, and yet there he was, standing on a beach in Donegal. The shock was incredible. But he hadn't tried to deceive me. He hadn't pretended to be dead, as I have. Ah, I don't know what to do, Shona. What will I do, darling girl?'

Shona looked over at Sonia and burst out laughing.

'What's so funny?' Sonia asked.

Shona laughed even more but managed to splutter. 'In my twenty-three years, abuela, nobody has ever asked my opinion on anything as monumental as what you have asked. Nobody has ever considered me worthy of an opinion on things that matter. I'm usually the one who causes the problems not solves them. So, I have to say it's a breath of fresh air to meet somebody whose problems are so bad that they need *my* opinion on how to go about to find the answer.' She stopped laughing and held Sonia's hand.

'A family vote, Granny. That's what we'll do. You, Enrico, me, Tommy, Paulina and Daniela. If it's a tie, we'll ask Ruby to be the tie-breaker.' Sonia roared laughing.

'Shona Moran, you are so like your mother. That's exactly the ridiculous kind of rubbish that she would have come out with too.'

'So, can you come up with a better solution, Granny?'

'No, my love. There are only ridiculous solutions for situations as ridiculous as the one that we're caught up in.'

'Seriously, though,' said Shona. 'Let's take matters one thing at a time. Let you and me get to know each other first, and then we'll decide what to do about Anna, Fiona and Eileen.'

'That's what we'll do, darling girl. Now this flight that Tommy has booked for tonight. Can we talk him out of it?'

'I doubt it, Sonia. He had to pay extra to change the flights.'

'I will pay extra again for you all to go back another day, Shona, and I'll reimburse him for today's extra. Please. Ask him. I want you to stay a little longer, but I would so love it if you kept Princesa Ruby here for a while longer too. And Shona ... before you go, this evening or otherwise, there is something I want to say to you. Meeting you, our Maria's child, and hearing how Anna is doing, has given me and Enrico so much joy. To have you both as our grandchildren is so special. Your mother was somebody that we created together, so you and Anna are an extension of that. To hear you calling us abuelo and abuela, your granny and grandad, is like sweet music. It would be so perfect to see Anna too.'

Shona burst into tears and threw her arms around Sonia. 'Abuela, I love you so much already. So, whatever Tommy decides to do, I'm going to stay on a bit longer. I'll see you tomorrow and for so many tomorrows after that.'

'Don't cry, my beautiful Shona, my namesake. I love you too. Be good now and stay out of trouble, and I'll see you tomorrow morning. I'm totally exhausted from the day's activities.'

'Bye, abuela.' Shona took a tissue from the table and blew hard and walked off to find Dani and Enrico in the garden.

'You look a mess, Shona.' Dani smiled and gave her a hug. 'Hey. I just called Tommy. I got him to speak to Enrico here, to persuade him to stay on for a few more days. Abuelo will pay for your new flights when you decide to go home, but for now, there is too much unfinished business to walk away from.'

'Oh, Enrico, I'm so glad. I called my sister and told her about Sonia and you, and she's so angry. I've disturbed a wasp's nest with all this.'

'Shona, think about it. This is not yours or my doing,' said Dani. 'The people who came before us made decisions that wrecked other lives. This is not your fault, and for us here in Spain at least, you are good news. You have made Enrico and Sonia so happy. You and the beautiful Ruby. I'm so happy that you're not going home yet. I want to get to know you properly now that I've got over my childishness about our abuelo. It would be so good to meet Anna too.'

'Dani, I don't want to take anything from you. Not your grandfather or your home. Nothing. I want my family. I want to belong.'

'So welcome to the Sanchez–Almez family, Shona. Let's see if we can make it all work for us.'

CHAPTER FORTY-FIVE

Shona sat on the beach on the spot which her grandmother had told her had been her own favourite place as a teenager growing up in Spain. In front of the house, Sonia had said, far enough away to feel peaceful, but near enough to hear her father shout for her. There was almost a full moon. Dani had told her that it would take another two days of changing tides and weather before the moon was completely full. Right now, the stars reminded her of the hundreds and thousands her mam had sprinkled on her chocolate cakes as a child. Her upbringing had been so different to Sonia's. She had wanted for nothing, but she had thrown it all back in her parents' faces.

She took out her phone and keyed in her dad's name. She wanted to tell him all about her adventures and hear Des Moran laugh his hearty laugh and say *never a dull moment since the day you arrived, Shona Moran.* Shona was desperate to hear his lovely voice. She was blessed to have her family, both adopted and biological. He didn't answer, so she tried her aunt's phone instead. She got voicemail there too.

'Hiya, Aunty Margaret. It's Shona here. You're probably never going to speak to me again after the way I spoke to you on the phone the other day, but, well, I'm ringing to say I'm sorry and …' Shona's voice broke. 'And, oh, I can't believe the things I said to you. I'm so sorry. Will you ring me back? Please? We're not coming home yet, Margaret. Tommy's calmed down and we're staying a bit longer. I want to get to know everyone here a bit better. My God, the stories I have to tell you … the things I've found out over the last few days …Ring me.'

She would have to save the rest for when Margaret called her back. *If* she did. Shona couldn't blame her if she didn't, but she was hopeful. Margaret had always forgiven her for everything before. She took a tissue from her pocket and blew her nose. She would be better off not blubbing on the phone to Margaret. Better to speak to her later.

Paulina got up from her chair and opened the shutters of her bedroom window. The spring sunrise poured into the room, and she enjoyed the familiar feeling of being wrapped in its warmth. Her *early morning hug* her mamá had called it when she was a child. It was one of the few familiar things left in her life. First Sonia had come back to Spain, saying she wanted nothing to do with her family home. She wanted to leave Enrico's daughter and granddaughter living and working in the guest house they had called home all of their lives. Eventually, she had relaxed, and the panic of Sonia's homecoming had faded.

Now Sonia's granddaughter was here, and she and her sister Anna had the strongest claim on the ownership of Paulina's home. Their conversation of the day before had made Paulina feel a little more at ease, but she had still woken this morning with that sick feeling in her stomach at the possible loss of the bricks and mortar she held so dear.

'You've nothing to worry about on my account, Paulina.' Shona's words were there to calm the tension that had pushed itself between them, causing a rift before they had even had a chance to get to know each other better. 'Meeting you and Dani has been amazing. I mean, think about it. You were my mam's sister, Paulina. If you want us to get a solicitor involved, we can; but you have my word. I came here to find the man who was the love of my grandmother's life. I never expected to find

Sonia herself, and to find that your dad is actually my grandad; that you're my aunt, and Daniela is my cousin. I promise you it feels like a fairy tale. My week has been a carousel of emotions, amazement, happiness, some sadness thrown in too, but most of all it's been about love.'

'I want to believe you, Shona, but my life since Daniela was born has not been easy. Her father's family caused me such problems, and I've found it hard to trust people I don't know since then. Whatever about losing my home, almost losing Dani was heartbreaking. I don't want solicitors. I had enough of all that when Daniela was little. If I brought you to court, I would lose. This house belongs to Sonia, to Fiona, to you and Anna, officially.'

'It belongs to Sonia, maybe; but she has only sad memories here, and the rest of us have no claim to it. You and Dani were born here. You've built this place into the happy place it is today with your mother before you, and as much as I've fallen in love with the place and the sense of belonging that it brings, Dublin is my home. It's where I grew up, and it's where Tommy will be. Ruby's daddy and I might be able to get together and make a life with each other, and then we could come over here for holidays and Ruby could get to know our Spanish family more as the years go by.'

'You and Dani have certainly sorted out your differences. I'm so glad. She's my pride and joy that girl. I love everything about her.'

'You're so lucky to have each other. I'm amazed at the close relationship that you seem to have. You're more like sisters than mother and daughter. My mother, Norah, who brought me up – we've spent most of our lives fighting with each other. I only found out about my adoption a few years ago. I went completely mad with drinking afterwards, but Norah stuck by me. It's taken time, but I eventually realised that she's a brilliant mother and a fantastic grandmother. She made a mistake, though, by keeping my birth secret from me.'

'Speaking of grandmothers and secrets; I think Sonia has made a big mistake keeping her supposed death a secret from her daughter. I wish she would tell her.'

'She might yet. It's early days. Let Anna think it over for a while. See what happens.'

Paulina sat in the early morning thinking about Anna. Whatever she decided to do would have such a great impact on all their lives. This young woman who she'd never met could change everything and the pessimist in Paulina was getting the better of her. Anna might decide that she had a claim to Paulina's home. What then?

CHAPTER FORTY-SIX

Shona got out of the taxi with Tommy and Ruby outside Enrico and Sonia's villa.

'It's very different up here in the pueblo than it is down by the coast,' said Shona. The cobbled streets with their white-washed terraced houses, bedecked with colourful flowers, were a stark contrast to the beaches with their bars and restaurants. 'Enrico told me that they were left this lovely house by a friend of his called Roberto, who was a Nationalist soldier in the civil war, but helped the people on the other side. He said this man risked his life daily to do right by people like Enrico. Apparently, if it wasn't for Roberto, my grandfather would never have made it through his time in prison. Sonia says Enrico doesn't like to talk about those days too much.'

'Here he comes, the man himself,' said Shona, as Enrico hobbled towards them using his cane. 'You look like the cat who got the cream, abuelo.'

'If you mean I look happy because my Sonia is home where she belongs, and I've been released from the hold of my fussing daughter, then you are absolutely right. Welcome to my house.'

Sonia walked out the door at that moment, leaning over her frame, but managing without help from anyone else. Shona thought that these two people were at their best when they were with each other. It must have been so awful for them when they had been apart all those years.

Ruby wriggled free from her father's hand and went running to Enrico first for hugs and kisses and then to Sonia. Sonia sat on a nearby chair and patted her lap for Ruby. 'Up you come, Princesa Ruby. Come and tell abuela all about your holidays.'

Ruby climbed up on her great-granny's lap and snuggled in close. In a short time, she had decided how much love was been thrown around here and who was giving it most, and she chatted away happily.

'Come on inside, Shona and Tommy,' said Enrico. 'It's early in the year for it to be this warm.'

Tommy followed Enrico without a second thought inside to the air-conditioned villa. 'Would you like a beer, Tommy?' asked Enrico.

'Ah, maybe later,' said Tommy. 'If you have a mineral, that would be lovely for now.'

'A what?' said Enrico.

'He wants a fizzy drink,' called Sonia from outside. She smiled up at Shona. 'The Irish should come with their own dictionary,' she said. 'Isn't he good not to have an alcoholic drink when you can't have one?'

'What do you mean?' asked Shona.

'It's hard living with an alcoholic when they can't have a drink and you'd like one.'

'Right. Well, tell it as it is, Granny, why don't you?' Shona was put out by Sonia's straightforward statement.

'Well, you are an alcoholic, aren't you, darling? Your great-grandfather was, and your mother was a drug addict. Genetically speaking, you didn't stand a chance, but you seem to be doing okay since your little lapse earlier this week. Am I right?'

Shona sat down on a chair beside her grandmother. 'There's not much escapes your eyes, is there? Yes. I've been such a good little girl, Granny, and I promise I'll be good for the rest of the holiday.'

'Sarcasm will get you nowhere, miss. Your mammy spoke to me like that all the time in her last few years with me. She was a little pup, but she was as gorgeous and charming as you are, so she got away with it most of the time.'

'Can we talk about something else? I don't mean that I don't want to talk about my mother, but I certainly don't want to talk about all the bad points that I've inherited from her.'

Shona blinked back tears. She wanted her time with her grandparents to be special, and that didn't include hearing about all Maria's bad points.

'Ah, I'm sorry, Shona. When you're my age you get a little cranky. I'll behave, I promise.'

'And I will too. I promise,' said Shona, smiling. Enrico came out with a large jug of iced water and two glasses. Shona noticed he hadn't asked her what she would like to drink. She would have to get used to that – to being different. Right now, she would give anything for that glass of iced water to be a vodka and orange juice. Would she always feel like that she wondered? Or would it get easier? But if it meant that Tommy might stay with her for as long as she was sober, then the prize was worth the effort ten times over.

She smiled up at her grandfather as he put the glasses and jug down on the table in front of them. 'Thank you, abuelo. Exactly what we need.'

Enrico made a dramatic attempt at a bow and looked down the road as if he was expecting someone. 'Daniela is coming up soon and she has made some lunch for us all. She says she can't stay as she has to work, but she promises me that it is a feast fit for a king.'

'Dani shouldn't have gone to all that trouble, Enrico,' said Sonia. 'I could have put something together with my lovely family here. Shona could have helped. I'm not incapable, you know.'

'You are certainly not that, my love. But—'

'But what?' Sonia looked ready to lose her temper with Enrico.

Enrico took a deep breath. 'We are having visitors, mi amor. Some very special people have travelled a very long way to see us. Dani picked them up from the airport, and they're on their way here now.'

'Who, Enrico? Who is coming? Don't mess with me, I'm too old for playing tricks. I don't like surprises, you know that.' Sonia was getting very agitated. Ruby slid off her lap, sensing her great-grandmother's tension.

'I know, Sonia, but I won't tell you who it is yet. Now you're not to trouble yourself about it. You know what the doctors said. You have to relax. I'm going back inside, and you can wait here for our visitors or come inside with us.' He turned and left them.

'Shona, do you know who is coming? Somebody from the past? Maybe an old school friend of mine? But he said that they are coming by plane. Oh, I could kill the man. I had better go back into my room and change into something smart. Men never think about things like that. I wore this old shirt over trousers because it was comfortable, but I know it does nothing for me, and I would have liked to put a bit of make-up on. Will you help me, Sonia? I can't meet anyone looking like this.' Sonia pulled her frame over and made to pull herself up.

'I think you're too late, abuela. I see Daniela's old banger coming down the road now, and she has passengers. Oh my God. Oh, my good God.'

'What is it, Shona? Who is it? Tell me. I can't see.'

The car drew nearer, and Dani pulled up outside. She jumped out of the driver's side and walked around to help one of her passengers from the car. Sonia had pulled herself to standing by now but was none the wiser about who was in the car with Enrico's granddaughter. Enrico came out of the house as fast as his stick would allow him, followed by Tommy on his walking stick.

Sonia froze as her old friend, Eileen, walked around the front of the car towards her, leaning on the arm of a young woman. She felt as though she couldn't breathe. She certainly couldn't speak. Eileen walked, slightly bent, straight passed her oldest friend to stand in front of Enrico who was grinning from ear to ear at having brought the two women together again after all these years. He certainly wasn't expecting it when Eileen brought her arm back and swung her hand full force across the paper-thin skin of Enrico's old cheek.

Everyone took an intake of breath, but Shona moved quickly to catch her grandad as he fell backwards in the doorway he had walked out of moments before. The shock was there on everyone's face except Sonia's. She was nodding her head as though she knew exactly why Eileen had done this to Enrico.

Tommy was the first to say anything. 'Who the fuck are you, and what do you think you're doing walking in here and smacking an old man across the face?'

Eileen was rubbing her hand and her arm. The exertion of what she had done was obviously causing her discomfort. 'You can bring me back to the airport now, em … Gabriella? Whatever your name is. I've done what I came here to do, and from the look on Sonia Dooley's face, she has a fairly good idea of what I think of her deceitful, bitch-faced ways of living her life. Your daughter Fiona will never know what you have done, Sonia. I hope she will never feel the hurt and rejection that I felt when Anna came to tell me you were still alive and asked me what I thought we should do.' She turned to her travelling companion. 'Anna, you can stay if you like but I'm leaving right now.'

Sonia was startled again. 'Anna?' she asked.

Anna nodded, not able to say anything. She walked towards Ruby and picked her up in her arms, not sure if she was protecting the child or herself from the madness.

'Aunty Anna? Who's that bold lady?' Ruby asked.

Eileen started to walk back to the car but turned back towards Enrico, who was crying now and leaning against the door frame. 'Bold, is it? If she wants bold, she should be looking towards her great-grandparents. And to think you let me send those Christmas cards to you, Enrico, and letters and photos telling you about your granddaughter Anna as she grew up. You miserable, two-faced little shit. I poured out my heart to you about how much I missed that fucking cow of a friend of mine. I thought I was writing to someone who felt the same love lost. And all that time you were enjoying each other's company while you rejected the rest of us. How the fuck could you do that? What gave you the bloody right to make the call on being dead?'

Eileen was raging. She walked back towards Sonia, who was beginning to bring herself around to what was happening. Eileen was almost on top of her before Tommy got between them and took the blow that was intended for Sonia. Daniela was beside her grandad now, wrapping her arms around him, soothing him with Spanish endearments.

'Enough now.' Tommy was beginning to understand what all this was about. 'I know you're angry, and you deserve to be, but we all need to calm down and go inside to work out how to sort the problem out.'

Eileen tried to push him out of her way; the effort of which made him smile. That was all Eileen needed to lose her head completely. 'I don't know who the fucking hell *you* are and what you think gives you the right to tell me how I should or should not react to that pair of conniving Spanish bastards. Let me at the bitch. I'll make her wish she *had* died years ago.'

Eileen grabbed at Sonia's sleeve. Tommy had dropped his cane by now and was trying to hold Eileen back without falling over himself. Ruby was crying, so Shona came over and took control.

'Okay, guys. As Tommy said earlier, enough is enough. You're upsetting my daughter and I'm not having any more of it.' She looked up at Tommy as she passed and took in his look of complete bewilderment at the antics of this nonagenarian madwoman. If it hadn't been so sad, it would have been comical.

'Inside everyone,' she said. 'Eileen, I can understand exactly how you feel. Secrets like this are shite. But Daniela is not taking you back to the airport until you and Granny have had a chance to sit down and talk this out with each other. Sonia's been very ill. She's barely out of hospital, and she's supposed to be taking it easy, not taking abuse. Let it go. At least, let *her* go.' She prised Eileen's fingers from Sonia's blouse. 'Now come on.'

Sonia and Eileen stared at each other. Sonia tried to reach out her hand towards her old friend. Her look was pleading. Tears were streaming from her rheumy, brown eyes, eventually becoming a sob. 'Oh, Eiley, Eiley. I'm so sorry. I should have died back then. I should never have been given this time with Enrico. I didn't deserve it. I have nothing to say to you in my defence. You're right. What we did to you all was unforgivable.'

'You've got that right. I would never in a million years have left my daughter standing on a beach in Balcallan looking out at the waves that she thought had taken her mother, when all that time, that same mother was living it up in the south of Spain.' Eileen wriggled away from Shona and backed up.

Sonia sank back down on the chair she had been sitting on earlier. 'Oh, I was never living it up, Eiley. My heart has been breaking all these years, yearning for my daughter and for all I'd left behind in Donegal. I was a madwoman who ran from a life that I thought that I couldn't cope with. By the time I realised what I had actually done, I couldn't turn around to you all and tell you I wasn't dead after all. I took the way that seemed to be easy on everyone.'

'Easy on you, you mean,' spat Eileen. 'It was certainly not easy on the rest of us. If it hadn't been for that one,' she said, pointing her bony finger at Shona, 'raking up her hornet's nest as she seems so good at doing, you'd have gotten away with it all and brought your dirty secret with you to your grave.'

Shona had had enough. She put the still-whimpering Ruby down on the bench beside Sonia and put her hands on her hips. 'This is most definitely not my fault, Eileen Sharkey. I only came over here to find out a little more about Sonia, my grandmother. How was I supposed to know that she was still alive?'

'Exactly, Shona. Nobody would ever have thought that anyone could think up such a terrible thing to do to the people who had loved her for most of her life, so she could be with some fella who she knew briefly as a child. But she did think it up, and she carried it out, and no matter who brought it all about in the end, nothing can change the way that things have turned out.' Eileen turned back to Sonia. 'I loved you. We were like sisters. You helped me care for my mother. I helped you care for Manus. I can't work out how this could have happened. How you could have thought that this was okay? I can't … Oh, good Jesus, Sonia … why? Why?'

And Eileen dropped herself down on the bench beside Sonia and threw her arms around her. 'You're alive, Sonia. I can't believe it's you. You're alive, you stupid, fucking bitch. I love you. Thank God, I've found you before we both died.'

'I love you too, Eiley. I'll never forgive myself for what I've done. I'm so happy you're here. So relieved. And you're right about one thing. I can never let Fiona know what I've done. It wouldn't be fair to her.' Sonia turned away from Eileen to look at Anna who had walked with the whimpering Ruby to the end of the garden. 'Is that really our Maria's Anna? Two granddaughters in one week. I can't believe it.'

Ruby stopped crying as her daddy walked over and took her from Anna. She glanced cautiously as she walked past the two crazy old ladies on the bench and clung to her daddy's hand. Shona joined them and hugged her little family to her. 'Come on inside, Ruby, and we'll see if Grandad has any ice-cream. Come with us, Anna. You can properly meet Grandad and leave Sonia until Eiley has calmed down.'

'You come inside too, abuelo, and I'll put some ice on your cheek,' said Daniela. 'It's getting very swollen, and maybe you can tell me a little more about what has happened here this afternoon.'

'I'll be damned if I have a clue, querida,' said Enrico as he stumbled back inside the villa, away from all the craziness that they had witnessed in the heat of the Andalusian afternoon.

Outside, the two old friends sat and chatted for an age, each one outdoing the other with news and anecdotes about their lives in Ireland and Spain. Eventually, the talk came back around to Sonia's leaving and the devastating effect it had left on her family. Eileen was adamant that Fiona shouldn't be told that her mother was still alive.

'Sure she's only getting over the news that her sister was murdered all those years ago and never took her own life as we previously thought. T'was that Shona one that raked that one up and all. She's a divil for the truth, no doubt about it.'

Sonia stared at Eileen. 'What do you mean, Eiley? Maria killed herself. She overdosed.'

Eileen realised her blunder, but it was too late. She would have to tell Sonia the truth now about how her daughter actually died, and she knew it would break her heart.

CHAPTER FORTY-SEVEN

Margaret had spent two sleepless nights worrying about Shona and decided that she couldn't take any more. She needed help and advice. She knew from Shona's social media that she was physically all right, and that she had obviously been playing with her emotions on the phone. Margaret had tried to convince herself that Shona was far too horrible to warrant her getting involved in another of her shitty messes, but then she had left her a message of apology. Being Margaret, she knew that eventually her love for her crazy goddaughter would wear her down, and she would dive in with Shona and end up pulling her to safety again.

It wouldn't be a good idea to ask Norah or Des to help out. Shona had spent so long getting her mother and father to forgive her for past demeanours that it wouldn't be practical to rock that particular boat. The more she had thought about it, the more it seemed that the best people to go to for advice were Fiona and Gerry. Or perhaps she would give Tommy's father, Stephen, a call. This was mostly about Ruby's future after all, and Ruby was his granddaughter.

'Hello, Stephen. This is Margaret. You know, Shona's aunt?'

'Of course I know, Margaret. How are you? And how are the Spanish brigade getting on? I'm not getting too much information from my son.' Stephen was laughing on the other end. He had such a lovely laugh.

'Em, well, I hear that Ruby has been having a ball. A complete lover of sand, sea and sun. But ... Well, I was wondering if I could have a chat with you, Stephen, about Tommy and ... eh, Shona?'

'Ah, not exactly my favourite person. If you're going to tell me that she's been fecking up my son's and granddaughter's lives again I'll go berserk.'

'Look, I hate phone conversations, Stephen. Can we meet up? I'll even come northside.' She laughed. The last time they had met, Stephen and Margaret had been teasing each other about their respective sides of the city. It was a long time since Margaret had thought about anyone in that way, but Des had insisted that Stephen was flirting with her that day, and to be honest, she had enjoyed every moment of his company.

'Grand so. I'll text you my address and you can let me know what time you'll be here.'

An hour later, Margaret was going through her very sad wardrobe and disregarding everything in it.

'You're a fucking eejit, Margaret,' she said to herself. 'What in God's name would that fella see in an old spinster like yourself? Get a grip.' Margaret grabbed her ancient comfort coat and ran down the stairs and out the door and into her battered Fiesta. Forty minutes later, she was sitting outside Stephen's terraced house and wondering what on earth she was doing here.

Standing in the porch waiting for the door to open, she felt a flutter in her stomach that she hadn't felt since her teenage years, back in the days when she actually believed that there would be somebody out there for her. 'Pull yourself together, you ancient biddy, you,' she said to herself as the door opened and Stephen stood there smiling and gesturing for her to come in.

The usual rigmarole with the teacups and kettle and the small talk that went with it was eventually over, and it was time to get down to talk about what she had come here to say.

'Stephen, I need to ask for your advice. It's about Shona.'

Stephen breathed in and let out a great big sigh. 'How can I give you advice about a girl that has me absolutely baffled since the day that I walked into her house to meet her and your sister, Norah. I have to be honest with you, Margaret. It took me a long time to get to the stage where I didn't want to throttle the girl. Or at the very least get her to the stage where she was as far away from my son as we could possibly get her.'

'Stephen,' interrupted Margaret, 'I know she's had her bad times, but lately she's been wonderful. She's completely off the drink. She's being a fantastic mother to Ruby. There even seems to be a bit of hope that herself and Tommy might sort out their differences and get properly together.'

'No chance.' Stephen was in with the negativity before she had had a word in. 'I know they're gone on holiday together, but that's for Ruby's sake, and because Shona's parents offered to finance it for them. It's great for Ruby that they've decided to be civil about being parents together, but that's as far as it goes.'

'I don't think so, Stephen. There's been a bit of a romance going on between them for a while now, I think. I mean ... Shona seemed to think there was a chance that—'

'Well, there isn't. No way. Margaret, you're a lovely lady, and I know that you've given so much of your life to sorting out Shona, catching her when she falls. And you better be ready because she will fall again, that's for sure. I'm sorry, but I don't want Tommy to spend his whole life having to pick up a wife or girlfriend off the floor.'

They sat in silence for a while. Margaret felt close to tears, and she knew that it wasn't only Stephen's attitude to Shona that was hurting her. She knew that if Stephen didn't want to have anything to do with her goddaughter, then he certainly wouldn't want to have anything to do with her aunt.

'What was it you wanted to ask my advice about anyway, Margaret? As I said, I probably have nothing much to say about her – nothing very nice any way.'

Margaret stayed quiet. She took a deep breath as she was on the verge of losing her temper with Stephen. He had every right to have his own opinion on Shona, and her goddaughter had given him every reason to say the things that he was saying, but it still rankled. Apart from revelations from the phone call that Margaret had had with her recently, and the further bad news from the call she had subsequently had with Tommy; Shona had been really trying hard to make things right in her own life and that of everyone else around her.

'Yeah, well, the more she's expected to fuck up, the more fucking-up she will do. That's for sure.' Margaret stood up. 'Thank you for the tea.' Turning on her heels, she began to head towards the door, but Stephen caught up with her and turned her around.

'Margaret, I'm sorry. Listen to me. Think about it. If Shona wasn't your goddaughter; if she was only someone you knew as little as I know her, then …'

'Then I wouldn't go around slandering her name when I know absolutely nothing about her or why she might be the way she is.'

'Tommy is my only child. I brought him up by myself, and I was never sure from one day to the next whether I made the right decisions about how I did that. But whatever I did, I must have done something all right, because he is one gorgeous young fella. He's intelligent and kind and great fun to be around. I nearly lost him in a car accident, thanks to Shona's shenanigans, but now, thanks to his determination and hard work I have a son who is back at university, albeit with a limp and a walking stick at twenty-four years of age. I'm sorry, but every time I look at Shona Moran, I think about the trouble she's caused and likely to cause in the future.'

'I'm wasting my time completely. You have your mind made up about a young kid who has been through hell over the last five years or so. But instead of losing everything, she is now back in the driving seat and being a great mother to your beautiful granddaughter. Have you thought about that at all?'

'You know, Margaret, you're some woman.' Stephen was smiling broadly, one hand on the wall and one hand on Margaret's shoulder. 'I admire you for the way you are.'

Margaret couldn't believe that she had been taken in by this man's flattery and flirting. She realised that she had only travelled across Dublin because she had wanted an excuse to see Stephen again. The man's middle-aged, rugged good looks had pulled her in. Right now, he was looking at her in a way that was making it very difficult to do what she knew she should be doing. Walking out his front door and not coming back near him again.

'Before you storm off, Margaret, hear me out for a minute.' *What was he? A mind reader?* 'Do you think Tommy had an easy childhood? His mammy was gone before he was old enough to know she was there. And would you believe, even in these times, there were those who thought it might have been better off if I had put him into fostering or adoption? That a young fella like myself might not be able to bring up a baby alone. I lost a lot of friends when I told them all to go fuck themselves.'

Margaret shivered in the hall. 'It's freezing here. Can we go back inside if we're going to continue with this?'

Stephen stood back and there was that flirty smile again. 'Is it cold or is my northside bad mouth too much for your southside ladyship?'

Margaret didn't know what to make of this man. She burst out laughing. 'If any other man spoke to me in that way, I would have been out the door and gone in a flash.' But she couldn't fault the man for being himself, not if she was asking him to excuse her niece's behaviour. And was she? Asking him to excuse Shona?

'But you're still here. Does that make me special?'

Margaret was shaking her head, still smiling, and turning to go and sit back down in her earlier seat.

'Not so fast, lady. I think we should go out to a nice restaurant I know nearby and work out all our problems over a lovely meal. And we'll pretend that that's exactly what we're doing and not in any way look on it as a first date. How about that?'

Margaret froze as she realised that he was standing so close to her that there was no room to back away. So, when he reached in and kissed her full on the lips, she had no choice but to stand there, unmoving, even if she had wanted to move. Which she didn't.

It was inevitable that, two bottles of wine, two Irish coffees and a whole lot of laughter later, Margaret and Stephen decided that it would be a great idea to book themselves on a plane to Andalucía the next day to help the kids sort out their lives for once and for all.

CHAPTER FORTY-EIGHT

Shona woke early the next morning to the sound of the waves. The next sound that she heard was the guest house kitchen coming to life. She smiled at her still-sleeping Ruby, in her put-you-up-bed a few feet away from her mother, her sweet little face damp from the heat. Margaret and Stephen's arrival the day before had shocked her and delighted her in equal measures. And there was something weird about both of them. Stephen had been so nice to her all evening, and Margaret had been different somehow. Younger-looking. Smiling more. Definitely strange, but it was great to see them. There had only been the one twin room left at the guest house, but they had jokingly agreed to put up with each other for a few days.

Margaret had persuaded Tommy to take some time away from Ruby today to head into Malaga with Shona, to give them time to talk about what had gone wrong this week.

'And every other week before that,' said Stephen. But when Margaret smiled at him and said, 'Enough,' he had actually winked at Shona and smiled in a way Shona had never seen before.

Listening to Tommy's gentle snores, Shona was a bit anxious about what the day held for both of them. They had said they would head off early, so she reached over and shook him gently. She tried to gauge from his waking whether he was looking forward to the day ahead or dreading it, but he threw off the sheet and headed for the shower as quickly as his *morning leg* – as he called his aches – would let him, so she didn't have time to read him.

Ruby woke with the sudden noise and sat up. She looked so adorable with her wakey-up smile and crazy hair that Shona vowed to herself that she would do everything she could to make sure that Tommy continued to let her look after her when he was at college. Unless, of course, things turned out even better than that, and she and Tommy ended up back together. Was it a pipe dream? There was no doubt that Tommy was happy to be with her earlier that week. If she could only bring him back to that way of thinking.

Throwing back the light quilt, she reached over and swept Ruby up onto her lap. There was nothing like that sleepy hug where Ruby quietly lay her head on Shona's shoulder and allowed herself to be held. The smell of last night's bath still clung to her skin, and Shona was filled with a love so utterly complete.

She whispered into her daughter's ear. 'Ruby, I will never risk losing the right to be your mammy. I'm all yours and you are mine. Mine and your daddy's. No matter what happens between us, that will never change.'

Ruby sat up and stared intensely at her mammy, and Shona was rewarded with one of her most beautiful smiles. Tommy was coming back from the shower and as he reached the bed, he dropped the towel from around his waist, leaving him there for Shona to gaze at. Pulling a clean shirt and shorts from his case, he turned and winked at Shona.

'Enjoying the view, are we?'

'Immensely,' she said, and they both broke down in a fit of giggles. Ruby had no idea what the joke was, but she joined in the laughter and clapped her little hands together with the joy of the moment. Tommy bent down and kissed the top of Ruby's head. Then as Shona turned towards him, he cupped his hands around her face and kissed her on the lips. Shona felt there was more love in that small kiss than there ever had been between them before.

'Tommy, I …' Shona began but was interrupted.

'Save it for later, Shona. We have all day to ourselves, and we'll have plenty to talk about. Okay?' Shona nodded.

'Come on, Ruby and we'll get you changed and dressed.'

There was a knock on the door and Tommy ran for the bathroom again. Shona went to answer it and was surprised to see Paulina.

'Come in. How are you? Sorry, were we making too much noise?' Shona asked and Paulina shook her head. 'No, no. I have this for Ruby.' She held out a shopping bag and Shona opened it to find a beautiful Spanish-style dress inside.

'Oh, it's gorgeous,' said Shona. 'There was no need. You're too good.' Carrying Ruby on her hip, she kissed Paulina on both cheeks. 'Thank you so much. You've already given us too much, opening your house up to us. You've made us very welcome, and now with Margaret and Stephen suddenly here, you've been wonderful.' Shona put her arms around her aunt and hugged her, and Paulina, although not sure what to do, put her arms up and patted Shona on the back in return. It was the most demonstrative she had been since they had arrived there. They both withdrew from each other awkwardly.

'You were just on time. I was getting Ruby ready for her day without her mammy and daddy. So now we can leave her dressed like a princess for the day. Look at this, Ruby. There won't be a princess in Andalucía to compare with my girl.'

Paulina nodded and smiled again and headed for the door. After she had left, Shona got down to getting herself and Ruby ready for their separate days. She was filled with a happiness she hadn't felt for so long. If ever.

Margaret and Stephen were already in the breakfast room when the trio eventually emerged. Once again, Shona noticed a closeness between the two that sounded alarm bells in her head of, well … something amazingly lovely happening. From the look of them,

Shona was sure that only one of the twin beds in their room had been used the night before. When had this begun? Shona wasn't sure how she felt about it all. Obviously, she was delighted that Margaret had someone in her life at long last, but Stephen? It kind of felt all wrong, but then again, who was Shona Moran to question other people's relationships? These two people needed someone else, and they had found each other through her. She smiled, and kissed Ruby who ran into Margaret's outstretched arms.

'Everything she needs for the day should be in that bag, Margaret, but if she needs anything else, then here's the key to our room.'

'If I was able to mind Shona Moran at that age, I'm sure her daughter will be a doddle. Now scat the pair of you and go bring about world peace.'

'Hah. Thanks,' said Shona. 'I think it might be best if we got going early, Tommy, and we'll get something to eat along the way. We'll let these two lovebirds coo over Ruby and play happy families for the day.'

Shona winked at Stephen and was rewarded with a goofy-looking smile that said she was absolutely right. Tommy raised his eyebrows at her, and she said, 'I'll fill you in on the bus.'

Taking Tommy by the hand she led him away as he looked back at his dad while trying to figure out what was going on and what Shona had meant.

Later that day, after a huge feed of tapas, washed down with iced tea, Tommy and Shona were sitting side by side in a pew in Malaga Cathedral. They were looking up at the enormous altar and the almost scary statues and tapestries depicting Spanish Catholicism down through the years.

'We learned a lot about the history of Spain in our Spanish class at school,' said Shona, 'but looking at everything we've seen today brings it all to life. Especially after hearing Enrico's and Sonia's stories about their part in that history.'

They sat in silence for a while and Tommy reached over and held and squeezed Shona's hand. Shona felt a sense of belonging in Spain that she had never felt before, but it had as much to do with Tommy being with her as it had to do with her Spanish relations. She leaned over and put her head on Tommy's shoulder.

'Tommy. We were supposed to spend today talking about … well, stuff about us.'

'Yeah. I know.'

'Well?'

'Well, what?'

'Don't brush it off, Tommy, please.' She sat up and turned towards him, taking his other hand too. 'What will happen when we go home, Tommy? Where do I sit in your and Ruby's future?'

Tommy stared at her and smiled nervously. 'Where do you see yourself sitting in my and Ruby's future, Shona?'

'If I tell you, then you'll laugh at me and get up and run out the door and back to the airport as fast as you can.'

'I promise you. I'll sit here and listen to every word. Now, spill.'

Shona took a deep breath. Could she tell him exactly how she felt about him, and how she felt about being Ruby's mother? The simplicity of what she wanted from her life didn't seem simple at all, but she would put it in the easiest words she could. Straight out and from the heart.

'I love you, Tommy. Not only as a friend, although you're the best friend I've ever had. Obviously, I adore Ruby. These past years have been hell on earth for you. It hasn't been all roses for me either, but, unlike you, I deserved what I went through. I would give anything now to be a part of your lives. A proper family. I think that we could make it work. I'll understand if this is the last thing you want. I'll be heartbroken, but I'll accept it. Whatever happens, please don't keep me away from Ruby. Please, Tommy.

'Last week I fell off the wagon too easily, and nobody was more shocked at that than I was. I still am. Obviously, I've a long way to go to get free from drinking, but I promise you that I will give it everything I've got … I'm rambling … Say something, Tommy.'

At least he was smiling, and he hadn't got up and walked out on her second sentence. He let go of her hands and she felt the loss. She dropped her head and tried to stop herself crying, but Tommy lifted her face up again and leaned in. His kiss was both beautiful and filled with desire. The tears fell then, and she let them. She was filled with so many emotions at once.

'Believe it or not, I love you too, Shona. When I thought you had slept with someone this week, I was livid, yes – but mostly I was hurt. That you could lead me to believe that there was a future for us and then dump me on the same night. That hurt made me realise how I felt about you. So, yes, let's give it a go. Move in with Ruby and me when we get home. I can't promise you perfection, Shona. We're only in our early twenties, and as you said, our first years around each other were absolutely crazy, but we'll try. We both want it to work, so that's a good start. I want to let you into our lives for good, because otherwise, I'd spend the rest of my life wondering what if … And something else. I need you. I've always believed that it was you who needed me, and I suppose I liked being needed, but now I know that I need you too. You and Ruby.'

Shona put her arms around Tommy and squeezed hard. 'This week started out as a disaster, Tommy, but it's turning out to be the best week of my life. I thought I'd lost you and Ruby completely. I won't forget how that felt.'

'Now, I think it's time to remove ourselves from the front pew of this cathedral before the dirty looks we're getting become physical.' Tommy pulled away slowly and stood up with the aid of his stick; a constant reminder of all that had happened between them. But they were still here, and who knew, they might even make it through.

In the morning Shona turned towards the window as the light filled the slats of the shutters and fell across Tommy's face. She got a fright momentarily when she saw Ruby's bed was empty, but then remembered that she had gone to sleep in Daniela's room the night before. Going to bed last night she had wondered if Tommy and her could finally make love to each other after what had happened between them this week. When she had been under the quilt for a few minutes, she had felt him slide in beside her quietly. Gingerly, she had reached her hand over to his and Tommy had interlaced his fingers in hers and squeezed gently.

'You frightened the shit out of me this week, Shona.' Tommy had said.

This had puzzled Shona. 'I don't understand, Tom,' she said. 'I know I've been an absolute bitch, but frightened? Why?'

'Tomorrow,' he said. 'I'm absolutely exhausted after today's travels. Goodnight, Shona.' He slid his fingers along her lips, and Shona had been filled with so much love and desire for him. But she had waited. Now it was morning and she reached over to trace her own fingers along Tommy's lips. Sure enough, it woke him. Shona had hardly slept wondering what this morning would bring with Tommy. To her delight he smiled a sleepy, lopsided smile.

'Morning.'

'Morning, gorgeous man,' she said.

Shona wondered should she bring up the half-conversation from the night before or would that break his good mood. They had another week together before they had to go home, and she didn't want to mess up again. She inched herself closer and then breathed a sigh of happiness when Tommy put his arms around her. With her head on his chest, Shona couldn't bear to break the feeling by starting a conversation. She draped one leg over Tommy and nestled it carefully between his. Tommy winced, and Shona went to pull away.

'Ah, I'm sorry, Tommy. Did I hurt you? Is the pain bad today?'

'No,' Tommy said. 'Come back. It's only achy from all the walking yesterday. It's nothing.' And he wrapped his good leg around her too.

'Another reminder of the crap I've put you through,' she said. 'But you're still here, Tommy.'

'I'm still here, Shona. Maybe when that fella rammed into me in his car, he damaged my head as well as my leg. But for now, I'm still here and those gorgeous curves of yours are calling out to me at this very minute.'

Shona didn't need a second invitation. She smiled fit to burst and dropped her hand further below the sheet. 'My curves are all yours,' she said. 'I'll swap you for …'

But she didn't get to finish as Tommy rolled over and covered her mouth with his and took possession of her curves quietly. There was plenty of time for discussing their future later.

CHAPTER FORTY-NINE

Enrico

'Here's your cup of tea, Sonia, with your milk and two spoons of sugar. You sure picked up some terrible habits those years you spent in Ireland. Two plain biscuits on the saucer for you to dip. Everything the way you like it.'

I place it on the small bedside table and sit on the bed beside her and wait for her to stir. Sonia loves her siesta in the afternoons, but she's not very quick to wake up from it these days.

'All the family are coming in about half an hour, Sonia. I can't believe they're all going back so soon. Their time with us flew. But now that you're better and getting stronger every day, there'll be many more visits no doubt.

'I'll be back in a minute. Up you get now and drink your tea. I know you're still grieving since you heard what actually happened to our Maria. I am too, but there'll be plenty of time to talk about that another day. Now get up and put on a nice dress, but don't take too long.'

I potter around the sitting room as Sonia likes to call it, checking that she didn't forget anything for the table. It is heaving with food. She had told them to drop in for a drink before they got ready to leave, but of course she has prepared enough nibbles to feed each of them their dinner twice. It's still very quiet in our bedroom. Has she fallen back asleep?

Putting my head around the door, I call her name again. 'Sonia.' She hasn't moved since I was here five minutes ago. I go around to her side of the bed and lean over her, giving her a gentle shake. Still no movement.

Immediately, I know, and I am as still as Sonia. A soft meowing noise comes from my throat followed by a gasp and the words 'No, no'. The room is quiet, and I can hear my heavy breath. I turn and stumble around to my own side of the bed, my body still bent over. I lie down and put my arm around Sonia. I have about twenty minutes left before the others intrude. I curl up beside her, as we have done almost every night since we arrived back in Spain from Ireland.

'You're leaving me again, Sonia, and all I want right now is to go with you. But yes, I hear you telling me that I still have things to do. I'll make everything right, mi amor. Paulina will have her guest house. This house will belong to Shona and Anna, and of course, the most beautiful princess of all, our darling great-granddaughter, Ruby. She is the future, Sonia. Our legacy.'

All the time I'm speaking to her, salty tears fall in my mouth and trickle into my ears, travelling over the wrinkles that have been etched across my face with every hardship that I have borne.

'Your face looks peaceful, darling. Please tell me that you didn't suffer. Was it your heart? I hope it happened in your sleep and that you didn't wake from it.

'Will you say hello to our parents, Sonia, wherever it is that you and they are now? Rosita who was your mother by birth, and Cristina who was your mother by right. And your father, will he be in heaven? It seems crazy now to believe that I was responsible for his death; but they were different times, and it was the only way to keep your mother alive. I can't remember what my parents and brothers looked like, but I have no doubt that they went straight to heaven when they died. I hope that Roberto was forgiven for being a Nationalist. He did so much good that he must be somewhere within reach of heaven. These years with you have been worth the years that Roberto willed me to live through the horror, when all I wanted was to let go. Remember me to your brother, Miguel, who was a brother to me in so many ways. And Rosa, Sonia, she will be somewhere at the head of all the angels. She was goodness personified. Look out for our Maria. I wish I had had a chance to know her. So many regrets in our lives but so many joyous times too.

'But do you know what I don't regret, Sonia? I don't regret loving you or persuading you to leave your life in Ireland and coming here. We deserved these years, snatched from the ashes of what went before. You wanted to see Fiona one more time, but now that's not possible. Our love caused enough hurt in the lives of your Irish family, and it would do no good to rake that up once more. Fiona and Manus must never know what we did to them. Anna has told us how Manus has been sober all these years, and such a good granddad to her; so in a way, we did good by leaving. Sometimes it's better to lie than to hurt. No?'

I hear two cars pulling into the gravel driveway. Footsteps of people we love empty onto the garden, and laughter and giddy voices drift in around us. In a few moments they will start to call our names, and eventually, they will find us here. Paulina will admonish us for our laziness before she realises what has happened. They will come in then and try to prise me away from you. Eventually, I will yield. There will be so many tears for you, my beautiful Sonia. I will dry my eyes soon so that I can help soothe their grief.

'Papá! Sonia!' Here she comes. 'Papá, what are you doing still in bed? Do you not know the time?' I turn towards her, and she sees my eyes, sore from salt and she knows. 'Oh, papá. When did this happen? What happened to her? Oh no, papá. Come. Take my hands. Sit up. Oh, my poor, poor papá.'

Paulina tries to ease me away from Sonia but I'm not ready yet. My body clenches up in anger with my daughter. I know she only has my welfare at heart, but as always, she doesn't see me; she doesn't feel me.

'Please, Paulina. Give me some time with her. Then I will come out to you all. Sonia prepared food and drinks for you all before she … slept. Please.'

So, she lets me go and I relax once more. I curve myself further into Sonia's body. She is warm. I could pretend she was still sleeping. I close my eyes, and the reality of the situation takes me over and my sobbing begins. I feel the reluctance in Paulina's retreating footsteps. I hear her muted whispers as she explains to our family in the sitting room what has happened.

I hear cries of disbelief. I hear little Ruby chatting away, ignorant of what has happened around her. She will hardly remember her beautiful great-grandmother. She will never know how much love Sonia poured over her in the short time they had together.

'I'll keep your memory alive, my Sonia. I've been lying still for too long now. These old bones of mine tell me of all the falls, the beatings I've had, and remind me of how many times I have had to get back up again. I will get up now. I can do this for you and for the family we have created between us. I love you, my Sonia. I have always loved you, from the day that you hit me with your slate in school for teasing you to this day, and I will always love you.'

'Abuelo.' A hand touches my shoulder, and I recognise the voice of my granddaughter, Shona. 'Abuelo, I'm so, so sorry.'

Dani is beside her, and another voice, Anna, my other granddaughter. One voice so familiar and the others so new, but all three so dear to me. I shift slightly away from Sonia and turn towards the girls. They are holding hands, united in grief. I try to sit up and they reach out to help me. Dani passes me my stick.

'Gracias.'

I stand as straight as my back allows and I look back once more at that face that is etched in my memory. Sonia the lively, vulnerable child. Sonia the loyal woman, torn between two countries. Sonia, the old and wise companion. All these pictures are there for keeps.

The girls help me into the sitting room, and I look around at the people, new and old to me, sorrow and disbelief written on each face. Tommy holds out his arms to Shona, and as she sinks into him, I know that these two will be all right. I ask Sonia to watch over them. Eileen is sitting in Sonia's chair, her loss filling her, absorbed into her body as she bends, doubled over with the pain. She has spent too many years grieving for Sonia, and now she must go through it all again. I hobble over to her and sit on the arm of the chair. I put my arms around her and hold her close.

I feel the hive of activity around us as phone calls are made. Ruby is the centre of so much love as Sonia's family use her to put their sorrow on hold. Nobody touches the food that Sonia had prepared so lovingly, only hours ago. Paulina and Daniela go back into the room where Sonia is. I will leave them to prepare her and to choose her dress.

Shona's godmother and Tommy's father sit uncomfortably in the corner. I can't put names to them right now. They are not sure what to do, who to speak to. He nods at her and takes her hand and leads her away. I recognise the way that they are together. There is no need for speech. They communicate with their eyes. They know that this house is not the right place for those who did not know Sonia.

'I want to see her.' Eileen pulls away from me and walks to the room where my Sonia is sleeping. I will leave her in the care of the women in her life. I fall into the warmth of the chair that Eileen has left, and I lean my head back and close my eyes. I am empty. Many years ago, in the cell in the north, I thought I had reached the emptiest a heart can be, but back then there was hope pushing to the fore of all my wretchedness. Sonia was out there somewhere, but now she is never going to come back. This is final. 'Good night, my Sonia,' I whisper. 'Sleep easy.'

Ruby climbs up on my lap, sensing the sadness in the room. I put my arms around her and try to stave off my tears.

'Where's Granny Sonia?' she asks.

I haven't believed in God for most of my life but when I reply I almost believe it's true. 'Sonia's in heaven, niña,' I say, 'and nobody deserves to be there more than she does.'

CHAPTER FIFTY

The group of seven coming through arrivals were a sombre-looking lot. Particularly Eileen, who seemed to have aged a decade overnight. Even Ruby looked washed out. Anna looked over at Shona's mam and dad, Des and Norah, waiting in arrivals for them. She knew of the hardships that Shona had put her adoptive parents through for most of her young life, and yet the love that poured from them when they talked about their daughter was wondrous. Both she and Shona were very lucky with the parents who took over the role that should have been Maria's, had she not been killed.

Later, they would drive everyone to their respective homes, but first they were all going back to Des and Norah's house for lunch. Everyone had argued over the last few days whether or not to include Fiona in the knowledge of Sonia's deception and recent death. Anna said that mourning your mother's death once was hard enough without having to go through all the pain of grieving once more. Eileen reminded them that finding out that her sister, Maria, had been murdered and had not overdosed had already unleashed a second round of grief for Fiona. Shona had been persuaded that it would be sheer cruelty to put her through that once again. It was Tommy who thought that it was madness to try to keep such a huge secret from her, but as he said, he wasn't family, and it was up to them.

As Shona reached them, Norah and Des put their arms gently around their daughter and granddaughter, bringing on a fresh round of tears from Shona. Anna gently picked up Ruby and cuddled her. She looked like she needed a bit of love and understanding. She cradled her in her arms and wished a happy carefree life for her beautiful niece. Judging by the way Tommy was looking at Shona, her sister had gotten her wish for a closer relationship with Ruby's daddy.

Shona let go of her parents and waited for Stephen and Margaret to catch up. Norah raised her eyebrows at her younger sister holding hands with Tommy's father of all people. Margaret burst out laughing.

'Close your mouth, Norah, and stop catching flies,' she said. Norah shook her head in disbelief.

Des clapped Stephen on the back. 'You lot can't stay away from our family, can you?'

'Oh, you're an attractive lot, all right,' answered Stephen, looking sheepishly like the cat who'd got the cream.

The solemn mood was broken, and a more relaxed group of people made their way out of the busy airport towards the cars left in the long-term car park.

Sitting around the table in the house where she grew up made Shona feel wrapped in comfort. She was sitting next to Tommy, their thighs touching, and his hand on her knee making her feel safe and loved. Ruby was happily entertaining everyone around the table, revelling in the attention of all those who treasured her so much. Her daughter would never worry about where she belonged in this world, and Shona would never worry about that again either.

Looking around the table, she allowed her feeling of being in the right place to envelop her. She had buried her grandmother only a few days ago, but she felt blessed to have known her and loved her for that short time.

Through the buzz of conversation, she smiled over at her sister, Anna.

'Are you looking forward to getting back to your mam and dad?' she asked her.

'Aye. But I think having mourned her own mother all those years ago, it would be heartless to put Mam through it all again. I know how you feel about living a lie, Shona, but sometimes a lie is the only kindness, and in this case, it's true. I was thinking that I'm so glad that I came over to Malaga when you asked. Getting to know our grandparents and their story was amazing. What they did was wrong in so many ways, but I am glad that they had that happiness in their life eventually, and I'm looking forward to going over with you again to see our grandfather and Dani. Though all of this came with a mixture of heartache for so many, and then there's the selfish side of me who wonders why Granny's daughter and her granddaughter were not enough for her.'

Eileen had been sitting quietly through the lunch but now she sat up and looked around the table. 'I'm the only person here who knew Sonia. I lived with her for all those years when she pined for Enrico. When Manus decided to marry Sonia, he knew he was marrying a woman who loved another man. Sonia never pretended anything else. Maria was all that Sonia had of Enrico, and when she lost her youngest daughter, she couldn't cope with the emptiness that was left. I spoke with Sonia for hours, actually, for days before she died. I realised the sadness that leaving Fiona and Anna left her with. You say that she had happiness in her life eventually, but I'm not sure that's completely true. The blackness of letting *us* go, so she could be with Enrico, never left her.'

Eileen picked up her napkin and dabbed her eyes and blew her nose into it. 'I'm happy that you came to me about Sonia, Anna. I'm so happy I got to see her again and that she met you and Shona. But it hurt. When I first saw her sitting there outside her villa, looking as if she hadn't a care in the world, I wanted to throttle her. I took it out on Enrico, God love him. He still wore the bruise on his face at her funeral. But as I said, I knew Sonia. I know what she and Enrico went through in their lives. I forgive them both, but I'll go to my grave without telling Fiona. What good could that do? Would Sonia still be alive now if I hadn't let the truth slip about Maria's death? Possibly. I opened a fresh grief there that her poor, tired body wasn't able for. So, I think we should make a promise around this table to keep it from Fiona at all costs.'

She put the napkin down and Anna reached over and held her frail hand. 'I second that, Eileen.'

All the heads around the table nodded quietly, except Shona. She still wasn't convinced.

Shona caught her father's eyes on her. He had a questioning look on his face. *Sometimes a lie is the only kindness*, Anna had said. Shona had fallen apart over a lie and only now was she putting her life back together. She smiled and nodded at Des and blew him a kiss across the table.

Des and Norah had lied about her birth as a matter of what they thought was kindness and perhaps they were right. Maybe the child that was Shona would not have managed the truth. Today her truth was all around her. Her parents who had painstakingly brought her up. Her godmother who had been her absolute rock all her life. Her sister who had stuck with her over the last few crazy years. Tommy's dad who seemed to have somehow forgiven her misdemeanours, or perhaps he was too enamoured with his new girlfriend to notice anyone else.

And Tommy. She reached under the table and slipped her fingers through his and he squeezed them gently. They turned and looked at each other and Tommy winked at her. The butterflies in Shona's stomach did a little somersault and she knew then that this love wasn't only about being safe. It was passionate. It was real.

Ruby was sitting on Stephen's lap beside her, and she turned to her mammy and climbed up onto her lap. Shona squeezed her and kissed her button nose and held her close, breathing in her smell. When she had first realised that she was pregnant, she had thought her life was over, but this child had been the beginning of a new and better life. She thought for a moment about Jameel's child that she had lost. She would never forget that baby, and she had quietly passed many sad anniversaries of that day. But there was no reason why Ruby shouldn't have a brother or sister someday, and perhaps that loss would feel less painful.

The doorbell rang and Des jumped up to answer it. There were hushed voices in the hall for a few minutes and the door opened. Shona sat still and stared at their visitor – her birth father. She had last seen Danny when she visited him in prison a few weeks before she went to Spain.

'You're out?' she said.

He nodded. 'I'm out. Good behaviour and all that. I didn't tell you that my solicitor was launching an appeal, in case it wasn't successful, but it was and here I am. I've done my time for something I never meant to do, and I can stop living my life looking over my shoulder and move on.' He looked around the room. 'I'm sorry to intrude like this, but Des asked me to come over.'

Norah stood up and took him by the arm. 'Indeed, you're not intruding,' she said. 'Pull up a chair behind you there and sit down beside your daughter. Will you have a bit of dinner?'

'I've already eaten, Norah, thank you, but I wouldn't say no to that gorgeous-looking cake.'

It was exactly the right thing to say, and Norah busied herself getting a plate and fork and one of her beautifully ironed, white napkins.

Shona stood up and gave her birth father a hug. 'It's so good to see you, Danny.'

'Did you bring what I asked you for, Danny?' asked Tommy. Shona looked questioningly at Tommy as to what Danny could have that Tommy could possibly want.

'I did, son.' He reached into his jacket pocket and handed a small, silky bag across to Tommy. 'I bought this for your mother, Shona, when she was pregnant with you, a couple of days before our lives fell apart. I never got to give it to her, and I never wanted to part with it, but when Tommy spoke to me about how he felt about you, then I realised who the ring should go to.'

All eyes were on Shona and Tommy. With his gammy leg, he wouldn't be able to kneel down or do anything dramatic, so he turned to Shona and held out the ring. 'Well?' he asked.

Shona looked down at the emerald ring Tommy was holding out to her, while Ruby wriggled in her lap, not liking being held so tightly. 'Well what, Tommy Farrell?' She smiled at him enjoying the moment to its full capacity.

Tommy jokingly went to put the ring back into its bag. 'Well ... if you're going to embarrass me in front of all these lovely people, then surely I'm doing the wrong thing.'

'If you don't want it, Mammy, I'll have it,' said Ruby. She grabbed hold of the ring, then and as she went to put it on, she dropped it in Shona's leftover cake and cream. Laughing, Shona prised it out and held it out to Tommy with her right hand, extending her ring finger towards him as she did so. Tommy slid the ring onto her finger. It fit perfectly.

'So, Shona,' he said. 'With this slimy, cakey, creamy ring, I'm asking you to marry me.' He didn't wait for an answer. Shona's face, smiling, and her eyes filled with happy tears, were all the answer he needed. Those around the table, some surprised and some not so, stood and clapped and cheered, while Shona licked the cake away from the ring.

Shona felt her grandmother in the room with them. She was in no doubt that Sonia had been the catalyst that had brought this day to fruition. Sonia might be gone, but her presence would be with her granddaughter for always. She closed her eyes and wiped away the tears.

'Gracias, abuela,' she said to herself, and when Tommy put his arms around her and Ruby, Shona felt that everything had fallen into place. Now it was up to her to keep it there and for the first time in her life, she trusted herself to do exactly that.

ACKNOWLEDGEMENTS

- To Neil, to whom this book is dedicated. He has been my absolute rock for thirty-five years, but particularly throughout the last seven years of operations and recoveries. Without his love and care I would never have been able to take up the pen anew and to put the writer in me back out there.

- To my children and their partners; Aoife; Katy and Brian; Méadbh and Warda.

- To my parents, Joe and Bridie; my siblings, Doreen, Joseph, Siobhán, Colum and Lorcan; and my extended family, who nurture my confidence.

- To my friends who constantly cheer me on.

- To my writing friends, especially to Tara Sparling and Kathryn Crowley who helped re-draft early manuscripts.

- To fellow authors, for their friendship and support.

- To the Castle Writers: Joan, Tara, and Bernadette, who have been my constants for about twelve years.

- To all my creative writing students who have given me the joy of sharing the craft.

- To Teresa Barker and Sally Dunne for much needed peace of mind.

- To Jeremy Murphy, Parvathi Venkitaraman and all at JM Agency, Publishing Consultancy for such a wonderful publication.

- To Parvathi Venkitaraman and Aoife Copland for the beautiful cover design.

- To the staff of Benalmádena library in Malaga, Spain, who helped me through the maze of research into Malaga in the time of Franco to the present day. They provided me with books in English, sourced from many other libraries and helped me with interviews of people who were experts in this area.

• To my brilliant, thought-provoking, gold-mining editor, Book Nanny Bernadette Kearns, for her incredibly talented and insightful work.

• To Zoe Miller, for her constant encouragement and for her enthusiasm in launching *Mosaic*.

• To loyal readers and the reading community of librarians, book sellers, book bloggers, and reviewers for supporting and spreading a love of reading. I hope you enjoy this book.

Previously by Carolann Copland

Summer Triangle

Shona and Majid are living very different, but ordinary, lives on opposite sides of the globe, when both their worlds are shattered.

Majid, who witnesses the death of his fiancée, a bomb victim at an Irish/Saudi festival, is so distraught he runs from his problems - right into the arms of Islamic fundamentalists.

Together his new allies and he plot to show Ireland exactly what they think of its cooperation in the US war against terror, but will Majid really get the closure he so desperately craves? Meanwhile Irish teen Shona falls pregnant following a drunken party and stumbles through early motherhood in a haze of alcohol. An overheard conversation about her past leaves her wallowing in the self-pity of betrayal and ripe for falling into the wrong hands.

When an attack in the city threatens to become Dublin's very own 9/11, will a chance meeting of the two teenagers hasten their road to self-destruction or help them rise from the ashes of the past?

Print: **www.buythebook.ie**

ebook: **Amazon and other major eBook platforms**

Scarred

Rory McGee is obsessed. The man who murdered his girlfriend, Maria Dooley, must be brought to justice.

Ex-IRA activist, now politician, Fergal O' Gorman, is accused of murder on live television during elections, causing a media frenzy. Rory's quest to expose the truth threatens to destroy the family he fought so hard to rebuild, and he's dragging Maria's daughter Shona Moran through the mire with him.

Rory needs to overcome the guilt he feels about letting Maria's death go unpunished. In a story of buried love and exhumed hatred, revenge can only be achieved at a cost. But how much is Rory willing to pay?

Print: **www.buythebook.ie**

ebook: **Amazon and other major eBook platforms**

ABOUT THE AUTHOR

Carolann Copland is an author and creative writing facilitator from Dublin. She lives and works between Ireland and Spain. Carolann worked for twenty years as a primary school teacher but now works full-time in writing. She has been facilitating writing workshops and retreats in Ireland and Spain for over ten years through *Carousel Writers*.

Carolann has a BEd in English and drama. Apart from her hometown of Dublin, she has lived in the United Arab Emirates, the United Kingdom and Spain. Outside of writing, her interests include reading, travelling, theatre, and socializing with family and friends. She is married to Neil and they have three grown-up daughters.